Maya Blake's hopes of becoming a writer were born when she picked up her first romance at thirteen. Little did she know her dream would come true! Does she still pinch herself every now and then to make sure it's not a dream? Yes, she does! Feel free to pinch her, too, via Twitter, Facebook or Goodreads! Happy reading!

Emmy Grayson wrote her first book at the age of seven, about a spooky ghost. Her passion for romance novels began a few years later, with the discovery of a worn copy of Kathleen E. Woodiwiss's *A Rose in Winter* buried on her mother's bookshelf. She lives in the US Midwest countryside with her husband—who's also her ex-husband!—their baby boy, and enough animals to start their own zoo.

SNOWBOUND WITH THE IRRESISTIBLE SICILIAN

MAYA BLAKE

AN HEIR MADE IN HAWAII

EMMY GRAYSON

MILLS & BOON

First published in Great Britain 2023
by Mills & Boon, an imprint of HarperCollins*Publishers* Ltd,
1 London Bridge Street, London, SE1 9GF

www.harpercollins.co.uk

HarperCollins*Publishers*, Macken House, 39/40 Mayor Street Upper,
Dublin 1, D01 C9W8, Ireland

Snowbound with the Irresistible Sicilian © 2023 Maya Blake

An Heir Made in Hawaii © 2023 Emmy Grayson

ISBN: 978-0-263-30705-4

12/23

This book is produced from independently certified FSC™ paper
to ensure responsible forest management.
For more information visit: www.harpercollins.co.uk/green.

Printed and Bound in the UK using 100% Renewable Electricity
at CPI Group (UK) Ltd, Croydon, CR0 4YY

SNOWBOUND WITH THE IRRESISTIBLE SICILIAN

MAYA BLAKE

MILLS & BOON

CHAPTER ONE

Dr Giada Parker clutched her travel coffee mug, her eyes stinging a little as the Antarctic wind picked up speed and whipped across her face.

She smiled through the discomfort.

Her triple-insulated weather gear protected her from the worst of the freezing temperatures, and, if needed, she could retreat to the significantly less chilly staff quarters below deck of the research vessel she'd called home for the last four months.

This was her last chance to see this intensely breathtaking landscape before her stint was officially over and she wasn't about to miss it.

She sipped her coffee, welcoming the scalding heat but not the reminder of what awaited her back home in London. Or Rome. Or wherever her mother decided they would spend Christmas this year. As of their last, terse conversation a month ago, Renata DiMarco hadn't decided where she would be dragging Giada and her identical twin sister to for the festivities.

With every bone in her body, Giada wished she could be spared the ordeal. Perhaps it was blasphemy to admit it, but Christmas wasn't her favourite time of year. Hell, she'd go as far as to say she detested it. Too many occasions over the years filled with too many harrowing scenes of Renata acting out after the inevitable several glasses of champagne had ruined the holiday for her. Her sister, Gigi, had weathered the storms better than she had, but then hadn't their mother accused Giada of being too sensitive, *too square*, among her many sins?

'*You should be more like your sister. She knows how to enjoy life...*'

That particular piece of unsolicited advice had been given when she'd sent her mother an invitation to her graduation. Predictably, Renata DiMarco had found somewhere else to be as her daughter had earned her PhD in marine biology.

Giada had assured herself she didn't care that neither Gigi nor her mother had made it or that the father she could barely remember hadn't even bothered to RSVP. But the thorns of anguish in her heart as she'd walked across the stage to collect her certificate had labelled her a liar.

She took another sip, more to calm her jangling nerves than for warmth. Staring across the blinding-white frozen tundra, she made a half-hearted wish for deliverance.

Then laughed in nervous shock as the vessel lurched, forcing her to reach for the railing to steady herself.

A warning that she shouldn't tempt fate, perhaps?

She snorted under her breath.

Yeah, right. Fate had a habit of ignoring her most ardent wishes. Giada was sure she wasn't about to start granting them now.

The only guaranteed thing was that she would at least get a few days' respite in her London bedsit before the summons from Renata arrived. A few days to shore up her emotional defences against the parent who didn't see anything wrong with denigrating her at every opportunity—

'Giada?'

She turned her head, startled to see Martin, her boss, standing a short distance away wearing a concerned frown.

'I'm sorry, Martin, I was miles away. Did you want something?'

The frown dissipated and a smile peeked through his months' old beard. 'I was a little worried you'd turned into a statue, you were so still. Anyway, you got a call five minutes ago. Your sister? I came to get you. She's calling back in ten.'

A ripple of anxiety washed over her.

In the four months she'd been away she'd spoken to her sister three times, all calls Giada had initiated, not the other way around. Gigi habitually forgot she had a twin for weeks at a stretch, and, while Giada knew it was extreme absent-mindedness coupled with the hard partying her influencer sister indulged in, it occasionally sharpened that same pang of unhappiness Giada had lived with for most of her life.

'Did she say what it was about?' she asked Martin, her stomach tightening involuntarily as she followed him across the snow-covered deck to the stairs leading to the lower levels.

He shook his head. 'She didn't. If it's helpful, she didn't sound like something was wrong.' He flashed a reassuring smile and gestured for her to precede him down the stairs. 'It sounded like she was in a bar, actually. God, I'd give my arm for a pint in a warm pub right now.'

She smiled but didn't bother to tell him Gigi would sound laid-back in the middle of a blazing apocalypse. Giada used to envy her sister's ability to remain unflappable in the face of their mother's melodramatic tantrums and the resulting angst-filled days Giada had endured.

Now, as she hurried after Martin, she sent another frantic prayer that she hadn't inevitably invited one of those tantrums with her foolish Christmas wish.

By the time she reached the small, dank office Martin and a few of the senior crew used, she was willing her hands not to shake or her mind not to create wild scenarios. She took a fortifying sip of her coffee after Martin left, then almost jumped out of her skin as the phone trilled.

Calm down.

Taking a deep breath, she answered. 'Hello?'

'Gids, is that you?' the lazy voice, gone sultry over the years from fits of smoking to sound uncannily like their mother's, answered. Giada grimaced at the much-hated nickname Gigi had taken to calling her lately. There was no point asking her to stop. Her sister, like their mother, did what she wanted when she wanted.

'Yes, it's me.' She clutched the phone tighter. 'Is everything okay?'

'Well,' came the sighed response. 'I'm dying to say yes, sis, but I'm kinda in a spot of bother.'

'Kinda? Either you are or you aren't. Which is it?' she demanded, her voice an octave higher and sharper than she'd intended.

'Goodness, Gids, I knew you'd hit DEFCON Five before I said two words.'

Giada could hear the eye roll in her sister's response. 'Gigi, we haven't spoken for weeks, and you've never called me while I've been away. I think it's fair to presume this isn't a welfare call. Whatever it is, just spit it out.' She squeezed her eyes shut for another fortifying moment before she blurted, 'Is it Mum?'

Her sister snorted. 'Way to lay the guilt trip, sis. And no, it's not Mum. Last I heard, she was in Rio getting a custom-fit costume done for Carnivale in February.'

'Please tell me she's not planning on staying there for Christmas? Or expecting us to join her?'

'Who knows? Though I think Christmas in Rio might be fun. I haven't been in ages.'

'Gigi.' Exasperation bled through her voice as she imagined a hellish two weeks with her mother and whatever menagerie of friends she'd picked up between London and Rio. She shook her head and zeroed in on what she could control. Like why her sister had called. 'What did you want to talk to me about?'

'Hold on,' Gigi yelled.

Giada gritted her teeth as raucous laughter and clinking glasses echoed down the phone. Then it quieted, indicating her sister had moved to a quieter area. Which disturbed Giada even further. Gigi didn't usually put much stock on discretion. 'Okay, first promise me this will stay between us?'

'What will?'

'Promise me first, then I'll tell you,' Gigi demanded.

'I've never betrayed your confidence.'

Unlike you.

She didn't add that, mostly because her twin didn't see anything wrong with blurting Giada's business to their mother, and also because her anxiety levels were climbing at an alarming rate already. She didn't need further angst.

'Yeah. Okay, fine. I may have taken possession of something that didn't quite belong to me.'

Giada inhaled sharply. 'Excuse me?' Her sister was many things, but she wasn't a thief. Until now apparently.

'Don't jump on your judgey horse so fast, Gids. There was a reason for it.'

Giada pulled off her woolly hat, suddenly feeling warm despite the cold dread coursing through her. 'What did you take? And what do you mean *was*?'

Her sister remained silent for several uncomfortable seconds during which Giada's vow to stay calm frayed badly.

'I took something important from this guy I was hoping to work for. Something that means a lot to him. And he's a very powerful guy.'

'Why?'

Gigi sniffed. 'Because he deserved it,' she spat without remorse.

At times like these, Giada wondered how they could be identical when their characters were night from day more often than not. 'Gigi—'

'Look, I was a little drunk when it happened, okay? And

also, people shouldn't make promises they don't intend to keep.' Giada barely stopped herself from laughing hysterically, then offering the pot and kettle example because how many times had Gigi airily made a promise then promptly broken it? She was glad she didn't laugh, or she would've missed her sister's less heated, 'Especially men.'

Thoughts of laughter evaporated. 'Did he hurt you?' The memory of their mother's boyfriend who had ingratiated himself into their lives when they were fifteen and earned their trust only to emotionally abuse them was an unwanted but vivid memory. It was also one of the few times Giada and her sister had bonded in their pain.

If Giada were being meticulous, it was probably that incident that had triggered Gigi's dissonance with emotional responsibility. Deep down, Giada couldn't blame her. But it still hurt that *she'd* been swept up with the masses. 'Gigi, what did he do?' she prompted when her sister remained ominously silent.

'I met him a few months back and we sort of moved in the same circles for a while. I helped him to get info from someone I knew and he said I could work for him. Then he humiliated me publicly, claimed I was flighty and didn't have what it takes to be one of his precious team.'

Giada exhaled, her tension easing a touch. 'So this is about a job? Nothing else?'

An affronted huff echoed down the line. 'It's not just a job, Gids! Do you know the kinds of doors it will open for an influencer if I have Alessio Montaldi's endorsement?'

'No, I don't, since I don't have a clue who he is,' she responded. 'And what exactly were you offering to do for him?'

'Whatever he asked. I would've done anything for him.'

Giada's eyes widened at her sister's low, husky and desperately voiced response. Another swell of dread washed over her. 'So he refused you the job. And you did what, exactly?'

Again, Gigi hesitated for heart-racing seconds. 'The thing I took…it was a family heirloom, Gids. And I…' She stopped and sucked in a breath and Giada took one right along with her, because she knew whatever was coming was big. And dreadful. 'He'd been looking for it for ever and had just found it the week before; was pretty obsessed with it actually. I think it played into some grand plan he was cooking up. Anyway, I thought he would take me seriously if I kept it for a while and then returned it.'

The creaking of plastic and the lance of pain through her fingers told Giada she was gripping the receiver too hard. 'When did you take it, Gigi?'

'Three weeks ago. I'd been trying for months to get him to change his mind about hiring me. I thought this would get his attention.'

'Look, just return his property and cut your losses. I'm sure you can find another—'

'I can't,' she interjected.

'Of course you can. Just return the thing, and apologise—'

'I can't return something I no longer have!'

'What do you mean you no longer have it?'

'Because I lost it three days ago.'

Giada dug the heel of her palm into her eyes, the dread she'd tried to hold at bay unfurling through her. 'Oh, God, Gigi.'

'I need you to help me, Gids. Please.'

'What can I do? I'm half a continent away.'

'But you're heading home soon, aren't you?' Gigi asked.

'Yes. For Christmas. With you and Mum.'

'That's not for another few weeks. I need you to help me out now. If Alessio discovers I've lost his property, I don't know what will happen. He's powerful and ruthless, Giada, and his reputation for not suffering fools isn't a joke.'

The protectiveness that was never far beneath the surface made Giada snap, 'I don't care about some power-hungry Italian who clearly likes to throw his weight around. When I get back you and I will talk to him and explain what's happened.'

Her sister snorted. 'He's not Italian. He's Sicilian. He already thinks I'm some useless airhead. I don't want to prove him right, Gids,' her sister said with a clear pout in her voice.

Giada wanted to roll her eyes at that but the lingering irritation wouldn't let her. 'Which is why I think you should come clean. Tell him what you've done and then speak to the authorities about recovering it.'

She could almost see her sister's careless shrug. 'I guess you don't care about me that much or the possibility that he can destroy my career with a few phone calls—'

'Gigi…'

Her sister huffed again. 'Are you going to help me or not?'

No.

The word hovered on the tip of Giada's tongue, ready to be set free.

But she knew how much her sister cared about her career. Plus Giada hadn't heard that thread of alarm in her sister's voice for over a decade. Ever since that final confrontation with Tom that had made her mother stare at Giada with something very close to hate ever since.

The harsh words spoken that had burst the false family bubble their mother had clung to, ignoring the emotional devastation going on under her nose. Giada knew Renata had never forgiven her for shattering that illusion.

'What do you want me to do?' she asked her sister.

'I need you to buy me time to find the heirloom.'

The speed of Gigi's response suggested she'd given it a lot of thought. Which was either a good thing or a bad thing. 'Fine. Give me this guy's number and I'll—'

'No. Jeez, Gids, you think I'd be calling you if a simple phone call would've cut it?'

'Then—?'

'I need you to distract him by pretending to be me for a few days while I try to find his item,' Gigi blurted.

'*What?* No. Absolutely not! You can't compound taking and losing his property by tossing subterfuge on top of it!'

'So you're saying I should just show up empty-handed and confess and hope he doesn't destroy my career or press charges against me?'

For the first time in a long time, Giada heard real desperation in her sister's voice. 'Gigi...'

'I know I don't have a PhD like you or some hotshot CEO but I know I can be a great fixer.' Her laugh was alarmingly self-deprecating. 'Hell, I do it for free for my friends all the time. All I'm asking is your help in fixing my mistake, Gids. He won't know who you are because you, shockingly, have zero social media presence. Trust me, I checked. Plus, only like...two people know I have a twin. So...please?'

Giada shut her eyes as her sister's plea bit into that vulnerable spot in her heart. As dread feathered down her spine.

Because she knew what her response was going to be even before she'd taken her next breath.

'How hard is it to find a slip of a woman who likes to give Bacchus a run for his money in the drinking stakes? Have you checked the cocktail bars on the French Riviera?' Alessio growled into the phone, his temper nearing simmering point.

These days, he prided himself on remaining unruffled. He expressed *some* emotions, sure. But letting any particular one—anger, bitterness—gain precedence over another?

Never. Not anymore.

There was a time when he'd been a slave to his emotions. But he'd learned, over long and arduous years, that there was untold advantage in doing the opposite. That his enemies writhed in indecision, wariness and suspicion when he displayed zero emotion. Just the way he wanted them. Those three flaws without fail granted him a means to exploit the chink in their armour that led to their downfall.

It'd served him well.

Except now he couldn't locate calm to save his life. Especially since all he heard at the end of the phone was nervous silence. 'Speak!'

A throat cleared. 'Apologies, *signor*. We've kept an eye on her usual haunts and explored many more. We've come up with nothing. She hasn't posted anything on her social media in over a week and she didn't go back to her apartment after her night out five days ago. My men searched the apartment, but we came up empty for the item.'

'So what you're saying is she's sniffed you out and gone to ground?'

'It seems so,' his trusted employee admitted with much chagrin.

While Alessio was furious at the outcome, he experienced the tiniest sliver of admiration for Gigi Parker. Perhaps he shouldn't have dismissed the airhead socialite quite so quickly. The team of fixers he'd sent after her were top-notch. Not his absolute best—they were currently engaged in another important task of ferreting out the last of his family's enemies and ensuring the final traps were properly laid for the reckoning he intended to deliver.

After years of meticulous planning, the perfect timing had been set—his mother's favourite time of year.

But he realised he'd underestimated Gigi. The flighty woman who'd imagined she could cajole and seduce her way into a job with him had some depth after all. At their meeting three months ago, he'd used the short ash-blonde hair, bold make-up and skimpy, thigh-skimming dresses to prejudge her.

His ultimate opinion *had* been cemented during the woeful fifteen-minute interview he'd had the misfortune of enduring with her. Perhaps if he'd stretched it to the full hour…?

Alessio dismissed the thought. It didn't matter. Yes, he'd been busy chasing the last cog in the wheel of restoring his family's honour and had taken his eye off the ball. But she'd stolen from him on a frivolous whim because she didn't get what she wanted.

Even worse, the Cresta Montaldi, the item she'd petulantly helped herself to, was one he'd spent the better part of a decade trying to retrieve.

There was no coming back from that.

If only Massimo could've been trusted to do his part, Alessio wouldn't be juggling a dozen balls in the air. How was it that the only person he came within a whisker of trusting turned out to be his playboy brother who didn't care a jot about the vendetta that had driven Alessio all his life?

He gritted his teeth and was about to issue a new set of ultimatums when the other man spoke. 'We talked to one of her friends. He said that she had plans to go to Switzerland. To Gstaad specifically.'

Surprise jolted him, then suspicion surged high.

'She's headed here? That's a little too convenient for her to be heading two hours away from my current location, don't you think? Surely, she wouldn't be that foolish?' Unless it was deliberate.

Was she taunting him?

While it wasn't rife public knowledge, it also wasn't a secret how much the ruby-encrusted family crest meant to him. With the astronomical sums he'd promised for the heirloom's retrieval, it'd been whispered about enough for its value to be known.

'We thought so too but…isn't it worth exploring? Maybe she's trying to make contact through your brother?'

Alessio frowned, casting his eyes upwards as if he had X-ray vision that could see through the ceiling into the bedroom where Massimo was currently sleeping off another hangover. Alessio had thrown in the towel at three a.m., but he knew

Massimo had stayed up with his friends until sunrise, which meant, despite it approaching noon, his brother wouldn't surface for another hour or two.

Alessio had come to Switzerland to drag his brother back to Sicily, to a family Christmas neither of them relished but that had to be performed for the sake of vows made to their mother.

After being apart for so many years due to circumstances beyond their control, it was an unyielding stipulation that they spent holidays and birthdays together. They hadn't missed one event in the last seven years.

Massimo had been his usual stubborn self, however, and Alessio had allowed himself to be talked into a rare weekend doing nothing but skiing and drinking, with the proviso that, come Monday, Massimo would get off his backside, off this mountain and onboard the private helicopter waiting to transport them to the airport.

Returning to Sicily was imperative to show his enemies that change and retribution were coming. That reclaiming his family name and everything else they'd cruelly ripped from the Montaldis was only a matter of time.

'You've been tracking her for three weeks. Has she had contact with Massimo?' he pressed.

'Not that we've noticed. But your brother is an easier man to track than you.'

Teeth gritted, Alessio accepted that unfortunate truth.

While his younger brother had memories of what had happened to them in the past, he'd efficiently blocked it out by delving neck deep into a playboy lifestyle that usually set Alessio's teeth on edge and caused the endless headaches. But Alessio had made a vow to his mother on her deathbed that he would protect his baby brother come what may.

Vows were sacred.

If Massimo was somehow involved in this, Alessio suspected Christmas would be even more strained.

And if Gigi Parker was aiming to gain leverage by using his brother…well, that was something else he hadn't seen coming with this woman. But at least, he mused as his blood rushed faster at the thought of putting this nuisance to bed and being reunited with his possession, he was in the right place at the right time.

He took a deep breath as he relished teaching the little thief a lesson. It would be his pre-Christmas present to himself while righting a wrong.

Win-win.

'Look into it and give me an update immediately. Don't let me down,' he tossed in the warning. Keeping his men on their toes reaped results.

'Se, signor,' came the quick response.

He hung up and turned away from the desk in the study of the luxury chalet he'd owned for years but barely used himself. Striding to the wide rectangular window, he stared at the stunning white-out landscape.

Much as he preferred the warmer climes of Sicily, he couldn't deny that Gris-Montana in winter was stunning. Before it'd caught his interest, the sleepy town had been gaining popularity, though at a slower pace than its more flashy neighbours of Gstaad and Montreux. He'd taken steps to keep its charm, and it was a little gem he hadn't minded using for the odd weekend.

But this wasn't the time to stand idly admiring his view.

He had more important things to do.

Like bringing those who'd shattered his family to heel.

For that to happen, he needed to retrieve his possession from the elusive Gigi Parker.

Preferably on this side of Christmas.

A mere three hours later, Alessio was having to put the former on hold in favour of the latter. His men had pulled out all the stops to get him the answers he desired.

Gigi Parker was indeed in Gstaad.

She hadn't bothered to hide her movements, another reason she would be no good to him as a fixer. Above all else, he valued discretion, unless a certain...flair was required.

Like publicly ousting a certain president in Cardosia not so long ago. When he'd helped his friend Severino Valente to eject the corrupt head of state, Alessio had partly done it to show his enemies how long his reach extended.

But that was a one-off.

Gigi Parker's kind of flamboyance he could live without. Perhaps he'd teach her a lesson that would make her change her ways in future.

Or not.

He didn't really care one way or the other. All he cared about was retrieving his property.

Snatching up the keys to the fastest car in the fleet Massimo intended to test-drive before no doubt offering one up as his preferred Christmas present, Alessio stepped into the wide hallway of the sprawling chalet.

Massimo was swaggering down the stairs in black jogging bottoms and nothing else. He raked back his overly long hair before frowning at Alessio's coat and the gloves he held.

'You're going out?' he griped. 'After badgering me to get out of bed?'

'I need to head into Gstaad to retrieve something. I'll be back shortly.'

Massimo rolled his eyes. 'Of course, business finds you in the middle of a nowhere ski village. Do you ever let up?'

'No.' The growled answer made his brother's face tighten. The petulance left his expression, his eyes growing solemn as they regarded each other. 'I will never let up until my promise to Matri is kept.'

After a moment, Massimo's gaze dropped. He gave a curt nod before veering in the direction of the kitchen, probably in search of a hair of the dog. 'See you later, then. I might meet some friends for a late lunch if you're not going to be around for a few hours?' he threw over his shoulder.

Alessio exhaled irritably. He couldn't keep his brother under lock and key. Massimo was a grown man of thirty, if a little directionless, but Alessio planned to have another *direction* talk with him over the holidays.

Until then…

'Ciao,' he said, then paused with his hand on the door handle. *'Frati?'*

Massimo looked over his shoulder. *'Se?'*

'I'm meeting Gigi Parker. Do you know who she is?'

Massimo frowned. 'No. Should I?'

Alessio prided himself on spotting liars at a dozen paces. His brother's confusion was genuine. 'No. *Arrivederci.'*

The custom Lamborghini consumed the miles between Gris-Montana and Gstaad and delivered him to his destination in a little under two hours. By then the latest update had arrived. Despite it being only mid-afternoon, his team reported Gigi was in a well-known ski-resort bar. Touted as being exclusive, it'd long lost its right to exclusivity, Alessio knew, when financial constrictions had forced it to open its doors to all sorts of characters.

Features twisting with distaste, he tossed his keys to the valet and strode into the dark interior. Eyes tracked him and whispers followed soon after as he headed for the so-called VIP lounge. If nothing else, the owner of the establishment would get increased traffic over the holidays when it was announced Alessio Montaldi had dropped in.

Buon Natale at te.

Sneering at the sardonic thought, he stepped into the lounge.

In one corner, a raucous group high on their post-ski celebrations were downing shots as if a drought were imminent. Pockets of revellers gathered around fat armchairs while scantily clad waitresses darted back and forth, frantically serving clientele who were determined to outdrink each other.

The group that caught and held Alessio's attention, though, was the large one in the middle.

Specifically, the woman holding aloft a champagne bottle as if she were Lady Liberty herself while the other hand was propped on her curvy hip.

A craftily placed spotlight shone on her long ash-blonde hair, highlighting the thick, wavy strands that normally fell halfway down her back. With her head raised to the ceiling, however, the tapered tips caressed the top of her ass, drawing Alessio's attention to the rounded globes moulded by her silver sequinned dress.

The dress itself ended just below the tops of her thighs in a band of wispy feathers that swayed when she rolled her hips in time to the sultry music.

At her next risqué pose, the group cheered then started chanting her name. 'Gigi! Gigi! Gigi!'

She rolled her hips faster, the motion hypnotic, as she fell under the spell of the music and her adoring fans.

Slowly, her body pivoted his way, presenting him with her profile.

Alessio frowned as heat swelled in his middle, then flowed up his chest to his throat. His hands clenched within his coat pockets, his shoulders tensing for reasons he couldn't fathom.

Had the Gigi he met months ago gained curves since their last meeting? Were her lips a little fuller, too?

And the look she was casting the males in her group seemed almost…coquettish, whereas she'd been brazen with Alessio.

Had he also missed the fact that Gigi Parker possessed impressive chameleon-like tendencies? His nostrils flared with irritation. Because again, what did it matter? Their final interaction wouldn't extend beyond tonight. Once he retrieved his property and delivered his lesson.

Which he couldn't do from across the room.

So why couldn't he move?

Why was his gaze rapt on the woman putting on a tasteless show for half a dozen men and women who seemed equally enthralled? And why did their slavish attention send a pulse of fury through him?

'Sir, can I get you—?'

Alessio dismissed the waitress with a curt head shake, his total focus on the woman now crooking her finger towards one man in the group. The guy fell out of his chair onto his knees, then eagerly crawled to deliver himself at her feet.

The slim arm holding the champagne slowly lowered and tipped towards the young man, who happily opened his mouth to receive the fizzing liquid. More laughter broke out as Gigi anointed him with her drink, drenching him in the process to his utter delight.

When she paused, he surged forward eagerly, bracing his hands on her hips.

Alessio's feet moved, fury inexplicably mounting.

He told himself it was because he'd had enough of this spectacle. But as he approached them, the urge to remove those hands from her hips grew into unreasonable proportions, until he could feel a growl bubbling in his throat.

'Who. Is. Next?' The object of his focus cocked her hips sharply as she shouted the question, effectively dislodging the hands on her hips and lowering Alessio's temperature.

'No one. Because your little party is over.'

Shouts of outrage erupted and died just as quickly when heads swivelled his way and expressions morphed from surprise to shock to wariness as whispers travelled through the crowd.

In the centre, Gigi froze, her smoky-grey, almond-shaped eyes widening before her mouth fell open.

He had to give her credit for her acting skills.

The rapid rise and fall of her chest and the light quiver that seemed to go through her, making the magnum of champagne slip from her wet grasp to thump, forgotten, on the cheap carpet, was a good touch.

The fast blink as her gaze left his face and did a quick scrutiny of his body before she sucked in a shaky breath? An ace performance that would've fooled a slow-witted man.

But he'd been subjected to far too many forms of deceit for it to work with him. And despite the curious heat unfurling through him, he tightened his jaw, one eyebrow elevated as he waited for her next move.

Her eyelids descended for a moment before she raised them to meet his gaze again.

'Mr Montaldi… Alessio, what a lovely surprise!'

CHAPTER TWO

GIADA WILLED HER heart to stop attempting to escape her rib-cage.

Her nerves were already eating her alive. The last thing she wanted was to worsen her predicament by collapsing in a heap. For starters, it would put a swift end to her ruse and blow her cover wide open.

Plus, she suspected the black carpet beneath her feet held substances she wouldn't like her skin to come into contact with.

But try as she might, she couldn't stop her racing pulse. Because it was registering far too late that clicking through hundreds of internet images of this man from the safety of her London bedsit was one thing. Being confronted with the flesh-and-blood version, the mile-wide-shouldered and tow-ering-several-inches-over-six-foot version, was a whole different ball of yarn.

Not to mention those eyes.

In the dark interior of the club, she couldn't tell whether they were dark gold, bronze or hazel. But she knew how ef-fectively they could reduce mere mortals to stupefied messes because they were scrambling her brain cells *right now.*

She'd been deeply sceptical when Gigi had insisted she only needed to install herself at L'Illusion in time for the *apres-ski* crowd to draw the attention of Alessio Montaldi's team of fixers.

Truth be told, Giada had tried not to think too deeply about how invasive Alessio would have to be to locate anyone at his whim. Then she'd hoped he'd send his minions to buy herself some time before she met the man himself. Because even two weeks after that phone call with Gigi and agreeing to this mad ploy, Giada had known she wasn't ready.

Exhibit one—the way she'd greeted him just now.

She'd forgotten to ask Gigi how to address the imposing, dynamic man looking down at her with hooded eyes, disdain dripping from every bronzed, polished pore.

With every bone in her body, she yearned to turn away from his judgemental stare, brace her hands on her knees and suck in the much-needed oxygen he'd seemingly depleted from the room with his presence.

But she'd promised her sister she would do whatever it took to buy time for Gigi to rectify her mistake. She couldn't let her down at the first hurdle.

Before she could speak, though, Jean-Luc finally rose from his submissive position on the carpet, his arm creeping around her waist as he smiled down at her.

'Everything okay, *chérie*?' he slurred, totally oblivious to the fact that his champagne-drenched shirt was sticking to her bare arm. Or that he'd drawn the merciless attention of their visitor.

Giada shimmied away from him with a light laugh she didn't feel. 'Of course!'

She'd noticed very quickly that Jean-Luc was the handsy type, prone to caressing a wrist, arm or hip in the name of tipsy friendliness, and had been inventing creative ways of combating a situation Gigi would've laughingly indulged.

Her heart jumped into her throat when Alessio's eyes shifted back to her and narrowed.

Had she given herself away already?

Swallowing, she went for broke. Striding forward on precariously spindly high heels, she rested her hands on his arms, raised herself on tiptoe and brushed a kiss across Alessio Montaldi's cheek.

Dear God...he smelled amazing. Like the ocean blended with wood smoke.

She trapped a stunned moan before it escaped, just as the thick arms beneath her fingers went rigid, then flexed, right before his body froze.

Was it her imagination or did he suck in a sharp breath?

When the heat pulsing off his body threatened to scramble her brain further, she hurriedly cleared her throat. 'I didn't know you were in town.'

His jaw rippled, his gaze fixated on her when she took a vital step back. 'Did you not?'

The sound of his voice, a deep, low rumble of oiled gravel, quaked right through her, leaving tiny explosions she barely stopped from gasping out loud.

Snatching in a breath, she widened her smile. 'Of course not. I would've made sure we connected for a drink. For old times' sake, if nothing else.'

He stared at her for several terrifying seconds before he exhaled. 'I'd advise you not to play games with me, Miss Parker.'

When the group inhaled a collective breath, Alessio slowly turned his head to survey the band of merry acquaintances she'd fallen into forty-eight hours ago. Giada wasn't sure whether to be glad or insulted on their behalf that he'd already forgotten about them.

'I will pay your tab for the rest of the night if you leave us,' he offered silkily, his tone totally belying the tempered rage vibrating off his body.

The ragtag group stared slack-jawed at him. Then excited whispers broke out.

When Jean-Luc attempted to reach for her again, his fingers inches from her bare shoulder, Alessio speared him with laser-sharp eyes. 'Now.' The directive was soft and deadly.

A split second later, with a chorus of *'au revoir'* and air-kisses, they rushed to the bar, eagerly shouting their orders at the bartender.

Alone with Alessio Montaldi and his laser gaze, Giada could barely breathe. Tension mixed with panic churned her insides as she forced another smile. 'Oops. Looks like you've scared my friends away. What am I going to do with myself for the rest of the evening?'

He took a step closer, forcing her to tilt her head to meet his gaze. His hands remained in his pockets but his gaze roved freely over her face, neck, down her throat to the risqué dip in her dress that exposed far too much cleavage.

When it rose again, the disdain had thickened, but something else lurked within the dark depths. Something she couldn't name but which sent a lance of dangerous heat through her.

'Here's a suggestion. With one phone call, I could have you arrested. Would you prefer that?'

Wild panic seized her before she breathed through it. With a move worthy of an academy award, she dragged her fingers through her hair in the slow, languid way she'd seen Gigi perform a thousand times. Breath held, she watched him track that motion too, a peculiar flame leaping in his eyes. Could she get away with licking her lips now? Or would it be too over the top?

Giada didn't want to decode why heat unfurled in her pelvis at the thought. Instead, she settled for tilting her head to one side and delivering a slow, heated smile, hoping it didn't betray the nervous yet weirdly powerful sensation flowing through her. 'Of course, I wouldn't prefer that. But you don't need to prove you're the big and powerful Alessio Montaldi. I know I'm completely at your mercy.' She dropped her gaze to examine her scarlet-tipped nails. 'Or am I?' she taunted softly, the way she'd seen Gigi tease men far too often.

Pivoting away from him without waiting for his response—mostly to hide her nerves—she sashayed over to the low sofa that backed against the wall of the lounge, supremely conscious of every inch of her body.

Lowering herself into it, she made a show of crossing her legs while she watched him from beneath her lashes.

His eyes narrowed to slits and his jaw turned to stone as he prowled forward. Fully expecting him to take the seat next to her, she was stunned when he perched on the coffee table directly in front of her.

With his hands out of his pockets, elbows braced on his knees and his body angled forward, he'd effectively blocked her gaze of the lounge, making himself the total focus of her attention. 'I caution you against toying with me, Miss Parker.'

She flipped her hair again. 'It's Gigi. I'm sure I've told you to call me that before?'

'You have. And do you remember my response when you did?' he batted back, his incisive gaze giving her nowhere to hide.

Oh, no.

Giada lowered her lashes. She couldn't keep staring into those piercing eyes and not give herself away.

What had Gigi advised?

'Keep the conversation general. He has a mind like a steel trap. He'll eat you alive on the specifics.'

She waved a carefree hand then dropped it onto her thigh. When his gaze followed, she fought the urge to fidget. 'Probably something formal and stuffy. But as you can tell, I'm not one for following rules.'

'Believe me, that hasn't escaped me. Where is my property?' he snapped.

She jumped, then forced another laugh. 'Straight to business, I see. Not even going to buy me a drink first?'

'No. And you and I have no business together. You stole something that belongs to me. You're a fool if you think you have any leverage at all in this situation.'

A flash of fury lit her veins. 'I don't like being called names, Alessio.' Especially that one. Her mother had called her foolish far too many times for every action Giada had taken that wasn't rubber-stamped by Renata DiMarco. Like Giada wanting to further her education. Or refusing to endorse her mother's extravagant spending sprees to Paris with money they couldn't afford. 'In fact, being insulted makes me very disagreeable.'

'You don't?' he taunted. 'That's surprising since you're actively collecting them with your every action. Another one that springs to mind is thief,' he tossed in cruelly.

Giada knew she—or rather her sister—deserved that one. But still her ire rose. 'If I took your property, and I'm not admitting to anything, did you stop to think it was to prove a point? That I might even be helping you?' she challenged.

Gigi's actions had been misguided and unfortunate, and her insistence that Alessio would *eventually* appreciate the reason had sounded sceptical to Giada. Only pure desperation made her toss it at him now.

From the furious incredulity on his face, he thought so too. 'No, because whatever point you were hoping to make lost relevancy when you resorted to stealing.'

It chafed that he had a point there too. In innumerable ways, what Gigi had done was wrong. But after meeting Alessio Montaldi, Giada could guess what had driven her sister to such rash action.

The man was fascinating. And unnerving. Infuriating and wholly possessing of a dynamism so hypnotising, she could see how everyone cowered and fell silent when he spoke. How, even now, the waitresses gave him a wide berth and the crowd watched him furtively, on the edge of their seats as if awaiting some marvellous exhibition they could later recount with bated breath.

She couldn't blame them.

She was on the mental edge of her seat. Toss in that sense-scrambling scent of ocean-cum-smoked wood aftershave pulsing from his skin, and the effect of those dark burnished eyes, and she feared she would soon be on the *literal* edge of her seat.

Unless she pulled herself together. Now.

'Even if the alleged act was exposing the flaws in your security? Perhaps you left yourself wide open and someone getting their hands on your property…hypothetically…may or may not have been a piece of cake.'

His jaw turned to granite. 'You have exactly one minute to tell me where my property is or—'

'I think we've established by now that I don't rise to threats, Alessio,' she interrupted, twirling a strand of hair around her finger even as her heart beat wildly like a trapped bird. 'So whatever you're planning on terrifying me with next, I'll probably just…you know…*scoff* at.'

His nostrils flared. His eyes darkened. Whether it was out of fury or because hearing his name might have triggered the same reaction it did in her, she wasn't willing to explore.

'During our last meeting, you struck me as many things, Miss Parker, but extremely reckless didn't strike me as one of them.'

Her heart stuttered at his arctic tone.

Giada should probably have dialled down the taunts then. The furious man before her was clearly running out of patience. But for the life of her, she couldn't back down.

It felt weirdly *invigorating* that she'd managed to needle him. Twirling another strand of hair, she smiled. 'Call it a new skill if you want.'

His head twitched back. Only by a tiny fraction but she could see the sliver of bewilderment in his eyes. As if he could barely believe her audacity.

Giada was marvelling at her gumption when he surged to his feet.

For an age he stared down at her. Every atom of her body was infused with so much electricity, Giada believed she would spontaneously combust.

His gaze slowly raked over her. Once. Twice.

Heat dragged up from her toes and she knew her lips were parted, her breasts straining against the already tight material of her dress. When her tongue dashed out to ease the tingle in her bottom lip, she allowed it.

She told herself it was okay to react this way because her sister had never been shy of embracing her sexuality. Gigi would never feel uncomfortable under such blatant male scrutiny. She would revel in it and give as good as she got.

But while Giada would withstand such a bold, unapologetic stare, she couldn't bring herself to return the favour. Not when the man in question was so...*potent*. So overwhelmingly untamed and *sexy*.

As much as Giada didn't want to admit it, Alessio Montaldi was an exemplary male specimen. The kind she wasn't in the habit of fraternising with...ever. The men she usually encountered were scientists who lived and breathed their jobs or benign betas who were friendly enough and nowhere near intimidating.

Alessio Montaldi *breathed* superior alpha male. He was the king of all he surveyed and with every bone in his body he owned it.

But he doesn't own you.

The tiny little but empowering thought raised her chin, sparks of defiance igniting through her as he stared at her

That defiance took a steep nosedive, however, when in the next moment he bent low and scooped her up.

She yelped as dizziness rushed her and her world turned literally upside down. Before Giada could fathom what was happening, Alessio was striding through the throng of clubbers.

Dear God, he'd tossed her over his shoulder!

'What the hell do you think—?'

'If you know what's good for you, you'll stop talking right now,' he growled.

Giada opened her mouth to rip a volley of words at him, but her throat dried up when warm hands landed at the backs of her thighs, sending sizzling showers of heat all through her body.

She knew it was only to keep her from tumbling over his shoulder, but the moan that escaped unbidden from her throat was luckily drowned out by the music and chatter that greeted the spectacle she no doubt made being carried out like a sack of potatoes.

Heat that had nothing to do with her inverted position, and everything to do with her way her breasts were pressed into his back, rushed into her face. The way his muscles rippled beneath her hands when she had no choice but to grab his coat to steady herself pushed her to ignore his warning. 'Put me down right now!'

'Are you sure? You seem to enjoy making a spectacle of yourself. I'm only obliging you,' he drawled, his voice still that infuriatingly steady rumble that burrowed into places she didn't want to name.

Giada sucked in a breath when he took the stairs that led outside in quick strides, uncaring that he was jostling her against his body. When she reached out to steady herself once more, her hands grabbed the firm hard globes of his ass.

He stiffened, then stopped.

Giada squeezed her eyes shut as mortification erupted through her.

She opened her mouth to say something, *anything* to abate the charged atmosphere she'd created. But Alessio was snapping something at the nightclub staff, who were hurrying to respond.

Then he was striding out of the entrance.

His threats weren't working.

Alessio couldn't recall the last time he'd been so thoroughly stumped.

He would've been inclined to believe Gigi Parker was off her head with drink or perhaps even drugs, had he not looked into her eyes. Stunning eyes that sparked with equal parts defiance and intelligence. Eyes that dared him to do his worst while holding a touch of nervous…anticipation?

Hand her over to the authorities. Let them deal with it.

He knew several high-positioned individuals in law enforcement across two dozen countries, including this one. He could have her in handcuffs within the next fifteen minutes.

So why was he hesitating?

And why the hell was he unable to take his eyes…or hands…off her?

She'd barely registered on his radar in the two weeks he'd spent in Europe during the summer when he'd been fixing a few problems for several members of royal families who'd repeatedly got themselves ensnared in scandals.

She'd been on the fringes of a particularly hard-partying bunch of socialites and trustfundistas who'd consistently ended up in the tabloids. Alessio had only taken note of her because her passable PR skills had come in handy when his team had needed it.

He wasn't entirely sure why he'd agreed to her request for an interview. Perhaps he'd had one too many whiskies? Or he'd

been frustrated that his efforts to locate the Cresta Montaldi
had repeatedly failed?

Whatever the case, he'd seemingly created a monster by
obliging her.

But had his monster been *this* beguiling?

What did it matter? Acting like a caveman wasn't his preferred behaviour. But he couldn't allow her to continue to
twirl her hair and bat her eyelashes at him as if he were some
simple hormonal teenager eager for attention from a beautiful
woman. His phone contacts were filled with women ready to
share his bed at the crook of his finger.

So why are you so affected *by her*?

Because she was in possession of the very thing his father
had died for.

The object his mother had despaired would never be re-
gained and returned to their family in time to restore their
reputation before she died. She'd faded away without that
hope ever being realised. It stuck in his craw that this slip of
a woman could be so cavalier with something so profoundly
fundamental to who he was. To *what* he was—the firstborn
of a once-respected Sicilian family going back generations. A
family he was determined to make whole again.

So *se*, he planned on delivering a few lessons before he
was done with her.

And if that meant suffering through his brain latching onto
how smooth her skin was, how her curves sank into his body,
how lush her ass seemed from the corner of his eye? *Bene*,
suffer he would.

'Put me down right now,' she shouted.

Jaw gritting against the insufferable heat surging through
his veins and pooling in his groin, he stepped out of the club,
strode to where the valet had fastidiously parked his vehicle,
and lowered her unceremoniously to the ground next to his
passenger door.

Alessio then watched her blink rapidly and scramble to push back her long silky hair, refusing to imagine if this was the way she looked when she was thoroughly made love to in bed. He almost welcomed the spiky glare she sent his way. The fact it only raised his temperature created a rumble in his chest he barely managed to stifle before it ripped free.

'Where's my coat? It's freezing out here.'

He wanted to snap that she should've thought of that before defying him, but he suspected it would only instigate more stubborn rebellion.

Instead, he found himself shrugging out of his own coat, stepping close to tuck it around her shoulders before gathering the lapels closer.

For a frozen moment, he thought he caught stunned surprise in her eyes at his gesture, before the entitled pout made a return, her glare turning fiercer as he reached for the door to his sports car.

'I'm not leaving without my—'

The words died in her throat as, per his instructions, the bouncer approached with her belongings. When she immediately went to shrug off his coat, he stepped back, a firm reluctance to have her take it off tunnelling through him.

'Keep it. The sooner we get out of here, the safer you'll be from my urge to throttle you.'

Again, he caught a flash of surprise at his heated words.

Se, he was mildly astounded himself. Was he a red-blooded Sicilian prone to vividly imagining how he would take down his enemies? *Certo*. Was he prone to blurting out those urges as if he were starring in a mindless reality TV show? Absolutely not.

'Get in,' he clipped out, yanking the door open the moment she'd snatched her purse and a wholly inappropriate sparkly coat from the bouncer—without a word of thanks, he noted

She opened her mouth, no doubt to throw another taunt his way.

Alessio hardened his features, letting her see how close she was to breaking his last straw.

Luminous smoky-grey eyes blinked again.

She glanced inside the car. Her throat started to move in a nervous swallow, but she halted the move at the last moment. He'd seen it though, and satisfaction pulsed through him.

Good, she wasn't utterly devoid of a sense of self-preservation.

But when she glanced at the door to the nightclub, he stepped into her eyeline. 'You're not going back in there. At least not tonight. Accept that and get in the car. This game you're playing ends tonight.'

The faintest fluttering of her nostrils, and she shrugged off all concern.

For a fraction of a moment, Alessio envied her easy ability to bat off responsibility and burdens. It'd never been a luxury he could indulge in. Not since his childhood was mercilessly ripped from him.

He smothered that bite of envy when she responded. 'You're right. Let's do this. The quicker we both get what we want, the quicker I can get back to my friends, right?'

His nostrils flared as she angled her body with exaggerated grace that nevertheless consumed all his attention, his compelled gaze falling to the long, exposed legs she lifted off the ground to slide into the footwell.

Dulce cielo.

He shut the door with suppressed emotion and rounded the car.

Sliding behind the wheel, he willed his senses to calm. Willed the tingling and fury and bewilderment to cease.

He had duties to perform. Wrongs to right. And this woman…sexy and infuriating—*why was her scent so intoxicating?*—wasn't going to stand in his way.

Alessio glanced at the clock. Time he didn't have was ticking away. 'You have thirty seconds to decide where we go once I start the car. I suggest the destination be wherever you're hiding my property. And don't say your hotel room to buy yourself more time. I have it on good authority it isn't there. But be warned, if you don't tell the truth…if you let me decide what happens next, you won't like the consequences.'

CHAPTER THREE

GIADA PRETENDED TO look out of the window at the neon sign of the nightclub to buy herself thinking time. To swallow the trepidation thickening in her throat.

According to Gigi, Alessio was a cold, unfeeling shark. An entitled alpha male with a rock for a heart who ruthlessly shredded opponents in his wake.

Well, his actions in the last ten minutes indicated otherwise. Even now, emotion pulsed from him, his fingers clamped around the steering wheel, chest rising and falling as he speared her with volcanic eyes. She still hadn't quite worked out their colour but they burned holes into her skin.

With every moment that passed, though, she grew more impressed with his rigid control. Just as she'd been awed by the hard, packed muscled beneath his—

No.

She was absolutely not going to think about his body. About that granite-hard jaw, those chiselled cheekbones and the way their perfect angles crafted his breathtaking face. About the sensual mouth that hinted strongly at his Latin blood and barely restrained passions—

Enough.

She shook her head to dispel the sensual web weaving dangerously around her. Giada wasn't sure why he affected her so strongly, but she wouldn't allow this insanity to continue.

Think, think. What had he said again?

Right. More threats about jail or worse.

She took a deep breath, almost groaning in despair when, from the corner of her eye, she saw his fingers tighten harder around the wheel.

No, he most certainly wasn't unfeeling when it came to his possession.

Scrambling to recall everything Gigi had said, she cleared her throat and faced him. 'I'll return your item. Before that, though, you owe me.'

Cold incredulity flashed in his eyes. *'Sei serio adesso?'* *Are you serious right now?*

'Sì, io sono.' Giada wasn't sure why she answered in her mother's language. Why uttering the husky words sent a pulse of...*something* through her veins. Or even why Alessio inhaled sharply, as if the same *something* spiralling through her afflicted him too.

All she knew was that she had to take proper control or, *dear God*, she risked losing her mind and scuppering this mission before she was of any use to her sister.

Fingers gripping the rich woollen coat doing a sterling job of warming her body, she ploughed ahead. 'I'm only asking for what you failed to deliver during our last meeting. For starters, you cut the interview short. You said some pretty unpleasant things and you prejudged me without giving me a chance to defend myself. I think that was wrong and unfair. If nothing else, you owe me for helping you with the situation in Monaco.'

Giada secretly exhaled in relief for delivering it with confidence. Somehow, she'd suspected it might come in handy.

She'd made Gigi repeat this part over and over so she didn't get it wrong, all while being secretly appalled her sister wanted to work for this man in spite of the awful way he'd treated her.

That confidence threatened to dissolve when Alessio narrowed his eyes. 'You're serious,' he mused harshly, in English this time. 'You want me to interview you right now? After your actions, I'd be a fool to let you anywhere near my business.'

Giada forced a shrug, even as apprehension at delving deeper into this subterfuge ate like acid through her bones. 'Or you'll get the chance to see my full potential. After all, if I can swipe your precious family crest right from under your nose...'

His jaw gritted at the reminder. 'What you're forgetting is that I employ fixers, not con-women or cat burglars. And most definitely not petty thieves.'

'And I'm none of those things. I told you, it was a spur-of-the-moment thing to prove a point. Oh, and I don't just want an interview,' she tagged on bravely.

'*Santi copra,*' he cursed under his breath.

She rushed on before the volcanic rumble became a full explosion. 'Your reputation as a hard taskmaster is well known. But so is the fact that you can be even-handed when it suits you.'

His gaze threatened to flay her. 'You think pandering to my vanity will swing things your way?'

In truth, she'd hoped it would.

Men in his position tended to love shameless sycophants. But clearly this man was cut from a different cloth. 'No. I suspect you believe you have the biggest balls when you walk into any room whether anyone cares or not. But I *am* hoping you have the integrity to go with that ego. So this is my ask—set me a task. Let me fix something for you. If I fail, you get your crest back and we go our separate ways, no harm no foul.'

'And if you pass?' His tone held decisive scorn, his belief that she would fail throbbing through every syllable.

Giada's fingers tightened around his coat to hide their shaking, praying she wasn't digging a deeper hole for her sister by heading down this perilous path. Giada didn't have the first clue how to be a fixer for a molten-eyed Sicilian who looked set to emulate the emblematic volcano that soared its majesty in his homeland. 'You give me a role on your team or write a good enough reference for me to land a similar job elsewhere.'

Silence, thick and charged, reigned in the car for a full minute.

Giada urged herself not to fidget.

When it got too much, she flicked her gaze up from where she'd pinned it on the dashboard. As suspected, his gleaming eyes were fixed on her, his expression inscrutable. Calculating. She didn't dare be relieved he was no longer furious, not when he was examining her like a specimen under a powerful microscope.

'You want a job with me this badly?' he drawled, his accent a little more pronounced, drawing further tingles over her body.

Saying yes felt like admitting to much, *much* more. But she'd boxed herself into this corner. She had no choice but to respond. 'Yes, I do.'

'Where was this fire back in Monaco? Back then, you were more interested in the perks of the job, not the job itself, if memory serves.'

Giada silently berated her sister for her flakiness. Then shrugged again. 'That was then, this is now. Do we have a deal?'

She hadn't seen it happen, but Alessio's fingers were no longer clenched around the wheel. Somehow one wrist rested on top of it now, and he'd angled his body and draped his other arm over the back of her seat. In the semi-dark interior of the car, his large body reclined like a lazy predator sizing up its prey.

The knots in her belly tightened as awaited his answer. She had zero recourse if he decided he'd had enough and handed her over to the authorities. Her only hope was that he wanted the quickest path to retrieving his property and wouldn't want to bother with the bureaucratic red tape of dealing with the police.

Or, as a fixer, he might want to do things his own way...

Caution whispered through her, diverting her focus from his far too fascinating face to the door.

From the corner of her eye, she caught his hard smirk. 'Re-thinking your own ultimatums, Miss Parker?' Silky, dangerous words that feathered alarmed tingles over her body.

Giada tried to hide her shivery reaction by boldly meeting his gaze, chin raised. 'Not at all. I'm only wondering how long you intend to keep me in dramatic suspense.'

A ripple went through his jaw but before he could respond, an incoming text beeped loudly.

Panic rolled through Giada as she frantically tried to recall if her phone was still off.

They'd agreed on radio silence until Gigi found the heirloom, lest it tipped Alessio off, but Gigi marched to the beat of her own drum.

Relief coursed through her when Alessio fished his phone from his breast pocket. Irritation flashed across his face as he glanced at the text, his face clenching even tighter at whatever he read. Then she watched his fingers fly over the screen for a minute in a series of quick-fire responses before he thrust the phone away.

He exhaled, then pinned her with his laser gaze. 'You have your deal, Miss Parker.' Before she could accommodate the tiniest sliver of triumph, he was continuing, 'But it will be conducted on my terms.'

With a flick of his strong fingers, the powerful engine roared to life.

Like a candle exposed to a gust of air, her relief snuffed out. 'What's that supposed to mean? What terms?'

He didn't answer immediately.

Instead, he leaned forward, making her shrink back in her

seat as he reached for her seat belt. He saw her reaction, a thin, cruel smile curving his lips, content to keep her in alarmed suspense as he secured her belt, then dealt with his own.

Then with the adeptness of a man in supreme control, he shot the car into traffic.

It wasn't until he'd pulled up at the first traffic sign that he answered. 'I've wasted enough time chasing after you. From now until this farce is over and you accept that you don't have what it takes to make it on any of my teams, I own your time. And you,' he finished in a silken voice fat with satisfaction. 'But a word of caution. Attempt anything underhanded and you'll learn the true meaning of consequences. *Capisci?*'

She'd got what she wanted and bought Gigi the precious time she needed. So why were alarm bells tolling louder in her ears? Giada tried subtly shaking her head to dispel the klaxon, but it only grew louder.

'I said, am I understood?' he pressed, that false indolence making him all the more terrifying.

Giada realised then that the tolling wasn't just in her head. The lights had turned green and horns were blaring behind them. Alessio ignored the irate drivers, his gaze fixed on her as he awaited her response.

'Yes. I understand,' she blurted, then gulped down her apprehension as satisfaction spread on his face.

His thigh muscles rippling beneath his trousers, he slid the car into gear and shot forward. Despite the glitz and glamour of Gstaad in winter, heads still turned as he cut through traffic.

Giada's thoughts continued to spin, alternating between being thankful she'd bought Gigi much-needed time, and fretting about what exactly she'd let herself in for.

Which was why it took depressingly long minutes to realise Alessio had driven to the cheap hotel she'd booked into. It didn't take as long to read the disdain on his face, however.

'You have ten minutes to pack your things,' he announced, his gaze flicking from the shady entrance to her face.

Her heart flung itself against her ribcage. 'Pack my... Why, where are we going?'

One silky eyebrow arched. 'Questioning me already?'

'I'm not following you blindly, if that's what you think,' she whipped back, more out of apprehension than anything else. Because that bell? It was clanging louder and this time it had nothing to do with irate drivers. 'And I suspect no one who works for you does either.'

Something glinted in his eyes, gone too quickly for her to decipher. 'I'm returning to Sicily in the morning. Tonight, we're spending the night at my chalet in Gris-Montana. Your interview will begin when we reach the chalet. You now have seven minutes, Miss Parker,' he warned with deadly softness.

Fevered questions tumbled on her tongue, but instinct warned her that Alessio would leap on any excuse to default her. For Gigi's sake, she couldn't hand him that excuse.

Aware of the seconds ticking away, Giada opened the door.

The two-star hotel located on a quiet side street with dim lighting and kitsch decor had seen better days, and, unlike the plush resorts and five-star hotels, the icy pavements hadn't been well swept or at all in some places.

Forgetting that she was wearing the sky-high heels her twin favoured and was way more adept at walking in, Giada stepped out, took a single step and immediately teetered wildly.

Dread and impending shame scrambled through her, a help-less cry breaking from her throat as the pavement rushed up at her.

At the last moment, and with dizzying speed that snatched her breath away, a thick, muscled arm swept her off her feet, as Alessio pulled her back against his hard torso.

Despite the layers separating them, his body heat suffused

hers, his scent wrapping around her so entirely that Giada barely managed to bite back a moan it was so appealing.

Her limbs went weak and loose, her head spinning from the effects of the near accident and his hard embrace. She wasn't sure how long he held her, only that she could feel every twitch and play of his muscles. Feel the intense awareness of his manliness. Reminding her that she hadn't been held like this for a very long time.

Not since her last, brief relationship fizzled and died under the stress of long-distance apathy.

An engine backfired in the distance. Above them, a weak bulb flickered.

Giada shook her head, willing back a modicum of the perspective she seemed to lose around this man.

'I… You can let me go now. Thanks,' she tagged on hurriedly, then cringed when her voice emerged low and husky. Almost…*turned on.*

He didn't respond or heed her request. Seconds ticked away as he held her.

Giada pressed her lips together, a little reticent to speak again in case her breathlessness betrayed her.

Alessio walked forward, still holding her captive, until they reached the double doors that led to the dingy little hotel lobby. His breath washed over her cheek, her only sign that he was leaning in closer still. 'Five minutes,' he said, low and fierce in her ear.

The second he set her down, Giada pushed away, eager to be free from his intoxicating presence. Because for several seconds, all she'd wanted was to remain plastered against the pillar of masculine heat, to receive every ounce of warmth from him and not the coat she still held onto.

She didn't need to look back to know he was watching her like a hawk, probably even following her into the building. Deciding to shun the elevator and take the stairs since she was only on the first floor, she rushed away, the giddy pounding of her pulse making her question whether the course she was taking was a wise one.

Batting away the warning—because, really, what choice did she have?—she went down another dimly lit hallway and pressed her key card to the lock.

Since she'd been on tenterhooks and out of her depth to do more than grab what she needed when she needed it, she hadn't fully unpacked.

In under a minute, she was done.

She considered texting Gigi to let her know what was happening but decided against it. It was too risky—

Thoughts and body froze when she opened the door to see Alessio leaning against the wall opposite, his hands once again shoved into his pockets.

'You didn't need to follow me up.'

'Didn't I?' he rasped with a lifted eyebrow that mocked her question.

'What do you think I was going to do? Run away? After getting you to agree to what I want?' she scoffed.

For an instant, a vicious harshness flared in his eyes. Giada wasn't sure which part of her response had caused it but she was relieved when it disappeared just as quickly. 'As long as you're in possession of what belongs to me, you can be assured that I won't take my eyes off you.'

Why that sent a sizzling trail of fire down every inch of her spine was too unsettling to contemplate. Then he was robbing her of breath all over again by stepping forward abruptly and relieving her of the small suitcase.

Giada told herself he'd done it out of suspicion, not chivalry. The tension riding him as he headed for the stairs without looking back said so.

His clipped, 'It's been taken care of,' when she approached

the reception desk to pay her bill and check out sent yet another spark of alarm through her.

The strange sensations continued to course through her as he stowed her case in the car and pointedly held the door open for her.

She found her voice a minute later, frowning at his stiff profile. 'I was perfectly capable of checking out for myself. You didn't need to do it.'

His mouth twisted, dragging her attention to its sensual curve. 'I didn't do it for you, *duci*. There's only so much of the stench I could breathe in from that filthy lobby before I caught something incurable.' He slanted her a glance, his voice dripping more of his seemingly customary disdain. 'I'm beginning to understand the gravity of your need for employment.'

Since Giada couldn't state the truth or confess that she hadn't given the hotel much more than a cursory glance after ensuring it had a bed she could sleep in and was priced within her budget, she had to let his comment slide despite its harsh sting. Keeping her gaze on the road, she shrugged. 'How far are we going?'

She felt his sharp look on her face.

'Eager to get back to your friends?' His tone held a distinct note of displeasure, making her hesitate before issuing a resounding *yes*.

She was supposed to be eager for a job, after all.

'Not at all. You'll recall I mentioned I wasn't going to follow you blindly. As for my friends, they'll be here when you and I are done.'

If anything, the atmosphere grew more charged. A little bewildered, Giada glance at him. His gaze was fixed ahead, his hands curled around the steering wheel in an easy grip that didn't disguise his tension as they stopped at another red light.

'Including the charming Jean-Luc?' The question was

snipped and chilled, the gaze he now directed to her face narrowed with irritation. 'You seem intimate with him.'

Surprise spiked her eyebrows. 'Who? Jean-Luc?'

His hot, probing gaze rested on her, his mouth a thin, formidable line.

Giada shrugged. 'I only met him a few days ago.'

His gaze remained on her. Narrowed. She curbed the urge to squirm. 'I don't even know his last name. I find that's the minimum basic requirement for someone I choose to sleep with.'

Dear God, why had she said that?

Something shifted in his eyes. Satisfaction? Triumph?

But even when the lights turned green and his gaze returned to the road the intensity remained, cranking up until it took complete hold of her.

'We're going to Gris-Montana,' he finally delivered.

That ended their conversation for the rest of the journey. She told herself to be thankful as they turned onto a lane marked *Propriété Privée.*

For the last twenty minutes they'd steadily climbed the mountain the area was named after, the accumulation of snow on the treetops and the landscape giving breathtaking white views as far as the eye could see.

But she couldn't stop the butterflies flapping their wings harder in her belly as the chalet came into view.

Giada couldn't suppress her gasp when she saw the structure. Partly lit by the surrounding white landscape, partly by strategically placed lights, the chalet was huge and golden and so magnificent she couldn't stop staring at it.

Made entirely of what looked like treated cedar logs, it soared against a backdrop of a snow-white mountain, a warm beacon in an otherwise chilly landscape. Wide windows broke the layers of wood and snow-topped slanting roof and, above it, a chimney sent out tufts of smoke into the sky.

It was picture-perfect and remote in the way only the super-rich could afford. The thought sent another dart of alarm through her.

Suppressing it, she turned to find Alessio examining her with the same intensity with which she'd just examined his chalet. A sardonic look followed the scrutiny, but he didn't say anything as he shoved his door open and came around to open hers.

Again, Giada was struck by his chivalry.

Again, she cautioned herself that it meant nothing.

In fact, everything she'd learned about Alessio Montaldi so far indicated that he was the kind of man who would smile and offer you your dreams on a silver platter…right before he destroyed you.

She stepped out, pulling the coat firmer around her when the freezing wind sent a chill through her. She realised she still wore his coat, and her gaze darted to him but he was walking away, her suitcase firmly in his hand.

She followed gingerly, cursing herself for not changing into the sturdy boots she'd brought. Then she reminded herself that she was playing a role. One that didn't feature sturdy work boots more suited to trudging through Antarctic snow running after penguins.

The wide breadth of his shoulders blocking the doorway stopped her from seeing the whole room save for the rich rugs that covered the polished wood floors, an opulent painting here and sumptuous velvet sofa there, until Alessio stepped aside to shut the wide door behind them.

Confronted with the floor-to-ceiling window and seeing the splendour of the snow-covered tall pines rising like giant white needles into the sky behind the chalet, Giada stopped in her tracks.

'Oh, my God, this is amazing!' The words slipped out before she could stop them. Then to cover the unguarded gushing, she hurriedly continued, 'You must love waking up to a view like this every morning?'

His shrug was cold and unaffected. 'It's a good place to own in my line of business but I rarely come here.' He turned away and headed down a hallway that opened into another small foyer, before pausing at the bottom of the stairs leading to the first floor. 'And small talk won't be necessary, Gigi. Neither will pandering to my ego aid your cause.'

She gritted her teeth. 'You're annoyed with me. I get it. But surely, this would go more pleasantly if we made an effort to get along?'

For a moment he seemed stunned.

Then his face clouded over and the cynical amusement returned as he folded thick arms across his chest. 'Keep telling yourself that if you need to. You may think you hold a hand worth bluffing with but understand this—things *will* go my way eventually. How long you're willing to keep up this game is entirely up to you.' He looked past her and nodded. Only then did Giada see the formally dressed butler waiting discreetly a few feet away. 'Johan will show you up to your room. Come and find me in the study in fifteen minutes. We'll begin with your first task then.'

Alessio stood at the wide window in his study, irritation biting greedily at his mood. It *was* irritation, he assured himself. Any other emotion was unacceptable because that would mean he was affected by his unwanted guest. And he absolutely refused to accommodate that. Refused to assess the dash of pleasure he'd felt from witnessing her unabashed appreciation for the very view he was staring at now. The view that had swayed him into buying this chalet.

So what if Gigi Parker liked it?

Her presence was a nuisance he would delight in doing away with as soon as possible. *Why* did he need constant reminding? As if not doing so would be…detrimental? Why couldn't he switch off his brain from recalling how soft and firm she'd felt when he'd stopped her from falling outside that deplorable place that dared name itself a hotel?

He'd performed an involuntary act he would do for most. Then he'd never wanted it to end. He'd breathed in the scent of her shampoo. Then wanted to remain exactly where he was with her locked in his arms, devouring every ounce of that glorious scent.

Diu mio, was all this snow freezing his brain? Because that could be the only explan—

The buzzing of his phone released a long-overdue growl from his throat. While he could operate from anywhere in the world, Palermo was where he thrived. It helped that it was also where his enemies were. They could cower in his presence, know the true fear of waiting for his axe to fall.

He should've put his foot down with Massimo and left days ago, he vexingly accepted, snatching his phone from his pocket.

Speak of the devil…

He read and reread his brother's text with disbelief and frustration. *'Figghiu ri—'*

'Is this a bad time?' a husky voice asked.

Alessio bit off the curse and whirled around.

She leaned in the doorway, slim arms crossed and one eyebrow raised in mild teasing. She'd changed from the cocktail dress into something equally scandalous—a pair of denim shorts that barely covered the tops of her thighs paired with a sweater that left most of her shoulders exposed and contained enough slashes and holes to render it useless. And… *Diu*… was that a neon-pink feather boa wrapped around her neck?

Had Alessio believed in the fates, he would've pleaded with them to spare him this insanity.

'I can come back later if you want?' she added, the merest wisp of amusement curving her pillowy lips.

Before he could disgrace himself with another uncustomary curse, Johan appeared, pausing a few feet from Gigi. Alessio didn't know why the presence of the butler so close to his unwanted guest riled him. Surely it couldn't be because Gigi Parker's endless expanse of killer legs was on display? Or that she followed his gaze and gifted his butler a stunning smile that made the older man's ears redden a little?

Jaw gritted, he raised his own eyebrow. *'Se?'*

His butler startled a little before inclining his head at Alessio. 'Would sir like me to serve dinner? I wasn't sure what time you would be returning but I have prepared several hot and cold meals for you to choose from.'

Alessio waved him away. 'There's no need. If everything is prepared, we'll serve ourselves when we're ready. You may leave for the day.'

If his butler was surprised by his response, he didn't show it. The older man had been employed based on his ability to exercise the utmost discretion, a trait Alessio demanded at all levels with his subordinates.

When Johan nodded and took his leave with zero fuss, Alessio sucked in a deep breath. Only to lose it again when Gigi glided into the study, her hips swaying with hypnotic rhythm he would have to be made of stone not to appreciate.

'I guess I not only need to earn my keep, I need to earn a meal too?' She stopped in front of his desk, dropped her arms and ran the tip of her finger over the polished surface. 'Then I guess we should begin.'

CHAPTER FOUR

GIADA KNEW SHE was playing with fire by goading Alessio this way.

But somewhere between leaving him in the foyer and staring cringingly at the revealing clothes she'd let Gigi talk her into packing, she'd decided that the best way forward was to keep him unsettled.

He'd agreed to her demands when he was frustrated.

He'd looked surprised when she'd admired the view from his chalet.

He'd sported a very puzzled look when he'd watched her climb the stairs to the guest room.

Somehow, for good or ill, she was doing things Alessio didn't expect. How long that remained the case, she didn't want to guess. But while he was on unstable footing, at least it would gain her some insight into how she could better deal with him.

So she'd chosen the stupidly skimpy shorts that made her insides recoil with mild horror. The sweater had been no better, with gaps that exposed most of her upper body including the skin-coloured bra she wore.

With no vest or scarf in sight, she'd had no choice but to add the feather boa to conceal *some* skin.

She looked ridiculous and felt uncomfortable. Gigi would be getting an earful the moment this infernal exercise was over.

But for now—

'What the hell are you wearing?'

The snapped query did its job of ratcheting up her unease. The seductive finger-glide stuttered and died, a tremor seizing her as she sucked in a breath.

To cover it up, she rested her hip on his desk and raised an eyebrow. 'I'm wearing *clothes*, Alessio,' she said, faking long-suffering patience.

His jaw gritted at her dry tone, but it didn't stop him from conducting a searing head-to-toe scrutiny. 'It's minus seven degrees outside.'

'Then I'm thankful you're not skimping on the heating in this lovely space.' She made a show of looking around the spectacular study, wondering whether she would get a chance to explore the floor-to-ceiling bookshelves before he tossed her out.

Gigi might abhor any literature that didn't relate to a cocktail menu but maybe Alessio didn't know that.

After several seconds' silence, she dragged her gaze from what looked like a bookcase filled with first editions to find him watching her with narrowed eyes.

Had her interest in his books given her away?

Heart dropping a little before it began thumping wildly, she straightened and forced herself to walk away from the shelves. 'Since I suspect I'm not going to win by indulging in a staring contest, shall we begin?' she pushed.

Giada had learned early on that burying one's problems or fears didn't make them go away. This situation wasn't going to get resolved until she bearded the lion in his den.

Still watching her with intense eyes, Alessio waved her to the sofas grouped in front of an exquisite fireplace. She didn't need a second bidding to relocate herself out of his direct gaze. She chose the single, sumptuous armchair, tucking one leg beneath her and quickly arranging the boa so it covered a good portion of her bare thighs.

The tingles rushing beneath her skin suggested he was still watching her but she averted her gaze, taking slow, steady breaths to compose herself.

It all proved useless when his low, deep voice rumbled across the room.

Her gaze flew up. Their eyes met.

And it belatedly registered that he wasn't talking to her. Alessio spoke with rapid-fire Sicilian into the mobile phone pressed to his ear.

Giada, being half Italian, understood enough of the conversation to know he wasn't pleased about the other person's absence, enough to glean that Alessio's growled demand for Massimo—his brother, apparently—to return immediately was falling on deaf ears.

Her cheeks burned when he uttered an earthy curse, followed by dire threats. Which didn't work, if the fingers he abruptly dragged through his hair were any indication.

Fascinated against her will, Giada watched the thick waves fall into sexy disarray as he spun around to face the window.

'This is not what we agreed, Massimo,' he gritted out in fiery censure.

Giada's breath shortened, her eyes riveted to the wide breadth of his tensing shoulders.

God, he was breathtaking.

Icily disdainful or fierily pissed off, Alessio Montaldi was captivating.

Far too captivating.

She needed to focus so she didn't mess things up for her sister. And yet, she couldn't take her eyes off him. She watched him pace in short strides, his patience rapidly fraying before he issued the final ultimatum for Massimo to present himself at the chalet by morning.

Ending the call, he tossed the phone onto the wide desk. Nostrils flared in temper, he abruptly shrugged off his jacket and tossed it over the chair.

Then those golden eyes snapped to where she sat. Without taking them off her, he sauntered close, the image of control again, as if those last minutes hadn't happened.

Giada thanked heavens she'd taken the lone seat far enough away because his very presence overwhelmed her. Stopping before the wide sectional sofa, he didn't immediately take a seat. Instead, he took his time to tug out his diamond-studded cufflinks, sliding them into his pocket before slowly folding his sleeves.

She wasn't going to stare at his brawny forearms.

She wasn't…she wasn't…she—

The flex of muscle seized her attention, the silky wisps of hair just perfect enough to make her thighs clench.

God, what was wrong with her?

Thankfully, she was saved from dwelling on the disturbing question when he folded himself into the seat and crossed one leg over the other.

Long fingers tapped his knee for several seconds. 'My client is the head of an international conglomerate.' He named the company and her eyes goggled. He saw her reaction, and one corner of his mouth twitched. 'I see you've heard of them.'

She might spend a significant portion of her time in a lab, on a research vessel or on some wide, forbidden expanse with only a handful of people, but even she'd heard of the entertainment giant. 'Anyone with a passable internet connection probably has.'

He gave a brisk nod. 'Three weeks ago he discovered that his younger brother had gambled away almost forty per cent of the revenue of the subsidiary he's in charge of and leveraged another fifteen per cent to several…unsavoury individuals.'

He named the subsidiary that streamed music and videos via an app she had on her phone.

Giada's mouth gaped. His sardonic delivery made her wonder if she'd misheard. His laser eyes said otherwise. 'You're not joking, are you?'

'I rarely joke about my business, Miss Parker.'

She exhaled in stunned alarm. 'But that's…'

'Hundreds of millions and counting. And with the brother now in rehab for his gambling, the situation is enough to plunge them into serious trouble and invite an investigation from the financial authorities if it's discovered. Simply put, should this come out, it'll end the company.'

She shook her head, unable to fathom the enormity of what he was saying. 'How did no one notice this was happening?'

Something bitterly dangerous flickered in his eyes. 'You'd be surprised how eager family are to turn a blind eye to flaws. How far they're willing to go to fool you because they know you care for them,' he said with a grating inflexion that made her tense.

Her breath locked in her lungs. Surely…he wasn't talking about her? Did he know?

Her gaze dropped to the feather boa, her fingers fussing unnecessarily with it as her brain spun. But then, her gaze slid to the discarded phone on his desk, and the snippets of frustrated conversation she'd overheard.

'Are you talking about your brother?'

He tensed, the muscle beneath his shirt rippling as he dropped his leg to the floor and leaned forward to plant his elbows on his knees. Just like in the bar, Giada was immediately aware of his power and presence. Of being the sole focus of his ferocious attention.

As if she'd ever been in danger of forgetting him, she silently scoffed.

'This isn't about me, Miss Parker.'

Are you sure?

The words hovered on her lips and she was glad she hadn't uttered them. This man had the ability to exercise supreme control, but it didn't alter the fact that, just beneath the surface, Alessio Montaldi's passions and emotions strained on a very tight leash.

For an insane second, Giada wondered what it would look like *unleashed.* Whether the very earth beneath her feet would quake with the eruption of his passions.

Thank goodness you'll never find out...

She ignored the bubble of hollowness in her belly at that thought as he continued.

'My personal life isn't up for dissection or discussion. *Caspisci?*'

His voice was a lethal blade whispering over her, dragging every nerve ending to life. It took every ounce of composure to remember she was supposed to be Gigi. Supposed to be unfazed by men like him.

'Sure,' she dismissed with an airy wave. 'I just wanted a bit more insight into the man I hope to work for.'

Derision rippled across his face. 'Counting your chickens already?'

She shrugged. 'Pessimism is a waste of good energy.'

'As is overconfidence, I imagine.'

'True. That's why I prefer a comfortable midpoint between the two. So, you were saying?'

Another flash of emotion crossed his face, this one echoing bewilderment. Giada reminded herself it was a good thing. She was keeping him unsettled.

Yet she almost regretted it when he leaned back, assuming his previous posture. 'My client wants his problems to go away before the annual board meeting in three weeks. Which also happens to be when his father turns ninety. And they announce a merger with another *FTSE 100* company.'

The sheer magnitude of the miracle he…or *she* needed to perform threatened to make her jaw drop again. It was at once exhilarating, daunting and overwhelmingly personal.

Despite their billions, a family stood on the brink of being shattered beyond repair because of the actions of a brother and son. Hadn't Gigi mentioned something about Alessio helping to orchestrate the ousting of the corrupt president of Cardosia in favour of his nephew?

Were his 'fixes' personal? Was that why he did it? What did it matter?

'Tell me how you would go about fixing it,' he invited in a silky tone, much like a snake hypnotising its prey before it struck.

Giada licked her lip, her heartbeat not at all interested in settling down. 'Well, for starters, three weeks is out of the question. I'd find a way to buy more time.'

His mouth twitched again and she found herself tracing the curve with her eyes. 'That is not an option,' he stated un-equivocally.

'Then it's impossible.'

'Throwing in the towel so quickly?' he taunted. 'I guess this interview is going to be even quicker than the last one.'

He started to rise. Panic raced up her spine. 'No. Wait.'

One eyebrow rose. And he waited.

'I… I need time to consider how to go about it. And more information about the family.' She cast a glance at his bare desk. 'Surely you have a file somewhere?'

'I do. But giving you the broad strokes is one thing, disclos-ing the finer details of the situation is another. Not that I won't sue you for everything you possess…' he paused, his gaze rak-ing mockingly over her attire '…and ensure you never hold a relevant job anywhere for the rest of your life, if you breathe a word of this to anyone.'

Giada shrugged as if his words didn't sting. 'I won't. But

if you like, I can sign one of those non-disclosure things,' she said, hoping he'd refuse. Gigi didn't have a discreet bone in her body, which really begged the question why she was so keen on landing a job with Alessio Montaldi.

If he was surprised by her offer, he didn't show it. Frankly, he looked bored. 'Contracts like that aren't worth the paper they're written on if one party has nothing to lose. Tell me, Miss Parker, what do you have to lose?' The words were soft, deadly, couched with more than a bite of suspicion.

'Far more than you think,' she said before she thought the better of it.

That got his attention. Glinting eyes pierced hers. 'Please. Enlighten me,' he invited silkily.

'Wouldn't that be falling under the personal label you wish to avoid?'

Touché, his expression said, but he didn't vocalise it. Nor did his gaze leave her. Whether this was his way of disarming his prey or he found her singularly of interest, Giada couldn't tell. She needed reprieve from it. While at the same time absurdly…craving it.

Since there was no way she was going to tell him that her work as a senior research scientist attached to one of the world's leading public think tanks would be seriously jeopardised should her activities come to light, she kept her lips sealed and awaited his next move.

Which was an indolent shrug interrupted by her loudly growling stomach. With another sardonic look, he rose.

Even from across the short distance between them he towered over her, overwhelming her anew. But the relief she expected when his gaze left her to flick to the window didn't arrive.

Outside, the last of the day's winter sunset broke through grey clouds to glint off the snow. But she suspected Alessio wasn't glancing out to admire the snow. Sure enough, he strode briskly to his desk and retrieved his phone, peppering the silence with a quick text.

Giada watched his lips firm when the answering *bloop* sounded. Tossing the phone back onto the desk with suppressed anger, he strode for the door, glancing at her over his shoulder.

'Come. We might as well have dinner. Perhaps you'll be more efficient once you've eaten something.' He paused with his hand on the handle. 'Unless you're in the grip of one of those fad diets that consist of alcohol and not much else?' he added.

Her face stinging with heat, she wanted to refuse his offer on principle alone. But she was starving, having barely eaten more than a ridiculously tiny but overpriced bowl of olives and cheese at the bar, and a slice of toast with coffee as her meagre hotel breakfast this morning. As much as she wanted to emulate her twin in this regard too—since Gigi could seemingly survive on air and alcohol—Giada couldn't deny the vital sustenance she needed to function.

Especially now.

Her discomfort ramped up as she recalled her mother's mockery of her voracious appetite.

'You double my food budget when you're here. Why can't you be more like Gigi?'

'Are you coming?' Alessio bit out, impatience pulsing off his body.

Giada rose, then felt even more self-conscious when the boa fell away, leaving her once more with several acres of skin on show.

Whether that was why Alessio's hand tightened on the handle or because this whole situation was highly vexing him, she chose not to examine as she crossed the room.

'Food sounds great. Thanks!'

Without replying, he walked off, leaving her to follow.

Beyond the study lay a sumptuous dining room, all twelve

places set with exquisite silver-and-grey-toned tableware that complemented the soft grey velvety chairs and smoked-glass table.

Alessio bypassed it, heading deeper into the chalet, to what she discovered was a masterpiece kitchen, complete with a wide island with further places set.

As Johan had detailed, a long side cabinet held several heating domes emitting incredible aromas, while, on another side, cold dishes were served on silver platters.

The large spread gave Giada pause. 'This seems a lot for two people. Are you expecting company?' Why did the thought of him entertaining guests, maybe *a woman*, make something sharp catch in her midriff?

Alessio paused on his way to the charcuterie board holding at least ten kinds of ham, cheese, olives and mouth-watering golden tarts. He grabbed one tart and tossed it into his mouth before turning sideways to glance at her. 'Would that have stopped you from striking your deal with me?'

'Of course not. But I don't recall you cancelling any plans either, so…'

Why the question brought a bite of irritation to his face, she discovered a second later. 'My brother has been using the chalet for the last week. His guests drift in and out as they please. I didn't plan on staying this long when I arrived on Friday. He was supposed to return to Sicily with me.' His eyes sharpened. 'But then you know most of that already, don't you?' he tagged on, a chilled note in his voice.

It was one question she could answer guilt-free. 'No, I really didn't.'

Gigi had made a wild guess on Switzerland, but she'd also mentioned Alessio had winter chalets in Val-d'Isère and Aspen, all rarely used by the workaholic billionaire. She didn't know why her sister had settled on Gstaad and she was glad she hadn't asked.

Alessio slanted her a disbelieving look before turning to fill his plate.

Giada chose to remain on her side of the kitchen.

The first cloche offered up a mouth-watering dish of thick lobster bisque with warm, rich rolls, the next a stuffed vegetable pie that suffused the air with garlic and rosemary. Grilled cutlets of lamb and feta almost made her groan in delight.

She helped herself to the bisque and added a salad, then joined Alessio at the kitchen island. Since he didn't seem in the mood for further conversation, she busied herself with unfurling her napkin and pouring herself a glass of water.

Then, the aromas growing irresistible, she took the first bite. She couldn't help herself. She moaned, indescribably good flavours exploding on her tongue.

Alessio's hand tightened around his fork, then he jerked to his feet and stalked away without a word.

Giada watched him leave, her skin jumping with trepidation. She was slowly chewing another mouthful, wondering what had happened, when he returned. She refused to acknowledge the tiny burst of relief when he held up a bottle of red.

She was no wine connoisseur but just by reading the label even she knew the rare vintage he held was worth several thousand euros.

'I'm assuming this is to your liking? If you prefer cheap champagne, I'm afraid you'll be disappointed.'

She exhaled in a rush, fire lighting her belly at his edgy dig. 'This is getting old very quickly. It's clear you're in a terrible mood but I suspect it's not all down to me and this situation we find ourselves in, so can you please stop piling on me?'

Fierce eyebrows clamped thunder on his features. 'Piling... on you?' he echoed with a puzzled rasp, fingers curling around the neck of the bottle.

The weirdest thing happened.

Giada laughed, the burst of mirth erupting from the depths of her frayed nerves.

Alessio's eyes widened. Right before his golden eyes darkened and latched onto her mouth.

'It means—'

'I have a fair idea what it means, Miss Parker,' he interjected, his voice still curiously husky. A moment later, he exhaled. 'You're correct. It's not often I let other matters get in the way of what I want.'

The admission sent shock waves through her. She didn't need to spend a considerable length of time with him to know Alessio Montaldi wasn't a man who disclosed such things freely. From his disgruntled expression, she suspected he was equally alarmed by the revelation.

He gave a brusque shake of his head and held the bottle higher. 'Wine?' he bit out.

Indecision prickled her.

She rarely drank beyond the occasional birthday or celebratory toast. And as she'd learned in the few hours she'd been in his company, she needed to keep her wits about her. But those same wits could glean quickly that she would be acting out of the norm if she refused, since her sister was a keen supporter of the 'it's five o'clock somewhere' attitude to drinking.

'If you're planning on getting me drunk then pumping me for information on your property, it's not going to work,' she said, hedging to buy herself some time.

His head snapped back, his eyes boiling with fury.

Giada wanted to rush to apologise but something held her back. The same absurd urging she'd had earlier on.

The need to see him lose control.

'I have very little doubt that you'll spill the goods sooner rather than later. And it won't involve underhanded tactics. At least not on my part.'

The last bit was aimed squarely at her and the shame that

unravelled through her, heating her face and robbing her of breath, was evident for him to see.

He gave a mocking smile of acknowledgment of his bullseye strike. Then he reached for the bottle, uncorked it and poured the glass she'd so clumsily attempted to refuse.

Now with little choice if she didn't want to appear churlish—and to save her speaking and disgracing herself further—Giada snatched the glass and took an unwittingly large gulp while her mind raced for ways to extract herself from this.

Several minutes later, her senses were still swimming, and, while she suspected most of it was due to Alessio and his infernal *presence*, she knew some of it was due to the wine, too.

Watching her mother and sister make spectacles of themselves after imbibing alcohol had made her shy away from the stuff, earning her another of the myriad names they liked to label her with. But here she was, skating dangerously close to edges she normally stayed far away from.

And not just that. She was also risking giving herself away.

Thank goodness he'd given her a reprieve from the interview for dinner. She stared into her glass, wondering if he'd suspect anything if she announced she was going to bed after their meal.

Since it was barely eight p.m. that would definitely raise suspicion.

'So what else is getting in the way of what you want? Besides me, that is?' she said in the silence. Having polished off her first course, she hedged for a few minutes before deciding she wasn't going to cut off her nose to spite her face when she was dying for another helping.

Hell, if the worst happened and he threw her out, at least she'd have a full stomach.

Scooping up a helping of lasagne and adding a gooey square

of garlic bread plus salad to it, she turned to find him watching her.

His gaze went from the plate to her face and Giada stiffened.

'Your appetite is more robust than I remember,' he observed with something like approval coating his voice.

She sent a quick plea that the blush creeping up her chest wouldn't reach her face. 'I wasn't aware my appetite was a thing of interest to you.'

'It isn't. But I recall you barely touching any food the last time we were in the same place together. Booze was more your speed.'

Since she didn't want to incriminate herself, Giada waved an airy hand. 'My appetite comes and goes. And when the food is this amazing, how can I resist?'

His gaze dropped to her mouth, then progressed down her throat and body. 'Interesting.'

Oh, God.

Giada turned back to the buffet to hide her dismay.

Did he believe her? Forcing her brain to stay on track, she cleared her throat. 'You haven't answered my question. And before you say it's none of my business, you opened the door.' Glad her voice was brisk with no signs of her inner turmoil, she returned to the island. 'So?'

He waited until she sat, then topped up her wine glass before she could stop him. Rising, he went to replenish his plate too, choosing giant meatballs smothered in tomato sauce, and *garganelli*. 'My brother assured me he would be here so we can return to Palermo together tomorrow for the holidays as per our family tradition.'

Something sharp knifed her gut. It felt uncomfortably like envy.

She'd stopped wondering what it would feel like to have a warm and comforting tradition set in stone, to not live with the uncertainty of wondering which whimsical place her mother would choose and what atmosphere awaited her when she inevitably dragged herself there. 'You spend holidays with your family in Sicily?'

'*Se,*' he responded, a bite of something earthy and solemn in his voice. 'Don't tell me, you prefer the company of a big, rowdy crowd made up of acquaintances you barely know to lose yourself in?'

She forced herself not to react because what he'd said was partly true.

Much as she'd yearned for the close comfort of her small family in years gone by, she'd come to accept that would never happen. These days Giada would much rather stay on a research vessel and work through the holidays than put herself through her mother's inevitable roller-coaster cycle of emotions. It seemed the older her mother got, the more erratic the occasions were destined to become.

'You know me well,' she quipped, assuring herself that leaning into Alessio Montaldi's stereotyped assumptions was better than revealing the stark bewilderment of her dysfunctional family.

His lips compressed, disdain reigniting in his eyes.

Giada told herself it was better this way, but she couldn't stop the hollow yawning in her belly. 'The evening is still young. Time enough for your brother to return. So what's the problem?'

'The problem is Massimo took my helicopter. And informed me by text half an hour ago that I shouldn't expect him in the morning because he's planning to spend the day with friends in Verbier. So the very earliest I can hope to leave this place is tomorrow evening.'

'And to a man like you, a few more hours in a gorgeous chalet is a fate worse than death?' she attempted to tease.

His eyes narrowed. 'When this isn't where I want to be or the company I desire? *Se*, it most definitely is,' he bit out without mercy.

Was she shocked that he didn't bother to hold back that her company was the last thing he wanted? Probably not. But she *hated* that intensifying hollowness in her body.

Because it reeked far too much of the dejection she suffered whenever she was with Gigi and her mother. She hated that she'd never managed to wrestle away the *yearning* and the *hope* and fruitless *wish* for a better connection with the only family she had. Especially during the holiday season.

There was a time in the distant past when Christmas had been a true time for joy. When her mother had come within a whisker of being happy, when Giada and Gigi had the promise of a proper family within reach. Perhaps that was why she hated this time of year. Her foolish heart never failed to *yearn*.

And reality was always, *always* worse than the expectation.

'You find my words harsh? Or just personal?'

She startled and looked up to find his gaze near her plate. Following it, she saw how tightly she'd gripped her fork.

She relaxed her fingers. 'Do you care?' she countered, pride sparking anger. 'We're using each other as a means to our own ends, aren't we? Like you said, our personal lives aren't part of the deal. My feelings in this don't matter. The fact that you might be my potential employer shouldn't change anything. You employ thousands of people. I'll do my job and we don't even need to see each other again after tonight.'

For some reason, he looked even more disgruntled. He set his own cutlery down and picked up his wine glass.

Giada couldn't stop herself from glancing at those capable fingers wrapped around the delicate crystal. Remembering how they'd felt against her skin when he'd thrown her over his shoulder and stormed out of the club in Gstaad. How his touch had branded her.

Heat rose to blend with the other sensations swirling through her. She shifted in her seat, willing them all away.

But they remained, intensifying as he lifted the glass, his eyes fixated on her as he took a healthy gulp.

'I stay in constant touch with my teams. I find face-to-face interaction produces the best results. Things have a habit of… festering in the dark. Assuming things are running smoothly out of sight is asking to be stabbed in the back.'

His nostrils thinned and a shadow moved over his face as he spoke. Before she could begin to work out what that meant, he continued, 'I've learned not to allow that to happen. So should you, in the unlikely event, find yourself contracted to me, you won't have the freedom of running around thinking you can do what you want. Perhaps you should consider that before this goes any further?' There was a slice of something smug and almost…*anticipatory* in his voice.

As if he relished the opportunity to toy with his prey.

A shiver raced over her. The notion that she'd be required to be at his beck and call every hour of every day—because she suspected there was nothing as mundane as a nine-to-five with this man—*excited* her.

Well, not *her*.

Gigi.

There was that hollow again.

What was wrong with her?

Sucking in a breath, she reached for her glass of water with a touch of desperation. It would do her more good than the wine. 'That's good to know. And no, that won't change my mind. I still want this job.'

His eyes glinted with a mixture of mockery and begrudging…respect? When the latter eased a touch of that hollowness, Giada suspected that her brain and body were playing tricks on her.

Because that would mean…

She jerked away from the table, and when his eyes narrowed, she picked up her half-finished plate and headed for the sink.

'What are you doing?' he growled behind her.

'I've finished eating. And as you dismissed your butler for the night, I'm clearing up.' She shrugged, not turning around in case he read her befuddled feelings in her expression.

For several seconds, silence reigned behind her, then she heard the distinct sound of his chair scraping back.

Giada's skin tightened as he strolled closer. As his scent hit her nostrils. As he paused behind her before stepping next to her, his plate in hand.

As she felt the singe of his regard before he drawled, 'I'm reluctant to admit you've done the impossible, Gigi. You've surprised me. Whether that's a good or bad thing, I'm yet to make up my mind. Perhaps having another day I don't want freed up in my schedule may not be a bad thing after all.'

CHAPTER FIVE

HIS WORDS MADE her nervous, Alessio could tell.

For some reason he welcomed it. Relished it in fact because it eased some of the unsettled feelings rushing freely through him. And while he wanted to blame Massimo and his infuriating avoidance antics for those emotions, Alessio knew most of it stemmed from this woman.

Diu, his confession was ringing in his ears and he *still* couldn't believe he'd given his potential adversary an insight into his thoughts.

And she was an adversary. Just because she didn't seem like the entitled princess he'd initially written her off to be didn't mean he could lower his guard.

She was still withholding his property from him, after all.

But even her nervousness was a surprise.

The Gigi he'd encountered before didn't have a nervous bone in her body. She'd been the typical brazen, party-addicted socialite chasing her next adventure, not this seemingly conscientious individual who baulked at drinking wine and tidied up after herself without whining about the absence of servants.

She's playing a part...

The realisation sent a bolt of ire—and alarming disappointment—through his gut.

He watched her closely, saw her visibly relax her shoulders and breathe out, while avoiding his gaze and throwing open cabinets until she found what she was looking for—the dishwasher.

With a touch of that bewilderment that irritated him, he watched her place her dish and cutlery within, before pointedly looking at his. When he didn't move, her gaze flicked up. The hint of nerves and spark of fire within stoked his own.

A little bemused by the whole situation, Alessio—who couldn't remember the last time he'd stacked a dishwasher—stepped forward and slotted in his used plate and cutlery.

Then straightened, his hands propped on his hips.

Your move.

She licked her lower lip, then bit the inside of it as her eyes darted once more around the kitchen, avoiding his. When she spun away from him and hurried back to the stool, he couldn't help but stare at her lush behind, a groan rising forcefully in his throat before he swallowed it back down.

'I've had an idea about your problem.'

'You mean your problem, don't you?' he countered, striding after her with a compulsion he couldn't stop.

She shrugged, and while she dragged her wine glass towards her, she made no move to drink, contenting herself with running a slim finger along the edge. 'I guess. Okay, here's my idea. Since it's a subsidiary, would your client be prepared to sell it off quickly? Get rid of it so it's no longer part of the whole? Surely the new buyers would agree to take the other thriving businesses at a renegotiated deal than saddle themselves with the problematic subsidiary?'

'They probably would, if the problem wasn't being kept under strict wraps. This subsidiary forms part of the deal. Suddenly selling it off would raise more questions and invite more scrutiny. And you also forget the issue of the fifteen per cent in the control of others. That isn't a problem that can be wrapped up as neatly as everyone would want.'

'Why not? Who are these people?' she asked, her eyes wide

with curiosity and speculation. 'You mentioned they were un-savoury. Just how…umm…unsavoury?'

Alessio's jaw tightened. 'They're the kind of vicious leeches who target and prey on weak individuals. The kind who shouldn't be allowed to get within a mile of someone like my client's brother, and yet it's inevitable that he'd fall within their clutches.'

He hadn't meant that to come out so forcefully. Hadn't meant to let on that crushing the kind of parasites he abhorred had been the only reason he'd taken on this particular client.

'Why is it inevitable?'

'Because people have the unfortunate habit of believing the worst can never happen to them. That they're safe trusting the best of people who lie and cheat their way into positions of power. Right up until they discover differently. Almost always by then, it's too late.'

As it'd been too late for his father, his mother and far too many members of his family. In the space of one lazy Sunday afternoon, his family had been decimated by men his father thought he could trust.

The speculation in her eyes deepened and he wondered why the hell he couldn't shut up. She didn't need to be a rocket scientist to work out that there was some *personal history* behind his clipped words.

He turned from her, stabbing his fingers through his hair as the roiling intensified within him. He'd never been great with being away from Sicily at this time of year. It had been his mother's favourite season, every moment before Christmas Day a time of joyous celebration. Even after the tragedy, despite her sorrow and heartbreak over her dead husband, she'd been determined to put on a brave front for her sons.

Of course, it also inevitably reminded him of all that had been taken from him, and reignited the vow he'd made to make his enemies pay.

Maybe that was why all these useless emotions were leaking from him.

Basta...

Massimo had better present himself tomorrow or he would hunt him down and make him regret these silly games he was playing with him.

Until then...

He turned back to her, his gut clenching again when he found her eyes pinned on him. Her expression was a mix of sympathy and heated curiosity. He hated the first, was unwillingly drawn to the second.

Alessio couldn't...didn't feel inclined to look away.

Something in Gigi Parker's eyes drew him. A spark within the smoky grey that propelled fire and need through him that had nothing to do with the turbulent situation with his brother, his client, his stolen heirloom or the outside world, and everything to do with the comprehension that he was *attracted* to her.

Diu mio. A growl left his throat before he could contain it.

She startled in her seat, but surprisingly, after a beat, said, 'Well, the only way forward that I can see is for your client to come clean or to buy off these people who own the fifteen per cent. As much as it sticks in my craw to help them profit further, sometimes it's better to cut your losses.'

Interesting. 'And if they won't go away?'

Her eyes widened into sparkling pools that he wanted to get lost in. Then a shadow crossed her face and she lowered her gaze for a second before meeting his again. 'Everyone has a price. Or barring that...'

Her voice drifted off and a look came over her face, a reluctance as she took a breath.

'Or what?'

Her lips firmed, then she forced the words out. 'A weak spot that they don't want exposed?'

Now it was his turn to burn with curiosity. The depth of feeling in her voice told an intriguing story. The need to know pounded through him, boundaries be damned.

He forced himself to suppress the need to demand to know what it was.

'You recommend that I exploit that weak spot?' he asked, quietly impressed and intrigued.

'Aren't you going to anyway?' she returned, mild challenge and…something else in her eyes.

Something that resembled… She wasn't *judging* him. Was she?

'You find something wrong with the way I fix problems, *duci*?' he asked silkily, wishing his earlier fury with her would return. Because, really, who was this creature to judge him? She was a *thief.* A common, albeit alluring, mercenary. 'Aren't you, right in this moment, playing dirty to get what you want?'

She had the grace to blush—another intriguing ability he wouldn't have believed her capable of at their last interaction. Alessio followed the pink trajectory, an urgent craving to trace his fingers along her skin attacking his insides.

'Would you have given me a chance any other way?'

'No.' Alessio didn't have any qualms about admitting it. After the harrowing experiences he'd endured, he apologised for very little. Still, he avidly watched her reaction to his response.

She shrugged. As if she didn't care one way or the other.

His disgruntlement rankled again. Along with his reluctant admiration.

This woman had a thicker skin than he'd credited her with. What else lay beneath that satin-smooth skin? His tongue thickened in his mouth as other, more carnal, demands arose.

'So are you going to?'

'*Cosa?*' he asked in his mother tongue, his thoughts firmly mired in carnal filth.

'Explore their weak spots on behalf of your client?' Her tone still held a measure of judgement.

Yes, he wanted to reply. But the pang stopped him. Which was ridiculous.

He should have no reservations about dishing out retribution where it was deserved. 'Ultimately, if that path is taken, it'll be the client's call.' Her gaze stayed on him a fraction longer, and he gritted his teeth when the pang sharpened. Enough of this. 'But whether I do or not shouldn't stop you from finding alternatives—where are you going?' he asked sharply when she pushed her glass away—still half full—and rose.

Her gaze darted to the window and the darkness that had encroached while they'd been eating. 'I'm going to bed. If we've got all day tomorrow, I'd rather approach this with a fresh perspective in the morning.'

Another jolt of shock rocked him.

She was calling it a night? *She* was taking herself off to bed when he was wide awake?

Every single, sexually available woman he knew would've taken swift advantage of the hunger he knew blazed in his eyes and thrown herself at him by now. Curiously, this woman was almost jumpy with denial and nerves she was doing her utmost to hide, her gaze darting to then away from his as he stared in blatant disbelief.

She wasn't playing hard to get.

Alessio had been well versed in that particular game since he was seventeen and navigating his way through boyhood into manhood under circumstances that would've felled a lesser man.

No, she was genuinely walking away, leaving him to cool his heels.

He wanted to deny her escape, to state unequivocally that *he* would decide when she went to bed. But even in his head, it sounded churlish and borderline childish, the actions of a weak man, and he, Alessio Montaldi, was anything but weak.

Besides, he had a few dozen tasks demanding his attention. Tasks that would ensure he didn't give this creature a single second more than he'd already wasted on her.

He'd barely managed a curt nod of dismissal when she stepped away from the island, that ridiculous boa trailing on the floor. He watched her nervously pluck at it as she stared at him, her lips moving but no words forming.

Was she rethinking her decision? Had she rightly realised she was letting an opportunity pass and was about to suggest the much clichéd and highly suggestive nightcap—?

'See you in the morning.'

Another rumble of disquiet held him still and mute. But it didn't stop his gaze from tracking her when she headed for the door.

Nor could he drag his gaze from the lush swaying of her hips, from the delicious curve of her ass and the sculpted legs he could imagine wrapping around his hips as he drove into her.

That was not going to happen! Remember who she is. Why she's here.

'Gigi.' His voice was a touch untamed, echoing his feelings inside.

Did her shoulders hitch with tension before she faced him? 'Yes?'

'My property, it is safe?' Alessio despised the throb of emotion in his voice, even more so when her eyes widened at hearing it. Perhaps that was why her gaze dropped. Why she slicked her tongue over her bottom lip.

His reputation was ruthless enough for people to believe he had no emotions. Maybe this creature had believed it too. Was he embarrassing her?

For some absurd reason, Alessio wanted to reassure her that he was human.

Thank God, he killed that notion quickly.

Her gaze rose again. 'You have my word that you'll be reunited with your property once we're done here.'

By the time she reached her room, Giada was drowning in guilt. Sagging against the door after she shut it, she took a deep breath, tried to reason with herself.

He'd asked for reassurance. She'd given it without truly knowing whether she was able to do so. But what other choice had she had?

A low moan escaped her and with every sinew in her body, she wanted to rush across the room, dig out the phone, and call Gigi. Demand to know precisely when she was retrieving Alessio's heirloom and to hell with the radio silence they'd agreed on.

But even as the thought tempted her, she knew she couldn't risk it. Aside from the threat of exposing her sister, that look on Alessio's face just now was enough to stay her hand. That tiniest sliver of vulnerability quickly doused but present enough to have made her breath catch. To have triggered a yearning to know exactly what the family crest meant to him. Why he was so desperate to have it returned to him.

Of course, she hadn't dared. She might have fast-talked her way into this position but the last thing she wanted to do was taunt the dragon.

Her gaze fell on the bed, and she moved towards it.

A quick shower and bed.

Tomorrow would be here soon enough. A day she'd have to spend in the chalet with Alessio, waiting for his brother to return.

Another moan slid free before she could stop it but, feeling a little fed up with herself for her wilting-rose performance, she straightened her spine. Crossing the room, she reminded herself that had Alessio given Gigi the full interview as he'd promised or not humiliated her enough to anger her, they wouldn't be in this situation.

He was merely reaping the consequences of his actions.

The shower was glorious, the full jets easing a few layers of her tension but by no means all of them. Giada suspected she wouldn't be able to fully relax until she left here.

Whenever that was.

The thought led to tossing and turning for hours after she slid between the sumptuous sheets. Without her phone or a watch, she had no idea what time she eventually drifted off, but she knew she'd slept way longer than usual when she jolted upright with a sinking feeling in her stomach.

The rich, heavy curtains blocking the wide windows had effectively kept the white landscape from disturbing her but she still frowned as her feet hit the floor.

Something had definitely woken her.

Padding barefoot towards the door, she pulled it open, only to freeze when the sound of a very angry, very frustrated male reached her ears.

Giada frowned down at the flimsy nightgown Gigi had packed for her. It was barely more than a few strings of lace and netting. Shaking her head at how her sister could wear this—or any other items of clothes she owned—she gladly tugged it off and reached for the silk bathrobe she'd found in the bathroom last night.

It covered her from neck to calves more fully than anything else in her suitcase. Feeling better armoured, she brushed her teeth, pulled her hair into a ponytail and stepped out of her room.

The hallway was deserted. As were the foyer, dining and living rooms.

She hadn't actually had a full tour of the chalet so she wasn't sure where the irate conversation was taking place besides Alessio's study, which also turned out to be empty.

But as she was heading for the kitchen, she spotted the staircase leading to a lower level. And from the stairwell, she heard Alessio snapping in quick-fire Sicilian at some hapless recipient of his ire.

She debated the wisdom of bearding the lion in his den, especially without the bolstering foundation of coffee. But her feet, apparently possessing a mind of their own, propelled her down the stairs before she could stop herself.

The basement was a sublime revelation that would no doubt register properly when her attention wasn't entirely absorbed by the man pacing the heated flagstones.

As she took him in, panic of a different sort joined the roiling in her belly.

Alessio wore only a pair of black cotton lounge bottoms, sweat dripping down his very bare, very sweaty torso. The discarded boxing gloves on a bench nearby indicated what he'd been doing when he'd been interrupted.

Fireworks exploded beneath her skin and Giada was thankful her robe was thick enough to hide her body's reaction from him. Otherwise she would've needed to throw herself into the large indoor-outdoor pool sparkling invitingly just beyond a set of wide glass doors with wispy strands of steam rising off it.

Alessio hadn't noticed her yet. When he paced away from her, she gaped at the sight of his bare back, and the tattoos inked deep into his skin.

The first etching was of a sword, hilted with what looked like a ruby and emerald, with a fist clenched tight around it. Then followed a set of black roman numerals from where the tip of the blade ended, all the way down to the bottom of his spine.

It was mesmerising and she knew deep in her bones it meant something deeply personal to him. Her fingers itched to touch so badly, a sound broke from her mouth before she could stall it.

Breath held, she watched him spin around.

Alessio's flaming eyes fixed on her, his phone still glued to his ear as he rasped in Sicilian, 'This is unacceptable. I need to get out of here.'

In the throbbing silence, she heard a hesitant voice make a suggestion he evidently found displeasing, and his already statue-like form stiffened further.

'Absolutely not. You will get off the phone and find a different solution. One that doesn't involve— *Ciao? Ciao?*' He yanked down the phone and stared at the screen, incredulity mounting on his face. *'Figghiu ri—!'* He bit off the end of the epithet, his lips thinning until they were a white tense line as he sucked in a long, sustained breath.

'I'm guessing saying good morning won't go down well right now?'

Dark eyes regarding her from beneath thunderous eyebrows, his fingers tightened around his phone. 'No, *duci*. It is far from a good morning.'

Every instinct screamed at her to leave, but her body refused to obey. 'I was about to get myself some coffee. Do you want one?'

For another uncomfortable beat, he stared at her as if having a hard time deciphering her words. Giada pivoted towards the stairs, concluding that he'd either ignore her or take her up on her offer.

She was nearing the top when she felt his presence behind her.

She concentrated on putting one foot in front of the other and thankfully made it to the kitchen without stumbling. Relieved that the elaborate coffeemaker had already been set up to dispense the heavenly nectar, she glanced over her shoul der at him. 'Double espresso?'

A flash of surprise lit his eyes before he gave a single, curt nod. While she busied herself making their beverages, he prowled from one end of the kitchen to the other.

The moment she turned with his espresso, he stopped moving, his eyes once more riveted to her. Giada didn't want to know why his singular focus affected her so viscerally.

It meant nothing. Absolutely nothing.

And yet her belly flipped as she handed him his cup. Watched him stare into its black depths for a handful of seconds before he tossed it back in one brazen swallow.

An act she found far too sexy for her sanity.

Cradling her own cup of standard coffee—if the rich smooth Java the likes of which she'd never tasted before could be called standard—she attempted to alleviate the tension whipping around the room.

'More problems with Massimo?'

Impatient irritation flashed across his face. 'I haven't spoken to my brother this morning. There's no point now.'

'Oh, I...' She frowned. 'Wait, what do you mean there's no point?'

Narrowed gold eyes bored into her, as if trying to decipher what seemed to be a ridiculous question to him. 'Have you looked outside at all?'

'Outside?' she echoed. 'No. Why would I need to—?' Giada turned as she spoke.

At first, she couldn't tell what he meant. Then, obviously impatient with her inability to grasp his meaning quickly, Alessio stalked to where she stood, took her by the elbow and marched her to the window.

Where she bore witness to the near apocalyptic white-out that stretched as far as the eye could see.

It was eerie in its beauty and terrifying in its meaning. Because she'd seen this type of snowstorm before, but thousands of miles away, in the Antarctic, where it was a run-of-the-mill occurrence. Where it was common and expected and often even celebrated from a safe distance.

But here? Now? The unwelcome implications tumbled through her head.

Her gaze flew to his, probably seeking some reassurance that her eyes were deceiving her even as she shook her head. 'No,' she breathed, her voice diminished with shock.

Which seemed to please him if the sinister smile that danced around his no longer thinned lips was an indication. 'Oh, yes, *duci*,' he stated with cold finality. 'Courtesy of a freak storm last night, we're snowed in. Which means neither you nor I are going anywhere any time soon.'

For a full minute, panic prevented her vocal cords from working. When they did, her frantic gaze returned to the window. 'That's impossible.'

The warmth of his breath brushed her ear a second before he responded, 'Not only is it possible, we're about to be hit by a harder one in the next hour. If you don't believe me, just look up.'

She did. And her stomach fell. Snow-laden clouds overhead hung thick and low, a sure sign that another fierce storm was imminent.

She sucked in a panicked breath and turned to him. 'So what's the plan? How do we get out of here?'

One sardonic eyebrow rose. 'Did you not hear what I just said?'

Because she needed space from his proximity to think and to formulate an escape—because getting cooped up in this chalet with him was *not* going to happen—she hurried to the island and braced herself against it. With her roiling insides, thoughts of caffeine no longer appealed, so she set her cup down.

Then resolutely faced him. 'But you…you're Alessio

Montaldi, world-class fixer. Surely, we're not just going to sit here for…however long it takes for this to clear, are we?'

She realised she was wringing her hands when his gaze fell on them. But even as she froze the motion, he was leaning back against the very same window, toned arms folding contemplatively as he watched her. 'Why, Gigi, you seem overly agitated. Wasn't this what you were angling for all along, a chance to have me all to yourself? I thought you'd be more excited that Santa has delivered your Christmas wish much quicker than you expected or, I dare say, even deserved?'

The reminder that Christmas was fast approaching, and that she would be stuck impersonating her sister, sent bolts of panic through her.

More, her mother would be *livid* if Giada ruined whatever plans she had up her sleeves. 'Believe it or not, this isn't what I want at all.' This was supposed to have been a *brief* stalling tactic to buy Gigi time she needed to relocate Alessio's property.

His gaze hardened. 'Do you not have the courage to grab the opportunity this presents to you? Or is the distress because there's not enough of an audience here to keep you entertained? Your penchant for dancing on tables and pouring liquor down your throat does not offer the same satisfaction when you have only me for company?' he mocked.

The impulse to deny it all was swift and hot. But she forced herself to lift her chin, to stare him down with a taunting, bored gaze of her own. 'Maybe. What's wrong with wanting the company of friends? Especially around the holidays? I want this job, yes. But I also have a life beyond this. So yes, I have plans that don't include being cooped up here with you.' Her very being shook with uttering that last sentence. Because the reality grew more unnerving with each passing second.

'Except it isn't just the holidays with people like you, is

it?' He tightened the screw with cynical judgement dripping from his dark gold eyes. 'Life is a year-round party, isn't it?'

She rolled her eyes. 'And you have a problem with it, I'm guessing? You'd rather everyone in the world walks around like a brute with a vendetta or some other carnage brewing in their eyes the way you do?'

Thick, charged silence rushed into the kitchen, the heartbeat drumming in her ears amplifying her foolishness. She knew it from the embers sparking to life in his eyes. From the way her fingers and toes tingled from the force of his incandescent stare. Before she could think *What would Gigi do?* Giada was rushing into speech. 'I'm sorry, I didn't mean—'

He swatted her apology away with a wave of his hand. 'I don't care what you think about me. I would happily toss you out into the storm so you can be reunited with your cheerleading squad, if your risking death didn't mean loss of my property.' He straightened and his arms fell to his sides as he strolled towards her with the false indolence and grace of a panther. 'Tell me where it is, and as soon as my team recover it, you can brave the elements back to the bright lights. Far be it for me to keep you from cheap booze and mediocre conversation.'

Oh, he was good. Breathtakingly so.

Giada's head spun with the way he'd turned the tables on her.

Her fingers knitted again—a habit she couldn't stop—and her brain scrambled feverishly. 'Who were you on the phone with earlier?' she demanded, sidetracking to buy herself time to frame an answer. 'I heard what you said about needing to get out of here. If it wasn't your brother, then who were you talking to? Was it someone who could get us out of here?' She knew her questions were too eager but she didn't care. Not if his answer was *yes*.

His pitying look said her prayers were about to be denied.

He came even closer, arms extending to rest on the countertop on either side of her hips, effectively caging her in. The scent of sweat mingled with pure man should've put her off. Instead, she had the wild desire to place her nose in his throat, *breathe him in*.

'If you heard that part, then you also heard my response. As much as you wish it, the answer is no, *duci*. The lines are down, which means no phone calls. No internet. There's no getting off this mountain. Not until the series of storms have passed. As much as we both loathe it, we're stuck with one another.'

She was absorbing the fact that Alessio Montaldi didn't find her a mere nuisance but actually *loathed* her presence when he lifted a hand.

Giada shouldn't have noticed how elegant his fingers were, with the neatly trimmed nails and the wisps of hair that dusted the back of them. But as with the tattoo that rippled and writhed with each movement, she was completely absorbed.

So much so, she didn't...*couldn't* utter a word as he slowly traced her bottom lip with his forefinger. As his piercing gaze absorbed every flicker of expression as if it were his due. As her body trembled and roused with eagerness at his electric touch and she had to scramble madly to prevent the moan that eagerly rose to her throat from escaping.

'So tell me, are you going to play a good little houseguest or are you still intent on taking a chance with the elements?'

Since she wasn't stupid and since she of all people knew first-hand how dangerous the ice could be, no matter how entrancing it was to look at, she had little choice but to give him her answer. 'I'll stay,' she said, but the next words were unplanned, falling from her lips without her permission. 'But nothing has changed since yesterday. If you're expecting meek and mild, you're going to be very disappointed.'

She'd held her breath, anticipating his displeasure or temper.

Alessio had just stared down the blade of his nose at her, that disdain surging to full force. The next instant he straightened and exited the kitchen without a word.

Leaving her to stagger back to the window, disbelief still deadening her limbs at the situation she'd found herself in.

How the hell would she survive days in this chalet with Alessio Montaldi?

And why did it send a flurry of *excited* butterflies through her belly?

CHAPTER SIX

THAT HAD BEEN three hours ago.

Alessio didn't make an appearance when she ventured out of her room and, unable to sit still with her senses jumping over the nerve-shredding situation she found herself in, she toured the rest of the chalet.

It was much bigger than she'd initially realised.

Besides the kitchen and dining areas, she discovered another, larger living room towards the back of the chalet, complete with two fireplaces, enough seating for a very large gathering, and—breathtaking enough to stop her in her tracks—a white ceiling-grazing Christmas tree, decorated exclusively with dark gold and the occasional dark green ornaments she was certain didn't come from a high-street department store.

Venturing closer, she noticed that the larger adornments contained small velvet boxes with discreet designer labels of famous jewellers giving a strong hint as to their contents.

Giada's eyes widened as she skirted the base, quickly losing count of how many such baubles graced the stunning tree. Over the mantelpieces was even more jaw-dropping opulence, little expensive gifts cleverly hidden within the strings of Swarovski crystals expertly trailed through the holly wreaths and the remaining decorations.

Had she been here under other circumstances, she would've

been thrilled to explore some more. But Giada couldn't stem the trepidation pulsing through her and the one thought pounding in her brain.

She was stuck here with Alessio Montaldi. No end in sight.

The thought eventually drove her back to her bedroom, frantically looking for a way out. All that greeted her when she looked out of the window was the last snow dump two hours ago, and the promise of more in the laden skies resting over the valley.

A sound of apprehension-laced frustration erupted before she could quell it. Which made her berate herself. Since when did she dissolve into a helpless puddle at the first sign of adversity?

Since you were locked in with a man who makes your pulse skitter like loose marbles tossed on a stone floor!

Enough.

Going to her suitcase, she dug out her phone, a pang of regret piercing her. She should've texted Gigi last night instead of playing it extra safe. Powering it up, she paced her room, praying for a single bar.

After a futile half-hour, she gave up and turned it off again.

Before she'd put it away, the butterflies were kicking around again, her senses jumping. She discovered the reason why when she stepped out of her room and found Alessio in the hallway.

He'd showered and changed, but evidently it'd done nothing to ease the stark displeasure etched into his face.

She'd known she couldn't avoid him for ever, much as she wished to. But knowing didn't prepare her for coming face to face with him again. For the flurry of excitement that rushed through her when he moved closer.

Her breath caught and held as he examined her much like the specimens she pored over on her research missions. He didn't care that time grew uncomfortably long between them, nor did he give an inkling as to what he was searching for.

Whether he was satisfied at finding it or he gave up, he turned away, leaving Giada to expel a silent, pent-up breath.

'We may be temporarily stranded here but there's no reason why we can't pick up where we left off last night,' he said.

For another charged moment, her thoughts flew helter-skelter, until she realised he was referring to his client's problem. To the interview she was purportedly here for.

'Oh. Yes, of course.'

He strode a few steps away, then paused when he realised she wasn't following. 'Are you coming?'

Her gaze flew up from where it'd dropped to his backside. One eyebrow arched, his mocking eyes landing on her scorched cheeks.

Oh, God...

Had she really been checking him out as if he were a side of prime beef? Flinging her gaze to a point over his shoulder, she tried not to trip over her own feet as she followed him downstairs, and into the kitchen.

'There's more than enough from last night or fresh cold meals in the fridge for lunch. Are you okay with vichyssoise and a salad to follow?' he asked over his shoulder.

She nodded hurriedly. 'Of course.' When she found herself watching him avidly again while he performed the mundane task of pulling dishes out of the fridge, Giada shook her head. 'I'll go and set the table in the dining room, unless you want to eat in here?'

'The dining room will do. But the table is already set,' he murmured.

She hid her grimace as she remembered seeing it before. 'Oh...yes.'

'Feel free to choose wine. The cellar is through there.'

She followed his direction and went past an industrial-sized pantry stocked to the gills with enough food to feed an army for several months.

Praying fervently they wouldn't need more than a fraction of it, Giada went through swinging doors into another room stocked brim-full of wine and spirits. Red, white, and everything in between flashed at her, leaving her with a momentary pang of disquiet. Every bottle looked vintage but, like last night, their exclusivity screamed at her. Indecision made her pluck out and return several bottles, her lip caught between her teeth.

'Problem?'

She jumped, her heart lodging in her throat, to find Alessio disturbingly close behind her. In the enclosed space, his scent assailed her, the combination of fresh ocean breeze and virile man wrapping its intoxicating effect around her.

Shifting away before he saw how her nipples had peaked, how she was struggling to breathe, she shook her head, brazening it out. 'Not at all. I was just deciding which white to choose.'

Facing the wall of chilled vintage whites, Giada went in blind. 'This one, I think.' She pulled out the Chardonnay and passed it to him.

Alessio stared at the label with another arched eyebrow, while she fought not to squirm. 'Interesting choice.'

Unsure whether he was mocking her, she blurted, 'Why?'

He displayed the label to her and she read it properly. 'Maison de Montaldi. You have your own label?'

His mouth twisted in that musing way that wasn't pleasure nor displeasure. 'It was payment from a particularly grateful client. I look forward to tasting if it was worth it.'

'You mean you were given a vineyard as payment, and you've never even bothered to try the wine?'

He shrugged and waved her towards the door. 'I'm more partial to Sicilian wine. My French client was nearer this side of the border, which was why I had it sent here. This is only my second time visiting here since so, no, I've never had a chance to try it.'

She frowned as she preceded him out of the kitchen and down the hall to the dining room.

Once they sat down, Alessio opened the wine and poured her a glass. He twirled his own glass as she helped herself to a bowl of vichyssoise and warm bread, nodding imperiously when she indicated his own bowl.

She served him, then found herself waiting with bated breath as he sampled the wine, then shrugged.

'It's decent enough.'

Giada tried not to roll her eyes at the dry response, even while a part of her eased and dared to hope that this enforced proximity might not be so hellish after all.

The melon, prosciutto and pea salad that followed was mouth-watering. But the *pièce de resistance* was the tray of chocolate truffles he slid towards her after they'd taken their used dishes to the kitchen.

It was so heavenly it drew a small moan of delight from her.

When he stiffened and a wave of something intense washed over his face, she hurried to dissipate the approaching turbulence.

'How long have you had this place?'

He waited a beat, then, 'Six years.'

'You've only visited the chalet twice in six years?'

'I will endure it if I must, but I prefer warmer pastimes to skiing.'

'Which begs the question, why buy a remote chalet in a country that prides itself on its winter activities if you don't even like it here?' she asked.

His eyes rested on her puzzled face for a moment, as if gauging if her interest was genuine, then he nodded behind her.

'You see that mountain behind you?'

She turned and looked out of the window at the stunning view. Through the falling snow, she saw the large silhouette rising into the sky. 'Yes.'

'I own it.'

Her eyes widened. 'You own it? The whole mountain?'

'And the village. And every tree, stream and building in the five-mile radius. But I bought this place primarily for the mountain. On the infrequent occasion the mood takes me, I know I can ski without being disturbed.'

Giada realised her mouth was gaping and hastily closed it when she caught his amusement. 'Shouldn't…isn't there some sort of law against being so…?'

'Yes?' he encouraged when she paused. 'A law against wanting privacy for myself and the clients who need it? Against bailing out a micro-economy that was at risk of being exploited by commercialism?'

Surprise popped like a cork in her brain. 'You mean you saved this place?'

He shrugged. 'It was in danger of becoming a mini Verbier or Val-d'Isère. I stepped in and stopped it.'

'And yet somehow I don't think you did it solely out of the goodness of your heart,' she ventured dryly before she could stop herself.

His teeth flashed in a shark-like smile and her breath caught, both at his breathtaking male beauty and at the fact that the gesture didn't reach his eyes. 'Do megalomaniacs love boasting that they skied on *my* private mountain? And do they get charged ridiculous sums for the privilege? *Assolutamente.* There's no law that says I can't make millions while saving a small corner of the planet, too. Not *capitalising* on that is just pure naïveté, *cara.*'

She hated that his argument was sound. That he was finding ways to shatter her preconceived notions about him. Hated that all the reasons she shouldn't find this magnetising man attractive were being blown to smithereens. And that her re-actions were getting stronger by the minute.

As she wrestled with her feelings, he tilted his head to one side, studying her with a shrewd look in his eyes. 'Am I turn-ing out not to be…what did you call me? A carnage-and ven-detta-loving brute?'

Heat surged into her face and her gaze danced away from his, the look in his eyes too intuitive to engage with. His low laugh had the desired effect of raising her hackles, though. Her chin went up before she could register that a part of her enjoyed this challenge, this parry and thrust with him. Maybe a little bit too much. 'I only go on what I see.'

'Do you? And yet you condemn me for doing the same?'

Thrust.

Her soft gasp at the low condemnation drew a smile, this one more circumspect. Perhaps even a touch pity. Before she could take offence, he continued. 'I don't blame you. It hap-pens. My job title is ambiguous enough to draw certain pre-conceived notions and, I dare say, intrigue.'

She couldn't deny it. She *was* intrigued. Just as she'd been astounded by her sister's interest in being in this man's orbit.

The urge not to dwell on just how intrigued she was pushed her into speech. 'How did you become a fixer, anyway? As far as I know there's no degree course for it in mainstream education.'

One corner of his mouth quirked, then his face grew seri-ous. Solemn.

Giada even thought she spotted a flash of bleakness be-fore it disappeared. Suddenly, the lightness in the room was gone. Her heart hammered steadily as she wondered whether he would answer.

He set his wine glass down, but his fingers remained wrapped around the delicate stem. 'From a very young age, my father drilled into me the advantage of being useful. To those with power, sure, but also to those without. There was no telling when the people who served you might be swayed away from you by someone with more power. If you treated everyone equally and with respect, you were always guaranteed loyalty, no matter what.' His mouth twisted and harshness etched with grief on his face. 'A good enough lesson, but unfortunately not one everyone ultimately believed in.'

'What do you mean?'

One shoulder rolled, as if the memory unsettled him. When he dragged his fingers through his hair, Giada got her first glimpse of a ruffled Alessio. 'People can be swayed by other things besides power and respect. They can be swayed by greed and jealousy. By the need to inflict cruelty. My father found out the hard way when he was betrayed by people he trusted. They colluded to lure him into a trap, and he paid the ultimate price.'

Not for a single moment had she expected the conversation to turn so dark and heart-rending. Or for the urge to offer sympathy to be so forceful. 'Oh. I'm sorry, Alessio.'

He stiffened for a moment, his glance finding hers and staying, a look she couldn't quite fathom. Dismay? Surprise? Acceptance? *'Grazie.'* The response was low and husky.

For the next minute, he did nothing but stare at her, as if trying to work her out. Tension slowly wound its way through her.

Had she given herself away somehow?

She swallowed, casting around her mind desperately for something to dilute his intense scrutiny. But the only thing that came to mind was the subject they were discussing. 'Does that mean you don't agree with the lessons your father tried to teach you?'

He exhaled, his gaze moving slowly over her face once more before he answered. 'Not at all. But there was one ingredient I wish he'd taken into account when practising what he preached. Perhaps he would still be alive today.' There was bitterness and a touch of *longing* in his voice she couldn't miss.

'What lesson?' Giada asked, the need to know this man more digging deeper into her.

One curve of his mouth twisted. 'Trust but verify. Or some words to that effect, I think the saying goes.'

'But you don't trust easily.'

He didn't refute it. 'Or rarely at all,' he confirmed. 'I find it serves me better that way. Blind trust is an exercise for fools.' The certainty of those harsh words sliced across her skin, as if his words were personal when they absolutely shouldn't be.

Beyond this elongated, enforced moment in time, they would never set eyes on one another again. Never share a meal or wine or the pain that resided deep in their souls.

And yet... 'You can't go through life that way,' she muttered, almost compelled to reach for a ray of light. To what? Guide him away from his pain? What right did she have?

'Can't I? Tell me, Gigi. Who do you trust?'

Caught firmly between the curious ache in her chest from hearing him call her by her sister's name, and the vastly exposing nature of his question, Giada could do nothing but shake her head and drop her gaze, desperately buying herself time to think.

They were long past frivolous discussions of wine and capitalism and mountains. Now they were venturing into territory that lay too close to her heart. Subjects that could bruise and torment.

And while she stalled, he leaned closer, mockery gleaming in his eyes. 'You see? Taking advice isn't as easy as doling it out, is it, *duci*?'

She boldly met his gaze. 'Maybe not. But I don't write people off before I allow myself the chance to know them.'

Dark amusement returned. 'Is that aimed at me? Would you like to know me better, *bedda mia*?' His husky tone thickened, morphed into something else. Something that stirred her blood in a different way. They were ricocheting between subjects with dizzying speed.

She opened her mouth to steer things back to safer ground, but different words tumbled from her lips. Words she hadn't for a single moment anticipated. 'What's wrong with that? It's not like we're going anywhere in a hurry.'

'Are you ready to expose yourself in return?' he challenged, his eyes fixed squarely on her.

Her breath strangled in her lungs. In the short time since they met, she'd witnessed myriad expressions from the formidable Sicilian. The look he cast her now cut through all the previous ones, as if he'd been toying with her before and was now revealing his truth.

Or hers.

Dear God, did he know? If so, how?

Had their phone service been restored without her knowing and he'd somehow discovered her real identity?

'I… I don't know what you mean.'

He continued watching her with those laser eyes. 'Perhaps I'm finding your whole…enthusiastic approach to working with me still too good to believe. I'm still trying to discover what happened to the "work less party always" woman I met a few months ago.'

She just about managed to pull off a flippant shrug. 'Maybe she's wised up to the fact that there are other forms of fulfilment in life? Speaking of which, should we discuss your client?' she tossed in, praying she would distract him even as she sensed that Alessio Montaldi wasn't a man who allowed himself to be distracted very easily.

When his gaze swept down and a corner of his mouth lifted, she held her breath, certain he'd seen through her ploy. When dark gold eyes returned to hers and he nodded, she sensed too that he was merely humouring her. 'Very well.'

She licked her bottom lip and tried to gather her thoughts. 'I don't think there's a way for your client to get out of this without taking some pain. You mentioned his father's nine-tieth birthday is approaching. Didn't he start the company?'

Alessio nodded. 'Above a Chinese takeout shop in Brooklyn several decades ago.'

'Then get him to announce that he's holding onto the ailing company out of nostalgia until his death, at which point it'll revert to the new buyer at a discounted rate. Just buy your client some time to fix what's gone wrong. Everyone loves a bargain. And if you link it to a huge PR event with his birthday celebrations, there's a lower risk that the buyer will walk away without seeming greedy or losing face.'

When that rousing gleam entered his eyes, Giada told herself not to react. Not to squirm with anticipation at his response.

And when he rose and plucked up the bottle of wine, strolled lazily behind her to top up her glass, she ordered her breath not to stall, her senses not to glory in his nearness.

But it was all useless.

Because when he lingered after he was done with refilling her glass, with one hand on the table and his body bent over hers, every cell in her body screamed to a new dizzying layer of life.

Which only intensified when he murmured low and hot in her ear, 'There should be punishment for hiding this level of brilliant strategic thinking beneath gaudy clothes and cheap champagne, *duci.*'

Giada was desperately attempting to calm the runaway heartbeat that pulsed in her chest and between her legs when he abruptly left the dining room.

It was one thing being a billionaire with clout.

But when that clout couldn't be exerted because said billionaire was combating Mother Nature, not even the world's best fixer could win.

So for the next two days, Giada watched Alessio grow increasingly disgruntled as the blizzard raged on and off with frustrating frequency, while they warily skirted each other, sharing meals in near silence before he stormed off.

Giada suspected too that his revelations during their dinner had been more personal than Alessio had intended. While *she* couldn't replay every moment of it without her heart, mind and body reacting in varying degrees of intensity that shocked her, forcing her to scramble for a distraction.

On the fifth day, seeking another form of distraction, she walked into the basement level at sunrise, intending to wake herself up with a vigorous swim...to find Alessio had beaten her to it.

Every self-preservation instinct shrieked at her to turn and walk away, return when the coast was clear.

But firstly, she was over walking on eggshells around him. It wasn't her fault they were stranded here. Okay, maybe not totally. If he hadn't chased her down in Gstaad, he might've boarded the helicopter with his brother.

Secondly, the way Alessio moved in the water was almost transcendental in its splendour.

His powerful strokes were hypnotising, making her footsteps slow but not stop entirely as she was propelled to the edge of the sparkling pool.

Whether he was totally oblivious to his audience or knew she was there and was ignoring her—her money was on the latter—he kept swimming for another five laps. Her bet proved right when he stopped directly in front of her.

She stiffened, expecting more of the chilly atmosphere they'd inhabited for the last few days. Instead, he stared at her with open interest. Not warm, but not frosty either.

Then he took in the swimsuit she wore under her parted robe and jerked his head at the steps leading into the pool. 'Get in. I'll race you.'

Shock tightened her midriff before she grimaced. 'That's

hardly fair, is it? I was just watching you. I know how fast you are.'

The glint in his eyes made her yearn to know what he was thinking. 'Maybe not. But life isn't fair. I'll tell you what, let's make it interesting. I'll give you a two-lap head start for a five-lap race.'

Was it insane that she'd expected something entirely different? Something more…daring?

His eyes gleamed some more as he watched her, the dark gold stare seeming to decipher her thoughts. 'And when I win…'

Her breath caught. 'What happens when you win?'

'I will demand something from you that you'll willingly give.'

'What happens when I win?'

He shrugged. 'You will demand the same of me.'

Her eyes bulged, the tiny fireworks beneath her skin igniting faster. 'That's…' she paused and frowned '…surprisingly broad but weirdly acceptable.'

His lips twitched in a smile that said only he knew the kind of web he spun, just as he was sure it would eventually capture her.

It was a warning she needed to heed.

And yet, her feet propelled her to the edge of the pool, then down the steps, all while he watched, his eyes devouring every inch of her skin as if he had a right to it. *To her.*

He remained at the deep end, content for her to swim to him. Giada was aware the wild beating of her heart wasn't great for a race that hadn't even started, but she couldn't calm it.

Couldn't do more than remain poised beside him, ignoring the danger signs lurking in his eyes. 'Ready?' he drawled.

She licked her lips, the water she was treading gliding over her body like cool silk. 'Yes,' she breathed.

He nodded, then remained silent for a fistful of heartbeats. Before, 'Go,' he ordered, his words just about a silky murmur.

Giada struck out with one huge breath held in, exhilaration kicking in as her year-long training for her recent Antarctic trek gave her a burst of speed that surprised her. She made it to one end on a single breath, then back to where Alessio waited on another.

She barely glanced at him as she reversed direction, but she knew the exact moment he joined the race, his powerful strokes creating mini tsunamis as he passed her on his first lap.

Unsurprisingly, he easily passed her on the last lap, strong arms cleaving through the water, and by the time she finished he was waiting for her, one eyebrow arched and his hand slicking back his hair.

Her helpless gaze followed the sleek play of muscle, her mouth watering at the drops of water that lovingly clung to his face and torso. 'Is this where you tell me I made a bad deal?'

'This is where I tell you I'm impressed. I knew I would win but perhaps not by such a small margin.'

The curiosity in his tone was wrapped around a question. One she couldn't answer in truth. Buying herself time by dipping her head back and smoothing her hands over her wet hair, she shrugged. 'I love to swim. I try to get to a pool as often as I can.'

His eyes narrowed a fraction, and her insides tightened. 'Interesting. I don't recall that about you.'

'It must be something to have perfect recall about everyone you meet. You must tell me how that feels some time.' She'd meant it to be offhand, but it emerged a touch frantic and breathless.

Desperate to salvage what could turn out to be a costly mistake, she turned away, trying not to cringe at the silence that trailed her. She felt his gaze on her as she left the pool, snagged a towel and headed for the sauna, her skin jumping with hyperawareness.

She'd barely taken a calming breath when he entered.

Against the backdrop of soft golden maple that lined the sauna, his bronzed skin rippled with vitality. And in the close confines of the heating space, there was nothing she could do but stare.

'Careful, *bedda mia*. I'm discovering that your occasional... prickliness intrigues me.'

'And I should be careful because...?' God, what was wrong with her? She should be keeping things between them strictly professional. Instead, she was openly baiting a restless lion.

'Intrigue is the one thing I can't resist.'

With monumental effort, she glanced away from him, reaching for the wooden ladle to scoop out water and toss it on the sizzling coal. Its sibilant hiss filled the enclosed space with wonderful steam and made her break out in fresh sweat.

She felt it drip down her throat and into her cleavage. Felt the almost inevitable tightening of her nipples as Alessio's gaze followed several drops of perspiration, her skin tingling as his stare slowed on the very visible signs of her arousal. 'Or it could be extreme boredom,' she said.

'You have my word that boredom is the last thing I feel right now.'

The sound that escaped made her cringe and shiver at the same time. Made her thighs squeeze together as need pounded through her, settling low in her belly and dampening her already soaked suit further.

Her fingers dug into the wood beneath her thighs, her gaze fighting not to catch his. The wisest thing was still to leave. So why couldn't she just get up and go?

'Look at me, *duci*,' he commanded in a low, deep voice.

Of course her body moved of its own accord, angling towards where he sat within arm's reach. Not nearly as far away as she needed him to be. She couldn't stop her tongue from flicking out to bathe her lower lip, then her teeth from sucking that same tingling piece of flesh into her mouth and worrying it the way she craved to worry his.

The towel he'd tied around his waist did nothing to prevent her from seeing how...*affected* he was too.

When her gaze rose again to meet his there was a hint of affront. As if her daring to call him bored greatly offended. 'You know the power of your allure. Don't insult either of us by belittling it,' he condemned in a soft, deadly tone.

Giada's jaw dropped. 'I...you...' Her brain froze as words failed her.

She was fully aware of how mentally dextrous this man was, and yet, once again, he'd pulled the rug from beneath her with a handful of words.

Words that veered heavily on the carnal but weirdly touched some soft and vulnerable place inside her. A place that needed an odd little accolade just like that.

She was a good researcher, knew that her place on any expedition team was valued, that her colleagues respected her work.

But in her private life, bolstering overtures were sorely lacking.

Knowing she affected such a powerful man, even on a purely physical level, felt like...nothing she'd experienced before. It provided balm and confidence, a thrill and yearning.

And it kept her in place when he lowered his feet to the floor, his eyes immobilising her as he crossed the small space in a single stride. As he placed both hands on the bench beside her and leaned in close until their noses almost touched and his breath washed over her parted lips.

'You have me at your mercy. Granted, it will be fleeting. So...' That infernal brow arched once more, golden eyes turned even darker with his turbulent mood, daring her.

To what?

To shatter every last crumb of self-preservation? Or grasp a once-in-a-snowstorm opportunity to know what it was like to taste a live wire of a man who made the world shake with his very presence?

Alessio's gaze dropped to her mouth, his tongue mimicking her own action a moment ago. Another whimper escaped and Giada chose to...

Shatter.

Their lips fused like a perfect, hot clay mould. Pressing, shaping, gliding and battling, she didn't know where their lips started and sensation ended as the tension of the past few days exploded in a flurry of clutching limbs and exploring hands.

Alessio pressed closer, easily prying her knees apart and slotting himself between her thighs. His towel and her swimsuit were scant barriers as he unerringly found the heated place between her legs and pressed himself against it.

A hoarse cry left her throat.

Fingers that had been eagerly exploring his hard, smooth muscles dug into his flesh as desire spiked her blood. He groaned against her mouth, a staccato burst of words smashed into incoherence between them as one hand found her breast.

Mercilessly, he pinched her nipple, then soothed it with his fingers as his tongue delved deeper. Heat built and strained and threatened to burst with their climbing need.

When Alessio's hand landed on her backside and used it to propel her even closer, her vision blurred. The edge of the cliff beckoned. All it required was friction of clothing, a thrust of clever fingers or—she shuddered at the very exhilarating thought—the tugging aside of inconvenient fabric, to experience the utter bliss of skin-on-skin contact in its most visceral form.

Giada passed these reckless but enticing thoughts through her brain and when the response was a *yes, yes, yes*, her fingers spiked into his hair, clinging on as he pushed her nearer the precipice.

'*Diu mio, Gigi,*' he muttered hoarsely.

She flinched, the iced water of reality that was her sister's name uttered into this space, this unique experience, yanking her back from the edge.

Giada pushed at his shoulders and when he stumbled one step back, she slapped her thighs shut, her breath puffing in desperate pants. Aware he was watching her, perhaps even puzzled by her reaction, Giada kept her gaze averted.

Sidestepping him, she hurried to the door of the sauna. And then, because the last thing she wanted or needed was for him to follow her, she paused. 'Your world may be unconventional but even I know it's a terrible idea to sleep with one's potential boss. That…' She clenched her belly, wondering why the words were painful to get out. 'That was a mistake. It won't happen again.'

The slightest hardening of his features was the only indication that he'd found her words objectionable. Lazily, he tugged off his towel and tossed it away, leaving snug trunks that left no doubt how affected he'd been by their encounter.

Still watching her, he sat down on the bench, then went one better and *reclined*, totally uncaring that his arousal was on full display.

'Tell yourself that if it aids your pitiful little retreat, *piccolo fiore*. But we both know you'll bloom for me again before long. Now go, you're letting all the cold air in.'

She didn't move, those words he'd said to her before the recklessness started ironically granting her the much-needed shot of confidence. She used them to straighten her spine, to let her gaze drift boldly over his body, deliberately lingering over his crotch.

'You'll survive a little cooling down. Looks like you need it. And no, I won't be blooming for you again. I've had a taste. Once is enough, I assure you.'

She turned and strode off, her face burning when, a few steps later, his soft laughter reached her ears.

CHAPTER SEVEN

FIRST BLOOD TO HER.

Alessio begrudgingly handed her the rare prize of shattering his concentration when, hours after the sauna incident, he found himself staring into the middle distance, reliving those glorious few minutes.

He growled under his breath when his body eagerly responded to the recollection of her scent, her kiss, the noises she'd made. Of how eagerly her fingers had sunk into his body, and the way she'd rolled those supple hips against him.

He still didn't understand her abrupt retreat. And something about what she'd said about putting professional distance between them didn't ring true. Especially when she knew his way of doing business was unconventional at best.

A laugh escaped him.

To think the thief who still held his possession hostage would dare to lecture him on professional etiquette?

It was maddening. But...*exhilarating.*

He tossed his pen away and surged to his feet, his temper worsening when his gaze landed on the snow falling relentlessly outside the window. He'd flicked on one of the many TVs in the chalet an hour ago and swiftly turned it off when the forecast had predicted nothing but more snow.

On his desk were a dozen urgent situations requiring his attention. And yet, he couldn't dwell on a single one, never mind attempt to resolve it, without the enigma of Gigi Parker rippling through his concentration like a stone dropped into a pond.

Alessio frowned, something irritating the back of his mind.

He was missing something. But what?

A chime erupted, deepening his frown.

Then he was spinning around, registering the sound as real and not in his head. He powered his laptop in time to watch dozens of messages flood his inbox, but it was his phone he reached for.

Massimo's message that he'd returned to Sicily triggered both relief and irritation. At least *one* of them would be at home for Christmas.

One of them would visit his mother's grave with her favourite flowers and to leave a box of Cuban cigars their father had been partial to at his tombstone. He wasn't so sure Massimo would renew the vow Alessio made to their parents each time they visited their resting places, but he could only hope.

He sent a curt reply to Massimo, his mood on being stranded here not calm enough for him to deal with his brother over the phone just yet.

The next message was from the head of his top team promising a fuller report on Gigi Parker within twenty-four hours. His irritation mounting at the disorganisation he suddenly found himself surrounded with, he read the remaining messages, including the one from his American client.

Appeased this was something he could control and resolve, he dialled the client's number, relaxing in his seat as it was answered on the first ring.

'I've been trying to reach you for days,' the harried CEO said. 'Do you have a solution for me? The potential investors are threatening to call off the deal.' The man sounded desperate to the point of pleading.

Alessio paused for a second, the solution he'd intended to

provide drying up on his tongue. Instead, he found himself offering up the solution Gigi had suggested, a strange mix of alarm and pride surging through him when the man enthusiastically embraced it.

'Yes. I'll get my PR machine on it right away. I've already told my father what's happened, and he'll be on board with this. You're a miracle worker, Montaldi.' Relief heavily laced his laughter. 'I've been getting ready to throw in the towel and risk tanking this deal, but not any more. I owe you big. Besides your fee, of course.' He laughed again.

Alessio gripped the phone, gritted his teeth before he confessed, 'You owe me nothing. It was a member of my team who came up with it.'

'Well, whoever they are, I'm happy to meet them when this is all over, express my thanks in person and pass on that favour. They're saving me and my family from a potential hostile takeover and being dragged through the tabloids.'

Pure, unadulterated jealousy jolted him, as alien as it was shocking. The idea that the woman currently trapped in the chalet with him could soon be free to accept accolades and gifts from men like this grateful CEO made a muscle throb at his temple.

Inferno, he wasn't a caveman. He knew and worked with impressively clever and formidable women. Had bedded several, in fact.

And yet he couldn't pinpoint what it was about Gigi that made him feel as if he wanted to delve ever deeper into her very soul and mind, while simultaneously devouring every inch of her delectable body.

Basta.

His body was reacting to a longer than usual absence of physical stimulation. As soon as he left this frozen hellscape, he would indulge until this hunger in him abated. A holiday gift to himself, perhaps.

But even as the thought formed, he was dismissing it in distaste. Just as he was begrudgingly accepting that the chalet wasn't so bad. There was a certain…freedom from being suspended from the pressure to act. To fix. *To avenge.*

It would return soon enough, he knew.

But perhaps for now, he could just *be.*

With her.

Alessio dragged frustrated hands down his face as the infernal hunger prowling within grew, demanding satisfaction. Demanding to see her.

'Like I said, that won't be necessary,' he reiterated, noting that his voice was edged in cold steel.

Silence pulsed at the end of the line before the other man cleared his throat. 'Sure, understood. I'll be in touch to let you know how it goes.'

'You do that.' He hung up and realised his other fist was bunched.

Consciously unfurling his fingers, he rose again from his seat.

Alessio wasn't sure why he felt the urge to inform Gigi that her solution had been well received, especially since he was still annoyed by how their interaction in the sauna had ended. And yet, he found himself mounting the stairs and heading down the hallway towards her room.

The sound of her low, agitated voice when he got close quickened his footsteps to her open bedroom door.

She'd obviously noted the internet connection was back because her phone was pressed to her ear, her fingers dragging through her long ash-blonde hair as she listened for a moment, oblivious to his presence.

The look on her face before she turned towards the window made him freeze in the doorway, the very strong urge to cross the room to her side and demand to know what was upsetting her shocking him into stillness.

Because these strong feelings he was experiencing around her? They needed to be killed.

Sooner rather than later.

'No, Renata, I didn't plan it. I may be capable of many things but even I don't have the power to command snow-storms.' Sarcasm was rife in her voice but then so was the throb of pain and distress behind it.

'Why do you even want me there? All we're going to do is disagree…no, I'm incapable of predicting the future, but it's a reasonable assumption when the same pattern repeats…' She paused and took a breath as a torrent of English-laced Italian ranted down the phone.

'Well, you're just proving my point. I'm already aware I'm a disappointment to you. Maybe it's a good thing I can't make it for Christmas. You can enjoy yourself without my disap-pointing presence to spoil the holidays.'

Another deluge shot through the handset, making her flinch.

The growl Alessio couldn't quite halt caused her to turn, stiffen, then pale as she saw him in the doorway.

'I… I have to go. Goodbye, Renata.' A look he couldn't quite decipher shot across her face as she glanced frantically around, as if searching for…or hiding…something. Then she speared him with furious smoky-grey eyes. 'Does the word privacy mean nothing to you?'

'Who's Renata?' he bit out before he could stop himself, ignoring the return of the tingling that insisted that he was missing something.

More shadows drifted across her face, and he gritted his teeth at her momentary look of desolation. 'She's no one I wish to talk to you about,' she answered, her beautiful chin raised in a challenge that made his blood hotter.

Santo cielo, did anything about this woman not fire him up?

'You're close enough that she's expecting you for Christ-mas.' His eyes narrowed. 'A relative, perhaps?'

She swallowed, her eyes shadowing darker as she turned from him. Like him, she'd showered after the sauna. But she hadn't bothered to dress. Instead, she wore the silk robe the chalet provided.

On any other woman, Alessio would've imagined it a form of seduction. But from the way the lapels were carefully pulled close at her throat, the belt securely cinched at her waist; from the way one hand hovered close to her thighs to keep the robe from parting, he sensed it was more of a covering than anything else.

Just as the feather boa had been? Or the multiple layers she wore that didn't make sense? From moment to moment, it was almost as if she were a different woman, with interchanging personalities.

For instance, the Gigi he'd encountered a few months back wouldn't be in such an emotional upheaval over something like this.

Which, considering he liked to distance himself from such a show of emotion, was a thing for him to be lauding her for. Instead, he was at once intrigued and irritated. Because, damn it, he *wanted* to know which one was genuine.

Diu, was he going out of his mind?

So what if everything he'd believed about Gigi Parker had been turned upside down? Perhaps under normal circumstances he would've been vexed that she'd kept an astonishing amount of intelligence hidden beneath that vacuous façade and hedonistic lifestyle.

But…he was enjoying this version of Gigi. Perhaps a little too much. And whereas with any other woman he would've quickly distanced himself, he only wanted to know more about her disagreements with the person on the other end of the phone.

His hand shot out to stay her, then he went one better and

slid his fingers into her hair, massaging the knotted tension in her nape as he peered down at her.

'What are you doing?' she demanded in genuine surprise, as if she found his gentle caress strange.

'You're distressed,' he responded, in that moment unwilling to probe just why her distress fed his unnerved state. 'Tell me why.'

'Wouldn't you be if your mother called you a disappointment?' she shot out, then her face immediately closed with a touch of dismay.

Alessio wanted to pull her into his arms, to offer her comfort. But he was already unsettled by his knee-jerk reaction. He wasn't ready to compound it.

And wasn't that the most infernal thing?

He slotted away the titbit of her referring to her mother by her first name and asked the more pressing question. 'On what does she base that accusation?'

Her lips parted, then clamped shut. 'I don't think you can—'

'We're past using our current circumstances as an excuse. No one besides my flesh and blood know what I told you about my father. I'm not even sure why I told you something extremely personal, *duci*. It would make me feel a lot better if you shared in return,' he interrupted, his voice thick with emotion he was unwilling to name.

Her eyes widened. Then she licked her bottom lip.

Alessio suspected she didn't even realise she was performing that nervous tic. *A tic she didn't have before.*

He frowned, his senses prodding him hard once more. But her lips were parting, and, because he craved further insight into this woman, he once again ignored the sensation.

She raised her gaze and for the next age her eyes caught his. Held and held. Until something sharp and demanding tightened in his chest. Then spiderwebbed throughout his body, unfurling agitation and need until Alessio couldn't remember whether he was breathing in or out. Whether his preference was to drown in her eyes or die between her thighs.

Her sudden laughter drew another inward frown.

The sound was off. Fake.

'It's really not a big deal.'

His fingers dug a little deeper into her tense muscles and his senses leapt with pleasure and satisfaction when she leaned into him. 'Your obvious distress tells a different story.'

Delicate eyelids descended but before he could ask her to look at him, she raised them again. 'I think you heard most of what it was all about. She's been disappointed in my life choices for as long as I can remember. Everything I do seems... to rub her the wrong way. Including the fact that I might be stuck in another country for the holidays. She's not thrilled about the fact that I'm breaking with tradition.'

Again Alessio sensed she was withholding something, not giving him the whole picture, and while it frustrated him at least she'd answered. 'You spend every Christmas with her?'

She nodded. 'Although we spend it locked in one disagreement or the other. I've stopped trying to work out why she wants me around when it's obvious we don't get along.'

'Then maybe you shouldn't. Just accept that some families thrive on heightened emotions and decide whether that's the way you want it to be with yours.'

She blinked at him. 'Even though it makes us both emotionally dysfunctional?'

'The ideal of a perfect family is a myth, *duci*. Consider whether, if you did everything she wanted, you would find fulfilment within yourself without feeling like you've sold out.'

Shadows appeared again. 'I probably would,' she murmured. 'But I'd like to think there's a world where we can strike a balance between the two.'

He tucked his thumbs beneath her chin and tilted her face up to his. The powerful urge to kiss her distress away struck again. He barely managed to suppress the need. 'You already know where the balance is. You're distressed because *she* doesn't accept it. But I'm also thinking you might be relieved to be apart from her this year?'

Her nostrils fluttered as she inhaled sharply. 'I don't... I can't... I feel like a terrible person, but yes.'

'Don't punish yourself too severely. You might be surprised how withholding can focus a person's true goals. It might even push her to behave herself next Christmas.'

'And if she doesn't?'

'Then you'll have this experience of what it's like to spend your holidays without her.'

She stared at him as if she wanted to argue, but beneath his fingers Alessio felt her muscles soften, the few layers of tension leaving her body.

A second later she stiffened again. 'Did you just attempt to *fix* my mummy issues?' She laughed a little forcefully.

There was that switch again.

Alessio frowned inwardly, the prickling in his brain growing more insistent. The dichotomy that had grated at first was now insistently pointing in a direction he needed to heed.

Because it was almost as if in certain moments she was... acting. Putting on an inauthentic persona. Like...displaying overt sexuality then a curiously shy innocence? Like...curves and a voracious appetite where there used to be obsessive diet-watching? Like...looking a little lost in his wine cellar and being reluctant to drink when he'd seen her knock back several glasses of alcohol without blinking?

And even with the wine...

Alessio breathed through the gut punch as another memory slotted into place and the dominos started to fall, astonished that he managed to control himself before blurting out the demand. He was pleased for that restraint.

'Alessio?'

She was intelligent enough to sense the change in the room. Her beautiful eyes had grown wide and wary.

'It's easy to see the woods for the trees from a distance.' And as he said the words Alessio knew they were meant for him too. He was better off viewing what he suspected from a sensible distance too. He needed to be sure, to give a benefit of the doubt because...

Because if he was right...

The depth of betrayal and disappointment churning in his chest made him suck in a slow breath.

'I am curious as to why you call her Renata though,' he said, more to distract himself than anything else.

Tension seized her again but he didn't make a move to alleviate it. Not without risking giving himself away.

'She was a teenage mother. She liked it when people assumed she was an older sister rather than mother and daughter. She forbade us...um...me from calling her Mamma when I started school.'

As he watched her Alessio realised one thing. Whether or not his instincts proved right—and that *'us'* just now was painting a definitive picture that made things so much clearer—didn't minimise her pain.

Not if such a simple thing as claiming the woman who gave birth to her by her rightful label distressed the woman before him. Perhaps her emotions ran much deeper than he'd initially believed.

Deciding it was time to return to the realm of distance and neutrality, he dragged his hands off her silky-smooth nape, ignoring the mournful loss of her warm, supple skin. To allay the effect, he shoved his hands into his pockets. 'I came here for a reason,' he gritted out.

A flash of something lit her eyes before she nodded. 'What is it?'

'I managed to get through to my client. He's going ahead with your suggestion.'

Genuine delight lit up her eyes, chasing away most of the shadows. 'He is? That's fantastic!' Her eyes searched his for a moment longer. 'Does that mean I've passed the interview?'

Alessio's insides tightened with that curious mix of pride and fury. Answering 'yes' drew a line beneath their association, got her off the hook from whatever game she was playing. He wasn't ready for that yet.

His gaze slid past her to the snow-white landscape and, for the first time since his arrival at his chalet, he found he didn't quite mind the deplorable circumstances he found himself in.

'Let's not jump the gun yet. There are several stages to get through first.'

'Like what?'

His gaze returned to her. Not so wise ideas tumbling through his mind, Alessio decided to try one last theory. 'Come downstairs. We'll celebrate this win and discuss next steps.'

Now that he'd accepted the high probability that this woman *wasn't* Gigi Parker, he was noticing further irregularities that made him kick himself. For instance, she had a prepossession, a stillness that her sister—and he assumed he was looking at a twin version of the woman who stole from him—that Gigi didn't possess. Even the way she gravitated to the Christmas tree when they entered the living room, looking at it with almost childlike delight when the other would've completely ignored it.

Alessio could barely keep himself from staring at how the festive lights twinkling on the tree highlighted her smooth skin and perfect cheekbones, the full curve of her lips.

But he wasn't here to be enthralled by her beauty.

He crossed the room, deliberately walking close. Whatever

she saw in his face made her inhale sharply, then pivot to examine an ornament.

'A drink? A cocktail perhaps?' he asked, watching her carefully.

She shook her head, then, catching his gaze, hesitated for a moment.

Another domino fell.

He recalled his thought that first night that she was playing a part. He'd believed it was just to secure the job. But she'd been playing a part because she wasn't who she claimed to be. *Santa cielo*. What an utter fool he'd been.

'Um… I'm good with wine, thanks. Then I need to make another call.'

A perfect opportunity. 'You left your phone upstairs. Here, use mine.' He plucked his phone from his pocket of his joggers, saw the blank space where the bars should be, and cursed.

Her eyes widened but he saw a flash of relief in the depths, shoring up his conviction. 'Don't tell me…'

'Yes, we've been cut off again. *Non importa*. We'll use the time wisely.'

Crossing to the drinks cabinet, he reached for his favourite cognac. After pouring her a glass of Merlot he brought the drinks to where she stood.

Their fingers brushed as she took hers, the expected sizzle of electricity arriving on cue. Alessio was close enough to see the pulse leap at her throat, to watch her take a sip and swallow. Despite the charged air between them, she didn't move to fill it with mindless chatter.

This woman who delivered succinct, invigorating conversation also knew the art of silence. Alessio hated how much he liked that.

Her gaze stayed on his for a moment before moving once more to the tree, her head tilting up to take it all in after she took a small sip of wine.

'What are you thinking?' Four innocuous words that shocked him to the core. Not once in his life had he asked a woman her innermost thoughts. Not once had he cared.

But he cared now, for whatever mystical reason. He *cared*. Because she'd pulled the wool over his eyes. And *not* because of the shadows ghosting over her face.

'It's Christmas in two days. I can't believe I won't be spending it with my mother and...' She stopped, blinked a few times, then dragged her fingers through her hair.

He tensed. 'Your mother and...?' he pushed, with a voice edged with emotions he didn't want to investigate.

'And whoever she's decided will form part of her festivities this year,' she responded. 'She turns it into a competition, you see. Makes her friends vie for the privilege of spending the holidays with Renata in some exotic place of her choosing.'

Alessio was certain now that, while she wasn't lying about her elaborate reply, she was holding something back. His thoughts leapt back to the report sitting in his inbox. The report he couldn't access without an internet connection.

She set the barely touched glass on the table and dragged both hands through her hair. 'Didn't mean for this to get so *deep*. Let's liven it up a bit, hmm? Maybe some music? Or I can solve another fixer problem for you?'

She whirled, then self-consciously caught the bottom of the robe when it flared to reveal a flash of her shapely leg.

Alessio set his empty glass down. 'We'll continue this in my study. There's an important report I'd like to access if the internet comes back.'

Her eyes searched his and she swallowed, attempting to hide her alarm. But then she nodded.

He motioned her forward with his hand, keeping his expression neutral.

With that fake smile still pinned in place, she fell into step with him as they exited the living room.

Alessio kept a tight grip on his emotions as they entered his study. From the corner of his eye, he watched her fuss with her belt, her gaze darting around the room. 'Actually, do you mind if we pick this up later?'

'Why?'

She stiffened, then immediately attempted to relax her body. 'What do you mean why?'

'You seem nervous. Why is that?' he pushed.

She shrugged. 'It's been a long and unusually…revelatory day. I think I need a little peace and quiet to process it all.'

It was close enough to the truth for Alessio to marvel how many times she'd given just enough without going all the way. Without doubt, the incident in the sauna after their kiss had been one of them. He didn't know whether to be angered or impressed at her cunning.

How ironic that she was exactly the sort of person he would pay a high premium to employ in a heartbeat. 'Is that all?'

Wide grey eyes blinked at him. 'What else could it be?'

He ventured closer, watched her throat move in another swallow. 'You wouldn't be running away from something else, would you?'

Did her breath catch? 'Like wh—?'

He reached for her, all sense leaving his brain as neutrality vanished. Even as he sealed his lips to hers, he cursed the sensation…the emotions he'd condemned for so long. Without it, he knew he wouldn't be feeling this charged *betrayal*. This potent *need*.

He would've seen this coming a mile off. He most definitely wouldn't have swallowed her husky moan as if it were manna itself, wouldn't have craved more of it as he nudged her back against the closed door and plastered his body to hers.

Santa cielo, she was so soft So addictive!

Before he could compute the wisdom of it, he wrapped an

arm around her trim waist and lifted her off her feet. Pinning her delicious body to his, he stumbled towards the wall.

'Alessio…'

Sense would've been restored if she'd pushed him away. But even as his name trembled from her delicious, duplicitous mouth, her fingers were digging into his nape, her eyes pools of pure temptation as she held onto him. As her legs parted and wrapped around his waist.

And while he was a strong-willed, ruthless man, there were some brands of temptation, he was discovering, that dissolved his control. *'Se…se…'*

They tangled in a frenzy of limbs, his hands already pulling her robe loose before roving her supple form, reacquainting himself with everything she'd denied him when she'd walked away from him at the sauna. Her breath gushed in his ear as he trailed his lips from the corner of her mouth and down her jaw and throat. As he lapped at the wild pulse beating there.

As he charted a path lower to the pebbled peak of one plump breast, groaning deep as he finally, *finally* captured the erogenous morsel. Her back arched, and his senses lit on fire.

One more taste, just *one more* and he'd…he'd…

'Oh, God…' Her gasped delight pushed him deeper into quicksand.

Diu mio. 'Gi—' He stopped short of uttering the name he knew wasn't hers.

Just as she stiffened. Then tried to scramble away from him. 'Stop.'

Alessio froze, ice drip-drip-dripping into the flames of his ardour, dousing them enough for him to refocus. To regain a crumb of control.

And remember. 'Why, *duci*?' he forced the drawl as he dragged himself away from her, watched the woman whose guilt was written all over her face. 'Because you're not Gigi

Parker? Because you've been lying through your beautiful teeth since we set eyes on each other?'

A look of horror overcame her face, followed swiftly by alarm.

Alessio saw the wheels turning as her eyes darted away from his. Luckily for her, she gave up the ruse with a swift inhale.

'How did you know?' Her voice was a husky, shaky mess she couldn't control, and the sound of it aroused Alessio even further. Evidently, there wasn't a single thing about her that didn't turn him on. At least, now he unequivocally understood why.

She was not Gigi Parker.

Remarkably, now it was confirmed, he was remembering even more differences. The occasional bouts of shyness, the way she blushed at the oddest times. His nostrils flared involuntarily, taking in more of her heady scent as he stared down at her.

'I suspected. You just confirmed it.' When her eyes flared again, he continued, 'Among other things, the woman I met a few months ago existed solely on shots and cocktails. You drink wine and not very much of it. You also pretend to love the limelight when in fact I suspect you hate it.'

The deep relish in his tone had her snatching the loosened ties of her silk robe to hide herself.

He grieved the covering of her sublime body but hardened his tone. 'A little late for that, don't you think?'

'You can't expect me to still...'

'What? Give into your desires the way you've been fighting all week?'

She paled a little, which only served to highlight the deep rouge of her well-kissed lips. 'Why didn't you say something?'

He shrugged, the pressure in his groin warring with the curious chafing in his chest. He wasn't coming down with something, was he? No. He never got sick. This must be some new adverse reaction of subterfuge. One that didn't just start and end in rage. Alessio wasn't sure whether to be thankful or resentful of the sensation he couldn't totally figure out.

Enough.

'Maybe I was biding my time, seeing how far you would take it. And you were prepared to go all the way, weren't you?'

Her face flamed and he smothered a groan. Even now, with bare-faced evidence of her duplicity exposed, he found her far too alluring. A tiniest sliver of him wished he'd kept his mouth shut.

A flash of something close to hurt crossed her face before she smoothed it out. 'I'd do anything to keep my family safe.'

The prongs of accusation in her response flattened his arousal. 'Do I hear judgement in your tone, *duci*?'

Incredulously, she waved him away as if he were a pesky fly.

Swallowing a growl, he countered it by approaching her, catching her shoulders within his grasp. 'This is the part where most people show remorse. It would be great if I didn't have to drag answers out of you.'

'Would it do any good? Only I get the feeling I'd be wasting my time.'

He dragged her closer, his senses unwilling to stand the small distance between them. 'Try it and see.'

She stared at him for an age before her gaze dropped. To his mouth. Alessio stifled another groan. But again, she wiped the hazy look within seconds and had he not been watching her, he would've thought he imagined it. Unlike her sister, she was better at caging her emotions.

Much like him.

Instead of the kindred feeling he expected, Alessio grew even more disgruntled. He told himself it was because he would have to work harder at exposing her weaknesses, but it didn't quite ring true. What did ring true was the smouldering need to know her thoughts. Her feelings.

Where they went from here.

This enforced stay must be wreaking havoc on his psyche. He'd actively discouraged his previous partners from expressing anything but their willing enthusiasm for sex. Dirty talk in bed was the only form of extra-curricular discourse he welcomed. And yet now…

He dropped her shoulders and turned away. Once again, he was losing sight of his priorities. Now she'd admitted her lies, several questions needed addressing. Instead of thinking with his shaft, he needed to get to the bottom of just how he'd fallen for this subterfuge.

'We'll address everything, including this—' he waved his fingers between them '—in due course. First, tell me your real name.'

Her eyes snapped with defiance and alarm, but he spotted something else. Relief? 'It's Giada. Dr Giada Parker,' she stated with pride.

Reluctant admiration unwound inside him. Of course, she possessed a doctorate. It took a special woman to pull the wool over his eyes for this long. 'So when you said your mother was disappointed in you it obviously wasn't for what I thought. So…?'

Her relief receded a touch to be replaced by some more shadows. He knew his question drilled into the heart of the fraught relationship she had with her mother. 'She mocked me for wanting a career. Then for going further to gain a PhD.'

He lifted an eyebrow, the question clear.

'I have a doctorate in marine biology, a career my mother thought was a waste of my life.'

Surprise mingled with all the teeming emotions. 'I admit you've stunned me, Dr Parker.'

Despite the tension whipping between them, a smile teased her lips. When she blushed, the storm of hunger raging through him intensified.

'It's a bit of a relief to be called that again.'

Alessio inhaled slowly, absorbing her name, her essence. His eyes raked her face, lingering longest on her lips from where her real identity had just tumbled. 'Giada.' He breathed it.

Diu, it felt good to speak her name. And as he repeated it mentally, he was even more irritated to realise he much preferred it to the more jarring *Gigi*.

Giada.

Her sharp inhale fluttered her nostrils. Alessio realised he'd spoken her name again, infused it with something of what he was feeling. He brazened his way through it, allowing a sardonic smile to curve his lips.

'Yes, I should punish you for letting me call you by another woman's name for this long. Your twin, I presume?'

At her nod, he leaned closer, frowning when she retreated a step. Then he was smiling again because she'd caught herself, that regal chin elevating to spear him with a glare.

Colour washed into her face, even as she shook her head. 'You seem to get off on punishing people. First with my sister, and now with—'

'Don't you dare flip this on me,' he snapped, his humour vanishing. 'I punish people who cross me. And in your case it would be the most delectable way possible. A way that is making your cheeks heat up right now just thinking about it. You can be outraged all you want but you can't deny your body language.'

She opened her mouth to protest, but he quickly interrupted. 'Now, tell me where your sister is. And I advise you to come completely clean. For both your sakes.'

Emotions cascaded through Giada as Alessio stared down at her.

Primarily, it was relief. Followed by shame that she'd let her sister down. Even though the relief would be short-lived, she let it loose through her limbs, welcoming the clichéd truth setting her free as she breathed easy for the first time in almost a week.

She would deal with what that meant when she caught her breath and could find a moment to think.

But right now, heat pummelled her, making her intensely aware of every needy cell in her body. Need she desperately suppressed so she could answer his question. Alongside that need though was a feeling of almost…shock. What she'd done…almost done with him was…

She shook her head, her senses still a jumbled mess. 'Right at this minute? I don't know,' she said in answer to his question.

Alessio's eyes narrowed, the passionate man of minutes ago, not completely gone, but retreating in favour of the formidable opponent intent on bending her to his will. *And, oh, how she longed to bend.*

At least now, she could bend knowing he wouldn't address her by her sister's—God, what was wrong with her?

His hands slid beneath her shoulder blades, up her nape and spiked into her hair, while her blood dance giddily in her veins. And when the fiery blush burned its way up her face, she wanted to die a thousand deaths, especially when those very flames seem to flare in Alessio's eyes.

'Are you ready to bloom, *duci*?' he rasped, his gaze scouring her face to settle firmly on her mouth.

'Most definitely not,' she retorted hotly, even as her nipples peaked harder, her thighs twitching with need.

'Then I suggest you come up with a more satisfactory answer, *duci*.'

Or what? she wanted to taunt, to test him, see how effectively, or not, he could hang onto that iron control. Because from the way he was breathing, from the way the need prowling through her was mirrored in his eyes, his control was on a knife-edge. As was hers.

Giada would never be able to explain how she bit back the words, how she managed to breathe through the insistent urges until they eased.

'It's true. I've received just one text since we arrived.'

'What did it say?' he demanded.

The words flashed through Giada's brain.

Still no dice. Might not make it home for Xmas. You need to stall for longer. G x

Her frantic calls to Gigi's phone had gone straight to voice-mail, which was why she'd called Renata. Giada hadn't even got round to asking her mother if she knew Gigi's whereabouts before Renata laid into her.

The all too familiar ripple of despair and helpless pain sheared off a trace of her awareness of Alessio. Which helped her take a step back as his hand rose. He still managed to caress her cheek, but the moment his fingers moved towards her jaw, she forced another step back.

The comfort he'd offered earlier had been far too welcome. Even now, she yearned for more of it. Yearned to step into the warmth of his arms and let the power of her mother's censure and disappointment bounce off her. But that way lay danger and recklessness.

She'd withstood her mother's harsh and callous views of her firstborn daughter. She would power through without help from the dynamic man whose words soothed but whose eyes promised danger.

'She asked me to stall for a little longer,' she blurted, unwilling to perpetuate further lies now the truth was out. Now she was free…

To what? Dive headlong into temptation?

Something close to disappointment and, puzzlingly, vindication, snapped in his eyes, as if she'd handed him confirmation of something on a silver platter. 'So when you gave me your word on our first night here that my property would be returned to me, you were doing so on a wing and a prayer? With no knowledge at all that you'd be able to deliver?' he condemned. But behind the condemnation, there was a bleakness and resignation that stuck sharp darts into her chest.

She swallowed. Almost of their own volition, her hands rose to his shoulders. He tensed at her touch, his eyes boring lasers into hers. 'I meant it. I'll make sure it's returned to you.'

For an age he didn't reply, just appraised her with eyes that spoke their own story. Disbelief. Rage. Desire. Formidable judgement. A promise of retribution. And finally, his gaze leaving her to drop down her body...a deep, dark resolution that sent a pulse of exhilaration through her.

Slowly, his head dropped, inch by excruciating inch.

Until the tip of his nose brushed hers. His eyes didn't waver from her.

'Listen well, Giada, as I make my promise to you. You will not leave my sight until what is mine is back in my possession. And even then, I reserve the right to hold you captive until I'm satisfied that you pose no nuisance to me or my goals.'

Absurd hurt lanced through her middle.

'Get away from me,' she managed, despite her body's screaming desire to remain exactly where she was, beneath this man's powerful will and blatant, furious desire.

'Are you sure that's what you want?' he mocked, his lips twitching when her treacherous hips moved of their own accord, straining towards him.

'Yes,' she squeezed out after a long, desperate inhale. 'I may be deplorable in your eyes but even I draw the line at sleeping with a man who intends to keep me prisoner.'

'Even though you strolled into my cage with your eyes wide open?' he drawled, his scent wrapping tighter around her.

'That's the difference between you and me, I guess. I'll do anything for my family, including walking into cages, yes.'

The heat in his eyes cooled but he remained where he was. 'You deem yourself better than me?' he rasped.

'I'm not the one tossing out threats and ultimatums. My sister made a mistake by acting on impulse, and I'm sorry for that. Can you not—?'

The plea dried up when he hauled himself away from her.

She watched, eyes wide, as he dragged impatient fingers through his hair, seeking that control they'd hungrily chipped away. Sleek, beautiful muscles rippled as he inhaled and exhaled to regain it.

Deeply mesmerised, she could only watch him, her heart hammering in her throat as she leaned against the wall. Her breath caught when he pivoted to face her, his face a thunderous cloud of censure.

'Shall I tell you what that item your sister petulantly helped herself to means to me? To my family?'

Giada stumbled forward, her legs almost too weak to keep her upright. Reaching the sofa, she perched on it, tucking her legs beneath her as he prowled the room. 'Please,' she invited softly, instinct warning that whatever he intended to divulge wasn't to be taken frivolously.

His narrowed eyes examined her, determining if she was worthy of this evidently sacred piece of himself. Without preamble, he spoke.

'I told you my father paid the ultimate price. What I didn't say was that he was killed specifically because of that heirloom.'

CHAPTER EIGHT

GIADA'S JAW DROPPED, her insides twisting with sorrow and sympathy for him, and fresh anger at Gigi for putting him through this. 'I... Oh, God, I'm so sorry.'

The bleakness she'd caught glimpses of arrived and this time it stayed, dulling his eyes and tightening his jaw. It didn't diminish him one iota though. His proud bearing grew impossibly prouder, her condolences bouncing off him as he continued pacing.

It took a moment to realise he was lost in thought, probably in the past he'd just revealed.

She cleared her throat, her body swaying closer of its own volition. Closer to him. 'How...what exactly happened?' she pressed softly.

A muscle ticced in his jaw and for the longest time, she thought he'd ignore her.

Then he shook his head. 'I've often wondered if it was hubris, blind hope or just plain naïveté.' His mouth twisted but even that motion didn't detract from her absorption in him. 'Maybe it was a combination of the three,' he mused harshly.

Gathering the robe around her, Giada stayed quiet. She understood the need to work through his thoughts at a time like this. She'd needed to do the same after every confrontation with her mother.

'The Montaldis have held a certain position throughout our

history. One of leadership regardless of personal desires or what the world thought we should be.'

She frowned. 'Which was what exactly?'

That twist of his lips again. 'I come from a long line of fixers, *duci mia*. One of my grandmothers many times removed was a powerhouse rumoured to be utterly indispensable to one of the popes. She birthed the legacy I've sworn to uphold.'

She didn't doubt him. 'And with that sort of power and legacy come enemies.'

His smile dimmed, still a harshly beautiful thing despite his haunted eyes and dangerous subject. '*Se*. Over the years, there have been challenges, regardless of whether or not some of the new generation just wanted a thriving family and to leave behind a legacy they're proud of.'

'Are you one of them? I'm finding that hard to believe since you're happily unattached and are swimming in the deep end of the dating pool, according to the tabloids.' Why saying that left a trail of acid in her throat, Giada refused to dissect.

She had no rights where he was concerned. None at all.

Nor did she want them.

Ignoring the void that insistence left behind, she focused as he paced towards her.

'My marital status doesn't change the fact that I'm a Montaldi. And that I'm duty-bound to right the wrongs done to a father who may have been overly optimistic in his thinking that he could change the course of tradition, but who still didn't need to give his life for instigating that change.' The thick, unshakeable vow fell like an anvil in the room from a man who would not be swayed from his destiny.

Giada didn't even need to voice the questions brimming on her tongue. She only needed to remain silent so he could spell out how very wrong Gigi had been in crossing him.

'My father was determined to steer the responsibilities of his birthright in a new direction, rather for just the wealthy and privileged—helping fix wrongs for those who deserved it. Those with integrity who would pay it forward so others benefitted. He studied to be a lawyer and he was exceptional at it. He was exemplary at being a fixer. I learned everything I know from him.'

'But not everyone agreed with the new path?' she guessed.

He exhaled deep and long. Then his lips twisted. 'No. The inevitable crooked politicians and underworld drug lords cropped up with alarming frequency. They wanted to use his services. But he wouldn't be swayed. He ignored all the warnings because he believed he was doing the right thing. And when he told me, I...feared for him.'

'But you were still proud of him,' she slid in, the note throbbing in his voice evident.

He looked startled for a minute, then he gave a single nod. '*Se*. Power needn't always come from being feared. He taught me that too as a boy.'

And in those words, Giada made a discovery.

It was both startling and alarming.

Because its effect on her left her frantically out of breath and on edge.

Alessio wasn't a man who sold his services to the highest bidder without qualms. Every client he'd taken on had something fundamentally personal at stake. Something, if lost, money wouldn't replace.

Underneath his ruthless, brooding exterior, the man she was snowed in with possessed an unyielding core of integrity.

And the reason she was so aflame at that discovery?

It ramped up the unstoppable appeal that seemed to grow and expand and seethe with hunger with every second she spent in his company.

'You looked up to him,' she added softly.

Again he looked mildly nonplussed, and, even though he didn't nod, the flash of pain in his eyes spoke volumes. 'He was a great father. He cared for his family and his integrity and honour never wavered regardless of the pressure from others on how he should lead the Montaldi family.'

'What did the crest have to do with it?' she asked when the silence stretched.

'In Montaldi tradition, the person who possesses it has the right to challenge the ruling family for leadership. My father believed he had nothing to worry about because our family had retained it for four generations. We were easily the largest and most influential family in Sicily. No other family had dared to challenge a Montaldi in over ninety years.' He paused, his eyes growing bitter and bleaker with harrowing memories. 'But he didn't account for the betrayal coming from within his own family.'

Her gasp echoed in the chilling silence of the room. 'Who?'

The haunted darkness intensified, and within it Giada saw the ruthless man forged from loss, betrayal and determination. A man who plainly and unequivocally meant to avenge his father. A man who would strike down anyone who stood in his way.

A man who would go to the ends of the earth to reclaim the very tool he needed to achieve that goal.

The bracing shudder that rushed over her brought blinding enlightenment. She barely managed to squeeze her eyes shut and moan in despair as the true repercussions of what Gigi had done slammed home.

She wanted to throw herself at his feet in that moment. To beg for whatever sliver of mercy resided in his heart. But he was speaking again, and in that nanosecond she realised she couldn't. They were stuck here for another handful of days at the minimum, a week if they weren't lucky.

Divulging that Gigi currently had no clue where the Montaldi family crest was would be like sealing herself in with a predator and hoping it wouldn't devour her out of sheer fury and frustration.

'My father had three younger brothers. They didn't like the new direction he wanted to adopt; they preferred to sell our services to the highest bidder. When he wouldn't be swayed, they took over...by force. They gunned him down in front of his wife and sons on a Sunday after attending mass and praying by his side. My mother went from being a beloved matriarch to being cast aside like yesterday's garbage, thrown out of her home with her sons. She went from donating large tracts of her time and money to charities to not being even worthy of charity herself because she'd been blacklisted by my uncles. We were forced to leave Sicily, to live in halfway houses across the country while she worked menial jobs. She died heartbroken and broken. But with her last breath, she asked me to make things right. So you see, Giada, reclaiming my possession isn't a trivial matter to me.'

That momentary urge to disclose the whole truth was smothered beneath the need to assuage the obvious hell of his confession.

It grew and grew until she couldn't hold still. Couldn't watch him suffer from across the cold distance between them. Before she thought better of it, Giada rose off the sofa and approached him.

'Yes, I see, Alessio. I see it clearly,' she murmured.

He watched her with eyes that didn't really focus on her, lost as he was in his tortured memories. The yearning to erase them drew her hands up, extended to him.

And when he didn't move away or reject her, she touched the backs of his strong hands with hers. The skin-to-skin contact was raw and visceral enough to draw a hiss from him. To make *her* gasp low and needy, every inch of her flesh straining for more.

She dragged her hands higher, up and over his wrists and

forearms, then higher still to his elbows. Then she changed direction, running her touch beneath his polo shirt and over his lower abs.

Packed muscles jumped beneath her hands, his eyes turning molten gold as he continued to watch her every move with avid eyes, his breathing truncating as she explored his tight six-pack.

'Be careful what you're doing, Giada.'

The sound of her name sent another bolt of desire through her, making her so thankful that she could now shed her false persona. That she could be who she was with him. Her hands drifted up, over his flat nipples. He hissed in another breath, his eyes growing even more hooded.

'Giada...' There was thick warning and barely leashed arousal in that single word, making her moan.

'You moan when I say your name. You like it, don't you?'

The rough arousal in his voice lit a fuse to hers, and the confession tumbled out before she could stop it. 'She may be my identical twin so I should be used to it but... I don't like being called by another woman's name.'

'I hardly called you Gigi anyway. Perhaps deep down I knew,' he rasped. 'Perhaps I should've analysed why I walked into that club certain I would be handing you over to the authorities immediately, but then...decided against it. Why watching you blush and try to hide your body from me made my senses tingle in warning that something wasn't right but I didn't really want to explore it anyway.'

It was the height of foolishness to attribute anything beyond simple intuitiveness to it, but something leapt within her, a revelry in his statement that made her sway closer, her senses alight with need. 'Whatever it is, I'm glad you didn't.'

His nostrils flared, her open confession seeming to affect him. He started to reach for her but then froze.

'Before we go any further, I need to know. Is there someone

in Dr Parker's life besides your mother and sister who will give you grief for your absence?' The question was rasped with a displeased bite that sent a shiver through her.

Her heart lurched, then thumped hard in her chest. 'Are you asking me if I'm attached, Alessio?'

Perhaps it was the unwittingly husky way she uttered his name that made his breath expel in that rapid way. Or it was all in her mind.

'*Se*. I am. Because I don't have qualms about stating un-equivocally that I don't share,' he warned. 'That I'm extremely possessive in the things I crave enough to keep.'

Her heart lurched now for a different reason, yearnings she was desperately unwise to harbour, surging high with what it'd look like if Alessio Montaldi craved her. Fought to *keep* her. But that would never happen because, even now, the clock ticked down to their eventual separation.

But until then, she wanted…no, needed this moment. And she intended to take it. And once again, it was so very free-ing to speak her truth. 'You don't need to worry about attach-ments. Possess away,' she invited boldly.

Within one breath and the next, he caught her to him, plas-tering her against the warmth of his body. 'This unrestrained side of you… I like it. I much prefer it to the pretence from before.'

Another moan slipped out, her hands stealing around his neck so she could strain herself closer to his hot body. So she could alleviate the hunger ripping her to pieces.

'I want more of it,' he demanded thickly. 'And you can start by telling me that you want me.'

'You have eyes and a brilliant mind, Alessio. You don't need confirmation.'

'Maybe not, but a man likes to hear that the prickly woman he's going slowly mad over is finally yielding to him.'

Her gasp echoed between their lips, the quirk of his eyebrow conveying that he enjoyed the effect of his words on her, that he was anticipating her giving him exactly what he wanted. And like a snake dancing to the tune of a hypnotist, she lost herself to everything about Alessio Montaldi as he swung her up in his arms, exited his study and hurried them upstairs.

In his bedroom, he stopped at the edge of the bed with one eyebrow raised in heated demand, awaiting the answer she'd yet to give.

'I want you, Alessio. Very much. Maybe *too* much.'

With drool-worthy smoothness, he divested himself of his polo shirt and designer joggers. Then he swooped down, stopping at the last minute so the brush of his lips over hers was a mere whisper. 'There's no such thing as too much when it comes to this.'

This entailed a caress on her waist, a trail of fire up her ribcage before his hands closed possessively over her breasts, moulding with a deep groan as his lips completed the journey, sealing over hers in a forceful play of lust that had her senses diving into free fall.

The dizzying pairing of his thumbs tormenting her nipples and his tongue delving between her lips to dance with hers weighted her limbs with desire. The sheer power of it was so astonishing and bright and new that she barely felt it when he nudged her one final time to fall onto the bed.

He followed, his body barely parting from hers, the move so smooth and seamless, she felt a momentary twinge at how expert he was at this.

Then she set the troubling thought free. It had no room here.

This moment was all about seizing transient pleasure. More, it was about offering herself as a balm and barrier to the tormenting memories their conversation had unearthed.

If the journey also delivered mind-numbing pleasure along the way, the kind she suspected her brief and unsatisfactory forays into her two previous relationships hadn't managed to achieve…well, then who was she to look a sublime gift horse in the mouth?

The thought settled deep, producing a smile and a punch of pleasure as she moaned and arched into his touch.

He lifted his head, stared down at her, his eyes aglow with desire. 'You smile like a siren of old and display this breathtaking body so delightfully, I'm almost daunted by the prospect of being a slave to your wiles.'

'Almost? Meaning you think you're immune to it?' she asked, a substantial part of her frozen in anticipation of his answer.

'*Se.* Because base emotion, no matter how divine and powerful, is transient. We can stoke it all we want, but there's a beginning and an end. Then we have no choice but to put the past where it belongs and move on.'

A pang seared her. Telling herself she shouldn't take it to heart, that he was referring to their discussion of his father and his own avenging role, his words, didn't work. It drilled into a soft and vulnerable place within her, warning her to take him seriously…or else.

But, his warning delivered, Alessio was sliding one strong arm beneath her, accepting the offering she'd foolishly made moments ago, and bringing her even closer against him until they were plastered from chest to thigh, until his powerful legs tangled with hers and the thick imprint of his erection left no doubt as to what was about to occur.

What she'd moaned and craved only a minute ago.

She still wanted it. She'd be a hypocrite to deny it. But perhaps he'd done her a favour by killing any thoughts of this being more than a physical exchange of pleasure. That she, with weighty family baggage of her own, could somehow help him carry his.

'I'm losing you,' he rasped with a heavy hint of displeasure.

Do you care? she wanted to throw back. She held her

tongue. Asking that suggested she wanted a deeper insight into and a connection with a man who had laid his cards on the table.

So she shook her head and spiked her fingers into his hair. Summoning another smile, she slicked her tongue over her lips, more out of hunger than a need to titivate.

That it drew a ravenous growl from deep within him was neither here nor there.

He wanted her.

She wanted him.

It only needed to be as simple as that.

And when he lowered his head and recaptured her mouth, his body pressing her deeper into the bed, while swiftly divesting her of her robe, Giada finally set her roiling thoughts aside and succumbed to his mastery.

Alessio couldn't stop the emotional claws from digging deeper into him.

And no, it didn't help that his brain mockingly reminded him that he'd thrown this door wide open himself. A door he hadn't opened in so long that he'd believed it'd rusted shut for ever.

Diu mio, he'd told her about his father.

About the uncles who, even at this moment, were squabbling among themselves while warily scheming about how to deal with their powerful, intensely vengeful nephew.

Most sacred of all, he'd told her about his mother.

It was as if the moment he'd turned on the tap, he couldn't shut it off. And then she'd further scrambled his brain with her giving touch.

While it'd turned lustful very quickly, Alessio knew it hadn't started out that way. She'd offered simple comfort, his stark words of loss and pain touching her enough for her to reach out. To display emotion he'd been utterly defenceless against.

But he'd salvaged the situation…hadn't he?

She moved beneath him, and he angled his focus to the stunning woman offering herself so willingly to him.

Yes, he had.

Hell, he'd gone one better and shattered any misplaced notions she held towards what this meant. Which meant everything was fine.

There would be no messy emotional fallout when this unstoppable chemistry ran its course.

He was safe.

Alessio repeated those three words to himself on a loop as eager fingers dug into him, his mouth trailing her silky-smooth skin, dragging sounds from her that lit up the erotic flames in his blood.

He was safe.

So he tasted her, licked his way down to the tight rose peak of her plump breast and helped himself to her decadent flesh. Groaned deep when her back arched, willing him on as he suckled and grazed, his fingers working down her belly to the delightful heat between her legs.

At her lust-saturated cry, he turned his attention to her other peak, delivered the same strokes of pleasure as he explored her feminine core. He slid one finger, then two inside her tight heat, thrusting in rhythm to her rolling hips.

'Oh, God, that feels so good,' she moaned.

He raised his head, eager to see her pleasure for himself, devour her open, passion-drenched features. '*Se*, and it will get even better,' he vowed throatily.

Because he needed to make her forget what came before. Needed to dwell on nothing else but the sublime bliss to wash away the vulnerable exposure that haunted him.

He groaned in satisfaction and a little wonder at how thrillingly responsive she was when she met his gaze and gasped, 'Yes, *please*.'

A different sort of recklessness overcame him, one that insisted he give her everything she desired, turn himself inside out to leave his indelible mark on this woman his subconscious had known much sooner than he had.

So he returned to his ministrations with renewed vigour and was rewarded with her deeper cries, the mesmeric sight of her chasing release only *he* could provide. And even as she fell into her first, mindless climax, Alessio was hungry for more, for a deeper connection that had him reaching for the condom and ripping it open with his teeth.

The tremors that seized his hands as he drew the latex down his length, he attributed to hunger. It could be nothing else. He wouldn't permit it.

But it seemed his little siren wasn't a passive participant.

She rose onto her elbows when he slid between her thighs, her gaze darting between his face and where he was poised at the heart of her.

'You like watching me possess you, Dr Parker?' he breathed against her lips.

A deep blush rushed up her neck, and, since he didn't have to hold himself back any more, he licked its path to her cheek, then the corner of her mouth, before, with a groan seeming to burst from his very soul, he fused his mouth to hers and thrust into her slick heat.

Her hoarse cry of pleasure was almost his undoing, her tight welcoming making him clench his jaw to hold onto control.

At the roll of her hips, Alessio let out a shout before the very devil took possession of him. Capturing her arms above her head, he drew back and thrust deeper, harder, a desperation to the joining that struck a sliver of fear through his heart.

Because it'd never been like this with any woman before Giada.

And with the depth of hunger still prowling through him, he feared the spell would only get stronger.

And he might not have a choice but to do something about it. Because his path couldn't change. Not when he was so close to righting the past's wrongs.

He took her like a man possessed.

And Giada loved every second of it, revelled in the sweat that engulfed them both, delighted in his harsh breaths and guttural Sicilian words he showered over her. Then his beastly roar as he found his own release.

Did it absolutely terrify her just how much she relished his touch? Oh, yes. But would she have stopped it if her very life depended on it?

No.

That realisation thumped its ominous beat inside her long after their gasping breaths had calmed and their racing hearts had decelerated. Long after the man who'd taken her with such magnificent mastery had drifted into heavy sleep, the thick band of his arm curled around her to keep her close to him.

And even as she called herself ten kinds of fool for succumbing to his captivating masculinity, another tsunami of longing was threatening to sweep her under, so strong, so powerful that she had to bite down on her lip to keep from moaning her need and despair.

Was this the type of heady sensations her sister and mother had been chasing for as long as she could remember?

Was this a warning glimpse of what this could turn into if she didn't put her guard back up and fast? This hedonistic sensation that only more of Alessio would assuage?

If it was then…perhaps she owed them an apology.

Owed them understanding. Because the very thought of being under this potent spell for a day longer, never mind how many days she was trapped in this glorious chalet, was terrifying.

And alarmingly exhilarating.

But...didn't she know how to survive sustained threats?

Yes, she did. How many times had she butted heads with her mother and held her ground? How many times had she withstood Gigi's mockery and walked away with the burning belief that she was doing what was right for *her*? So what if Alessio's brand of temptation was unlike anything she'd felt before?

She'd withstood the harsh and frozen wilderness of Antarctica.

She would survive cutting herself completely off from this too.

She must.

Resolution burning within her, Giada sucked in a sustaining breath and slid from the bed. Then glanced back, the compulsion impossible to resist.

He remained asleep, a thick strand of hair tumbling over his forehead. His sleek bronze upper body was on full display, the sheets tangled around his lean hips.

She turned away from the masterpiece that was Alessio Montaldi, her feet weighted with lead as she caught up her dressing robe and dragged herself along the darkened hallways and back to her room. To the cold sheets that should've restored a slice of sanity but only reminded her what she'd left behind.

It didn't...*couldn't* matter.

Now she'd placed most of her cards on the table, she needed to work on extricating herself from this nightmare. Her fingers trembled as she searched for the phone she hadn't used in almost a week and turned it on, hoping against hope that there was a signal now the snow had stopped.

But fate and the tech gods weren't in a giving mood.

Tossing it aside, she determinedly slid back between the sheets and closed her eyes, fully expecting to toss and turn till daybreak. But perhaps, because she was still caught in the aftermath of a thousand emotional cyclones, sleep swiftly overcame her. Sleep crowded with dreams of writhing bodies and thick words of passion that made her cry out in pleasure only to be thwarted at the final culmination, making a complete mockery of her restfulness.

Still, she told herself she'd done the right thing as she rose and showered, donning ripped leggings before adding her bra, the see-through top she still detested, and the sweater.

Feeling exposed, she stepped out of the bedroom.

The smell of coffee drew her to the kitchen, and when that turned out to be empty, to the dining room, and the man sitting at the head of the elegant oak table, his gaze on the inch-thick document next to his coffee cup.

Giada took a moment to ground herself, to will her mind away from what had happened last night. But the curtains were open, and the light was falling on him, and she was weak enough to just...*absorb* his dynamic beauty, which transcended extraordinary good looks.

Something so uniquely him she doubted it could be replicated in this lifetime or the next, despite him being dressed in a simple pair of cashmere sweats and a black T-shirt.

Giada tried not to stare at the corded muscles that rippled beneath the fabric when he sensed her scrutiny, lifted his head and caught her gaze from across the room.

Where she'd expected cold indifference, there was narrow-eyed scrutiny that held...pained affront. He tracked her as she crossed to her seat.

A tall carafe of coffee waited and, to her surprise, the domed dish he waved her to next to his.

She lifted the lid and saw crispy bacon and scrambled eggs. On the table, a silver rack of fresh golden toast waited. 'You cooked?'

One eyebrow arched. 'You seem surprised.'

She was. Except his expressive eyes said she'd wronged him anew.

'Did you expect to survive on leftovers indefinitely?' he asked.

'Well, hopefully not indefinitely.'

Perhaps he noted her desperation as her gaze flicked to the window. Or he was just vexed with her because when she looked back, his jaw was set.

'If you're hoping to make a quick escape, you're going to be disappointed. The weather forecast predicts much of the same for the next few days, at the very least. Looks like we're definitely spending Christmas here.'

A pained sound escaped her before she could stop it.

He stiffened, eyed her with deep sardonicism. 'Was I that bad in bed?'

She gasped as her head swung towards him. His face remained an irritated mask, but something lurked in his eyes. 'I… What do you mean?'

'You look downright wretched at the thought of spending a minute more in this place whereas yesterday you'd almost accepted the situation.'

She tucked her hair behind her ear, her senses leaping and twisting just from his scent and body heat. 'You can't deny that a lot has happened since yesterday, besides the…the…'

'Sex?' he supplied in a droll tone.

A blush ate up her face and his features thawed just a tiny fraction.

She licked her lips and almost moaned at their sensitivity. 'Not necessarily. I would've thought you'd like to get out of here even more than I would.'

He shrugged. 'Not enough to risk hypothermia or worse. As frustrating as it may be, I've accepted the situation. Until I can change it, there's no point in fighting it.'

Was there a warning in there? She shook her head.

'And…not necessarily?' he drawled.

Her breath shortened at the intensity in his eyes. 'So I wasn't entirely terrible, then?'

'You don't need your ego stroked in that department, surely?' she snapped.

He took his time to answer, lifting his espresso cup and peering at her over it. His throat moved in a strong swallow, and he set it down before one corner of his mouth lifted in a quirky smile. 'No, I do not. Although you've served me a first that…intrigues.'

Her eyes widened. 'A first?'

'You're the only woman to vacate my bed before I have to encourage her out of it,' he confessed, that edge back in his tone.

'You sound more peeved than intrigued.' She forced a shrug and cut up the bacon on her plate, even though she doubted she would be able to push down a bite. 'Maybe I prefer my own company in bed after…'

Low, deep laughter rumbled from him but when she glanced up she noticed it didn't quite reach his eyes. 'What an intriguing creature you are, Dr Parker. You're deliciously passionate in bed, yet you can barely mention the word sex without turning red,' he mused.

Giada ignored the heat intensifying in her cheeks. 'It doesn't matter one way or the other. What happened last night isn't going to happen again.' The words emerged in a rush so she could hide behind them. Because up until she actually uttered them, Giada had feared she would change her mind. Feared she would succumb to temptation again.

He tensed, every trace of humour vaporising. For an age, dark gold eyes scoured her face, a muscle ticing in his jaw. 'Tell me why,' he barked.

Mild shock shivered down her spine. 'Because it was a mistake.'

'You regret it.'

She pursed her lips, the need to say yes warring with the truth she loathed to admit, which was that she was terrified of the depth of her own need. So, hoping she had one last performance in her, she raised her chin. 'Yes. It shouldn't have happened in the first place.' When explosive silence met her words, she blurted, 'I'm not in the habit of sleeping with men I barely know, or...' She stopped, unable to clearly define what Alessio was.

'Or men you're in the middle of deceiving?' he bit out.

She flinched.

He saw it and his eyes gleamed. 'At least you seem to have the semblance of a conscience.'

Furious flames ate away the last of her nerves. Setting her cutlery down, she faced him, intent on setting him straight on a few things.

'I was never without a conscience, Alessio. What I did I did out of love for my sister. It's the same way you care for your brother.'

The flames in his eyes turned livid. 'You will not compare the two.'

'Why not? Because you deem yourself much more superior to me? To Gigi? Tell me you wouldn't do anything for your brother. Aren't you right this moment in the middle of a years-long campaign to avenge your father?'

He surged to his feet. 'Watch yourself, *bedda mia.*'

Hearing the endearment snarled with fury didn't stop her memory from reliving it one more time. Before she shoved it away and stood too, her chest heaving with affront. 'Would your father want you to do what you plan to your uncles? What about your mother?'

Alessio stepped up to her, his eyes twin flames of righteous fury. 'I watched my mother struggle through life with her heart torn from her chest, the extended family she loved almost as much as she loved her husband and sons mocking her as she struggled to feed her children. Every last one of them turned their backs on her and colluded to ensure she could never rise out of the gutter they threw her in. So yes, when my mother made me swear on her deathbed that I would restore honour to the Montaldi name, I promised her I would. And nothing is going to deter me from that path. *Capisci?*'

CHAPTER NINE

IT WAS ALMOST laughable the way she'd thought this Christmas might turn out to be different just because she wasn't locked in acrimony with her mother in some exotic location.

The location was intensely breathtaking, sure.

The snow had let up at last and, with the sunlight glinting off it, it was the purest illusion designed to make one forget one's problems.

Almost.

Because even as she stared at the enthralling landscape, even as she tried to see the upside of this Christmas Eve, the *thunk-thunk-thunk* of Alessio's boxing gloves as they connected with intent on the punching bag gave ample testimony that she'd swapped one emotionally charged arena for another.

The opposing characters might be different, but the theatre was the same. Which begged the question—was there something wrong with her?

Was she destined to fight futile wars with people she let close? And yes, Alessio Montaldi had slipped beneath her guard, had imprinted himself on a vital part of her she knew wouldn't fade away easily.

Even now, after he'd warned her off voicing her opinion about his great and noble plan for avenging his parents, her heart continued to ache for him. Had ached after he'd walked off and left her in the dining room. She would've retreated and hidden away in her bedroom if that hadn't felt like a cowardly thing to do.

She'd relocated herself to the cinema room instead, attempting to distract herself with a classic Christmas movie she could barely focus on, each *thunk* making her stomach churn. Making her hate herself for her inability to shut it out and—

'I can hear you thinking from out here,' he observed from the doorway.

Giada tried not to show that he'd startled her. That every cell in her body now screamed at his proximity.

Instead, she forced a shrug. 'Then, by all means, remove yourself,' she said with tart resignation. Because as much as she wanted to brush away or bury yet another confrontation with someone else she…she cared about, the same bruising sensation arrived. Then deepened. Branding pain and despair into her soul because Alessio Montaldi signified high stakes. She'd given him her body. And, she feared, a lot more besides.

Otherwise, would she be *this* disconsolate? Would she experience this perplexing urge to stand her ground and surrender at the same time?

'I could, but I fear it would just follow me around,' he said.

And because she was weak and needy, she turned on the lounge seat she'd thrown herself on at some point she couldn't remember and stared at him as he ambled towards her.

'Would you throw some more clothes on, please?'

He didn't bother answering, only smirked as he stopped beside her, a towering display of masculinity frying a shameful number of her brain cells as he slowly unwound the protective bindings around his hands.

'Is that why you're hiding in here? Because my half-dressed state bothers you?' he taunted.

'Not at all. I'm just giving you space.'

'No, you're not. You're discontented with where I stand on certain issues and how we ended things this morning'

'You're wrong,' she countered heatedly. Because admitting it to herself was one thing, blatantly exposing her vulnerabilities was quite another.

'I propose we put that to one side. I don't wish to be locked in battle with you.' His gaze fixed hard on hers, a sincerity glowing within that made her protest wither away. Made her realise something else.

This was unlike her fights with her mother. Truce-calling never came into play with Renata. They tended to fester underneath every conversation until they eventually parted ways, then inevitably picked up where they'd left off at their next meeting. Always worse, never better.

She exhaled now, her roiling insides settling a little. *Better.* 'I don't want that either,' she confessed, much to her surprise and alarm.

He nodded, then without ceremony tossed away the binding and stretched out on the leather seat next to her.

She gasped. 'What are you doing?'

One arm propping his head, he watched her in that unnervingly intense way. 'Making up. I'm told it can lead to all sorts of delectable outcomes,' he rasped, his accent slightly thickening.

Exasperation was timely in diluting the turbulence caused by his nearness, his seeming geniality, and the furnace blazing in his eyes. 'And you wouldn't know because no woman has ever disagreed with you, of course.' Her droll tone emerged a little acerbic, fuelled by the jealousy twisting inside her.

A very masculine, very smug smile graced his lips. 'Exactly so. My past experiences have been much more agreeable. But you'll be pleased to know I find your spirit quite stimulating.'

She jerked upright, dragging her fingers through her hair that had come loose. 'Alessio, this is a—'

His fingers meshing into her hair stopped her words cold. Or perhaps it stopped it *hot*. 'This really should've been my first clue,' he rasped, his eyes following his fingers through her hair. 'It was very different a few months ago. And it has a wildness to it that is quite captivating,' he murmured throatily.

'I can alter it if you want to forget that I'm not my sister,' she said much too bitterly.

Displeasure flashed gold flames in his eyes. 'Touch it and I *will* put you over my knee and spank that delicious bottom.'

Her nostrils fluttered, a decadent thrill rushing through her that shocked her even more than his salacious words. Because that *rush* suggested she wanted him to do just that. Which was preposterous, wasn't it? She wasn't into kinky stuff...of any kind. *Yet?* 'Still threatening me with corporal punishment, I see. How primitive of you.'

His head tilted, slanting a wave of chocolate-brown hair over his forehead. 'Is it though? I'm merely warning that I'm prepared to fight for what I want.'

Sensation rushed faster through her veins, stinging her like frantic little bees. Her nipples hardened and surged against her sweater. She mourned her exposing attire blatantly announcing his effect on her. As for the heat surging into her cheeks... she shifted closer to the fire, hoping he'd attribute that to her proximity to the flames.

But one glance into his smouldering honey-gold eyes and she knew he could tell exactly how his words affected her. Hell, his lips quirked with mockery as his gaze dropped to her chest.

She lifted one shoulder, feigning calm, attempting not to feel the heavy weight of the hair he seemed obsessed with brushing down her back.

Most importantly, she didn't want to reveal how deep his words settled into her soul. 'You...you want to fight for me?'

His eyelids swept down momentarily, shielding his emotions from her. But she caught the tic at his temple, saw the way his nostrils flared. 'When the alternative is to prowl the rooms and hallways of the chalet in a sub-par mood, then yes. I'd rather we were on more agreeable terms. Or at the very least the agita was one that brings us both satisfaction.'

He meant it in a purely physical sense, of course, but it

didn't stop her heart from lurching. From *yearning*. Because no one had fought for her before. Ever. All her life she'd fought for every crumb of regard or happiness.

So even if this was a temporary truce, even if they returned to disagreeing minutes or hours from now, for this moment in time she would halt the upheaval. Give into the soaring enticement and embrace the warmth that came with it.

It therefore was no task at all to sway closer, to moan when his fingers spiked into her hair and angled her face to his. To blink in impatience when all he did was hold her there, his scrutiny soul-deep.

'Alessio, please kiss me,' she gasped, something inside desperate to grasp the moment before it slipped out of her hand.

His eyes turned molten but he still withheld her wish. 'It is true that, right now, my immediate need is to bury my fingers in those lush curls, feel them come alive around my limbs and take it from there. But first, I need you to give me the true reason you didn't want this to happen again,' he breathed against her lips.

Giada's stomach dipped in alarm. She'd bared so much. As he'd said, once Gigi resurfaced with his precious heirloom, they'd never see each other again. In a matter of days, they would be memories to each other.

Past but not forgotten. I'll never forget him.

'Giada.' The rasped command was unmistakable.

She sucked in a breath, the hand that had somehow found its way to his bare chest digging into his flesh, as if he could stop the ocean of anguish from sweeping her away. 'I've striven so hard not to be anything like Renata. I know she's my mother and I shouldn't think badly of her but...'

'A part of you reciprocates the disappointment she strives, unjustifiably, I think, to find in you? And you feel guilty for it?'

Her gasp at his concise summation drew a ghost of a smile from him. 'Yes.'

'And you think sharing my bed, and wanting to do it again, makes you like her?'

'It's not…something I've done before.' And it terrified her how addicted she could get to, not just sharing her body with him, but even this…delving-beneath-the-skin thing she was doing.

A flame of triumph lit his eyes for the briefest moment. 'I'm glad to hear it, *bedda mia*. And that in itself should tell you that there's no slippery slope unless you create one yourself.' His thumb slid back and forth over her lips, his eyes darkening at her hitched breathing. 'This might feel like it's out of your control, but ultimately the choices you make are entirely within your power and no one else's.'

Perhaps this was the reason Alessio Montaldi commanded power and turned the world's most influential men into his willing acolytes. Because just then, Giada felt like she could move mountains with her bare hands. As if the years of clashing with Renata, while heart-aching, had forged her into a woman who could hold her head up and declare herself *enough*.

Tears prickled her eyelids as she opened her mouth, not entirely sure what to say to Alessio. Thank you, maybe?

But a heavy look was passing through his own eyes, a shifting in the air that said perhaps he knew what was happening to her. Was caught in it, too? A blink later, it was gone. And his head was descending.

'You will not regret this, *se*?' he rasped huskily. Insistently.

She shook her head, a glut of emotion overwhelming her.

'Say it, *tesoro*.'

'No regrets. Absolutely none.'

A thick groan erupted, then he was fusing his mouth to hers, nudging her back on the leather seat, his expert hands stripping them both.

And as he thrust hard and deep inside her, and she delivered herself up for the exhilarating ride to nirvana, Giada affirmed to herself that, no, there was no regret this time.

But there *was* possible collateral damage of her deeper emotions. Because Alessio Montaldi hadn't just woven magic on her body. He'd also claimed a part of her soul.

'Buon Natale, duci.'

Giada kept her eyes closed, but the smile that took hold of her face lit through her heart and soul. She was well burrowed into the rich cotton sheets they'd eventually pulled over themselves somewhere in the early hours, after the thrilling Christmas Eve that had included another sumptuous dinner, champagne, and an attempt to watch a Sicilian movie that had been interrupted far too frequently with seeking hands and lips, thick, sexy demands and throaty moans.

The best part of it all had been making love with Alessio against the window of his bedroom while the snow fell outside, knowing this memory was seared in her heart for ever.

Now, with the smell of coffee teasing her nostrils and the promise of a stunning, masculine vision when she rolled over...?

Best. Christmas. Ever.

She lingered in that incredible feeling for a moment longer. Then yelped when a cascade of light objects bounced off her body. Turning over, Giada inhaled sharply as the glittering baubles rolled over the sheets.

Beside the bed, Alessio stood holding the giant white crystal-studded bag he'd evidently just emptied over her. And the contents he'd just emptied? Her eyes widened as the countless sea of ornaments danced around her. The same dark gold globes she'd seen hanging on the tree. Filled with priceless gifts.

'W-what...what's this for?' she blurted.

One eyebrow arched in wicked teasing as he tossed the empty bag aside. 'It's Christmas Day. Take a wild guess.'

'But...we can't. I mean, this isn't a normal...we're just stuck here under...certain circumstances—'

'Which we've agreed we're going to make the best of,' he

said with an edge to his tone as he prowled onto the bed, sending a few of the baubles scattering. He settled over her, elbows on either side of her head as he brushed his nose with hers, then let loose a smile that stole what was left of her breath away. 'So once again, *Buon Natale,* Dr Parker,' he breathed against her lips.

Giada tried to stop the shameless melting. To stop her heart and soul from relabelling her thoughts from moments ago to Best Christmas For Ever. But she couldn't. Something fundamentally important and essential shifted inside her as she exhaled and responded, 'Merry Christmas, Alessio.'

They kissed as if they each searched for something essential in the other. As if this moment, while verbally unacknowledged, was significant. And when they parted, he stared down at her with heavy contemplation, his eyes boring into hers for answers she dared not give.

Even as he moved away towards the tray bearing coffee and breakfast things, the heaviness lingered. Two cups poured, he handed her one, then sprawled himself on the side of the bed, reaching out with his free hand to run a thumb over her lower lip for an age before he sat back.

'Open your presents,' he rasped, tossing her one orb before he lifted his cup to take a healthy sip.

Giada's fist closed around it, her insides twisting with feelings she didn't want to name. 'I don't have anything for you.'

His gaze remained long and steady on her, its focus far too probing for her liking. 'On the contrary, you've given me an alternative view of what this day could be. And I'm not altogether…unappreciative.'

'What do you mean?'

He looked a touch impatient, a touch chagrined, as if he hadn't meant to reveal that. Then he said abruptly, 'My Christmas Day is spent mostly visiting my parents' graves. It was my mother's favourite time of year. Massimo and I spend a significant portion of the day with her. It's a duty I'm honoured to perform, but it's not without its challenges.'

She couldn't pretend not to care, not to stop the swell of emotion for this man whose heart had been so devastatingly ripped from him by those who should've treasured him. The idea of him spending all Christmas Day at a cemetery or crypt with his mother felt too harrowing to conceive.

Tossing the present aside, she set the coffee down, rose and went to the edge of the bed, slid her arms around his waist. 'If you don't mind that you're stuck here with me, then I'm glad your day has been a little different.'

He exhaled sharply, then stilled, his eyes fixed on her up-turned face. 'Tell me something, Dr Parker.'

She excused the madness that made her insides thrill to hear him using her doctorate. If anyone had mentioned a charis-matic Sicilian man would make her feel so 'seen' she would've rolled her eyes and flaunted her feminist card. 'Yes?' she in-vited throatily instead.

'You've mentioned your mother a few times but not your father.'

Tension shaved off a layer of recklessness. When she tried to pull away, he held her still. Sighing, because, hell, she was in far too deep already. What was another revelation? What was open-ing her innermost heart and letting him see the real her, anguish, warts and all? 'That's because he's never been in the picture.'

'Meaning?'

'Meaning my mother decided when she was pregnant that she would be better off as a single parent. And my father ob-viously concurred because he moved to New Zealand and spurned any attempts I made to contact him when I was old enough. Call me naïve but I thought the man who insisted his children be given his name would be interested but...' She ignored the twinge of pain and shrugged, 'I stopped trying when I turned twenty-one.'

* * *

Alessio shook his head, sliding away from yet another strong impulse to ease her pain. But he couldn't stop the words that came. 'In my experience, it's a decision he will regret before too long.'

The eyes that met his glittered in the festive lights but he still caught the despondency within the alluring grey. 'You have a crystal ball, do you?'

'No, but I turn down more requests to fix family reunions than I care to count. It's often misunderstood that I'm a fixer, not a priest or mediator.'

'Why do you turn them down? You don't like the emotional baggage that comes with it?'

His jaw clenched before he consciously eased it. 'Since the baggage belongs to them, not me, no, I don't. I turn them down because more often than not they, like your father, were in the wrong in the first place and want an easy passage to absolution.' His gaze drifted over her face, imprinting every feature deep in his mind.

'Well, I'm not holding my breath. And if he doesn't it's his loss.'

'Exactly so,' he concurred.

He held his coffee in one hand while his other spiked into her hair and cradled the back of her head. 'You've turned out to be an unexpected surprise in many ways, *duci*.'

She wasn't sure how to respond to that. Or to the bewilderment that preceded the flame lighting through his eyes. And, like so many terrifying things to do with this man and the seismic shifts he caused in her, she let herself be swept away by another kiss.

Then he was pulling away, determination stamped in his face as he nudged her back. 'Presents. Now. Then I have very definite ideas of how else you can wish me Merry Christmas.'

The first orb contained a platinum bracelet with a stunning

sapphire stone in the middle. Then came a pair of diamond earrings. The third contained a QR code declaring it as a ticket to spend the day with—

Her jaw dropped when she read the renowned poet laureate's name.

'Alessio, I can't accept all this,' she protested after the twentieth priceless gem had fallen into her lap.

'You must. None of them are quite my type.'

Whose type are they? she wanted to ask. She didn't. Instead she raised an eyebrow. 'Not even the poet laureate?'

'I already met them after I ensured their favourite writing ink distributor didn't go out of business when the unfavourable economy threatened them.' At her gasp, his lips quirked in a shadowy smile, then he nudged a few more presents towards her. 'Be assured, *duci*, everything I need to make this a memorable *Natale* is well within my reach.'

She didn't need a crystal ball to know what he meant. But the knowledge twisted an ache in her heart and a graver comprehension that she was in much deeper than she wanted to be. That she already dreaded taking the road that led away from this place. Away from Alessio.

To hide the emotional earthquake juddering inside her, she reached for the nearest globe. Then the next. Opening presents she had no intention of taking with her.

And then making a great show of throwing herself into a day she was certain would haunt her with its near perfection because of the man who resided in the centre of it.

A series of loud pings echoed across the room, making her startle out of her Boxing Day, front-of-the-fire-post-lovemaking haze.

She tried to turn but Alessio held her captive, his lips continuing their lazy exploration of her neck. 'Alessio.'

'Hmm. I think I'm addicted to the way you say my name.

There's always a hint of exasperation in there that gives me great insight into how I affect you.'

'And that pleases you? Why am I surprised?'

His grin brushed her shoulder, and she tried desperately not to melt even though she suspected that, while her body might be willed into submission, her emotions were another matter entirely. She moaned as he licked at a particularly strong erogenous zone before his mouth drifted up to sear over hers. They were locked in another torrid kiss when another round of pings erupted into the air.

Alessio tensed slightly, the implications settling on both of them.

When he lifted his head, she sucked in a slow breath. 'The internet connection is back.' Why was there a hint of mourning in her words? Why did her heart sink a few feet too?

'Hmm.' This time, it wasn't the lazy purring of a satisfied jungle animal. It was sharper, tinged with acceptance. Purpose, even.

When his lips left her skin, she fought not to beg him to return. To forget the outside world.

He had a vendetta to complete. And she…

She had a mother to appease. A sister to locate. A job to return to shortly after the new year.

For the first time in her life, though, not even the job she loved could pierce the gloom settling over her as Alessio rose to his feet in all his naked glory and crossed the room to where his phone had been discarded what felt like a lifetime ago.

His profile turned serious, then downright forbidding as he read the torrent of messages. She sat up, wrapping her arms around her knees as she watched him. She should get up too, go to her room and fetch her own phone and get on with the business of the rest of her life.

But she couldn't move. Didn't want to leave this enthralling little bubble created despite the acrimony pushing at it. Despite every rationale shrieking that it was the very worst of ideas.

Frozen, she watched Alessio's thumb hover over the screen. Then dark golden eyes rose to pierce hers. She wanted to believe indecision flitted across his face. A nanosecond later, when his digit pressed firmly, she knew she'd been mistaken.

The ring tone echoed loudly, the sound almost alien after so much time spent without its intrusion. Then a deep male voice was answering, and Alessio was lifting the device to his ear. '*Ciao.*'

The conversation was short, to the point.

Yes, he was fine. Yes, he required his helicopter as quickly as it could be arranged to fetch them. And yes, they would be requiring his jet too to take them back to Sicily.

Them.

That finally roused Giada.

She surged to her feet as he finished the phone call. He stared at her with his hands on his lean hips.

'My Sicilian isn't great, but did I hear you tell them that you're returning to Sicily with me?'

He strolled in that loose-limbed way that made her insides turn liquid. When he reached her, he cupped her shoulders, before his fingers drifted up to spear into her hair. '*Se*, you did. Wasn't that what we agreed?'

She frowned. 'But I thought…' She'd agreed to this when he didn't know her true identity.

He lifted an eyebrow. 'You thought what?' Hardness had crept into his tone, the fingers in her hair applying slight pressure, a subtle warning.

A tremor awoke deep in her belly, the stirring of old anguish wearing a new face. 'You know now that I'm not Gigi. Surely you won't achieve anything by keeping me with you?'

Hardness settled in deep, sculpting his face into a chilling work of art without him moving a single muscle. For an age, he stared at her, strands of disappointment and almost pity weaving through those golden eyes before he slid his thumb slowly, contemplatively over her bottom lip. 'You think, because we've had the pleasure of each other's bodies, that anything has changed, *bedda mia*? That I should simply abandon my life's goal?'

Anguish intensified, mocking her for having the temerity to believe it would ever die. For daring to think that she had the power to move a man like him to alter his path. But, even if she didn't—and she realised now that it'd been a foolish dream—she still wouldn't hold her tongue.

'Do you hear yourself? How can this be your life's goal? You have so much already, the very world at your feet. Why can't you strive for reconciliation? For peace? For forgiveness? For...love?'

He stiffened into pure steel, his nostrils flaring before he surged closer still, their breaths mingling as he looked deep into her eyes. 'How can I find peace when those responsible for shattering my family still walk free?'

Her insides clenched, partly with sympathy, but mostly for the raw, unvarnished pain that bricked his voice. 'Alessio—'

His hands dropped from her as if he couldn't bear her touch any longer. 'I made a promise, Giada! And I mean to keep it.'

It wasn't a roar of intent, but the boom of it blasted through her nevertheless. And as she took one breath after the next, battling against the horrible, terrifying notion that she wasn't merely attempting to be the rock he needed but to form the foundation of what she yearned for with him, Giada realised there was nothing she could say. Nothing she could do.

She'd strayed so far from her usual tormented path, wandered much farther than she should've, that she barely recognised this new, more desolate landscape.

'I understand,' she said, not understanding entirely. Perhaps because even though he'd helped her reconcile herself to the possibility that hers was meant to be a fractured family, she couldn't do the same for him. Couldn't help him see beyond the red haze of the pain and grieving for everything he'd lost. 'But you should really ask yourself this—did the father who loved you and taught you a life of integrity and honour want you to lower yourself to the level of the very people who betrayed him, or would he want you to choose a different path? And would your mother have extracted that vow from you if she hadn't been blind with grief?'

His fists bunched and the brackets around his mouth tightened as he stared down at her, icily condemning her.

She raised her hand before he could flay her with words. 'I know you think I have no right, but isn't there a saying about an eye for an eye making the whole world blind?'

'Are you really preaching at me about turning the other cheek?'

She shrugged. 'Why not? I don't have anything to lose, do I?'

'You think not?'

She forced a smile she didn't feel. 'I have a few more days to spare. I'll come with you to Sicily. Let you toss me into another room so you can feel good about staying true to your vows and whatnot. Once Gigi returns your precious crest, we'll be truly done with each other. Does that work for you?'

He looked momentarily nonplussed, as if she'd disrupted his grand and mighty chessboard game and ruined his plans. If her insides hadn't been ripping apart slowly at the stark realisation that she would indeed be walking away from this man in a matter of days with a heart she suspected didn't belong to her in its entirety, she would've laughed.

Would've indulged one last time in the touching and banter and ease they'd found in the last few days. In the best Christmas she'd ever had.

Denied that—and knowing more heartache awaited, because hadn't she ignored all the warnings, breezily believed she could master these emotions?—she turned and walked out of the living room.

She didn't expect him to stop her and of course he didn't.

Their unplanned interlude was over.

He had an illustrious quest to complete, and she...

Giada swallowed hard, her steps quickening on the stairs, not because she was in a tearing hurry, but because she feared she'd be unable to suppress the sobs frothing up her chest, eager to vocalise her shattered emotions.

She made it to her room as the first one choked out of her. She clenched her jaw shut, furious with herself for this inability to rise above torment that shouldn't have been there in the first place.

Crossing the room, she dug out her phone and turned it on.

The void while she waited for it to power up felt like an eternity. But when it was done and only three meagre pings sounded, Giada wished she'd waited until she had herself under better control. Until she'd applied sound reasoning to everything that had happened to her and bolstered herself with every *I will survive* speech she could think up.

Then she would've been better prepared to accept there was no hope for the shattered family she'd been cursed with. Because only two further text messages awaited her.

After nearly two weeks since leaving London and having minimal contact with her sister. The first message she'd already seen when the internet briefly returned. The second came on Christmas Eve.

Renata says you're not joining her for Xmas? Are you still with him? WTH? Call me. G

Giada reread the second message, incredulity building when it registered that her sister was more irritated that she hadn't

made it home for Christmas and was still with Alessio. There
was a searing disbelief that Gigi could be this self-centred.
That maybe Alessio was right. She'd made far too many excuses for her sister in the past. Sucking in a breath, she clicked
on the third message. Sent on Christmas Day.

Call me now, Gids. Not sure what you're playing at! G

A sharp bark of incredulous laughter left her throat. She
stopped the next one for fear it would turn into something else,
like hysterical screaming.

Jaw gritted, she hit the call button. And listened to it ring
and ring, then click into voicemail. Giada cleared her throat.
'Hey, it's me.' She paused, her mind replaying everything that
had happened since she last spoke to her sister, shaking her
head when her emotions started to swell out of control again.

'I…we got stuck in a snowstorm…in Alessio's chalet.' She
gave a quick, impersonal summary, leaving out the bits about
her sleeping with the man she'd been sent to deceive. 'Anyway,
call me when you get this message. And please tell me you've
located his crest.' She paused, swallowed and delivered the
last, most important news. 'And, Gigi, Alessio knows I'm not
you. I don't know what that means for you, but please return
his item. It's more important to him than you know.'

She ended the call, her heart thudding dully in her chest.
Then, feeling his presence behind her, Giada turned to find a
fully dressed Alessio in the doorway, his eyes burning into her.

She didn't need to ask him if he'd heard any of what she'd
said. It blazed right there in his eyes as he watched her toss
the phone on the bed.

'I take it you didn't reach your sister?'

'You don't need to lurk in doorways listening to my calls,
Alessio. That's beneath you.'

Her probably unfair dig bounced off his shoulders, his hands slotting into his pockets as he leaned his magnificent frame in the doorway. 'But then how would I gain all the delicious information that serves me so well, *bedda mia*?'

The endearment threatened to weaken her knees, the way it had every time he'd drawled it. But the mockery attached to it steeled her spine. Kept her on track. 'No, I didn't reach her, but I'm sure she'll call back as soon as she hears my message.'

Heavy scepticism crossed his face. 'What will it take to lose this blind faith you have in her?'

She scrubbed her fingers through her hair, her emotions rushing wildly beneath her skin. 'Feel free to take the high road on what you think is right for your family, but don't you dare look down your nose at me for whatever you think are my shortcomings. Your opinions aren't wanted or appreciated. Now, is there something you want particularly, or can I assume this conversation over?'

He stiffened, then he straightened, his body filling the doorway. Slowly, he sauntered into the room. Her breath caught as he came closer, his gaze ablaze with the kind of righteous purpose superior beings possessed.

'There is such a thing as being far too accommodating, you know, *cara*?' he warned silkily.

She met his gaze boldly, because she sensed if she didn't, she would simply succumb to the tsunami of emotions churning ever closer. 'Are you annoyed about that because it's not directed at you? That I have the capacity to care about more than one person?'

His nostrils flared and she realised she'd scored a bullseye. Whatever this man denied he wanted from her, he wasn't quite ready to see her give it away to someone else. That thought brought a shocked laugh. 'You are, aren't you? Why is that?'

'Because I've seen first-hand what happens when people

think you're a soft touch. They will take and take and take until there's nothing left.'

'So your answer is to stop yourself from giving anything at all?' Her question was softly spoken, something inside *still* vulnerable for him. Enough to tread lightly with his wild emotions. 'To hold everything inside until it shrivels to nothing and dies? Is that really how you want to live, Alessio?'

'This isn't about—'

'You? Of course it is. You're hiding. And you're condemning everyone who isn't hiding like you.'

Just like in the living room, his expression flashed with bewilderment. Then he shook his head, freed himself from the feeling gripping him. Even before he spoke, she knew he was going to distance himself once more.

'Contrary to what you think, I didn't come to eavesdrop on your call but to inform you there's a window for our departure. My helicopter will be here in two hours. Make sure you're ready to leave.'

CHAPTER TEN

YOU'RE HIDING.

Alessio seethed at the words spinning in his head in sync with the helicopter's rotor blades above him. He didn't even bother wondering how she dared lay such accusations on him when no one else would be brave enough to speak to him that way. Dr Giada Parker had a streak of fearlessness and an unwavering spirit that had drawn him right from the start.

But she was talking nonsense, of course. Especially when her own record was so woeful.

The more in-depth report he'd finally been able to access about Gigi Parker—and the fact that she had a twin sister along with their Italian mother—when the internet was restored painted a vivid picture of the Parker family. They weren't as brutal as his own family, but the lifestyles of two out of the three made for unsavoury reading.

And yet… Giada had never once turned her back on her sister and mother, and even made excuses for their dysfunction.

As unworthy as they were, she'd do anything for them.

A puzzling, guilt-tinged sensation made him shift in his seat. When the compulsion grew too much, he slanted a glance at her.

Her hands were tucked neatly in her lap, her steady gaze on the endlessly white landscape. While it grated how easily she could ignore and dismiss him, he took advantage of it to break down just what it was about her that riled him so, start-ing with the differences with her twin. *Diu mio*, if everything he'd read was right, she was as different from her sister and mother as night was from day.

Her sister was living proof of the apple not falling far from the tree.

As for Renata DiMarco...

Alessio's growing fury at the distress caused by her mother was another surprising discovery, and it'd recurred enough for him to weather the bewilderment a little better. To accept that maybe this was par for the course when dealing with Giada.

Once they parted ways...

The thought screeched to a halt in his brain, his belly clenching in rejection of it.

Yes, he reeled a little at how differently Giada had turned out in comparison to the rest of her family. But it didn't grant her the right to issue judgements about him. He didn't care, he assured himself. Not when all his meticulous machinations were bearing fruit, even while he'd been snowbound with his duplicitous guest.

His uncles were *finally* feeling the pinch of the traps Alessio had set for them, some of them years in the making—they'd proved a slippery, elusive lot with more cunning than he'd anticipated—with more than half of their shady endeavours hitting the rocks. With the remaining soon to follow, the first tentative attempts at contact had already begun. It was even more imperative now that the Cresta Montaldi be returned.

The fire of anticipation burned bright, yet hollow at the thought that the years of plotting and planning were nearing an end. He could, *finally*, look forward to a new year with a clean slate. A new year with his family name restored and those culpable paying the appropriate price for their sins.

Hell, he might even consider an extended liaison with her...

No.

He removed his gaze from her smooth cheek and sleek neck when it registered he'd been staring at her long enough to draw a querying eyebrow at him. Long enough for that telltale blush that should've been a dead giveaway when they met to climb into her face. He balled his fist on his thigh when the urge to touch her unleashed another bout of hunger.

No. This was over.

Does it need to be?

He sucked in a breath when his gaze drifted to her again, to her pink lips, slightly parted as she took shallow breaths.

'Is there a reason you keep staring at me?' she enquired, but he caught traces of breathlessness, the touch of bewilderment he himself felt. As if what was happening between them was as peculiar to her as it was to him.

He was an expert fixer, arguably the best in the world, and yet he couldn't solve the conundrum of Dr Giada Parker and the riotous feelings she roused inside him.

Shelving the subject for now, he glanced out of the window, relieved to see the airport come into view. The sooner he got back to Palermo, the sooner everything would slot back into its rightful place.

'You look cold,' he said, evading her question. He couldn't very well admit that she captivated him on a level no other woman had been able to achieve. That even now, he couldn't go a minute without wanting to look at her...to touch her.

But she was an addiction he *would* break.

He shrugged out of his coat, ignoring her budding frown when he draped it over her shoulders. 'We're landing in five minutes. And in case you haven't noticed, the temperatures are still negative digits out there.' Alessio couldn't stop the mild punch of primitive satisfaction when her fingers gripped the lapels and drew them closer to her body. 'And next time you decide on another identity-switching escapade, perhaps you should put your foot down about packing more sensible clothes?'

'You have enough on your plate, Signor Montaldi. Let me worry about how I dress in future.' The saccharine smile she tagged on made him want to kiss her mouth all the more desperately, then drag a promise from her that she would never put herself in a similar situation for her undeserving sister again.

But he suspected his tigress would bite his head off. She was fierce when it came to her family.

Just…as *he* was.

He sucked another breath as that singular truth dug deeper into him. And for the rest of their transfer from chopper to plane and through the myriad phone calls he had to field while they flew to their destination, Alessio couldn't dispel the notion that they weren't so dissimilar after all.

Giada pressed her phone to her ear for the sixth time since she boarded Alessio's luxury private jet. She'd wanted to be relieved that he'd barely waited until take-off before disappearing through a door at the rear of the plane. But all she'd felt was increasing anxiety and a harrowing *loss* as they flew towards Sicily.

She'd seen the looks the airport staff and Alessio's employees had cast her in the VIP lounge and as she'd boarded his airplane. Now she was no longer playing a part and consumed with getting her sister out of trouble, she was even more aware of how out of his league she was. No amount of reassuring herself that she didn't care worked any more.

And he was taking her to the heart of his existence.

As much as she knew he put up a formidable façade, Giada had seen enough cracks to glimpse the pain that resided beneath that front. Having accepted that she *did* care, she feared her heart had different ideas. The foolish organ wanted to shield him, maybe even herself, from the true torment his vendetta had and would cost Alessio Montaldi.

So she kept calling Gigi. Kept leaving messages.

She was in the middle of leaving yet another when she felt him approach. Her very skin tingled and shivered, and her heart leapt in such an alarming way, Giada was already dreading looking at him.

Just as she was dreading looking deeper into the depth of her heart's desire when it came to Alessio. A desire she suspected had scaled the ultimate emotion…

But that same compulsive yearning made her lift her gaze to the man with his hands in his pockets, regarding her from a seat away. Whose gaze searched hers with an intensity she wanted to scream at.

When that gaze dropped down to the phone clutched in her hand, she was almost relieved. Until he spoke.

'If you're trying to reach your sister, don't bother. She's not going to answer.'

Anxiety tore through her. 'Why not? What have you done?' she snapped.

His features hardened. A muscle ticced in his jaw. 'I see you continue to think the worst of me. Does it give you satisfaction to do so?'

The silky query was at odds with the censure gleaming in his eyes. Giada felt a momentary pang of regret.

'I'm sorry, I shouldn't have automatically assumed. But I still want an answer. What's…where's Gigi? How do you know she's not going to answer?' Fear crawled up her throat as the questions spilled out.

Alessio advanced and sat down opposite her. 'She's unharmed.' His face twisted with that disdain she hadn't seen since before Christmas. Seeing it again sent a pulse of dismay through her. It didn't matter, she told herself. All she cared about was Gigi. But she knew it was a lie as the hollow wid-

ened in her belly. 'She's been seen with a particularly unsavoury group in the South of France, hired by two of my uncles.
The initial report is that she isn't there willingly.'

Giada jerked forward in her seat. 'What? Why?'

Another twist of contemptuous fury. 'It looks like she
trusted the wrong people.' He shrugged. 'Or she's clueless as
to who they truly are. Who knows?'

'And? What aren't you telling me?'

For an age, he simply stared at her. '*They*, and not your sister, are in possession of my crest. I suspect she's not answering your calls because she's unwilling to be forthcoming about
the true prospects of recovering what she took.'

'But she can't…she wouldn't just…' She shook her head.
'You said unsavoury. Just how unsavoury and why don't you
look more worried about your chances of getting back your
property?'

The look that entered his eyes left her without a doubt as
to the true nature of the man she was dealing with. 'The information is still coming in about your sister. As for worrying about my chances…' He gave an expressive shrug. 'You
forget that I'm a fixer, Giada. Which means I always come
out on top, especially where my own interests are concerned.
My property *will* be recovered.'

She didn't doubt him for a moment. So far only the most
extreme kind of *force majeure* had stood in his way. 'And
what about Gigi?' She hated how her voice trembled. Hated
how she feared his answer because it would break her heart.

His eyes turned into hard chips. 'I suspect she'll resurface
when she believes the coast is clear. But our deal still holds,
duci. You won't leave my sight until the Cresta Montaldi is
in my hands, *se*?'

Giada was certain she should've been more outraged than
she actually felt. But a numbness was overcoming her. And it
had nothing to do with discovering what her sister had been

up to. Or even Alessio's insistence on keeping her captive. No, it was more to do with how she felt about Alessio Montaldi. And the absolute certainty that he would shatter her before this was over. But her breaking heart still held enough concern and love for her twin. Enough for her to ask, 'Is Gigi safe?'

'At the last report she was fine,' he said coolly as an attendant approached to inform them they would be landing soon.

The drive from the airport to the Montaldi estate near Monreale was swift and conducted in silence on her part, and with rapier-sharp Sicilian conversation on Alessio's. At some point he switched to French, then to German. From the snippets she could grasp, several irons he'd placed in his fire before being snowbound with her were ready.

But despite the flash of triumph on his face after each call ended, he grew tenser as they passed beneath what looked like a caretaker's residence spread over towering iron gates.

Giada grasped the reason for the grand entrance when, after three heart-racing minutes driving along a tree-lined stone drive, an honest to goodness eighteenth-century castle unfolded into view.

Complete with battlements, turrets and pointed arches, it was straight out of a neo-Gothic fairy tale.

'Welcome to Castello Montaldi.' The throb of pride in his voice didn't defuse his tension as he threw open his door and held out his hand to her.

Giada followed him up a porticoed entrance and into a jaw-dropping marble foyer, determined not to be overwhelmed.

A single step later, she knew it was a lost cause. Everywhere she looked, Alessio's proud heritage loomed.

'I need to attend to a few things. Vincenza will show you to your room.' A middle-aged woman with a kind smile and greying hair stepped forward, her clothing and bearing marking her as the housekeeper. Alessio started to turn away, then veered back. 'Vincenza will also help you pick an attire for tonight. I've had a few delivered for you.'

'What's happening tonight?' she asked.

A hard little smile lifted his lips. 'A family party. You'll be attending as my guest, of course.'

Giada wanted to shout at him to come back. To curse him for springing this unwanted surprise on her. But she feared it would fall on deaf ears. Or worse, that she'd dissolve into hysterics. How foolish had she been to think leaving their snow-bound chalet behind would mean the end of this roller coaster?

And how especially foolish was she to experience that lingering thrill that she would spend at least another day with Alessio before—?

The bracing reminder of Gigi's plight shaved off several layers of her traitorous feelings as she followed Vincenza up one set of sweeping stairs.

'The *castello* is big, *signora*, so it will be better if a maid stays close by to bring you where you need to go, *se*?' Vincenza smiled when Giada nodded.

Several hallways later and a brief history that informed her there were nineteen bedrooms, a chapel, and a private park on the estate among many other eye-goggling facts, double doors opened into a stunning stone-walled room, complete with four-poster, antique sofas she was sure were as old as the *castello*, and blood-red velvet drapes tied back with gold rope.

And at the foot of her bed, a rail of exquisite gowns waited on hangers. A glimpse of the labels made her eyes widen, although, in hindsight, she shouldn't have been surprised.

She nodded through the quick tour of her suite, then as Vincenza prepared to leave after promising a tray of refreshments, Giada cleared her throat. 'Is the party for a specific reason or is it a yearly thing?'

Vincenza hesitated, then her eyes shadowed a little. 'The

Montaldi Christmas ball is a tradition started by his *matri* that Signor Alessio continues.'

A *ball*, not a party. Damn Alessio. 'I see.' Her gaze drifted back to the gowns. 'And what time am I to be ready?' she asked.

'It starts at seven. I'll return to help you get dressed,' Vincenza replied.

She wanted to tell the older woman not to bother, that she could dress herself, but something held her tongue. Alessio's tension suggested this wasn't just another traditional holiday event. The last thing Giada wanted was to compound her sins.

She murmured her thanks, and when the tray arrived, she nibbled on olives, parcelled meats and pastries, washed down with a gorgeous chilled limoncello. Then she took a long, leisurely bath, attempting not to succumb to the growing anxiety at Gigi's continued radio silence.

She chose the blood-orange velvet gown because it was festive, she told herself. Not because the Montaldi coat of arms she'd seen stamped on various items throughout her suite bore the same colour.

Vincenza's smile of approval when she saw Giada's choice eased her growing jitters. And by the time the older woman had expertly coiled and woven Giada's newly shampooed ash-blonde hair into an elaborate chignon, it was impossible not to feel a resurgence of overwhelming sensation.

Dragging her gaze from the woman in the full-length gilt-edged mirror, who was at once familiar and alien to her, Giada smiled at Vincenza. 'Thank you for your help.'

The housekeeper returned her smile, then reached for the velvet pouch she'd brought with her. 'From Signor Alessio. For you to wear, then meet him downstairs.'

Giada spun to face her. 'What is it?'

Vincenza pulled out a squat jewellery box and deftly flipped it open. Giada gasped. If she'd thought the perfect little gems from the chalet were breathtaking, this was on another level. The ruby and diamond necklace winked and sparkled its brilliance from its velvet bed. And, damn it all, it was perfect for the dress she'd chosen.

Giada thought of refusing but as quickly as the denial rose, she squashed it. There was no point.

Just as she'd left those treasures behind, she would merely use this for whatever part she needed to play until Gigi resurfaced. So she bit her lip and nodded at Vincenza, who smiled enthusiastically and fastened the necklace and matching earrings in place.

Checking her phone one last time and gritting her teeth at her sister's silence, she followed the housekeeper.

It was testament to the size of the *castello* that Giada hadn't seen or heard any signs of the ball beginning until they descended onto the ground floor and traversed a series of hallways.

Then she heard the strains of classical music.

'Buonasera, duci,' his deep voice murmured just behind her shoulder.

Giada spun around, her breath catching as she blinked at Alessio while his gaze raked her from head to toe.

'You look sensational,' he rasped heavily.

He looked sublime. Naturally. The soot-black tuxedo emphasised his physical perfection, the styled-back hair lending him an air of sexy danger that had her insides knotting with dizzy desire, her heart searching for a way out of a prison that had lost its key somewhere on the snow-covered peaks of Gris-Montana.

Because as her gaze collided with his, as she witnessed the heat and the anguish and the danger and realised that, alongside it, the shadows had grown, that tension from earlier had only intensified in the hours they'd been apart, Giada understood that she would do anything to take his torment away.

Because she loved him.

And when that crucial truth strangled her vocal cords, leaving her mute as he stepped closer, placed a finger beneath her chin to lift her face to his, she surrendered to the feeling. Because to fight it here and now was to bare it all to him.

To show him what her foolish heart had done.

'It's time.'

She forced herself to focus. 'Time for what?' she asked distractedly.

Darkness shrouded his face, and his jaw turned to stone as he offered her his elbow. 'Time to put beloved ghosts to rest, finally.'

He *needed* to do this.

Otherwise, what would've been the point of his life up till now? What would the years of scheming and sacrifice have been for?

Maybe it's time to let it go...

Similar words to the ones *she'd* spoken...*traitorous* words... this time spoken by his own brother a mere hour ago. Tonight of all nights, when he'd finally confirmed that every shady enterprise and support his uncles had relied on was dismantled and they were well and truly broken, when vengeance was within his grasp? When one uncle had fled Sicily and two others were here tonight, their tails between their legs, eager for his forgiveness?

Entering the ballroom now and seeing Massimo's half-pleading look made Alessio's gut tighten.

If he hadn't taken them at their word that they'd never met before, he would've believed the stunning Dr Parker and his brother were ganging up on him, breaking down defences he suddenly lacked the willpower to uphold.

Because what was worst of all? He'd entertained the possibility of *letting go* for a full minute, and, *santo cielo*, the lightness of being had taken his breath away.

But in that brief abandonment of his life's purpose, other *unattainable* yearnings had rushed in, tormenting him with impossible mirages of what his life could look like.

With Giada Parker.

With…love?

That was when he knew it would never happen. Because the ferocity of his need in that minute? It surpassed every crumb of vengeance he'd gathered to himself over the years. And it…terrified him.

So no, there would be no *letting it go*. Not even knowing deep in his bones that his mother was already resting easier knowing his crest was back in his possession, their family honour and respect well within reach.

Letting go meant being unmoored. Being alone.

And for the first time in his life, Alessio wasn't quite ready to face a challenge.

Cold dread seized Giada's nape as the ballroom doors swung open and several dozen heads swivelled their way.

Her fingers dug reflexively into Alessio's arm. He made a low noise in his throat but he didn't slow his steps. On the contrary, he all but dragged her after him, his fierce gaze cutting through his own guests as if they weren't there.

Someone approached with champagne. Giada took the glass just for something to occupy her. And when her eyes sought Alessio again, his tension had escalated even more.

'Alessio—'

'There you are, *frati*. I was beginning to think you wouldn't show.'

Giada turned towards the only person who'd dared to venture close, her eyes widening as she registered the man's resemblance to Alessio.

'Massimo,' Alessio bit out, confirming who the younger man was.

Massimo nodded at his brother, then his gaze shifted to her. 'I understand I'm to blame for you getting stuck with my brother.' Eyes a shade lighter than his brother's glinted beneath the ballroom chandeliers. 'Do I need to beg your forgiveness or—?'

'Is everything in place?' Alessio snapped, his jaw hard enough to crunch titanium.

Massimo's gaze flicked away from hers, a hint of hardness and something else…something she wanted to label compassion shifting through the gold depths as he looked at his brother. '*Se, frati.* Are you sure you want to do this? We can—'

'I'm sure,' Alessio interrupted.

Massimo paused a beat, then nodded at someone behind Alessio's shoulder. A man holding a large box under his arm stepped up to the dais where a quartet played.

When the music trailed off, Alessio eased her arm from his. Without glancing her way, he stepped up to the dais. A second later, Massimo trailed him and stood one step below.

Giada's heart thumped hard as a hush came over the crowd, their gazes commanded by their host.

'Everyone here is connected in some way to my family. So you'll know some or all of our history. You'll know the wrong that has been done to us.' He paused, his eyes narrowing as they tracked across the room. 'Some of those traitors are here tonight.' At the gasps that sounded, he smiled. 'They eat and drink from my table and dare to hope that I've forgotten. I…' his gaze darted to Massimo '…*we* haven't forgotten.' He gestured with his hand and the man with the box stepped forward.

Even before he'd opened it, Giada knew what it contained.

Sure enough, when Alessio lifted the lid to the sizeable antique box, the most exquisite ruby-and-emerald-encrusted crest about the size of a large dinner plate, the same winged roaring lions design as the monogrammed items she'd seen all over the *castello*, nestled on the blood-orange silk bed. He plucked it out and held it up almost indifferently, but the slight tremble of his hand and the ferocious look in his eyes relayed his tumult.

'Tonight, with this *cresta* returned to us, my brother and I reclaim our birthright, and I my place as the rightful head of the Montaldi family. Anyone who disagrees, speak now.'

A rumble tore through the room, but no one dared raise a voice.

Alessio gave a satisfied nod, then continued, 'We also claim the right to seek justice the way we see fit. The culprits know who they are. Present yourselves.'

The crowd slowly parted to reveal two grey-haired older men. They were a poor likeness of what Alessio would look like thirty years from now but the resemblance was patent. Giada had no doubt they were his uncles.

They lurched towards Alessio, hushed pleas falling from their lips. When they got close enough, they grasped Alessio's hand, dropped frantic kisses on it.

Alessio's livid gaze fixed on them, then unerringly found Giada's.

Perhaps she mouthed the *no*. Perhaps she only screamed it in her head. Either way, Alessio's eyes darkened, determination warring with bewilderment. His chest heaved frantically for a full minute. Then he stepped off the dais, leaving his uncles kneeling on the floor.

And he left the ballroom.

Giada knew if she didn't go after him, she'd lose him in the labyrinthian *castello*. At least that was the surface truth she told herself. The deeper one was the unrelenting need to take away his pain. To offer solace. So when she saw his tall figure stride down one hallway and enter what looked like a study, she tore after him. Only to pause in the doorway when she realised he was on the phone.

'And the Parker woman?' he rasped.

Giada's heart lurched, then grasped that he wasn't necessarily talking about her. He confirmed it a moment later. 'The deal was for the return of my property. Nothing else. She found her way into this mess. She can find her way out of it.'

Giada stumbled forward, unable to remain quiet. 'What are you talking about? Is it something to do with Gigi?'

Alessio swung around. The look in his eyes hadn't dissipated one iota. In that moment he was a man locked in full vendetta mode.

'Answer me, Alessio!'

He continued to regard her like a speck of dust on his clothing.

Then he reached for the door and shut it in her face.

When her shock wore off, Giada reached for the handle, then banged on the door when it didn't budge. 'Alessio!'

His voice rumbled on for another minute before he yanked the door open. He was no longer on the phone.

'What do you want, Dr Parker?' His voice was soft, tinged with fury.

Giada rushed into the room. 'What's going on? Who were you talking to? Call them back!'

'I will not. Your sister is no longer of interest to me. She's been warned never to cross my path again.'

A shaky breath exploded from her. 'You really are a cold bastard, aren't you?'

'Not at all. I think I've been exceedingly magnanimous in not having her thrown in jail.' He strolled to the window, then retraced his steps back to her. 'And I'm prepared to extend that generosity to you.'

For one foolish, traitorous moment her heart leapt. Then

the true meaning of his words imploded within her. 'To me?' she repeated.

'*Se*. You. I have zero interest in anyone else.'

She was grappling with the singularly vicious delivery when he continued, 'Since we've established that we're not entirely averse to each other's company, I'd like you to stay here in Palermo with me until the new year.'

The dark temptation in his voice, coupled with the trailing of his fingers over her jaw and down her neck to her shoulder, *almost* made her succumb.

'You really don't get it, do you? I can never be with a man who throws people away the way you do. So the answer is no. I won't be rolling around in bed with you while my sister's safety hangs in the balance. Whether it's her fault or not, I'm going after her. And I expect you to honour your offer not to call the cops on me. Or was that an empty promise? Because I'm leaving this place. As soon as you tell me where to find my sister.'

Giada could've sworn he'd paled a little; that he sucked in the smallest shocked breath, as if her outburst had thrown him. But when she searched for a chink in his formidable façade all that was reflected back at her was chilling indifference. Which he shored up with a shrug.

'If that's the way you feel—'

'It is,' she tossed back quickly. Because that flood of emotion was building again, threatening to weaken her the longer she stayed in his presence. And she was done being weak for this man. Done trying to make him see that the fervour with which he cherished his family was the same for her.

Could be the same fervour for each other.

'An address will be provided for you by the time your belongings are packed,' he said icily, then retreated to the window, his broad back a stone wall.

Giada's head spun with how swiftly everything was falling apart. She could barely remember the walk from study to bedroom. Could barely recollect shoving her clothes into her suitcase. But as she left the dressing room, she caught sight of herself in the mirror. She still wore her gown.

And the ruby and diamond necklace and earrings.

A half-sob threatened to escape. She swallowed it down forcefully, dropping her case so she could tackle the clasp.

It refused to budge a full ten minutes later. Giada stifled a tiny scream, the fever rushing through her bearing all the hallmarks of hysteria.

Dear God, if this was what love did to rational beings, she didn't want it.

Liar. You want it with every fibre of your being. And you want it with the man who's just broken your heart!

Another sob caught in her throat. She exhaled it in relief when she heard footsteps behind her. 'Vincenza, thank God. Can you get this necklace off me, please?'

Warm hands clasped her shoulders, making her yelp as Alessio breathed in her ear. 'Not yet. I've decided we're not quite done. I have some further things to say.'

'Are you serious? We have nothing to say to one another. Not after—'

The words died in her throat when she spun around and saw the anguish etched on his face.

'All this is your fault. You know that, don't you?' he accused thickly.

'Oh, yes, I'm aware that blame has landed on my lap since we met. But maybe you'd care to elaborate?'

His nostrils flared. 'In a matter of days, you've made me need so badly. I trained myself not to do that after my father died. Then I redoubled my efforts when I lost my mother. But you, *duci*. You...' He gave her shoulders a gentle shake. 'Don't you understand what you've done? Tonight I abandoned every vow I made, in the name of *mercy*. I told you I wanted nothing to do with your sister and yet I've just negotiated her release and put myself in debt to some objectionable individuals. She's on her way home and has promised to call you twice a week from now on until you say otherwise.'

He laughed harshly as she gasped, grateful tears springing to her eyes as he released her to drag shaking fingers through his hair. 'Nobody else gets a chance like this with me. No one else would get this far. If word of this gets out, my reputation will be in shreds,' he accused.

And yet there was no venom in his tone. If anything, Alessio Montaldi looked shell-shocked and a little vulnerable at the revelation.

The light that shone in his eyes was almost…pleading.

'What am I going to do now?' It was a hushed query, his eyes searching hers for answers. 'I've dismantled every nefarious dealing my uncles profited from. I have them in the palm of my hand. But I can't bring myself to crush them. And, *Diu mio*, I find myself considering granting them forgiveness. You've ruined me, Dr Parker.'

Her heart gave a wild leap. 'Have I? Or have you proved to yourself that you are and were the better man all along? That you're truly your father's son? Now you get to truly live. You get to remember your parents for the wonderful people they were without the burden of vengeance weighing you down. You get to love free and true…if that's what you want.'

'And what about who I want? What if it's too late for me… with her?'

Agitation rolled through her belly, decades-old fear attempting to take hold once more. But he'd taught her to be brave. So she would be brave, *for them*. She'd stare the possibility of rejection in the face, one more time, and take the greatest risk of her life. 'You're a fixer, the great and fearsome Alessio Montaldi. Are you going to let the possibility stop you?'

His hand dropped slowly from where he'd clutched his nape.

Eyes like gold lava stared into hers and his shoulders squared. He looked larger than life, but then, didn't he always? And yet, this time his mouth worked as if he was summoning up and testing words he was afraid to say.

Her heart lurched, fearful but eager. Willing him to say them. Because if he didn't…

She shook her head. *I trust you.*

She didn't realise she'd spoken the three little words out loud until his breath shuddered out of him.

'*Diu mio*, I don't deserve you. Or your trust.'

Her heart dropped six feet beneath her feet but she wasn't going to crumble. 'Why not?'

For the first time since she'd known him, shame and regret etched his face, sinking in deep as he shook his head. 'Because I *hesitated*, Giada. You asked me to save someone you love, and I hesitated because I was afraid. For myself. I was afraid what letting go would mean for me.'

She shook her head, puzzled. 'W-what do you mean?'

'Because it became clear that I would do *anything* for you. That I would lay down my very life for you if it came to it. I'm used to power and a lot of it. But…that sort of power, the kind you have over me, it's…'

'Terrifying?' she offered softly.

He made a rough, wholly animalistic sound at the back of his throat. '*Se,*' he agreed with an awed rasp.

'I guess that's that, then?' she dared. Then turned away.

He arrived in front of her with the force of a hurricane. Flames leapt in his eyes as he grabbed and held onto her upper arms. 'What?'

She shrugged even as her heart attempted to beat right out of her chest. 'If you're too terrified to face that power, then there's nothing more to discuss, is there?' She deliberately glanced at the door behind him. 'Maybe I'll take a holiday until my next posting. Find a man who   '

His untamed growl silenced her. 'I've just put one *vinnitta* behind me, *tesoro*. Do not let me pick up another.'

'There he is, my powerful Alessio. Are you going to do what it takes, then?' she teased.

His arms dragged her closer. 'Is this what you want? To see me at my most terrified? My most vulnerable? To know that I love you so much, that I'm besotted to a level that petrifies me?' The words were jagged, almost broken. And the tremble that seized him when he said them made her heart surge with emotion.

Giada lifted her hands, slowly because the wildness in his eyes needed to be handled with care. He was a man on the brink.

The brink of a discovery so deep it terrified her too.

'Yes, I do,' she stated without holding back. And when she saw the jaw-dropping shock in his eyes, she smiled and cradled his strong jaw, rubbing her thumbs over his stubbled skin, revelling in the shudder that went through him. 'Before you go thinking me cruel, just know that I want you this way, this open and honest and fearful, because it means you'll treasure the feeling. Just as you treasured the memory of your parents, you'll fight every day to keep this feeling alive because you'll know that it's returned. With an equally open and honest heart, Alessio.'

The shuddering grew until a relentless wave overtook him, his eyes darkening until they were barely gold, until they burnished with disbelief and then hope. Joy. Awe. 'Giada...'

'I lo—'

'No.' His fingers brushed over her lips. 'Before you say words I might be too selfish to allow you to take back, you need to be sure, *duci*. Once I grab hold of a thing, I tend not to let it go. I might get obsessive. I might rage and burn a few worlds down for it. You saw how I was with my vow to my mother. I hesitated and almost sacrificed someone you love.'

The last words were dredged from a harrowing place she knew anguished him now.

'Do you regret it?' she asked.

His face twisted. 'Every second since, *tesoro*. I'll regret for the rest of my miserable life.'

'Doesn't that tell you anything, Alessio? Because it tells me that you know where you went wrong. That it was a single-second mistake instead of a decision you acted on even though you knew it would hurt me. And don't forget, you still got her back. Life is a complicated puzzle we work through every day. You can't close yourself to love because of a mistake you made. And even if you do, I'll still forgive you for it.'

He swallowed, his chest heaving in a deep breath. 'I still think—'

'Mention that you're not worthy of me one more time and I'll walk out of here.'

His eyes flared again. Then started to lighten, the flames leaping higher. 'I love you, Giada. With every undeserving bone in my body, I swear I will earn your love. I will never make you feel unsure of my devotion. Bless me with your heart and I will make you a vow to treasure it as long as I live.' The smallest hint of a wicked smile twitched his lips. 'And I think by now you know how I am with vows.'

Tears filled her eyes again and she *finally* let hope soar. 'I do. And yes. To all of it. We will love each other and embrace the fear. And when our children are born, we will show them that love like that is worth it, a hundred times over.'

His throat moved again and he shook his head. 'I didn't believe in fate or luck. But I'm almost thankful that your sister stole from me. That I drove that day to find you. That I'm so *blessed* to have you, Dr Parker,' he finished gruffly.

'Can I tell you I love you now?'

'*Se, per favore,*' he whispered urgently.

She leaned up and brushed her lips over his, then pulled

back before he could take over and capture hers. *'Ti amo tanto, Alessio.'*

He swooped down and took her mouth then, every last emotion saturating their kiss until Giada was drowning in it and welcomed more.

'Chista è da me,' he breathed against her lips when they came up for air.

'Yes. I'm yours. Now and always. Now take me home, Alessio. We have a new year to welcome.'

'A new year *and* the rest of our lives,' he amended.

As she'd suspected he would.

And that was the only way she wanted it.

* * * * *

AN HEIR
MADE IN HAWAII

EMMY GRAYSON

MILLS & BOON

To Mr. Grayson, always.

To my favorite proofreading team, Mom and Dad.

To one of my biggest cheerleaders, Little Man.

To my Queen of One Lines, Katelyn.

To my friend who is stronger than she knows, Laura.

CHAPTER ONE

ANIKA PIERCE SAT back on her towel and gazed out over the pristine waters of Hanalei Bay. No one looking out over the calm, gentle waves would have guessed that just the night before the ocean had churned and frothed beneath the weight of a late-November storm. The heaviest rains of the season in the Hawaiian island usually didn't start until December. But the storm hadn't gotten the memo, barreling across the ocean and turning the midnight blue waves to black. She'd watched it from the hotel balcony, bewitched by the jagged bolts of lightning and the rumble of thunder that had made the windows tremble. The fierce beauty of it all had thrilled her, called to something primal deep inside.

Anika snorted. Or perhaps it had just been a perfect mirror of her mood. And all because of *him*.

Nicholas Andrew Lassard. The bastard.

She'd walked out onto the hotel's terrace that overlooked the waters of the Pacific Ocean just after breakfast this morning, soaking in everything from the soaring palm trees to the mountains that guarded the Hanalei Valley. She loved Slovenia and the small town of Bled that had become her home. But she was going to take full advantage of the summer-like weather. With a hot cup of tea in one hand and a book in the other, she'd been excited to lie out on one of the chaise lounges and enjoy her morning.

Until she'd turned and run smack into Nicholas. If there was one thing to take joy in, it was that her tea had ended up all over his crisp white shirt. He hadn't reacted with anger, even though the shirt probably cost as much as what she charged for a night at the inn. No, he'd simply smiled that charming Scottish smile and told her it was good to see her. Then, when she'd demanded to know what he was doing here, he'd calmly replied he was attending the International Hospitality & Tourism Conference.

Just thinking about the smug expression on his handsome face stoked the simmering embers of irritation into hot spurts of anger that roiled about in her chest. When he'd walked into the Zvonček Inn, three weeks ago with yet another offer to buy her hotel, this one with an increase of another hundred thousand euros compared to the offer he'd made over the summer, he'd seen the brochure for the conference on her desk. The arrogant jerk had even commented on it and asked if she was attending.

Had he followed her to Hawaii? Was he truly that fixated with buying the inn that he would fly nearly eight thousand miles and track her down?

Yes.

She had underestimated Nicholas when he'd swept into Bled a year and a half ago and begun construction on the Hotel Lassard at Lake Bled. A three-story luxury hotel with an on-site spa, restaurant and rooftop bar. Elegant, glamorous and ridiculously expensive.

And just down the road from the inn that had been in her mother's family since World War I.

The hotel had done their due diligence in sending a representative to meet with her and deliver a leather portfolio complete with architectural renderings of the future hotel. *"Community relations,"* the willow-thin girl in a fancy black suit had said with a huge smile that had reminded Anika of a shark. She hadn't been a fan of having another hotel so close to hers, especially one with all the modern amenities hers didn't have. But the kind of people who stayed at the Hotel Lassard were most definitely not the kind of people who stayed at the Zvonček Inn. They wanted marble bathtubs and grand chandeliers, not cozy fireplaces and handmade quilts.

She'd met Nicholas a week later at a breakfast hosted by the local tourism board. With thick, dark brown hair that looked artlessly windblown and an actual dimple in his cheek when he smiled, he'd had half the women of Bled in love with him before they'd sat down. Irena, an elderly shopkeeper with huge round glasses perched on her nose, had breathlessly whispered the silver watch had to be Cartier and the charcoal-gray suit tailored to Nicholas's broad shoulders and lean waist was most definitely from Savile Row in London.

"See how perfectly it fits his rear?"

The memory of Irena's croaky voice teased a reluctant smile from her lips. Yes, Nicholas was a good-looking man. She could even acknowledge handsome. Too bad his greedy soul was so ugly.

The wealth, the charm, all of it had put her on guard. Nicholas walked in far different circles than she did. That he hadn't bothered to come and deliver the news of his new hotel to her in person had shown her that Nicholas took care of the big, flashy things, whereas little people such as herself were fobbed off onto his underlings. Seeing him flirt with women of all ages at the breakfast before he'd delivered a slick presentation on what his hotel would bring to the community had cemented her impression of an overindulged lothario who liked playing at the hotel business.

Except, when Nicholas wanted something, he played hardball. She'd found that out the hard way this past spring when he'd surprised her by walking into the inn and requesting a private meeting. His sheer presence, from another one of those custom suits down to his shiny loafers, had grated on her nerves and made the worn rug in her office and the pots of snowdrops on the windowsill feel meager and outdated.

He'd smiled at her. She'd given him the tiniest one in return.

And then he'd robbed her of speech by sliding another leather portfolio with the embossed silver logo of the Hotel Lassard onto her desk, one with an offer to buy the inn for fifty thousand euros above its current value.

He'd taken advantage of her silence. His words had flowed out, smooth as brandy and just as potent, with that charming accent underlying his pitch.

He'd been satisfied, he'd said, with the property they'd purchased and its views of not only the lake but the island and its romantic church, the castle on the northwestern shore. Yet the one thing he hadn't gotten was lakeside property. He'd accepted it, he'd said with all the humbleness of spoiled royalty, content to have the views.

Until he'd taken a tour of the lake and seen her inn from the water. He'd even used the Slovenian term, *pletna*, for the gondola-like boats that ferried tourists around, smiling slightly as if he was proud of himself for bothering to use the word correctly.

Her inn, he'd explained, could be a perfect extension of the Hotel Lassard. With extensive renovating, the integrity of the building could be kept while adding the luxury and glamour that guests of the Lassard brand expected. It would also give his clients access to the small beach for swimming and lounging in the summer, as well as the dock for year-round boat launches.

Then he'd leaned forward and said the words that even now made her grate her teeth just remembering how self-righteous he'd sounded.

"I know the inn is in trouble. I can fix it."

To his credit, he'd only blinked when she'd said, "No." He'd leaned back, his chair creaking ominously. For once, she'd wished something in the inn would break and send him tumbling to the floor.

He'd asked why. She'd replied the inn wasn't for sale. He'd added one hundred thousand euros to the offer on the spot.

And damn it, she'd been tempted. For one horrible second, she'd been tempted. Yes, the inn was aging. It seemed like every time she turned around, mattresses were needing to be replaced, a window had to be repaired or one of the ancient water boilers was on the verge of dying. Decisions that had fallen to her more and more as her grandmother, Marija, had grown sick. Decisions that tangled with worry about her grandmother and weighed on her so heavily that some nights she would lie in bed and feel like she could barely catch her breath wondering how she would possibly overcome it all.

Accepting Nicholas's offer would have been the easy way out. The inn had been in her family for over a hundred years. Walking the halls where her mother, Danica, had grown up, reading on the same window seat and walking barefoot in the yard in the spring when the snowdrops the inn had been named for covered the ground in a blanket of white blooms, had been a lifeline she'd desperately needed. After Danica had passed, Anika had journeyed from the States to live with her only remaining family. Marija, and the inn, had saved her.

But it wasn't just her family or their legacy on the line. The guests who came back year after year considered the inn a home away from home. She wasn't going to let some arrogant hotel scion turn it into a ritzy getaway her clients would no longer be able to afford, to turn her inheritance into a splashy spectacle. All because the bastard wasn't satisfied with his views of the lake.

She'd said no again. The smile had disappeared, giving her a glimpse of what Nicholas Lassard concealed so well behind that pleasant face: a sharp, intelligent businessman who didn't like being denied what he wanted.

No. She was not letting him ruin something else on this trip. She was here for the conference. Hopefully she would pick up some ideas and make some contacts that would bring more business. But she was also heeding the advice Marija had bestowed on her that final week before she'd passed when she'd given Anika an envelope containing a plane ticket and a reservation for the conference they'd always dreamed of one day attending together.

"Go and enjoy yourself." She'd squeezed Anika's hand when Anika opened her mouth to protest, to point out the money would have been better spent on the inn. *"Do it for me, Anika. I'll be happier knowing you have a chance to live a little."*

The concrete dock jutted out into the water and offered the most incredible views. The end was covered by a canopy and offered several picnic tables as well as ladders for those wanting to swim off the pier. But at eight o'clock in the morning, the pier was blissfully empty.

Sailboats and a couple smaller fishing boats gently bobbed on the water. Tourists in kayaks paddled across the bay and into the Hanalei River. Beyond the water and the beach, mountains swelled up toward the sky, the jagged ridges hinting at the wildness beyond.

She missed home, missed the crispness of fall sliding into winter as snow danced down from the Alps and dusted the town and the adjoining lake. Lake Bled was becoming better known as a travel destination, although it had held on to its small-town European charm.

But Hawaii had rekindled a wanderlust she hadn't felt in years. She hadn't even known she'd needed to get away from Slovenia until she had stepped out of Kauai's airport into tropical heat that had slid across her skin like a lover's caress. Palm trees had provided shade, mountains covered in velvety green instead of snow had stood proudly against a turquoise sky and, perhaps her favorite part of all, were the chickens that had run about with carefree glee.

Determined to relax before she walked back up for the conference's opening session, she lay back on her towel. Slowly, she focused on relaxing her body, tension seeping out of her muscles as the sun gently wiped away her worries and lulled her into a dreamlike state. Schedules and overdue bills and marketing plans slipped away. For once her mind was completely, blissfully clear of everything except where she was.

The word drifted through her mind again—*heaven*—and she let out a sigh of contentment.

"Be a shame to burn that beautiful skin."

She froze as the deep, gravelly voice rolled over her, each of the words pronounced with emphasis and tinted with his rasping accent. The rigidity returned, invading her body and tensing her limbs into tightly coiled springs as her pulse kicked up a notch.

Because he's annoying as hell, she reassured herself.

A shadow fell over her, blocking the sun. Reluctantly, she opened her eyes and blinked.

"I was wrong."

Nicholas loomed over her, white smile flashing against tan skin that said he had recently been traveling, or more likely partying, abroad.

"About what?"

"I'm not in heaven. I'm in hell."

He threw back his head and laughed. She propped herself up on her elbows and glared up at him, trying to contain the burst of fury that raced through her. Normally Nicholas only inspired minor irritation, occasionally a dash of righteous anger.

But right now, when she had just achieved the peak of relaxation, she wanted nothing more than to shove him off the pier.

"It'll be hot enough this afternoon to count as hell."

"What are you doing here?"

He arched a brow as he crouched down next to her.

"Same as you."

"Trying to have some alone time?"

"Yes."

Her hands curled into fists. "The definition of alone means no one else around."

He glanced around the bay in a slow, considering manner that made her want to grind her teeth.

"Hmm. Must have missed the sign that said this was a private pier."

He pulled his sunglasses off as he spoke. A different type of heat rolled over her, swift and so shocking it made her lips part in surprise. She'd never had a physical reaction to him before. Maybe it was his proximity. Perhaps it was the woodsy scent of his aftershave winding around her.

Or you just haven't been on a date in forever.

Latching on to that rational excuse, she channeled the unexpected jolt into the glare she slanted at him. He arched an amused brow. The chiseled planes of his angular face and defined jawline made the contrast of deep blue eyes that always seemed to glint with amusement all the more alluring.

He's the enemy! her brain screamed. *Stop fantasizing!*

"Cut the crap, Nick. Why are you here?"

His grin flashed once again, confident and sexy. "I like that you still hold on to your American phrases."

"And I like you when you're not around."

"You wound me, Anika. We're not only colleagues but neighbors. Shouldn't we at least act hospitable to one another?"

"I'll acknowledge that we are, unfortunately, neighbors," Anika replied. "However, *colleagues* would imply we both work for a living. I work, whereas you splash your face on magazines and reap the money of the hard work done by your employees as you plot how to take over small businesses like mine and add to your treasury. So I think *colleagues* is a bit too generous a term."

His smirk spread into a smile. She blinked, uncomfortable with the heat flickering low in her belly. Yes, the man was handsome. But he was also a pampered, sneaky snake.

"This is fun. We should talk more."

"I'm insulting you, not conversing."

"Still, one of the more enjoyable conversations I've had in ages."

"Did you follow me here?" she asked, trying to get him back on track.

"I was invited to be a guest speaker for one of the conference's panels in the spring. I've been slated to speak for months."

"You might have mentioned that when I told you I was going," she snapped.

"And risk you canceling? I couldn't have that, especially," he added as his voice deepened, "as this might just be the thing to bring us together."

Alarm skittered through her. "There's no 'us,' Nick. Never is, never will be."

His smile didn't falter even as his gaze sharpened, intense and suddenly focused on what he wanted. There was the heir apparent to his father's hotel empire, the man who would stop at nothing to get what he wanted. The next time he'd visited the inn, a bigger offer in hand, he'd stood in her lobby like he already owned it. When she'd ordered him to leave, he'd listed all the repairs she was facing down, a list that had made her inwardly wince as he included the estimated costs for each repair. Yet it had also reinforced her resolve that he was the last person on the earth she wanted to hand over the inn to. That he had violated her privacy to such an extent, dug so deeply into her personal finances to acquire his own goals, had driven her to slide the offer out of the folder, hold it up and rip it down the middle right in front of his eyes.

He'd been back. Oh, he'd been back repeatedly through the summer, each offer more than the last.

Which made her all the more determined to keep his greedy hands off her family's inn.

"Why do you resist? My offer could do nothing but help you."

"I think you mean ruin," she shot back, hating that his tone stayed so calm and collected while hers vibrated with indignation. "With how much you're always off gallivanting around the world—"

"Miss me, Pierce?"

His hand came up and brushed a stray tendril of hair back from her face. Something crossed his face, something that made her stomach flutter.

Then it was gone, so quickly she wondered if she'd imagined it.

Get a grip.

Her reaction to Nicholas was simple biology. Whether she liked it or not, he was attractive. She hadn't dated anyone in nearly two years, and the couple of times she and Zachary had attempted sex, it had been less than satisfying.

Don't think about sex! Not around him.

"I miss the solitude and peace I enjoy when you're not around. Now go away, let me enjoy my morning and," she added sharply, "keep your fancy manicured hands off my property."

He reached down and, before she could pull away, threaded his fingers through hers and held up her hand. Their palms met, pressed together in an intimate caress that swept through with a fiery intensity. It took a moment for the reality of his calloused skin to penetrate her shock.

"I've never gotten a manicure."

His voice slid over her, his tone deeper, sultry like the warmth slowly building as the sun climbed higher in the sky. She should pull her hand away. But as his fingers drifted down, traced the lines crisscrossing her palm, then lower to settle on the pulse beating wildly in her wrist, she didn't move. When his gaze returned to her face, she couldn't stop her sharp intake of breath as she saw something she'd never expected to see in Nicholas's eyes.

Desire.

A memory of the last tabloid image she'd seen appeared in her mind. He'd been looking at his now ex-girlfriend with the same focused intensity, one hand resting casually around her waist as she'd smiled up at him on the rooftop of some famous museum.

Nicholas Lassard wasn't made for family, for commitment and wedding rings and babies. She wanted all of it. What she didn't want was to be the latest in a long string of conquests.

The thought gave her enough willpower to pull her hand away. She turned away from him, her eyes seeking out the palm trees swaying gently in the breeze. She breathed in deeply and refocused on the issue at hand.

Something needed to be done. She knew it, had known it as she'd arranged for the necessary repairs to the structure of the inn when paint had begun to peel and the carpets had become more worn.

Selling the inn might save her financially. But it would be saying goodbye to a legacy, watching it turn from a cozy haven into a swanky offshoot of a hotel that offered champagne in crystal flutes at check-in and heated outdoor pools. The essence of the Zvonček Inn would be lost.

As would the only thing she had left of her family.

"You run a resort that costs over a thousand dollars a night and twenty-four-seven room service. I work in an inn that uses antique keys." She glanced at his black T-shirt and linen pants. Even at the beach, his wardrobe screamed wealth.

"We run in very different circles. You stick to yours and stay out of my way, I'll stick to mine, and everyone stays happy."

His hand settled on her calf. She jerked at the feel of his bare palm on her skin, then inwardly cursed for reacting to his touch.

"Does it make you happier to be away from me, Anika?"

"Yes."

"I'm wounded."

Frustrated, she stood, so swiftly she nearly knocked Nicholas back on his rear. Satisfied in the most petulant way possible, she turned her back on him and whisked her dress over her head. A strangled noise made her look back over her shoulder.

Nicholas was staring at her. Was *stare* even the right word, she thought frantically as he rose, his eyes raking her body.

"What are you doing?"

"Going for a swim."

"Don't be a fool," he growled. "There's high surf in the winter and—"

"And a smart tourist just might ask the lifeguards over at the beach if today was safe for swimming before she went in," she snapped back. It was much easier to ignore the fire and possession in his gaze when he acted like a macho idiot. "Don't underestimate me, Nicholas. You'll lose."

With those parting words, she jumped off the pier into the waters of Hanalei Bay.

CHAPTER TWO

NICHOLAS ACCEPTED THE pen from the perky redheaded clerk behind the counter. He didn't miss the appreciation in her eyes, nor the brush of her fingers against his.

"We just need your signature here, here and here."

"Saying I won't sue if I get eaten by a turtle?"

The clerk chuckled. "To date, we've had no turtle attacks. Have you ever been on a turtle snorkeling tour, Mr. Lassard?"

"Snorkeling, yes, but not for turtles."

The woman's smile switched from flirty to genuine. "Then you're in for a treat. Their nesting season is from May to September, but we've had plenty of guests see them in the winter, too."

Nicholas returned her smile. "I'm looking forward to it."

"Do you think we'll see a dolphin, Mom?"

Nicholas glanced over to see a sandy-haired little boy excitedly tugging on his mother's shirt as they headed for the door. The woman smiled down at her son.

"I hope so."

"Or maybe a sea monster!"

Something in the boy's hopeful expression stabbed straight into Nicholas's gut. For a moment he saw David, sunny smile brightening his freckled face, his dark blond hair falling into his eyes because he'd refused to get it cut.

A smile extinguished in the span of a heartbeat by a careless driver who had missed a stop sign and changed his family's life forever.

His fingers tightened around the pen. He'd accepted, after years of counseling, that the driver had been at fault. An acceptance that had lessened, but not fully removed, the guilt that lingered beneath the surface. He'd been the one to suggest riding bikes that day, the one who had been looking the other way when David had ridden out into the road.

Behind him, he heard the door close and the sound of the little boy's chattering fade. The tightness in his chest eased a fraction. He finished scrawling his name.

"Thank you, Mr. Lassard." The clerk gestured towards a corner decorated with plush, vibrant blue chairs and a flat-screen TV mounted on the wall. "We have one more guest on the way. As soon as they arrive, I'll start the safety video."

He moved to a bank of windows that overlooked the harbor. He had been to Hawaii before with his parents, but they'd visited Maui on that trip. In the first ten years after David's death, the only time Nicholas and his parents had been happy was when they were on vacation. Thailand, Spain, Brazil, Alaska. They'd jetted all over the world, briefly escaping reality and indulging in adventure. As soon as they'd returned to their stately mansion in London overlooking Eaton Square gardens, his father had retreated to his office or flown off to take care of business somewhere else. His mother had crawled into bed and slept or taken pills to keep the grief at bay. They didn't talk about David. Unless they were on vacation, they'd barely talked at all.

He shoved his hands in his pockets and watched a family move toward the dock. This past summer had marked the twentieth anniversary of David's passing, and things had improved immensely in recent years. He didn't know what had finally driven his parents into counseling. But they'd recovered, slowly climbing out of their depression and rejoining life. It had been about that time that Nicholas approached his father about becoming more involved with the Hotel Lassard brand. His father had agreed with the stipulation that Nicholas work his way up. He'd started with a maintenance crew for the chain's flagship hotel in London on the weekends as he'd pursued his business degree at Oxford. He'd slowly but surely worked his way up to his current job as Director of Expansion.

Too bad that what had seemed like such a simple expansion, a way to achieve his vision for the Lake Bled hotel, had turned into such a chaotic mess.

Anika Pierce had caught his attention when he'd spoken to Bled's local business owners nearly eighteen months ago. Unlike the majority of attendees who had responded with wide-eyed excitement to his presentation, she'd been polite but chilly, asking intelligent questions that had heightened his interest. So had her overall professional appearance, from her dark hair caught up in a twist on the back of her head to her black trousers and a loose white shirt with a tie around her slender neck. But her frosty attitude had rankled. He'd ensured that representatives from the Hotel Lassard had connected with all of the local hotel owners in the area, to reassure them that he would be working with, not against, their interests. Perhaps Anika just didn't like having another hotel so close to her inn, even though his research and development team had assured him the inn and vacation rentals in the area were in an entirely different class than the Hotel Lassard.

Whatever the reason for Anika's snooty attitude, he was used to a different type of response from most women. Her lack of one, combined with the grudge she seemed to hold, had made it easy to not think of her when he'd left.

Business had taken him back to London, then New York and finally Bilbao in northern Spain. When he'd returned to Slovenia in the spring to see the construction, he'd taken the long route around the lake past the centuries-old castle that stood guard on the clifftops. He'd also booked himself a ride on one of the gondolas that frequented the lake's pristine waters. One of his father's most important lessons as Nicholas had ventured deeper into the family business had been to experience what his guests would as much as possible.

It had been on that boat ride, as the gondola circled the southern end of the island, that he'd looked toward the upper levels of the Hotel Lassard emerging above the treetops and seen the Zvonček Inn on the lakeshore. The simple beauty of it had hit him square in the chest, conjuring images of long-ago trips before David's passing, to destinations like the beaches of England and Ireland instead of cities bursting at the seams. In that moment, he'd had a clear vision of the future: the main hotel to the east, with an exclusive mansion for guests wanting more privacy or a room on the lake just a short walk away. The pier could be redone, with a terrace for dining and a dock for boat rides to the island. Luxury combined with the natural beauty Lake Bled offered.

When he'd toured his property in person, reviewed the aerial photos of the surrounding area, he hadn't even considered acquiring the inn. But once he'd seen it from the lake, nothing less than owning it would do. He hadn't analyzed the obsession that had suddenly seized him. Whatever was pushing him was pushing him in the right direction.

He'd gotten back in his car and turned at the wooden sign that advertised the Zvonček Inn. A small painting of the bell-shaped snowdrop flower the inn was named for had faded long ago, the white petals almost the same brown as the sign.

That had been his first clue of how the inn was doing. As he'd driven up the long drive, he'd given credit for whoever had planted the snowdrops blooming along the gravel, the simple charm further enhanced by the white lanterns marching up to the house.

The house itself had surprised him. Unlike the cottage style of so many buildings in the area, the three-story home reminded him more of Victorian-style houses he'd glimpsed on his trips to the Hamptons and Martha's Vineyard. From the tower topped with a conical roof to the expansive porch trimmed with intricate wood spirals that reminded him of a gingerbread house, it was the definition of quaint.

Or had been. Whatever pale color the house had once been painted had long since faded to gray. The porch sagged. Shingles were missing from the roof.

But there was promise. Nicholas had achieved far more with far less.

He'd anticipated Anika being a harder sell than most. But he never would have guessed she would be a flat-out denial. Not with the inn falling apart around her.

He'd considered approaching Marija Novack, Anika's grandmother. He'd met her a couple of times, including during the town's annual Winter Fairy Tale market, where she'd been manning a booth draped in evergreens and selling the inn's version of the traditional Bled cream cake. Aside from the tawny gold of her eyes, he hadn't glimpsed a single trace of Anika in the woman's deep smile or the feathery cap of silver hair on top of the narrow, slender face.

The sixth sense that had made him so successful, his ability to read people quickly and accurately, had noted the fatigue lurking in the crinkles by her eyes. The paleness of her skin. He might be resolute, tenacious, heavy-handed when the situation called for it. But he wasn't cruel. He wasn't going to press a woman who, at best, was getting on in years.

Unfortunately, his suspicions that something else was going on had been confirmed that summer. He'd backed off as Marija had neared the end of her life, had even sent flowers to her funeral and given Anika space to mourn her grandmother in private. He knew, better than most, how important it was to grieve. Especially when someone you loved so deeply was there one moment and then gone the next.

He turned away from the harbor and moved over to the table set up with fruit, coffee and *malasadas*, thick, chewy doughnuts that were a breakfast favorite in the islands. He poured himself a cup of black coffee, savored the underlying flavor of molasses and focused on the slight burning on his tongue from drinking it before it had a chance to cool.

Better to focus on that than the past.

Especially when the present, and more importantly the future, demanded so much of his attention.

Including one stubborn, infuriating inn owner.

He'd given her time, nearly three months after Marija's passing. But as the opening date of the Hotel Lassard had drawn nearer, he'd decided to press forward. When he'd heard that a tree had taken out the roof of one of the guest rooms during an autumn storm, he'd returned with an even higher offer and the opportunity for Anika to remain as the general manager of the property. It had been more than generous.

A view Anika had not shared, judging by how she'd ripped this one not down the middle but into long, thin strips she'd fed into the fireplace crackling in her office.

He'd been angry, yes. He wasn't used to hearing the word

no and, as he'd discovered over the last few months, he didn't like it. Some might argue he had been indulged too often. But when it came to business, it had nothing to do with being spoiled and everything to do with the fact that not only was purchasing the inn the right move for his hotel, but it was the best thing for Anika before that damned house collapsed on top of her.

Stubborn, prideful woman.

Yet beneath his annoyance, something else had started to simmer, then pulse through his veins when she'd turned to face him, crossing her arms over her chest and arching one eyebrow with a smug smirk on her full lips.

Desire. It had unnerved him to the point that he had left Anika with the less than witty retort of "This isn't over" before he'd walked out, putting as much distance between him and her as possible.

He enjoyed women. Their beauty, their company, their beds. He wasn't like some of his class who took a new woman out every night or, worse, balanced multiple lovers at once. But he wasn't a saint, either. He had no intention of marrying, of having children. Not after seeing the devastation David's death had wrought on his parents' marriage, straining it to the breaking point far too many times. Yes, they'd survived and eventually found a new kind of happiness. But years of his mother drifting about the house, a medicated wraith, and his father traveling so much he barely saw his wife and surviving son, had been enough.

Toss in the guilt that had never relinquished its hold on him and he was left with a firm commitment to bachelorhood.

And something about Anika, his reaction to her, told him it wouldn't be straightforward and easy. No, Anika Pierce was a challenging woman with hidden depths and a fire that would ensnare him.

A point proven by the eye-popping sight he'd witnessed yesterday morning. When Anika had stood and stripped off her dress, he'd nearly swallowed his tongue. Beneath the loose shirts and wide-legged trousers she usually wore back in Slovenia was an incredible body shown off to perfection by a deep orange bikini. A body that had made him uncomfortably hard as he'd taken in the subtly defined back, trim waist and generous curves of her thighs. When she'd turned, hair the color of dark chocolate streaming over her shoulders and fire snapping in her golden brown eyes, he knew he was in trouble. He hadn't anticipated how much he wanted to touch that pale skin, slide his hands over her hips and pull her against his body and find out just how much passion Anika had been hiding under that cool exterior of hers.

As if to further torment him, her husky voice sounded behind him, low and pleasant. Surprised, he turned to see her smiling at the red-haired clerk.

"I'm here for the turtle snorkeling."

He had never been jealous of a woman before. But in that moment he was fiercely, horribly jealous of the clerk. Anika was smiling at her like she was a long-lost friend. She brushed a lock of hair behind her ear, giving him a view of the excitement sparkling on her face.

"We'll be heading out in about fifteen minutes. If you'll just sign the waiver and then head over, I have one other guest needing to watch the safety video."

Anika turned, her smile fading almost as soon as she saw him. Irritated, he shot her a cocky grin and raised his cup. She turned back to the clerk and pointedly ignored him as she signed the forms.

"Anika, I didn't know you were coming on this excursion," he said as she slowly walked over to him when she was done.

"Are you following me?" she asked as she stopped a few feet away, arms crossed. His eyes slid down to the curves of her breasts pushed up past the scooped neckline of her vivid red tank top. With her hair once again loose, a straw bag over one shoulder and blue jean shorts that showcased those long legs, she looked incredible. She followed his gaze, pink staining her cheeks when she realized what he was looking at.

"It's rude to stare."

He blinked, taking another sip of coffee to hide his satisfaction at the breathlessness in her voice. She felt it, too, this sudden attraction snapping between them.

"I apologize for staring."

She tilted her head, her eyes narrowed. "Why do I feel like there's a *but* in there?"

He grinned. "Because there is. But I won't apologize for liking what I see."

The pink deepened into a red that nearly matched the color of her shirt.

"Stop it. I'm not one of your conquests."

"I've never seen you as a prize to be won."

"Just my inn?"

Beneath the bravado, he heard the tiniest thread of something he hadn't picked up on before. Fear. Anika started to fidget as he watched her, glancing off to the side then down at her feet before her head snapped up and she squared her shoulders.

"What?"

"I'm just trying to figure you out."

"Well, don't. It's pretty simple. I don't like you. I'm not selling to you. End of story."

"Are you ready for the safety video?"

They both turned to see the clerk, who was standing just behind the desk with a wide grin on her face, her head swiveling back and forth as if she were taking in a tennis match instead of two people about to kill each other in her lobby.

"Yes," Anika said quickly. She stalked past Nicholas and sat down on a leather bench in front of the TV. Nicholas debated for a moment before he sat next to her.

"There's plenty of other seats."

"So pick one," Nicholas replied casually. "This has the best view and room for three or four people. I want to make sure I get all the safety information needed to enjoy this trip."

She grumbled something under her breath that sounded suspiciously like how she was planning to murder him on said excursion, but he ignored it. The clerk hit a button on the remote, shot them another silly smile and walked back to the desk as images of turtles swimming through the ocean filled the screen.

"I think the clerk might be playing matchmaker."

Anika snorted and he bit back a laugh. He didn't know a single woman he'd dated who would have made such a derisive, uninhibited sound in his presence.

"Perhaps one of us should tell her that has as much chance as a snowball in hell."

"Snowball in hell," he repeated. "Another of your American euphemisms?"

"And an accurate one. Tell me," she said as her smile sharpened, "how does Hawaii measure up to the Caribbean? That was where you went after our last meeting, right?"

"Keeping tabs on me?"

"Hard to not overhear the maids gossiping about the fight

you had with your girlfriend at a beachside restaurant. You were even trending on Twitter."

He grimaced. "Ex-girlfriend."

Ex-girlfriend and one of his few mistakes. Sadly, it had been a catastrophic one. Susan, a textile heiress, had entertained ideas of changing her status from millionaire to billionaire through marriage. An idea she hadn't shared with him until she'd slipped "insider information" to a magazine that Nicholas Lassard, the renowned bachelor, would be proposing within the year. He could have easily told her he had no interest in proposing. Had she bothered to ask him, he could have told her all of it in a private conversation instead of a public display on the beach of his latest resort. He'd tried to escort Susan to his office, but she'd insisted on being out in the open.

He scowled. He should have known she would have arranged to have the entire debacle photographed by a paparazzo. She hadn't gotten a ring out of him, but she'd gotten some photos of her looking elegantly tragic, soft blond curls framing her face, tears on her cheeks and her hands clasped together in front of her ample bosom as her white dress fluttered around her.

He suppressed a shudder. The thought of being tied down to Susan until death did them part was enough to make a grown man weep. The woman thrived on drama, on being catered to and taken care of, a quality that had initially drawn him to her. He enjoyed playing the role of hero. He just hadn't planned on doing it all the time for such a self-obsessed woman.

"I'm sorry."

His head snapped around. Anika was still staring at the screen, but her expression had lost its edge.

"For?"

"The breakup. Whether it was amicable or not, break-ups are hard."

"Thank you." He took another sip of coffee to hide his surprise at the genuineness in her tone. He never would have described Anika as compassionate. Yet here she was, offering her sworn enemy words of comfort. "This one was for the best."

"Didn't lose the love of your life?"

"I will never have a love of my life. Susan, unfortunately, did not understand that."

Anika's body tensed next to him. He glanced over in time to see something flit across her face, something that made him feel, uncomfortably, like he had just disappointed her.

"Well, isn't she lucky you corrected her in that assump-tion." Before he could reply, she stood. "Enjoy the trip."

She walked out of the room without a backward glance.

CHAPTER THREE

STUPID, STUPID, STUPID!

Anika resisted the urge to physically smack herself as she stretched out on the trampoline mesh stretched between the hulls of the catamaran. The boat skimmed across the ocean, the sparkling blue waters of the Pacific passing by a dozen feet below her.

She was in Hawaii on the kind of trip she had always imagined. But instead of staring in awe at the islands dotting the horizon or the sharp, jagged peaks of the Nā Pali coast drenched in vivid green with waterfalls tumbling down from jaw-dropping cliffs, she was thinking, once more, about Nicholas Lassard.

I'm just trying to figure you out...

The memory of those words sent a shiver through her despite the sunshine warming her skin. When he'd looked at her like that, those blue eyes lingering on her body, followed by curiosity as if he had genuinely wanted to know more about her, she'd panicked. She didn't want a man like Nicholas taking an interest in her.

Not because she couldn't resist him, she reminded herself hurriedly. But something had changed between them. Yesterday on the pier, perhaps? Just now in the office? Or had something been there all along and they were just now becoming aware of it?

Whatever it was, it was dangerous. Nicholas was the enemy. And, thankfully, as he had reminded her, he was the exact opposite of what she wanted from a man. They had zero similarities when it came to what they wanted out of relationships. That she had been disappointed by his pronouncement of avoiding love was more than enough warning that she needed to stay away from him the rest of this trip.

The trampoline dipped. She turned her head to see a handsome man sitting down near her. His jet-black hair was buzzed short on the sides and long on the top. A light blue T-shirt clung to a muscular frame. His navy swim trunks were loose, but didn't hide the muscles in his legs that spoke to someone who kept himself in shape. He shot her a smile and she smiled back, waiting for her body to react.

Aside from a small, enjoyable warmth in her belly, there was nothing. Nothing even close to the heat that had bloomed low in her body and then snaked through her as Nicholas had raked his eyes over her.

Determined to banish Nicholas from her thoughts once and for all, she pushed up on her elbows.

"Enjoying the tour?"

"Oh, yes." His smile widened, flashing white against brown skin. "My uncle owns the tour company. I practically grew up on this boat." He held out his hand. "Adam Kekoa."

"Anika Pierce."

He hung on for just a moment longer than was necessary, appreciation warming his eyes.

"Your first time in Hawaii?"

"Yes, and I'm loving it."

"Good," he said with a hint of pride. "It's a beautiful island. Are you here for business or pleasure?"

"Mostly business. I own an inn and I'm here for a tourism conference."

The boat started to slow.

"Ladies and gentlemen, we're nearing our first snorkeling stop," the captain announced over the speaker. "We'll be issuing gear as soon as we stop. We have an even number of guests on board today and ask that you snorkel in groups of at least two."

"At the risk of sounding forward, do you have a snorkeling buddy?" Adam asked.

"No, but I—"

"Adam?"

Her pleasant feeling evaporated as Nicholas walked to the edge of the trampoline. Unlike Adam's casual attire, Nicholas still had on tan linen pants and a loose, grayish-blue collared shirt. He'd left the buttons at the top undone and rolled up the sleeves to his elbows, giving everyone a view of his toned chest and muscled forearms.

He should have looked prissy and spoiled. Not confident and sexy.

Adam turned, a small wrinkle forming between his brows.

"Yes?"

The sharp smile Nicholas sent his way nearly made Anika shiver.

"Your uncle asked if you would help him pass out equipment. One of his workers is helping a sick guest."

Adam frowned. "Okay." He glanced between Nicholas and Anika before seeming to come to a decision. "It was nice to meet you, Anika."

Anika waited until Adam was out of sight before she stood, gliding toward Nicholas with slow, measured steps as she fought the anger churning inside her.

"What the hell was that?"

"What?" The bastard had the audacity to look completely

innocent as he stared down at her. "I was talking with the captain. One of the guests got sick. He said he needed his nephew to help him. I offered to help and he pointed out Adam to me."

"I don't believe you for a second. You deliberately interfered because you saw that I was enjoying myself."

He sighed, as if he had the right to be impatient with her. "I did not poison anyone, Anika. I did not lie to Adam."

When he said it like that, her suspicions did sound foolish. But there had been something in his expression, something predatory when he'd looked at Adam, as if he'd wanted to wring the man's neck.

"Fine."

A wave smacked into the boat and sent it rocking. She started and stepped back, one foot landing on the trampoline. Nicholas snaked an arm around her waist and pulled her flush against him.

Oh, God.

Nicholas's body was hard and so deliciously warm she couldn't stop her harsh intake of breath at how good he felt against her. The press of his hips against hers, the hardness of his chest beneath her palms. The faint yet rich scent of his cologne, woodsy mixed with the warm, peppery smell of cinnamon.

She tilted her head back to tell him to release her. And froze.

His lips were less than a breath away. All she had to do was push up on her toes and they would be kissing.

She really wanted to kiss him.

Torn between the desire that had taken root inside her and panic that skittered through her, she lifted her eyes up to his. He was staring down at her, that greedy gleam back and burning in the blue depths, his fingers pressing possessively into her bare back and scorching her skin.

Then it was gone. He kept one hand at her waist and eased back. She nearly reached for him before she curled her hands into fists at her sides.

"Thanks."

"You're welcome." And just like that the casual, carefree Nicholas was back. "Ready to snorkel?"

"Yes."

She started to brush past him, but he laid a hand on her shoulder.

"Looks like you're stuck with me."

"What?"

She whipped her head around and nearly groaned. While she'd been fantasizing about Nicholas's abs, the rest of the guests had already grouped up. Some were already in the water, swimming about with their snorkel tubes bobbing above the surface. Another quick survey revealed Adam up top with the captain.

She sighed. Her stubborn streak demanded she go into the cabin or back on the trampoline and sunbathe, anything but go snorkeling with Nicholas.

But that would be the ultimate example of cutting off one's nose to spite their face. The conference registration had included several excursions. While she was looking forward to the waterfall hike tomorrow and a tour of a coffee estate later in the week, she'd been most excited about the snorkeling trip. She loved to swim in the lake back home. Missing out on a chance to swim in the ocean, something she'd never done before, and see a turtle up close wasn't worth it.

Minutes later, she slipped off the ladder and into the water. Her body, used to the chilly waters of Lake Bled, acclimated quickly to the cool temperatures of the Pacific. She treaded water as she waited for Nicholas, purposefully looking away from how perfectly his black trunks clung to his backside.

Damn Irena and her sharp eyes for pointing out just how attractive Nicholas's rear was.

Once Nicholas was beside her, she struck out with strong, sure strokes away from the boat. She kept inside the perimeter of the bobbers the captain had tossed into the water but distanced herself from the other groups. A quick glance back confirmed that Nicholas was keeping pace with her. She made a downward motion and, at his nod, dove beneath the waves.

The quietness of the water surrounded her. Peace bloomed in her chest as the tension eased from her muscles. She hung, suspended, thirty feet above the sandy bottom, looking out toward the darker depths that went on for thousands of miles. A sobering and yet awe-inspiring feeling, she thought, to realize how much more there was to the world than her tiny corner of it.

Movement caught her eye. Wonder spread through her as she looked down and saw a turtle swimming beneath her. It was massive, the shell nearly four feet across, its flippers propelling it at a steady yet leisurely pace through the water.

Excited, she turned and grabbed Nicholas's hand, gesturing toward the turtle. His eyes widened as he glanced down. She saw his eyes crinkle as he grinned around his mouthpiece. Together, they swam down a little more, still keeping some distance so they didn't spook the majestic reptile, but drawing close enough to see detail like a strand of seaweed trailing in its wake, the small tail peeking out from under its shell.

She waited as long as she could until her lungs started to burn. With one last look, she swam up.

"Oh my God!" she cried as Nicholas surfaced next to her. "Did you see that?"

"I was right there," he replied wryly as he pushed his mask up onto his forehead.

"I know, but did you *see* that?" She laughed. "I can't believe it. That was just…oh, it was just incredible." She sighed in happiness and tilted her head back, soaking in the contrasting shades of the deep blue of the ocean and the paler periwinkle of the sky. "Best part of the trip."

"It's not over yet."

Something in his tone chased away her contentment. Something dark that hinted at unsatisfied desires and carnal pleasures. She kept her gaze averted as restlessness moved through her. Restlessness and a hunger that frightened her.

"Doesn't matter," she replied as she pulled her mask back down, as much a shield against the seawater as the man treading near her. "Definitely the best part."

When she turned to look at him, she felt her chest lurch. It wasn't just the desire in his eyes that had her contemplating swimming as far away from him as possible. No, it was how he looked at her as if he really saw her.

As if he knew what she was thinking, the wild thoughts running amok in her head, his lips curved up.

"We'll see."

"Immersing yourself in the communities you invite your guests to, experiencing what they will experience, can help you offer truly personalized, unique stays. Thank you."

Nicholas inclined his head to acknowledge the applause. His presentation on designing excursions and trips for his guests had been well received by the nearly four hundred attendees seated in the ballroom.

He'd also managed to keep himself focused the entire

forty-five minutes. A feat, given that he'd spent the majority of yesterday and today thinking of Anika.

Something had shifted yesterday. Perhaps it was the visceral reaction he'd had when he'd been chatting with the captain of the snorkeling tour and looked down to see Anika in that damned orange bikini sitting next to another man. He'd never been the jealous type before, but had entertained a vivid fantasy of accidentally knocking the man into the water when Anika had smiled at him. When the captain had identified the young man as his nephew and mentioned needing his help, Nicholas had been only too happy to intercede.

He hadn't anticipated holding her, of having her nearly naked in his arms. But when she'd been there, he hadn't wanted to let her go.

Yet what continued to linger in his mind, late into the night when he'd gotten up to sip a glass of whiskey and gaze out his balcony doors at the moon casting silver shadows on the ocean waves, was when she'd spontaneously grabbed his hand, simply because she'd been thrilled by the sight of a sea turtle. And when she'd laughed, a look of pure joy on her face, he'd been hit with the realization that he had completely misjudged Anika.

Now, he was starting to genuinely like her. He needed to focus on getting the contract signed. But the more time he spent with her, the more he wanted to get to know her just a little bit more. Perhaps kiss her just once and find out for himself what she tasted like.

Probably for the best that as soon as they'd gotten back on the boat, she'd distanced herself from him and spent most of her time either in the cabin or on the trampoline at the front. Nicholas had given her space, needing a little for himself, too, to process how quickly their relationship was changing. Thankfully, Adam had been so busy helping his uncle he hadn't had time to approach her again. When the boat docked, Anika had hurried down the gangplank and driven off in her rental car before he'd even made it ashore.

He hadn't seen her since. A good thing, he reminded himself. It had provided him with a chance to take a step back from these feelings she stirred inside him and renew his focus.

"Thank you, Mr. Lassard." The moderator, a curvy young woman with a wide smile, gripped her microphone and turned to the audience. "We have ten minutes for questions."

Several hands shot up. Nicholas answered the questions with detail and a touch of humor. Public speaking, while not his favorite task, was a necessary component of serving in a leadership role. His father had made it clear that Hotel Lassard executives were considered the face of the company, a sentiment Nicholas agreed with. And, while he didn't care for it, he was good at it.

"Yes, the young lady in the back."

Awareness crackled over Nicholas's skin as Anika stood up, her slim form clad in a billowing yellow silk top and beige slacks that hugged her legs. With her hair pulled into an updo, he could see every line of her face, the long slender curve of her neck. Her mouth twisted into a small but devilish smile as she accepted a microphone from a conference worker. Anticipation flowed through him.

"You mention creating a one-of-a-kind experience for your guests by utilizing resources in the communities where your hotels exist, yes?"

"That's right."

"What happens when people in those communities don't like what your hotel is doing?"

He arched a brow in silent acknowledgment of the gauntlet she'd just thrown down.

"An excellent question. Understandably, not everyone is a fan of a world-renowned resort opening its doors." He added the slightest bit of emphasis to his words, savoring her narrowed eyes. "The biggest detractors are often other hotels concerned that we'll take away business."

"Don't you?"

Some people in the audience stirred, surprised by the unknown woman's audacity, but settled back down when Nicholas just smiled. God, she was glorious, standing there in sunshine yellow with lightning in her eyes.

"While it's inevitable that there will be some competition, the Hotel Lassard prides itself on community relations. That includes maintaining a team that travels ahead to any site prior to the beginning of construction and liaises with local hotel owners and managers. We strive to collaborate with them as much as possible."

"But what do you do when the interests of your hotel conflict with someone in the community? What then?"

If it had been just the two of them, he would have stood and applauded. She had him right where she wanted him, on the chopping block in front of hundreds of people. Her boldness excited him. Her daring impressed him.

And that beautifully haughty smile on her face made him want to pull the pins from her hair, tangle his fingers in the silky threads and kiss her senseless.

"It rarely happens. But in the event it does, we explore every possible avenue for collaboration. Not only is it not in our brand's interest to make enemies, but if we don't believe something is the right thing to do, we don't do it. You might argue," he continued as she parted her lips to do just that, "that we only do the right thing because the public is watching. And yes, especially in today's media-focused environment, the public is always watching. But we also do the right thing because it's the right thing."

"And what if the right thing is walking away?"

Challenge vibrated in her voice. The rest of the ballroom fell away as they stared at each other, two people at odds in every way except for the passion that had just flared from a simmer into a blazing inferno.

"The professional in me acknowledges that sometimes the right thing to do is walk away. But personally," he added with a wicked grin, "I don't lose."

The ballroom erupted into a frenzy of conversation. People craned their necks to see who had dared to take on the heir to the Hotel Lassard fortune, while others stared at Nicholas as they whispered and speculated.

Nicholas didn't pay attention to any of it. He just watched as Anika held his gaze, tilted her chin up in a clear gesture of contest. He let his eyes drop down, caress her body from afar, then looked back up. She was watching him, defiance still radiating off her in thick waves.

But he also saw the rise and fall of her breasts beneath her shirt, the faint color in her cheeks, her own perusal of his body as he stood up.

He wanted her. And, while it probably killed her, she wanted him, too.

Securing her signature on the sale contract paled in comparison to his new goal. By the end of the week, he would have Anika Pierce in his bed.

CHAPTER FOUR

TWINKLING LIGHTS CRISSCROSSED the air over the flagstone terrace of the resort. Tiki torches burned brightly. Waiters passed through the crowds of guests with silver trays, some carrying hearty fare like smoked pork with fried onions and guava jelly, marinated ahi tuna and honey walnut shrimp, and others with sweeter treats like slices of chocolate haupia pie, brown sugar–grilled pineapple and small bowls of passion fruit ice cream. Sensual jazz played from hidden speakers scattered among the lush blooms edging the patio. Beyond the green lawn, the waves of the ocean glowed in the light of the setting sun.

Anika sipped on her cocktail as she glanced around. She had been waiting all afternoon and well into the evening for Nicholas to seek her out. Ever since their verbal sparring in the ballroom, she'd been waiting to continue their battle, anticipating it.

Except he'd disappeared after the presentation. She hadn't seen him in the afternoon sessions she'd attended, not in the hallways in between workshops, nor in the tour she'd taken of the resort before dinner. The longer he stayed away, the more on edge she'd become, waiting for the proverbial ax to fall.

It had, she thought grumpily, cast a pall over her afternoon. Although the workshop on marketing on a limited budget had been helpful. The tour had been informative and fun. Still, too often her mind strayed to how Nicholas had looked as he'd said the words that had made her body go molten.

I don't lose.

The memory sent a shiver down her spine. She'd gone to his session as a sort of reconnaissance mission. The more he'd talked, the easier it had been to summon her old anger and dismiss whatever anomaly she'd felt for him on the snorkeling tour. When she'd stood to challenge him, she'd felt prepared, confident.

With every reply, she'd felt her resolve tremble. With every smile he'd directed at her, she'd felt her body weaken. By the end, when he'd uttered those fateful words, she knew she had to do something to reclaim her dignity. Talking to him, reminding him that just because they had a pleasant swim in the sea didn't mean she was just going to roll over and sign the contract, proving to herself that she could handle a conversation with him without thinking about his body pressed up against hers, had been the perfect solution.

One he'd thwarted by disappearing for the past nine hours.

She took a longer sip of her drink, the light and tangy flavors of lime, pineapple and vodka lingering on her tongue. Why was she continuing to let that man consume so much of her time and energy? Especially when she was in Hawaii, a tropical paradise where she was meeting with hoteliers from around the world?

A drumbeat filled the air. Anika turned with the rest of the crowd as a line of dancers clad in strapless red dresses with thick skirts filed onto the terrace. All of them wore crowns of leaves on top of their hair, with leis of the same leaves draped around their necks and matching strands circled around their ankles.

A woman with silver streaked through her dark hair broke from the dancers and stepped forward, a smile creasing her face.

"Welcome, guests from around the globe. My name is Kalea and tonight I am honored to bring the art of hula to you." The side conversations fell silent as Kalea's voice rang out, strong and proud. "Once a means of communicating stories about gods, goddesses, nature and things happening in the world around us, hula suffered over the past two hundred years. It was once deemed illegal to perform in public places, discouraged for decades by outsiders and considered a mere tourist attraction in my grandparents' time." Her gaze roamed over the audience. "The history of this dance was nearly lost. But thankfully, it has been revived in recent years. Tonight, we share our culture with you."

Kalea stepped back into the line. A moment later the dancers began to chant in unison, the song ringing through the night. Anika stared, mesmerized by the sharp, coordinated movements, the smiles on the dancers' faces, the passion in their voices.

"Incredible, isn't it?"

She started as warm breath teased her ear. Her fingers tightened around her glass. She could feel him at her back now, just a couple inches behind her as they watched the dancers spin as one in a tight circle.

"Have you seen a hula before?" she asked.

"My father took my mother and me to one years ago. I have never before seen, and likely never will again, witness such precision and perfection."

"Hmm."

"What?" His voice rumbled through her body all the way to her toes.

"For once we agree."

His chuckle caressed her skin. She swallowed hard and tried to focus on the dancers as their hands wove a story in the air, their bodies moving in perfect harmony. At the end they paused before lowering their arms to their sides. Thunderous applause broke out. The dancers bowed. As they walked off, a small orchestra set up on the adjoining patio began to play. A sensual, jazzy melody wound its way over the crowd.

Slowly, Anika turned to face Nicholas. Her breath caught in her chest. His all-black ensemble, from his coat and pants to the collared shirt with the undone top button giving a tantalizing glimpse of his chest, made her think of a demon.

Or the devil.

The man had certainly tempted her in more ways than one over the last couple of days.

He returned her frank perusal with one of his own.

"You look beautiful."

Pleasure bloomed in her chest. She glanced down at her dress, an off-the-shoulder sky blue gown with a bodice that clung to her like a second skin until it flared into a waterfall skirt that showed off her legs in the front and fell in gentle waves in the back down to her silver sandals. She'd discovered it in a secondhand clothing store back in Bled and bought it for herself.

But the heated gleam of appreciation in Nicholas's eyes certainly didn't hurt.

"Thank you." She cleared her throat. "I was worried."

A smile spread across his face.

"About me? I'm touched."

"Worried I might have sent you running back to your penthouse with your tail between your legs."

He leaned down. "I think you're more worried that I'm not scared off, Anika. It would be easier, wouldn't it, if I was, instead of thinking about you constantly?"

Speechless, she stared up at him.

"I need to mark this on my calendar. The first time Anika Pierce has never had a witty comeback."

Thrown by the heat in his words, scared by her body's response, she latched on to the first thing she could think of.

"Don't think you can seduce me into signing that proposal, Nicholas."

The teasing light disappeared in an instant, replaced by a harsh intensity that made her swallow hard.

"Dance with me."

Her mouth dropped open. "What?"

He grabbed her hand and pulled her toward the dance floor. She opened her mouth to tell him to go to hell, tensed her arm as she prepared to yank out of his grasp.

But she didn't. Because a wicked, decadent part of her wanted one dance, just one, with the man who made her feel sexy and beautiful and vibrant.

He's still a colossal ass. Doesn't mean you can't enjoy yourself.

Comforting herself with that thought, she followed him out onto the terrace, placing her now-empty glass on a passing tray. People were dancing, most just swaying in place, although some executed a few complicated moves that made her eyes widen.

Nicholas suddenly turned to face her. She managed to stop before running into him, but his abrupt turnabout left her mere inches from his chest. He released her hand and she knew a moment of embarrassment. Had he dragged her out here just to make a fool of her? Was this payback for her grilling him at the end of his presentation?

And then he touched her. Electric shock spiraled outward from where he placed one hand, possessively, on her lower back. His other hand rested briefly on her hip, then drifted slowly up her side, his fingers nearly grazing but just barely avoiding her breast before they trailed down her arm. By the time he wrapped his hand around hers and spun her into a turn, anticipation beat a tempo so fiercely in her veins she almost felt faint.

"I don't use sex to get what I want."

His words penetrated the haze of pleasure that had descended over her. She blinked, then focused on the irate expression on his face.

"I find that hard to believe," she managed to retort.

He pulled her against his body as he spun her around a couple wobbling back and forth. His leg moved between hers, the intimate move making her breath catch, before he guided her away from the other dancers.

"When you and I have sex, Anika, it won't be for any reason other than we want to."

A dull roaring drowned out the sounds around her. Each beat of her heart felt magnified, thundering inside her body as she stared at him.

"What?" she finally managed to gasp.

"You want me. I want you."

"I never said I wanted you," she sputtered.

Nicholas watched her, his fingers pressing more firmly against her back, his eyes glowing with that same predatory light she'd glimpsed on the catamaran.

"You also never said you didn't. So tell me now, Anika. Tell me you haven't thought about me kissing you. Tell me," he continued, his husky voice washing over her and sending sinful shivers racing over her body, "you didn't think about how we'd be together when you were in my arms on the boat. That you didn't imagine me tracing my fingers, my lips, over every inch of your incredible body."

Say something!

But she couldn't. Not when her imagination was conjuring up carnal images of her and Nicholas entwined, arms wrapped around each other as he trailed his lips over her neck, her breasts, his hips pressing against hers without any barriers between them.

"Ah." His smile deepened. "So you have thought about it."

"I…"

"I want you, Anika."

"You want my inn."

"They're two separate things."

"Not to me," she whispered, trying to hold on to her sanity. Trying to ignore that intoxicating woodsy scent, the way he looked at her as if he couldn't bear another night without her in his bed.

No one had ever looked at her like that. Not Zachary, not the handful of men she'd gone on dates with her first two years at university. There had been some pleasantness with Zachary and their physical encounters, but nothing close to this. Nothing like the fire burning inside her, this deep-seated need to feel Nicholas's body join with hers.

The song ended. The crowd erupted into applause. Nicholas held on to her for a moment longer before finally releasing her and joining them. Someone called out his name and he turned his head for just a moment.

A moment was all she needed to melt into the crowd. She hurried inside the resort, taking the stairs two at a time up to her room. She raced inside, closing the door behind her and locking both the doorknob and the dead bolt before she yanked the dress off and tossed it into the closet. When she'd first purchased it, it had been a symbol, a sign that she was doing something for herself.

But now, every time she looked at it, she wouldn't feel strong and confident. No, she would feel heat. Heat on her arm where his fingers had danced and grazed before he'd captured her hand in his. Heat between her thighs when she remembered how she'd wanted nothing more than to surrender to the lust that had descended on her and refused to release its grip.

With a muttered oath, she pulled a plain cotton nightgown out of her suitcase, then pulled one of the resort's robes out of the closet and thrust her arms into the voluminous sleeves. The thick, plush material enveloped her body, covered her skin.

But it didn't eradicate the desire that lingered in her blood. It didn't banish the memory of how Nicholas had held her, of how she'd wanted him to do more than just whisk her around the dance floor.

Her fingers fisted in the silky coverlet. What was happening to her? Marija and the inn had been the priorities in her life ever since she had arrived in Bled. She'd been able to indulge in her love of traveling the year after she'd completed her studies at the Bled School of Management, staying close to Slovenia but experiencing locations like Italy and Austria. She'd wanted to travel more, yes. But after a year when almost no one had traveled, followed by the rash of repairs and Marija needing more help, she'd put those dreams on hold.

She'd been disappointed, yes. But there had been comfort in returning to the familiar, an assuaging of the faint sense of guilt she'd experienced at not being around to help. There had also been satisfaction in her work, the camara-

derie with the guests, walking around the lake that always
made her feel like she was in a real-life fairy tale.

And family. She'd always had family. First her mother
and father, who had shown her what a marriage founded on
mutual love and respect could be like. Then her mother, a
woman who had survived the unexpected loss of her husband in a car accident and continued to shower her daughter with love. Followed by Marija, a grandmother she'd only
met twice in person before Danica's passing but who had
welcomed Anika into her home as if she'd been born and
raised in Slovenia.

Until now. Now, except for the inn, she was alone.

Is that it? she asked herself as she pushed off the bed
and stalked to the balcony doors. *Am I responding to him
because I'm lonely?* She closed her eyes. *Please let it be as
simple as that.*

Slowly, she opened her eyes. Her room was on the corner of the resort and overlooked Hanalei Bay and the night-
drenched waters of the Pacific Ocean beyond. Lightning
flickered in the distance, followed by a soft rumble of thunder.

She had a sickening feeling that the answer to why she
found herself so drawn to Nicholas Lassard was far from
simple.

A sigh escaped her as a fork of lightning stabbed down
toward the water, briefly illuminating the white-capped
waves. Which should she fear more? That Nicholas wanted
her in his bed?

Or that she wanted to be there, too?

Thunder rattled the windows of the ballroom. Voices quieted
for a moment, then rose once more as the rumbling receded.
The band struck up another tune, a rendition of a popular

pop song that made the ever-increasingly inebriated guests dance faster as they laughed, joked and enjoyed themselves.

It was the kind of party Nicholas usually thrived in. So why, he wondered as raised his glass to his lips, wasn't he out there with them? While he didn't let loose to the extent that some people were, he liked having fun. Meeting new people, sharing a drink with a beautiful woman, perhaps inviting her back to his room.

Except the only woman he was even remotely interested was nowhere to be found.

The whiskey hit his tongue, the oaky flavor pleasantly sweetened with sugar and enhanced with bitters. If he focused on the taste, the scent of orange curling up from the peel artfully arranged in his glass, maybe he could push thoughts of a certain feisty brunette out of his mind.

Except the shimmer of amber liquid in his glass reminded him of eyes crackling with fire. The citrus fragrance catapulted him back to how she'd felt in his arms, how hard he'd gotten just touching her hand.

A woman appeared in front of him, stunning with her black hair falling over her bare shoulders in thick curls and a fiery red evening gown. Her lips curved up as she eyed him with appreciation.

"Are you here alone?"

"I am."

She stepped closer and laid a confident hand on his arm. "Would you like to change that?"

He stared at her for a long moment, willing himself to feel something for the woman at his side.

But all he could think about was Anika.

"As beautiful as you are, I'll have to decline."

She eyed him for a moment before removing her hand

with a slightly disappointed smile. "Whoever she is, she's a lucky woman."

He grunted as the woman in red walked off, hourglass hips swaying enticingly back and forth. Judging by the look of near terror on Anika's face when he'd told her just where he saw this battle between them headed, followed by her flight from the dance floor, she most likely considered herself the unluckiest woman on the island.

But, he reminded himself as he took another sip, as much as she had wanted to, she hadn't denied their attraction.

He'd been able to deny it himself up until yesterday. Once he'd held her in his arms on the boat, experienced the novel emotion of jealousy seething inside him, felt the quiet joy of having her grab his hand and share that incredible moment beneath the ocean waves, he'd accepted that he wanted Anika.

Maybe she needed a little more time. Maybe they needed to settle this business with the inn first so they could just focus on each other as individuals instead of business rivals. How Anika thought she could possibly keep the inn running by herself as the repair costs mounted and the building deteriorated around her was beyond him. She struck him as an intelligent, driven woman.

So why did she insist on holding on to this? Surely she wasn't so emotionally attached to a house that she would risk it falling into ruin rather than let someone else have it?

An ugly thought invaded. Perhaps it wasn't just letting anyone else have it. Perhaps it was just him.

His fingers tightened around his glass. Never had he been bothered by someone in his world thinking negatively of him. Being liked paled in comparison to being respected.

Yet the possibility that he was the primary reason behind Anika refusing to sign grated on him. Yes, he was tough but fair. Yes, he had high expectations, but his employees and his guests reaped the benefits of the standards he set. Had Anika's inn been thriving, or even just quietly succeeding, he wouldn't have approached her in the first place.

But it wasn't. It was failing. It was failing and he could save it. She was just being stubborn because, for whatever reason, she'd had a grudge against him from the second she'd met him.

He tossed back the rest of his drink. Yes, they needed to settle the sale of the inn. He had been coming at it from the wrong angles, talking up how it could benefit the Hotel Lassard and how it could help her financially. After seeing more of Anika's emotional side the past couple of days, what he needed to focus on was how he could preserve the inn, the legacy that was so important to her.

And then, once she saw reason and he had her name on the contract, there would be no more obstacles between them and finally enjoying each other's company, both in and out of bed.

He glanced down at his watch. It was just before nine. Early enough to invite her to join him in the resort's cocktail lounge for a drink.

He started to pull out his phone when someone knocked into him. A moment later his shirt was covered in red wine. He looked up to see a wide-eyed older gentleman with a thick beard staring at his chest in horror.

"I say," he said in a thick Australian accent, "sorry about that." He glanced down at his feet and frowned. "I didn't think I was that munted." Nicholas bit back a sharp retort as the man awkwardly patted him on the arm. "I'll pay for the dry cleaning."

"No need."

"I can afford it, you know. I own four hotels in Sydney. Four!" the man insisted as he held up five fingers.

"I'm sure you can. Excuse me."

Nicholas walked to the elevators. Thankfully, he had the carriage to himself at it climbed toward the top floor. A minor setback, but once he changed, he would call Anika and—

A jarringly loud boom sounded overhead, one so deep it made the walls of the elevator shake. A moment later the lights blinked out and the elevator ground to a halt.

CHAPTER FIVE

ANIKA STOOD IN the open door of her balcony as the storm rolled over the mountain and swept across the bay. She swirled her wine in her glass, tilted it up to her lips and smiled as lightning lit up the enormous clouds rising above the island. Rain began to pelt the resort, big drops that rivaled the thunder's roar.

It rained in Bled fairly regularly. But nothing like this, this wild unleashing of nature's power.

Exactly what she needed to distract her from her earlier musings.

Thunder cracked overhead, an earth-shattering blast that rattled the glass door of her balcony. The resort plunged into darkness.

She sighed and leaned against her doorway. She had lived through plenty of blackouts, from summer storms in the Midwest and the occasional tornado threat to snowstorms leaving her, Marija and their guests cozied up for a day or two while the old generator had kept the bare necessities running. There had been a touch of excitement during those blackouts, a feeling like everything had slowed down and she was cocooned from the rest of the world.

Her phone rang. Irritated at having her moment interrupted, she pulled her phone out of her pocket and frowned at the unknown number.

"Hello?"

"Are you all right?"

She nearly dropped the phone. "Nicholas?"

His low chuckle washed over her.

"Were you expecting someone else to call?"

"No, just…how did you get my number?"

"I can't tell you all my secrets now, can I?" he teased, his voice husky. "But truly, are you all right?"

"Of course. Why wouldn't I be?"

"I wanted to make sure you were okay after the power went out."

Confused and touched by his thoughtfulness, she found the resolve she'd built up over the last hour starting to crack.

"I am," she finally said. "And you?"

"Stuck in an elevator."

"What?"

"When you're in the hotel business," Nicholas replied casually, "it's a given that at some point you will get stuck in an elevator."

Anika shuddered. The resort only had four stories, but the thought of being stuck in a metal box hanging a few dozen feet above a concrete floor sounded like a scene from a horror movie waiting to happen.

"Have you contacted anyone?"

"Just you."

"Nicholas," she said, exasperated. "I can't help get you out of an elevator."

"I know. I called to make sure you're all right. I'll get out when the power comes back on."

A beeping in her ear made her look down. She swore softly.

"What's wrong?"

"My phone's almost dead." She sighed. "I forgot to charge it last night."

"Distracted, Pierce?"

"Terribly. There's this pompous ass who won't leave me alone, and he's keeping me up at night."

"Do I keep you up at night, Anika?"

Flustered, Anika glanced out the window as the storm continued. His words from the dance floor washed over her. But instead of disgusting her, the memory kindled something deep inside her. A longing for intimacy. A hunger for passion, to experience the kind of satisfaction Nicholas promised with a single glance.

"Anika?"

"Yes?"

The word came out on a squeak.

"Good night." She heard the smile in his voice, could picture it vividly in her mind. "Sweet dreams, hopefully of me."

"Dreams of strangling you, perhaps." She paused. "What will you do?"

"Not much I can do. As much as I enjoy the Bruce Willis movie where he performs some impressive feats in an elevator shaft, I have no desire to be a stuntman or end up a smear on the floor. I know you would prefer otherwise—"

"Don't say that."

Silence fell. Anika wanted to take back her words, but she meant them. Much as Nicholas drove her crazy, and as much as she had loathed him before this trip, she'd seen a different side of him the past couple of days. Yes, he was egotistical and cocky and used to getting his own way. But he was also intelligent, confident and even kind. She'd seen him talking to a bartender, some of the employees on the tour boat, the "little people" so many looked past.

"I wish I had a pen."

"Why?" she asked quietly.

"To mark the day Anika Pierce no longer wished me dead."

"I don't think I ever truly wished you dead. Just…horribly maimed."

His laugh rolled over, pulled the breath from her lungs as she closed her eyes and imagined him lounging in one corner of the elevator, a seductive smile on his lips, a teasing glint in his ocean-blue gaze.

"Progress."

Her phone beeped in her ear again. She had maybe a minute left of battery if she was lucky.

"Where are you?"

"I told you. The elevator. I'm stuck—"

"I know," she replied impatiently, "but which one?"

"The last on the right on the east end of the building."

She mentally pulled up a map of the hotel.

"Stay where you are."

"Okay," he said slowly. "Not too hard to do when you're—"

Her phone died. Before she could lose her nerve, she ran her fingers through her hair and stepped into the hall. Emergency lights glowed white, illuminating her way down to the bank of elevator doors at the far end of the hallway. She walked up to the one on the far right and placed her hands on the cold metal.

"Nicholas?"

"Anika?"

She smiled, grateful to hear his voice reverberating through the door. "Thought you could use some company."

When he didn't respond immediately, her bravado started to slip.

"Thank you."

She let out a shuddering breath, surprised by how relieved she was.

"So…how are you?"

He huffed a laugh. "I've certainly been worse. What's it like out there?"

"Quiet. No guests out in the hall. I imagine if people aren't stuck down in the ballroom, they're in their rooms enjoying the ambience."

"Ambience?"

"The thunderstorm. It's perfect."

"Describe it to me."

Anika frowned. "What?"

"I've always pictured you as cold."

She frowned, more hurt than she liked by his comment. "I'm trying to figure out how, with compliments like that, you're considered one of the most eligible bachelors in Europe."

"I'm charming, I'm handsome and I'm ridiculously wealthy," he replied easily. "Cold and aloof was my first impression. But the more I get to know you, the more I realized how much more there is to you. You don't jump in headfirst like I do. You bide your time, evaluate, think, plan. So when I hear that dreamy note in your tone when you tell me a storm is perfect, it makes me very disappointed that I'm stuck in here and can't see your face. For something to bring that awe to your voice, it must be truly spectacular."

Shaken, Anika let her hands slide off the cool metal and stepped back. Her heart responded to the most beautiful words she'd ever heard by tripling its rhythm as she tried to rein in her runaway emotions.

"Am I wrong?"

"No," she finally replied. *Why,* she thought with some irritation, *are my eyes hot?* "I'm starting to see why so many women fall at your feet."

"Because of my handsome charm?"

She waited a moment, swallowed hard. "Because you know how to make a woman feel special."

"Feel?" His laugh reverberated through her as thunder boomed. "Anika, you are special."

Trembling, she sank down onto the carpet and tucked her feet under her. "Lightning's flashing over the water. It's this vivid scene of crashing waves illuminated for a moment in silver. The mountains make it look even more dramatic. And when I'm cozied up in my room, wrapped in a robe with a cup of hot tea or sipping a glass of wine, I feel like I could watch the storm for hours."

"Stunning." Nicholas paused. "My brother and I used to watch the storms at our home in Scotland. It was my favorite of the family homes, one my mother inherited and where we spent most of the first five years of my life before we moved to London. Stone, turrets all over, a massive fireplace in the library, perched on the edge of a moor with mountains in the background."

Anika closed her eyes, pictured two little boys with their faces pressed against the window as rain rolled across the grassy plains.

"What's your brother like?"

"He's dead."

Horrified, Anika's eyes flew open.

"Oh. Oh, Nicholas, I'm so sorry."

"It's all right. It was twenty years ago."

It might have been twenty years ago, but the raw grief threaded through his words told her he still felt it like it was yesterday.

"I'm glad you have memories with him," she finally said.

"Thank you. Since I've shared a bit from my past, why don't you share a bit of yours?"

"All right. What do you want to know?"

"How does an American girl from the prairie end up running an inn in Slovenia?"

She chuckled. "Put like that, it does sound odd." She traced a finger over the pattern in the carpet. "When I was twelve, my mother passed away from the same cancer that took Babica. Babica was the only family I had left. So I boarded a plane and flew to Slovenia."

"What about your father?"

"Killed in a car accident when I was five." She swallowed hard. "I don't have a lot of memories of him. But the ones I do have are good. My mother worked as a nurse in Kansas City. On days she worked, he would take me to school. We'd stop at a little bakery in town and get doughnuts." A smile crossed her face. "Doughnut Days with Dad. I'd forgotten he used to call them that."

"He sounds like a wonderful father."

Something in Nicholas's voice made her look up at the closed elevator doors. "What about yours?"

Nicholas took his time answering, finally breaking the silence with a sigh. "We're in a good place now. My father is still CEO of the company. My mother serves on the boards of several charities and volunteers at a library."

"A library?" Somehow she couldn't picture a woman swimming in the kind of money Nicholas's family had reading to groups of restless little kids.

"She loves reading, and she loves kids. It's been good to see how far she's come. They didn't take David's death well," he added, as if he'd sensed her unasked question. "Dad was gone all the time. Mom slept and popped pills. I spent most of my time in school or with the soccer team. It wasn't until I started university that they got better."

The image of two little boys at the window shifted to one grief-stricken child watching the storm alone. Her heart cracked. As someone who had always been surrounded by love, she couldn't fathom being a child left alone in the throes of grief.

"Nicholas…" She tried to come up with words of comfort, of support, of anything that didn't sound blasé or empty. "I can't think of anything else but I'm sorry. That sounds like hell."

His laugh was soft but harsh. "It was lonely. The cheeriest times were when we went on vacation. Brief escapes when we could be happy."

Realization hit her. "That's why you went into the family business, isn't it? Why you focus so much on experiences and such for your guests?"

Another period of silence passed, followed by a quiet chuckle. "I never thought about it too much. But yes. The best times of my life have been traveling. I want to give the best to our guests. Plus," he added in a tone more reminiscent of his usual arrogance, "I like to win. Always have."

She sighed. "You're awful, you know that?"

"You've mentioned something of the kind before. What have I done now besides make you feel wretchedly sorry for the poor little rich boy?"

"You're making me like you."

The words emerged, a truth spoken she couldn't, and didn't want, to snatch back. Before Nicholas could reply, something deep within the hotel groaned. The lights flickered back on. Startled, Anika got to her feet as the elevator doors parted.

Nicholas stood just on the other side, hands tucked casually into the pockets of his trousers, his shoulders thrown back in a confident pose that just a week ago would have grated on her nerves. But right now, with the intimacy of their conversation hanging in the air between them, his eyes glittering as he watched her with a possessive gaze, all she could feel was heat.

Smoldering, erotic heat. Making her chest so tight she could barely breathe.

"I have the top-floor penthouse." Nicholas held out his hand. "Join me. Let's watch the storm together."

She stared at his hand for a long moment. She should go back to her room. Yes, she wanted him. But he wasn't good for her. He wasn't what she wanted. And the more they talked, the more she got to know him, the more dangerous he was. She didn't want to like him. The more she liked him, the more she opened up to him, the harder it would be to walk away when the time came.

Which she would have to do at some point. Men like Nicholas Lassard didn't stay. Regardless of how high they took you, how much they charmed and seduced you, they always left with the remnants of a broken heart clinging to their heels.

The elevator doors started to close. Nicholas stepped into the doorframe. The doors shuddered, then slid back.

"One night, Anika. Stay with me for just one night."

He moved closer, his eyes fixated on hers. She watched as he drew closer, her body tight, blood pounding through her veins. If he had moved quickly, had shot her that trademark smirk or made a pithy, arrogant joke, she might have been able to reach deep down inside herself, grab on to some rational thought and pull herself together enough to walk away.

But instead, he reached up and cupped her face in one

hand, his fingers settling lightly on her cheek in a gesture of tenderness that destroyed the last, tenuous grasp she had on reason. She leaned into his touch, a soft sigh escaping her lips as her eyes fluttered shut.

Warm breath whispered across her lips just before his mouth closed over hers. One last bit of sanity tried to prevail, to warn her not to surrender to the man she'd sworn to fight at every turn.

And then he circled an arm around her waist, pulled her flush against his body, and all rational thought vanished.

Her lips opened beneath his. His tongue slipped inside the wet heat of her mouth, teased her with long, slow strokes that elicited a moan from somewhere deep inside her. Her arms looped around his neck and she leaned into his embrace.

He froze.

Oh, God. How could she have thrown herself like that at him? Embarrassed by her overly enthusiastic response, she started to pull away. She would thank him for the kiss, coolly and politely, then calmly walk out the door so he couldn't see her shame—

He grabbed her hips and pulled her back against his body, then stepped back into the elevator and slammed his hand against the button to shut the doors. Her gasp echoed in the car as his hardness pressed against her most sensitive flesh.

He placed a finger under her chin and lifted her eyes up to meet his. "If you stay with me, I'm going to make love to you."

Go! He was giving her the perfect opportunity to turn and walk away. To lay down the boundary once and for all.

Slowly, he traced his fingers up one arm. Her skin pebbled beneath his touch. A shiver rippled over her as she started to breathe heavier, faster. His hand moved up, grazed the sensitive curve of her shoulder and neck.

Before she could reach out and grasp the flimsy threads of rational reasoning, he ran his thumb over her bottom lip. The hardened desire in his gaze became a softer glow, one that could only be described as wonder.

"You are so beautiful, Anika."

Her eyes grew hot again. When he'd said it earlier, it had made her feel sexy, sensual. But now, when she was standing barefoot in a robe thrown over a cotton nightgown, her hair hanging in uncombed waves over her shoulders, she truly felt beautiful.

She reached up and slid her arms around his neck once more.

"Make love to me."

CHAPTER SIX

NICHOLAS SWEPT HER into his arms as the doors opened to the penthouse. He kissed her again as he stalked into the suite, his lips possessive and dominating. She surrendered to his touch. Her pulse tripled as he carried her to the massive bed. Lightning lit up the room as he laid her down, white light illuminating his handsome profile. Giving in to impulse, she pulled him down and kissed the hard line of his jaw, nipped playfully at his neck. He shifted, moved his body on top of her and pressed her down into the silky embrace of the bed.

"If you keep that up," he growled in her ear, "this won't last long."

A husky laugh escaped her lips. Delighted that she could affect him, she arched her hips up, savored the hardening of his jaw.

"Do I tempt you that much?"

"Do you remember that day in your office?" he asked as he started to trail kisses down her neck.

"Yes," she gasped as he eased the straps of her nightgown down.

Cool air kissed her bare breasts. Suddenly shy, she moved her hands up to hide her nakedness. He grasped her wrists and pinned her arms above her head.

"When you tossed the pieces of the contract into the fire

and looked at me with that smug smile, I wanted to kiss you." He placed his lips against the swell of her breast. "I wanted to push you up against the wall, wrap my arms around your incredible body and kiss you senseless."

"Why didn't you?" she asked, her voice hitching as he swirled his tongue over her skin.

"Because you would have smacked me."

"Or tossed you into the fireplace," she replied with a teasing grin.

He responded by sucking her nipple into his mouth. She cried out, arched into his embrace as her fingers slid into his hair and tightened in the silky strands. Pinned by the weight of his body, she could do no more than writhe beneath him as he licked, kissed and nibbled first one, then the other breast.

"Nicholas!"

He moved back up and kissed her mouth again. "I love hearing you say my name."

His fingers grabbed the hem of her nightgown. He tugged the material up, then tossed it onto the floor. The storm chose that moment to light up the room once more with a series of flashes, bright white revealing her in nothing but a pair of lacy black panties.

Nicholas pushed himself up and ran his eyes over her. She forced herself to lie there, to not reach for the sheet or a pillow. The almost savage expression of male satisfaction on his face eased her tension, rekindled some of her earlier feminine confidence. Slowly, she shifted her hips, smiled as fire flared in his gaze. Testing, taunting, she trailed one hand down her side, over her ribs, then teasing the hem of her panties.

Thunder rumbled, making the crystals of the chandelier above the bed shake. Rain started to fall again, a faint drumming that crescendoed into a roar. It was either that or the clamor of her heartbeat as Nicholas lowered himself back down and kissed his way from her lips down her neck, over her breasts, her belly and then lower still. He traced his tongue along the scalloped lace of her underwear. She trembled as anticipation pulsed in her, making her body feel as light as air.

He reached up, pulled her panties down over her thighs, her calves, kissing her legs as he did.

And then she was completely naked before him.

"You're still wearing clothes."

"Astute observation." He shot her a wicked grin as he settled his body between her thighs.

Her core throbbed as she watched him lower his head.

"It's not fair."

"Life's not fair," he replied as he pressed a kiss to her inner thigh.

"But…" Her words trailed off as he kissed higher, closer to her most sensitive skin. Nerves fluttered in her belly.

He glanced up at her. The sight of his dark head between her legs filled her with a perplexing tangle of apprehension and desire.

"What's wrong?"

"I…" She swallowed hard. "Just a little nervous. No one's ever kissed me…there. Before."

"No one?"

Another shiver wracked her body, one that left her weak at the possessive gleam in his eyes.

"No."

He watched her, waited, gave her time to tell him to stop. When she didn't, he lowered his head.

Pleasure speared through her, hot and so delicious it made her tremble. Her hands fisted in the sheets, moved restlessly as he kissed her, teased her until she was sure she was going to scream if he didn't do *something*.

And then he did, his tongue doing wicked things as he licked and stroked and loved her with every touch. Her hands moved down, her fingers tangling in his hair once more as she pulled him against her. The lightness in her grew, pulsing hotter, brighter until she could barely stand the sensation but dear God, she couldn't ask him to stop, not now, not when she was so close.

He pressed his lips to her. She cried out his name as the lightness in her burst. Her hips bowed off the bed as her entire body hummed with pleasure. He gentled his caresses but didn't stop, not until she dropped onto the bed, her body limp and trembling.

Thunder rumbled again, softer this time but more potent, the sound rolling through her body. Dimly, she heard the rustle of clothing, the rip of a wrapper. She opened her eyes to see Nicholas standing by the bed, gloriously naked as he slid a condom onto his hard length. She stretched her arms above her head, a satisfied smile crossing her face as he watched her every move with obsessive precision.

"You're very handsome, Nicholas."

He smiled down at her. "Thanks."

"I mean it." She rolled onto her side and let her eyes drift over his broad shoulders, the defined muscles of his abdomen, the tapered waist and thick thighs. "It's a little unfair that you have an actual six-pack, but given our circumstances tonight, I'm choosing to be grateful instead of jealous."

He stared at her for a moment before throwing his head back to laugh.

"How did I not see you before?"

Confused by the comment, she tilted her head. Then her

bemusement disappeared as he wrapped one hand around his erection and stroked. Aroused, pleasure still sparkling through her, she rose up on her knees and beckoned for him to come closer.

He stalked toward her. Her body shuddered, eager to feel his naked skin against hers.

Except he stopped a foot away from the bed, still running his fist up and down his long, thick length. When she reached for him, he stepped out of reach and chuckled at her soft growl of frustration.

"Next time."

She planted her fists on her hips, one brow curving up. "What makes you think there will be a next time?"

He moved with predatory speed, wrapping his arms around her and pulled her flush against him. Every hard muscle, every chiseled plane, pressed against her nude flesh. The delicious intimacy of it scorched her veins as he slipped a hand into her hair and tugged so that she looked up at him.

"Because once won't be enough, Anika." He pressed his hardness against her wet center, a triumphant smile crossing his face as she moaned. "Not for this."

What if one night's not enough?

The thought sobered her, took the edge off her desire. Surely she would be able to walk away. She liked Nicholas, certainly more than she had. But that didn't mean she trusted him, or liked him enough to want to sleep with him again.

Besides, as he'd made perfectly clear in his own words, he wasn't interested in forever.

He tumbled her back onto the bed. The feel of his hard thighs pressed against hers banished coherent thought. Restless, seeking, she ran her hands all over his body, indulging in the greedy need to touch him. He indulged her, dropping heated kisses on her jaw, her neck, her breasts.

Emboldened, she skated one hand over his firm behind, trailing her fingers over his rock-hard thigh, sliding between their bodies to…

"Minx."

He captured her wrist and brought her hand up. He kissed the center of her palm, a gentle gesture that made her sigh, followed by a yelp as he nipped the sensitive skin with his teeth.

"Next time," he promised, the words a whisper against her lips.

Alarm pulsed through her, quick and frantic. Then she shoved it aside. *Not now.*

He rested himself against her liquid heat, then started to press inside. She gasped as he stretched her.

"Am I hurting you?"

"No, just…" Her fingers tightened on his shoulders. "You're big."

He leaned down and kissed her, leisurely and sweet, easing her tension away with soft caresses until she relaxed once more. Slowly, he pushed deeper inside her until his hips rested against hers, his entire length buried inside her. She tightened her body around him and smiled when his breath caught.

"Careful, *bhrèagha*," he said tightly, his Scottish lilt more pronounced.

"Where's the fun in that?"

His lips twisted into a devilish grin. "Very true."

And then he began to move. Languid, deep thrusts that made her moan and gasp. Her hands moved on his body, gliding over his damp skin before settling on his hips and urging him deeper. Sensation built, blazing brightly where their bodies joined before it spiraled throughout her body, growing brighter with each movement.

He slid one hand into her hair, growled her name before covering her lips with his in a greedy kiss that sent her careening over the edge. He followed a moment later, his body tensing above her, his groan echoing in her ears.

He eased himself down on top of her, their breaths mingling.

"Am I crushing you?" he murmured against her neck.

She shook her head, too sated to even open her eyes. She couldn't say how long they lay like that, sweat-slicked bodies pressed together, his fingers drifting up and down her body. His touch was deceptively light. Each stroke etched something into her heart, kindled a need far deeper and more terrifying than the lust she had just indulged in.

"I'll be right back."

Cool air replaced Nicholas's heated body. But this time, instead of a balm to her overheated skin, it was a cold reminder of what she had just done.

More like who you did.

She rolled off the bed, wrapped a sheet around her chilled body and moved to the balcony doors. The chaos of the storm called to the hurricane spinning inside her chest.

If it had just been physical pleasure, that would have been easy. If it had just been about the incredible orgasms Nicholas had given her, she could have walked away without a backward glance.

Rain lashed the windows. She slid open the door, sucked in a breath as cold drops soaked through the sheet. Beyond the waving fronds of the palm trees, she could dimly make out the white-capped tips of the waves. Churning, frothing, stirred up by something unexpected.

It hadn't just been sex. Not after the glimpse she'd gotten of his tortured past and the man he'd become despite the loss. Not when he had cradled her with such unexpected tenderness one minute, then claimed her body the next with his dominating kisses, his commanding touch. Not when he'd held her gaze, his eyes burning with something that went deeper than mere desire.

You're imagining things.

She had to be.

She sensed him before his hands clasped her shoulders, drew her back against his body.

"What's wrong?"

His voice pierced the clamor of the storm. She tensed.

"Nothing."

"Liar."

The word whispered against her skin, an accusation without menace, but unfortunately accurate. She wanted to draw away, to hide. To take the coward's way out.

Except her mother and grandmother hadn't raised her to run.

"I never saw you and me ending up like this." She raised her chin up, staring into the heart of the storm. "It's unsettling."

He tugged the sheet down enough to bare her shoulders. "Because of the contract?"

Her breath hitched as he dropped a kiss on the skin he'd just revealed. "That's part of it, yes. But we're not together, like dating. I've never slept with someone I haven't been in a relationship with."

His hold tightened slightly. "Oh?"

"Don't." Irritated, she turned and faced him, ignoring the frisson of awareness when she realized he was still gloriously naked. "Don't you pull that macho routine where you go caveman on me because I've dared to have one lover while you've been strutting around like a damned rooster for years."

One brow curved upward. "A rooster?"

Her eyes dropped down to his half-erect hardness, then back up to his face. "An apt comparison. There was a rooster that used to strut around the yard back in Missouri. You remind me of him."

"Should I be flattered or insulted?"

"Both. A rooster mates between ten and thirty times a day."

Both brows shot up. "That sounds tiresome."

"I imagine you have a similar history."

His expression darkened. He tugged her closer, one hand sliding down her back and firmly molding her body to his. An illicit thrill snaked down her spine.

"I haven't been a monk, it's true. But even in my more… active days, I didn't go to bed with a different woman every night or even every week. If I had lunch with an acquaintance or business partner, the tabloids acted like she was a part of my harem. I haven't been with anyone in months."

"You and your ex didn't have a fling for old times' sake in the Caribbean?"

He leaned back, a satisfied smile tugging at his lips. "Why, Pierce, I do believe you're jealous."

"I am not," she lied. Because, she realized with horror, she *was* jealous.

"It's okay if you are." The smirk disappeared as he dropped his head. "I am. I almost tossed Adam off the side of that damned catamaran for daring to be close enough to touch you. The thought of anyone kissing you, touching you the way I just did, drives me mad."

Another tremble wracked her body, this one a deep, delicious quiver she felt all the way from her chest down to the swollen, slick skin between her thighs.

"Why?" she whispered.

"I don't know." He grazed his lips across hers, a light caress that taunted, exerted control. "I'll figure that part out later. But right now, I just want to do this."

He ripped the sheet from her body. Shocked, aroused, she stood just beyond the doors of the balcony, the rain hitting her bare back. His hands framed her face, slid into her hair as he kissed her, lips moving masterfully over hers. Gone was the gentle lover, the sweet seducer. In his place was a conqueror, a man who wanted to ensure she would never forget the feel of his body against hers as he tugged her down onto the floor, the taste of him on her lips as his tongue plundered her mouth.

This was what she needed. Hard sex, no kindness, nothing that could draw her heart into the equation.

Just once more. To get him out of my system.

He slid his hands up the backs of her arms, started to roll so that she would end up beneath him.

No.

This time she was in control.

She pushed back, knocking him off balance. She took advantage of his momentary surprise, planted her hands on his chest and pushed him down. Straddling his hips, she delighted in the flare of lust in his eyes as he grabbed her thighs. She reached between their bodies and grabbed his erection. The feel of his bare skin in her hand made her gasp. A mad desire shot through her, to feel him inside without any barrier between them.

"Condom," he ground out. "End table."

Thank God one of them had enough rational thought. She stood up and grabbed a condom packet off the table. After he slid it on, she wrapped her fingers around him and slid herself, slowly, down onto his hardness. He hissed, his fingers digging into her thighs as he tried to urge her to sink down further. She resisted, rising up until he was just barely inside her, before she lowered herself again, each stroke sending physical waves of pleasure through her body as feminine satisfaction wound through her at the frustrated need on his face. The cold rain at her back heightened each sensation, made her feel wild and uninhibited for the first time in far too long.

Finally, she sank down onto his full length, their moans mingling as they found their rhythm. He reached up and cradled her breasts in his hands. The light strokes, teasing touches, made her move quicker, reaching for that incredible peak he'd already brought her to twice.

They soared over it together. She collapsed on top of him, allowing herself the intimacy of being held by her lover as the storm continued to rage on outside the doors.

Anika blinked against the sun streaming through the windows. She mumbled her discontent and started to roll over, then sat straight up when she came face-to-face with Nicholas's smiling face.

"What are…?" Her voice trailed off as the night, and early morning, came back to her in a rush. "Oh."

"Good morning to you, too."

He surprised her by sitting up and pressing a soft kiss to her lips.

"Um… I didn't mean to fall asleep here. Sorry—"

"Don't hide from me, Anika. Not after what we shared."

Irritation replaced her embarrassment. "Excuse me?"

"I always knew you were a force to be reckoned with." His eyes warmed as they traveled down her naked body. She resisted the urge to cover herself with the sheet. "But the woman I saw last night was truly incredible."

What was she supposed to say when he sat there clad in

loose black pants and nothing else, morning stubble dark on his cheeks? Her hands itched to reach out and feel the roughness beneath her fingers.

"Thank you."

"You're welcome." His face sobered. "I ordered room service. We need to talk."

"Ah." She looked away, detesting the faint sense of dread that crawled through her. "The four words every woman likes to hear."

"Anika—" He swore as a ringing noise cut him off. "Give me a moment." He rolled off the bed, crossed to the glass doors and stepped out on the balcony, pulling his phone from his pocket and pressing it to his ear.

Alone, Anika released the breath she hadn't even realized she'd been holding. Spying her robe and nightgown draped over the back of a chair, she hopped off the bed and made quick work of getting dressed. Once the robe was firmly belted at the waist, she let out a sigh of relief. Clothed, she felt more in control, like drawing on armor as she prepared to do battle against her enemy.

Except at some point Nicholas had ceased to be the enemy. She bit down on her lower lip and glanced over at the balcony. He stood at the railing, his head tilted up toward the sky, his shoulders thrown back in a stance of confidence. Never had the sight of a man's naked back made her want to swoon before.

But it wasn't just his impressive physique or how he'd made her feel last night. His appreciation for the hula performance, his sharing the horrifically tragic circumstances of his childhood, had humanized him. He was still a cocky bastard, she thought with a small smile as she watched him start to pace back and forth, one hand gesturing as he talked.

He didn't want the things she did, which made anything beyond what they'd shared last night an impossibility.

Before this week, that thought had made her roll her eyes and thank the heavens she wasn't the kind of woman who interested a man like Nicholas.

But now...now it just made her sad.

She turned away from the balcony. The only thing she could think of that he would want to discuss with her was the inn. Had last night changed his mind? Had he finally accepted her answer, was perhaps even coming to respect her as a fellow business owner?

The scent of coffee penetrated her musings. She inhaled deeply as she walked over to the cozy white table and chairs set up in one corner of the room. An emerald coffeepot sat next to a matching cup and saucer, steam rising from the spout.

With a whispered murmur of thanks, she started to pour herself a cup.

And nearly spilled it all over the table as she spied the manila envelope next to the cup with the words "Zvonček Inn Purchase Proposal" written in black marker across the top.

She should be angry, she told herself as she set the coffeepot down with trembling hands. Angry, not hurt. Furious, not humiliated.

The anger was there, yes. It paled in comparison to the painful sorrow that left her hollow. It had been reasonable to assume that Nicholas would still want to talk about the inn. But had he really thought she would roll out of bed, march over and sign on the dotted line simply because she'd slept with him?

A sickening thought made her stomach roll. Had he had sex with her to make her more receptive to his proposal? Done exactly what she had accused him of on the dance floor last night? Using the desire between them to get what he wanted?

I don't use sex to get what I want.

He'd looked so fierce when he'd said it, had made her feel guilty for even suggesting it.

Except he'd also uttered another phrase that circled round and round in her mind.

I don't lose.

She had told him repeatedly she didn't want to sell. Her refusals hadn't stopped his relentless pursuit, and all because he was egotistical enough to want part of his new property to be on the shores of the lake, her inn be damned if it stood in the way.

Grateful for the anger creeping in, she grasped it, wrapped it around her battered heart. She had let her guard down, had let loneliness and lust guide her actions last night. Despite trying to hang on to some semblance of reality, she'd struggled to hold herself back, to keep her emotions in check.

Really, she told herself as she hurried toward the door, this was the best thing that could have happened. She'd needed this reminder that there could be no future between her and a man like Nicholas.

Resolved, she walked out of the penthouse and closed the door behind her.

CHAPTER SEVEN

Seven weeks later

ANIKA DRUMMED HER fingers on the arm of the plush tufted chair arranged in front of the marble fireplace. Never would she have pictured herself sitting in the lobby of the Hotel Lassard.

But then she never would have pictured herself having a civil conversation with Nicholas. Dancing with him. Sleeping with him.

Having his baby.

Her stomach twisted. She was seven weeks pregnant with the baby of a man she once had barely been able to stand. The man who had brought her to incredible, dizzying heights of pleasure.

The man who had seduced her even as he sought to try and buy the one piece of her family she had left.

That wasn't totally accurate, she grudgingly admitted as she stared into the hearth. She hadn't been just a willing participant in her own seduction. No, she'd been an enthusiastic contributor.

She sighed. She hadn't seen or even talked to Nicholas since the morning she'd walked out. She'd expected him to show up at her room demanding to know what had happened. When the minutes had turned into an hour, she'd glanced at her phone, not sure if she was hoping that he would call or that he wouldn't.

Her phone had stayed silent. Each passing hour without any communication told her what she needed to know. Whether Nicholas had slept with her to persuade her to sign the contract or not, what they had experienced had been a one-time thing. He had no intention of chasing her down.

Which is a good thing, she'd reassured herself as she'd hurriedly packed and changed her flight to an earlier time.

Yes, the night had been enjoyable. But it was just that: one night. Not to be repeated. Judging by how hurt she'd been at seeing the contract on the table, she was already in too deep emotionally. Any further intimate contact with Nicholas would just cause more pain. Some distance was needed.

Except that every time her phone had dinged the week following her trip, her heart had fluttered. Every time that it hadn't been him, she'd had to fight back disappointment.

So, she'd thrown herself into work, implementing the ideas she'd come up with from what she'd learned at the conference. The biggest change, adding a nonrefundable reservation fee like one of the workshops at the conference had suggested, had made her nervous. Not only had it not deterred guests from booking her inn based off some of the new social media campaigns she'd implemented, but she'd been able to use the fees to spruce up some of the rooms. Little touches, like new linens and hiring a local handyman to paint. But if she could keep this up, small steps, she just might make it.

We, she silently corrected herself as she glanced down at her belly.

She'd become aware of something different the week before Christmas. At first, she'd chalked up her bone-deep exhaustion to working hard and fitful nights when dreams

of her time with Nicholas invaded. Then, as her stomach
had rebelled every time she'd tried to eat breakfast, she'd
assumed she was getting sick.

It hadn't been until the day after Christmas, when her
breasts had felt swollen and heavy, that things had suddenly
clicked. A visit to the doctor had confirmed that she was
indeed pregnant.

She closed her eyes and let out a sigh. She'd always
wanted to be a mother. She had just assumed that title would
come with marriage to a man she loved, and one who loved
her in return. Not a one-night fling with an international
lothario.

She'd spent the week after trying to decide what to do.
Part of her didn't want to tell Nicholas. He had made it crystal clear on their trip that he had no interest in settling down.
If she told him about the baby, it would cement a connection
between them that would never be broken. Worse, it meant
she and her child would become a part of his life, even if
he wasn't physically present: the chaos, the constant media
attention not if but when the news came to light, the other
women who would no doubt drift in and out over the years.

That last thought had made her so nauseous she'd barely
stumbled to the bathroom in time.

But her mother and *babica* had raised her to be truth-
ful and honorable. Withholding knowledge of this magnitude would have flown in the face of everything she'd been
taught. And if her child ever looked her in the eye one day
and asked if she had told their father about them, she needed
to be able to say yes.

A quick search online had revealed that Nicholas was in
Dubai. Mercifully, the few tabloid photos she'd found online had shown him alone or with colleagues. It had been a
simple matter to check the online gossip websites. When one

article had touted that the "devilishly handsome Nicholas Lassard, heir to the Hotel Lassard empire" was on his way back to Lake Bled to oversee the final phases of construction and readiness before his newest hotel's grand opening in a few weeks, she'd called over to the hotel and confirmed that Nicholas was indeed on his way. The hotel had done a soft opening the first week of January and was hosting select, invited guests as it completed construction on some of the remaining rooms. Construction Nicholas was overseeing as he also wined and dined his elite clients. When the receptionist had asked why she was calling, she'd simply replied that she and Nicholas had attended the conference in Kauai together and she had something to give him. The receptionist had called back to tell her Nicholas would see her at seven o'clock.

A tiny smile tugged at her lips. Even if part of her was terrified, there was a small, villainous part of her that was looking forward to seeing the shock on his face when she dropped the news.

Awareness tickled the back of her neck. Her eyes opened and her head snapped up. Nicholas leaned casually against the fireplace mantel, his tall, lean figure draped in black, one leg casually crossed over the other. The angles of his face, from the sharp cut of his cheekbones and broad forehead to the tapered point of his chin, contrasted with the smirk lurking about his full lips. His hands were in his pockets, his deep blue eyes focused on her face with an intensity no doubt designed to intimidate.

"Well, well," Nicholas drawled. "I never thought I'd see the day you would set foot in my hotel."

She took a deep breath. "I never thought I'd see it either."

"Welcome."

He still smiled pleasantly, still sported a pleasant tone. But he was reserved, distant.

"Thank you." She looked around, taking in once more the Swarovski crystal chandeliers, the floor-to-ceiling windows that overlooked the circle drive outside, the fountain that would spring to life in the spring. "It's lovely."

"It is." He sat down in the chair next to hers, his nearness crowding her. "Frankly, Anika, after the way you left in Kauai, I'm surprised to see you at all."

She wanted to look away from his eyes, but forced herself to maintain his gaze.

"I should have at least said goodbye. That was unprofessional of me."

His reserve cracked as anger rippled off him. "Unprofessional? You didn't walk out of a business meeting. You completely disappeared without so much as a goodbye after we slept together."

"Keep your voice down," she hissed. A quick glance around the lobby confirmed that no one had been close enough to hear.

"Afraid what others might think of you if they knew you'd fallen prey to my charms?"

"I saw the contract, Nicholas." When he just stared at her, his brow slightly furrowed, she curled her fingers into fists. "The contract for the inn. Were you just waiting for me to put my clothes on before you handed me a pen to sign?"

His face tightened. "Is that what you thought?"

"Hard to miss when you conveniently left it on the same table as the coffee."

He sat back in his chair, his head swinging toward the fireplace. He stared at the flames for a long moment.

"Yes, I brought the contract with me to Kauai. I had planned on using some of our time in Hawaii to convince you to sell." His gaze swung back to her. "I had looked at it before I came down to the terrace that night. I laid it down on my way out the door. I hadn't planned on you coming back up with me. Nor did I plan on springing it on you that morning."

She stared at him, confused. Was he telling the truth? Had she misread the entire situation and acted like an adolescent teenager heartsick over her first crush?

"However," he said as he leaned forward, resting his arms on his thighs, "since you brought it up, we have unfinished business to discuss."

Fury surged through her. *Bastard.*

"No, we don't. Not in regard to the inn."

"So, what's the plan, Anika? You're just going to run it by yourself? No matter what you think you learned at the conference, it can't save the inn."

"I've already seen an uptick in reservations," she fired back. "I've been making improvements, upping our social media presence. It's slow going, but I'm doing it. And I'll continue to do it by myself."

"For how long? That building is one brick away from collapsing into a heap."

"Ah yes, the building you want so badly you're willing to pay triple the current market value. That makes sense."

"If you would stop being so bloody stubborn, you'd accept the help I'm offering."

She threw back her head and laughed.

"Is that what you call it? Help meaning buying out the inn that's been in my family for over one hundred years so you can raze it and make a replica of the monstrosity you've constructed here?"

His eyes darkened. "Careful, Anika. I'm proud of what I've built here."

The fight drained out of her as quickly as it had arisen. This was not how she'd pictured the conversation going.

"I didn't come here to fight, Nicholas." She glanced around as a couple wandered through the lobby, the man dressed in a black suit, the woman wearing a violet gown that probably had some expensive label sewed on the inside that made the dress quadruple the cost of what she'd worn in Hawaii. Acutely aware of her threadbare coat and thrift store trousers, she stood. "Is there somewhere private we could talk?"

He sighed, a thoroughly disapproving sound that increased her exhaustion.

"Fine. My office."

She started to stand, readying herself for the moment ahead, when her stomach rolled again. She froze. Fear dug into her stomach, clambered up her throat until she could barely breathe.

"I changed my mind. I'm sorry."

She turned away. She wasn't going to be sick. Not this time at least. But she wasn't ready. Not yet. She needed time, a little bit more time, some distance from the nasty confrontation they'd just had.

She'd barely made it three steps before she swayed. Exhaustion, the lack of food, her nervousness about talking to Nicholas, all of it came crashing down at once. Before she could move, Nicholas stepped forward and circled an arm around her waist. Panic skittered as his hand clamped down, his fingers brushing her belly.

"What are you doing?"

"You look like you were about ready to faint."

With a firm hand, he guided her down the hall.

"There's no need to support me. I can walk just fine—"

"You were going to topple over," he said frankly.

She glanced up at him, confused by his surly tone. What had happened in the nearly two months since they'd parted? Where was the man who teased and laughed and barreled through life with a carefree smile?

"I don't need you to manhandle me," she argued, some of her earlier bravado returning. Much easier to fight with him than to worry about how he might react to her unsettling news.

"Given your penchant for not taking care of yourself and preferring to work as hard as possible until you're on the verge of collapsing, I'm going to take responsibility and ensure that you get off your feet before we talk."

"I said I didn't want to talk tonight."

"You can say whatever you like. But you're not leaving here until you've had a chance to rest."

She ground her teeth together as he escorted her behind the desk past a wide-eyed clerk and toward his office. He strode in, kicked the door shut behind him and guided her to the couch. She looked around the room. Plush leather furniture, pale ivory walls that matched the winter landscape outside the large windows.

Nicholas circled around his desk, a gleaming mahogany behemoth, and sat down, the ice-kissed lake at his back.

Had she thought the worst part was telling him about the baby? She'd been wrong. It intimidated her, but it was the right thing to do. Once she told him, and he reiterated that he had no interest in being a father, it would be done.

But their argument in the lobby had stirred up the emotions Nicholas had brought to the surface in Kauai, from their shared moment on the catamaran tour of the Nā Pali coast to the conversation during the power outage that had led her up to his room.

No, the worst part of all of this, at least in this moment,

was that she wanted to believe him, wanted to believe that he had wanted to spend time with her, to be with her just because of who she was, not what she owned. She didn't like feeling this vulnerable.

She swept her gaze around his office, noting the various awards and pictures of him with famous people. Movie stars, politicians, CEOs of international firms. They came from two completely different worlds. All of the reasons why she had resisted him in the first place came rushing back. He had told her before that he had no interest in true love, no enthusiasm for the things that she wanted out of her life: a family, stability.

"If you think any harder, smoke's going to come out of your ears."

She sighed. "Always one with a quick compliment."

His lips quirked. She shoved away the sudden, deep desire to see him smile, truly smile like he had those months ago.

"I was just thinking of how different we are, that's all."

"Ah. Still going with how I'm nothing more than a spoiled man-child playing at the hotel game while you actually work for a living?"

She flushed under his scrutiny as he flung her words from the Hanalei Bay pier back in her face.

"Contrary to this image you have of me of some rich play-boy who just swims in money in his bathtub every night, I do care about my company and the people I work with," he said, an edge to his voice.

Ashamed, she looked down and stared at her feet.

"I said some horrible things before." She swallowed her pride as she forced out her apology. "I'm sorry."

"Why?"

"Why?"

He stood and circled the desk, trailing his fingers along

the surface. She watched, unnerved and fascinated by her body's immediate response.

"Why do you say things like that? Why did you run away in Kauai?"

"I already told you," she said, her voice breathless.

He advanced toward her, each step hiking the tension in her body.

"So why are you here now? What is it you want?"

Tell him! Tell him now and just get it over with! her brain screamed.

He stopped, staring down at her with his hands tucked in his pockets much the way he had been when the elevator doors had slid open and she'd fallen into his arms.

"Well," he finally said, "are you going to spit it out? Or are we just going to—"

"I'm pregnant."

CHAPTER EIGHT

BLOOD ROARED IN Nicholas's ears. He couldn't have heard her right.

"Come again?"

"I'm pregnant," she repeated, "and it's yours. I haven't been with anybody since our…encounter."

His heart pounded so hard it was a wonder it didn't beat right out of his chest. Disbelief was paramount, but beneath it churned shock and a heavy dose of fear.

When he'd come back in from the balcony to find Anika gone, he'd thought that perhaps she had gone back to her room to change. But as the seconds ticking by turned to minutes, he'd been faced with the fact that she had left. Snuck out the door and deserted him without so much as a goodbye.

It had grated, yes. It had been the first time a woman had ever left him like that.

But there had been more to it than simple ego. The hurt that had pumped beneath his damaged pride had been the driving factor in not reaching out to her. He didn't want another relationship anytime soon, not after the disaster with Susan. And if he ever did contemplate dating seriously again, it would be with a woman he could keep at arm's length. Not someone like Anika who stirred him up inside. A woman who made him feel possessive, jealous, borderline obsessed.

As the days had turned into weeks and then nearly two months without a word from her, he'd focused on work. Or at least tried to. How many times had he picked up his phone, wanting to text, to call, to hear her voice? Each time he'd set the phone back down. That he wanted to talk to her, not just enjoy her company over dinner or her body in his bed, was enough to convince him that she had done them both a favor. Continuing any association with her would have been inviting inevitable drama into his life when they would have to part ways.

As she'd told him, Anika was the kind of woman who wanted things he couldn't give.

Things like a baby.

His eyes dropped down to her stomach, concealed under a loose gray shirt. He swallowed hard.

"How? We used protection."

A light blush stained her cheeks.

"We did. But do you remember in the middle of the night…"

Nicholas's brain fumbled, trying to remember. And then the image came back to him with roaring clarity. He had turned to her in the night. They'd made love to each other with questing hands, seeking lips. At one moment, just one, he had slipped inside her before he'd remembered that he had not put on a condom. He had quickly withdrawn, peppering kisses down her breasts, her belly, over her hips, before he'd pulled out a condom and sheathed himself.

"It was only a moment."

"A moment was more than enough." She stilled, a distant look coming into her eyes, one that hinted at a pain she was trying to conceal. "If you want, I'm happy to provide a test and we can get blood work done so that you know for sure it's yours."

Nicholas was surprised to find that he didn't doubt a single word that Anika was saying. As little as they had gotten along in the beginning, the time that they had spent together in Hawaii had helped him realize just what kind of person she was. Even though he'd been angry and disappointed at the way she'd walked out, she was not the kind of woman who would make up a pregnancy. Especially, he thought to himself, a pregnancy with someone she could barely stand.

"I appreciate the offer." He walked back around the desk, needing the familiarity of his desk, something that made him feel in control. "What steps do we take next?"

"I'll continue to go to my doctor's appointments. I can keep you updated, of course."

"Updated?"

She frowned. "You told me from the beginning you had no interest in being a father or having a long-term relationship. I'm not going to make any demands on you."

Annoyance stirred inside him. Did she truly think so little of him?

"I'm not just going to stand by and live the rest of my life while you take care of our child by yourself."

Alarm flooded across her face.

"What do you mean?"

"I mean that I'm going to be involved."

"Involved how? I'm more than capable of taking care of this child by myself."

"How? You can barely keep your business afloat."

Too far, he realized as her expression morphed into anger.

"As I said," she replied in a chilly voice, "since I've come back, I've already increased reservations for the spring by fifteen percent over last year. It's starting off small, but it's working. Just like I told you it would."

He half expected her to stick out her tongue at the end,

she was so fired up. And damned if that didn't stir his blood, just like she had when she'd stood up in the middle of a ballroom full of people and sparred with him. Reluctant admiration filled him. He wanted that property and everything that it could bring the Hotel Lassard. Still, it was impressive how hard she was fighting to keep the inn up and running, how much she was accomplishing with so little. It also made him realize just how capable Anika would be as a mother.

His eyes drifted down once more to her belly. He'd never contemplated the possibility of having children before, despite his mother's growing hints in recent years. He'd only been eleven when David had been killed. But that event alone had cemented his commitment to never having children. He hadn't been able to keep his seven-year-old brother safe. How could he possibly trust himself with the responsibility of an infant whose existence would literally rest in his hands for the first few years of its life? Even if he could overcome that fear, he wasn't sure that he would ever be able to overcome the pain. The pain that had lingered from years and years of his parents drifting farther apart and wallowing in their own depression as he had been left to fend for himself.

His parents were good people. They had overcome the odds and eventually found their way back to each other, and to him. But that decade between David's death and their reconciliation had been lonely and bitter. If his parents had succumbed to loss and left him for so long, what would he do if he were to face a similar loss? Could he guarantee that he wouldn't do the same thing his parents had done?

That it was even a possibility had been enough for him to abstain from considering a family of his own. A child deserved more than he could offer.

Yet as the reality of the situation hit, something shifted

inside him. He might not be capable of providing a child with the kind of love and happiness that so many fathers could. But he had plenty of resources at his fingertips to ensure the child and Anika would never want for anything. He owed it to both of them to at least try to be involved as much as he could.

"Look, I know this was unexpected." Anika started to rise from the couch. "How about we sleep on it and talk tomorrow?"

Her face went pale. Nicholas was on his feet and by her side within seconds.

"Are you all right?"

"Yes." She attempted to wave him off, but he eased her back down on the couch. "The doctor said everything is fine. Just the usual first trimester symptoms."

"You're staying here tonight. You are not driving home when you look like death," he added as she opened her mouth to protest. "You need to rest, for both yours and the baby's sake."

She glared up at him.

"Is this how you're going to get your way for the next seven months? By using the baby?"

"Yes."

His blunt answer surprised a laugh from her.

"I'm too tired to argue."

"Good. The top floor rooms are finished. I'll take you up there."

"All right."

If she was acquiescing this quickly to his order, she definitely wasn't feeling well.

"Do you have any guests at the inn tonight?"

"No, not for a couple of days."

"Excellent. You can stay here."

"Don't push, Nicholas," she said with warning in her voice. "I'll stay here tonight. I'm not staying for an extended period of time. My home is at the inn."

He knew when to push and when to relent. For now.

"Tomorrow we'll have breakfast together and we'll talk."

"Talk," she repeated in a voice that said she would rather jump into the freezing lake.

"I promise not to bite."

His words charged the air between them. Was she thinking of the moment he was remembering, when she had been on her hands and knees before him, his hands tight on her hips as he'd driven deeply into her. She'd tossed back her head, her glorious dark hair spilling across her back as she'd cried out. He'd followed a moment later. As they'd drifted down from the aftermath of their shared pleasure, he'd gently tugged her up, pulling her back against his chest, tilted her face to his and kissed her. He'd nipped her lip, a playful caress that had made her moan into his mouth as he'd covetously run his hands up and down her body.

"Yes, well…" Anika cleared her throat. "Tomorrow, then."

Nicholas opened the door and gestured for her to go out before him. His hand tightened on the knob as her sweet orange scent drifted up, teasing him as she walked by.

He would do the right thing by Anika and their child. Including not indulging in this mad desire for her and upping the emotional stakes between them.

He could resist. Would resist.

Even if it killed him.

CHAPTER NINE

ANIKA STARTED AT the knock on her door.

"Coming!" she called as she glanced at the mirror and winced. Her face was pale, her hair a mess. She usually didn't bother about things like makeup. A simple brush through her hair, a dab of mascara and some tinted lip balm were enough to keep her going. But the prospect of seeing Nicholas looking like she'd just crawled out of bed made her feel embarrassed. He was used to glitzy, glamorous women clad in diamonds and sequins. Normally she wouldn't care. But right now, she did.

Damn hormones, she thought to herself as she moved to the door.

She twisted the knob, opened it and then stared as Nicholas smiled at her, a heavy silver tray in his hands. The brooding darkness that had clung to him yesterday was gone, replaced by his customary charm.

"Good morning," he said as he moved into the suite. "We missed breakfast the last time we saw each other."

She rolled her eyes even as her stomach rumbled at the scent of food drifting up from beneath the silver dome.

"I woke up to find a revised contract out on the table after we just had sex, Nicholas," she ground out. "Of course I left."

"Or," he countered as he lifted the silver dome off, "you could have stayed and we could have talked."

"I didn't want to talk. I felt embarrassed enough as it was."

Slowly, he set the tray down and then turned to her.

"I'm sorry for that. I never wanted to embarrass you, Anika."

Surprised by his apology, she looked down as her cheeks heated. "Um, thanks."

"I have a proposal for you."

Her head jerked back up and she eyed him suspiciously.

"Given how I handled your last one, and the numerous times you've brought it up since, perhaps you should cut your losses."

"Not losses," he countered with a confident smile. "Temporary setbacks. However, I think you'll actually like this one."

"Arrogant of you to assume."

"I propose that we put the subject of the inn on the back burner since we have a more pressing matter at hand."

Loath as she was to admit it, she did like this proposal. While she would prefer to get the business of the inn solved now, she also recognized that discussing how they were going to handle the baby was more important, especially since Nicholas did not seem to be wanting to take the easy way out and let her raise the child on her own.

He pulled out a chair for her and she sat, her eyes growing wide at the sight of fresh fruit, eggs and pastries. Her stomach rumbled. The first time she'd had an appetite in the morning in nearly two weeks.

"I wasn't sure what you would be hungry for, so I took the liberty of ordering a little bit of everything. I've heard the first few months of pregnancy can be quite challenging."

She took a bite of toast layered with butter and jam, moaning at the delicious berry flavors on her tongue. When she opened her eyes, it was to see Nicholas staring at her, his gaze riveted on her lips.

"Everything okay?" she asked nervously.

"You have a bit of jam…here."

He leaned over, his thumb swiping across her lip. The little bit of intimacy made her blush.

Nicholas cleared his throat. Embarrassment filled her. Had he noticed her reaction? Or had their one night in Kauai been enough to sate his attraction to her? Was she just making a fool of herself by mooning over him?

"Tell me everything you know so far about the baby."

Focus. He was being responsible. She needed to respond in kind.

"I'm seven weeks along. Due in early August. They picked up a very faint heartbeat at the beginning of this week. In a couple of weeks, I'll go in for an ultrasound and actually get to see it." Suddenly shy, she looked down at her plate. "You're welcome to be at that appointment."

"I would like to be there."

"All right." She took a deep breath. "Nicholas, I'm not saying you can't be involved. It's just not what I would have expected based on our conversations in Hawaii."

"Which is fair," he acknowledged. "I want to be involved at least on some level. I'm not content to simply be a bank."

The way he said "bank" made her tense.

"I'm not going to be coming after you for money."

"No, but I am going to make sure that you and the baby are well provided for. And that, Anika, is nonnegotiable."

She wanted to argue with him. But if she was being practical, she knew that she could not provide everything that was needed for herself and the baby off what she was making with the inn. If she accepted his help, she would be able to continue to focus her resources on repairs and getting back onto firmer financial footing.

"Fine," she agreed reluctantly. "Thank you. But nothing over the top. I'd never want our child to feel like I was using their father for money."

Nicholas surprised her by reaching over and grasping her hand. "I know you wouldn't. Whatever capacity I'm involved in when it comes to our child, I'll make sure that if that question ever comes up, they know, too."

Touched by the gesture, she gently squeezed his fingers then pulled her hand away.

"Well, is there really anything else? Once the baby's here, we can set up some sort of visitation schedule. Maybe based on your traveling—"

"What about us?"

"Us?" Anika repeated.

"Yes, us."

"There is no us. We had a one-night stand. Now we have a baby." Her chest twisted as for one brief, mad moment she let herself wonder what it could be like if they weren't two completely different people. "That's the end of it."

"But that's not the end of it. For us, and this child, it's just the beginning. We should focus on how our relationship is going to evolve moving forward."

"Did you not hear me?" Anika asked, frustration mounting. "There is no relationship."

How was she going to do this?, she suddenly wondered. She had planned on doing this by herself. Now Nicholas wanted not only to contribute financially and potentially be involved in the baby's life, but he wanted to be part of her life, too? How was she supposed to move on if he was always there, either directly in her life or haunting the fringes of it?

"There will have to be some type of relationship if we're going to maintain a positive environment for our child. I don't want to just get to know our baby. I want to get to know the mother of my child."

She tensed. She was not going to allow him any further into her life than she had to. Not when doing so would just deepen the pain of what could have been but would never be.

"Where do you see this going exactly? Because we're not a good fit. I don't see us dating, getting married, any of that. I don't want us to be together just for the sake of the baby."

"I don't want that, either," Nicholas replied. "As I told you before, I have no interest in marriage. That doesn't mean that I don't think that we should still have a healthy relationship."

"Okay," she said, "but you're always traveling—"

"I was already scheduled to be in Bled through early February for the last bit of construction and the grand opening. With it being the newest property, I'll also being making trips at least once a month, if not more, for the year after that."

Was that supposed to make her feel better? That he was steadily encroaching on her peaceful existence? She'd thought after the hotel opened he'd be gone, off to his next hotel and his next adventure.

"While I'm here," he continued, seemingly unaware of her inner emotional turmoil, "I'd like for us to spend time together. Get to know each other a little bit better."

She arched a brow. "Better than we already know each other?"

His smile turned devilish. "I wouldn't say no to a repeat performance of what we experienced in Kauai. But we don't know much about each other personally."

Embarrassed, she looked away. She was carrying the man's child and yet she didn't know much beyond the small bit he'd revealed and what she'd read in the tabloids.

"Okay," she finally said. "How do you propose we get to know each other better?"

"Let's start with something simple. Dinner, tomorrow night. There's a beautiful restaurant just a little way around the lake that I've been wanting to try. See if it will belong in our recommendations list for our guests."

"Lunch."

He frowned. "How is lunch different than dinner?"

Because dinner feels like a date. And I can't think about you like that.

"It works better for me."

She returned his stare with one of her own, willing herself not to back down. He was already throwing her carefully organized plan into chaos. She could force herself to accept his desire to be in their child's life, even be moderately grateful for it.

But she drew the line at anything that would pull her back to the emotional brink he'd brought her to in Kauai. That one fleeting night when she'd seen just why women fell for him. When she herself had teetered on the edge of something far deeper and more meaningful than a one-night stand.

Anika, you are special.

"Lunch this time," he said, his voice breaking into her thoughts.

She started and felt a blush creep up her cheeks. She had the disconcerting feeling that he could see exactly what she had been thinking about.

"Lunch," she repeated. "Good."

"This time."

Nicholas gazed out over the water. One of the things he appreciated about Bled was the constant views of the lake. No matter where he went, the lake seemed to be always in sight.

The castle, the church perched on the island, the Alps standing guard in the distance, all of it came together to create a fairy-tale magic. In the past three years, he'd focused on cities like Tokyo, Singapore, London and New York. Modern, forward-thinking cities with populations that flocked to the luxury offered by the Hotel Lassard.

But always in the back of his mind he'd envisioned branching out into communities like Bled. Smaller towns and cities that offered so much more than the standard five-star restaurants, museums and clogged streets. There was still luxury and glamor to be found, but against the backdrop of culture, of unique destinations one wouldn't find in the midst of a megalopolis.

Places like Bled. It was unlike any of the locations he had ever visited or opened hotels in before. The natural beauty reminded him of the trips to Scotland, of simpler vacations they had taken before David's death. A day at the beach in Cornwall, hiking at Killarney National Park in Ireland, weekend getaways to their home in Scotland. As much as the more glamorous, luxurious vacations of his teenage years had been fun, part of the enjoyment had been the respite from grief. True happiness, like he'd found on those family journeys, had eluded him thus far.

He had come to understand the driving force behind the obsession to possess the hotel, a realization that had come on the heels of his conversation with Anika during the storm, followed by far too much time to brood over the past two months. To succeed here, in a town that reminded him of those times, in a place that mattered, had become the most important thing in his life.

And yet, he thought as his gaze slid from the bare trees guarding the island church to the woman seated across from him, in just a short amount of time, it was no longer at the forefront of his mind. Her dark hair was gathered in a loose bun at the base of her neck that emphasized her cheekbones and large, golden brown eyes. She wore a collared white shirt with a row of pearly buttons down the center and a gray skirt. Before Kauai, he would have appreciated her figure but still classified the outfit as matronly. Now, with his intimate knowledge of what lay beneath the material, he was struggling not to entertain fantasies of unbuttoning her shirt, punctuating each undone button with a kiss to the skin he revealed.

His fingers tightened a fraction on his coffee cup. He forced himself to relax his grip. Judging by Anika's reaction to his quip about spending another night together, she would not be gracing his bed again. The attraction was still there. He hadn't missed the flare of interest in her eyes, the blush in her cheeks.

But she wanted to keep him at arm's length. Preferably, he imagined, even further than that if possible. She hadn't been excited about the possibility of him being involved with the baby. Not excited, but she'd accepted it. Something he'd been grateful for. If she had pushed back, he would not have hesitated to use every tool at his disposal to fight for a place in the baby's life.

What that place looked like was still to be determined. But he had a responsibility, and he would see it through. He would be there for his child as much as he was capable.

Although just how much he was capable of being there was yet another question he would have to figure out in the next few months. Because the more he'd thought about it, the more he'd realized that his initial approach of money and a modest presence in his child's life was no better than what his parents had done, especially his father. Henry Lassard had thrown money at the problem of his family's grief.

Luxury vacations, a private home in Bora-Bora, a Ferrari for Nicholas's sixteenth birthday. That had been easier than doing the hard work their situation had required.

As he'd walked himself through that unsettling realization, there had also been the ugly sensation, something that twisted in his chest, when Anika had emphatically said that she did not want to be married to him. Ridiculous, because marriage was certainly not in the cards for him. Yet ever since Anika had left him in Hawaii, he had been able to think of little else but her. She had popped up at the most inconvenient times. He'd imagined what she'd say to a particularly pompous executive during a contentious boardroom meeting with the Hotel Lassard's board of directors in London, pictured her by his side as he'd walked down the lantern-lined Charles Bridge in Prague. One moment he'd missed her, and the next he'd been angry, even furious that she had walked out on him.

Anger was better. Anger was easier than contemplating how, or why, she had crept into the deepest corners of his heart.

No matter what he felt for Anika, the thought of continuing his life as a bachelor, of traveling around the world while she stayed here in Bled and raised their child, filled him with something almost akin to loss. Thinking about the trips he had lined up after the grand opening and into spring made him feel like he was already failing.

That was partly why, in addition to working on the hotel, he had spent the last day examining all the ways that he could do something. He had already set up a trust fund and savings accounts, and altered his will. Their child, and Anika—whether she liked it or not—would be well cared for. Taking steps like those, concrete measures toward ensuring they would have a comfortable life, made him feel like he was at least accomplishing something.

"Have you been out to the island?"

He refocused on Anika, watched as she moved a cheese and potato dumpling around her plate and frowned. She'd eaten some at breakfast yesterday, but she'd barely touched her dumplings or her salad. Wasn't she supposed to be eating for two now?

"No, I haven't." He glanced out the window again at the tall, dark spire of the church stabbing up toward the sky, the red-orange roofs of the other buildings surrounding it. "I've been on a tour of the lake, though. I'll make it to the church one day."

"It's an amazing bit of history," Anika said with a genuine smile that made his chest tighten. "Marija and I used to go there all the time. On the southwest side is a stone staircase with ninety-nine steps. Legend has it that if a groom carries his bride up the steps into the church, they can ring the bell inside and have their wish granted."

He smiled. It was stories like that, bits and pieces of history and culture that, coupled with the luxury of his hotels, made the experiences his family's company offered some of the best in the world. The tourism manager he'd hired had already added excursions to the island for future guests, but he made a mental note to schedule a trip to the island before the grand opening.

"Marija mentioned you two spent a lot of time out and about the lake."

"I didn't realize you two spoke that much."

"Only occasionally," he said, noting the defensive set to her shoulders. "In town a couple times, at a tourism meeting. And once at the Winter Fairy Tale market."

She relaxed and he forced away his irritation. Had she

thought he'd been going behind her back, speaking to her grandmother and trying to convince her to sell? Or did she just not want him around her family? Thoughts of Marija stirred a sudden, fearsome thought.

"The cancer your mother and Marija had…is it genetic?"

"It is, but I'm not a carrier."

The tension that had seized his body loosened a fraction.

"I'm double-checking with my doctor, but the initial appointment I had said that unless you were a carrier of that gene, it's unlikely that our baby would be at risk."

Nicholas nodded. "This is all new to me."

"It's new to me, too," Anika said with a gentle smile.

"Let's talk about something positive. You seem to have fond memories of where you lived back in the States."

"I do. We lived in a small town outside of Kansas City just north of the river. The town was along the banks. Not mountains like this, but rolling hills covered in trees. We lived next to a large farm, but we also had a few animals— a cow, a couple of goats, chickens."

"Hence your knowledge of roosters."

"Yes." Anika grinned, the smile transforming her face. "My mother was a nurse, so we only kept a few animals. But it had always been her dream to have a farm. Well, hers and my father's." She glanced down at her plate. "I'm grateful for what I've had. But it seems like as the years go by, my family gets taken away from me bit by bit. I missed having a father, especially when I would come across something of his that told me a little bit about who he used to be. Who he could have been if he had been able to stay with us."

In that moment, Nicholas made a vow. To Anika, to their unborn child and to himself. He might not be the kind of father Anika had pictured when she'd envisioned a family of her own. But he would do what he could to give her as much of himself as possible.

Her eyes glimmered as she looked out over the water. He wanted to reach over to comfort her, to pull her into his arms. A move a boyfriend or lover might do normally. Not an appropriate gesture for a couple exploring nothing more than a co-parenting relationship.

He'd moved through his relationships, the occasional fling, with ease, confident in his every action. But right now, seated across from Anika, he wasn't sure what to do.

"It's the first time in my life I've been alone. After my father passed, I had my mother. After my mother passed, I had Marija. They were always there for me."

"I only met her the few times, but she was an incredible woman. She told me a little bit about your family's history here."

"Yes. It's been in our family since just after the first World War. My great-great grandfather bought it for almost nothing off of an American who modeled it after his house back in Virginia, but then missed his home too much to stay. The house was a great source of pride for Marija."

"But not your mother?"

"My mother always told me that she enjoyed growing up here, that it was a beautiful place to live as a child, but that she wanted more. She wanted to travel, see more of the world. That's how she met my father. She was a traveling nurse, but she eventually settled in Kansas City when she got pregnant with me. At that point she'd been traveling nearly a decade and decided that it was time to grow some roots."

Nicholas cocked his head to one side.

"Do you ever get the feeling of wanderlust that she did?"

Anika shifted in her seat, as if his questions were making her uncomfortable.

"Occasionally. But not really."

She was lying. To him, certainly, but perhaps to herself, too. One day he would push her. But not today.

She changed the subject to his recent trip to the Czech Republic. They talked about his hotels, about the places they had visited. Lunch came to a close on a succulent dessert topped off with powdered sugar and cherries.

"This was nice," Anika said quietly as they were walking toward her tiny car.

"You sound surprised."

"I am," she admitted. "I wasn't expecting to enjoy my time so much." She smiled up at him, a shy smile that hit him right in the gut. "But I'm really glad we did this. Thank you."

"You're welcome. It was nice getting to know a little bit more about you."

"Maybe next time I can learn a little bit more about you."

"What do you mean?"

"You got to hear quite a bit about my past. How I ended up here, my parents. We talked about your hotels and your travels, but I didn't really get to know much about you."

He shrugged.

"That's who I am."

She frowned. "Who you are today, yes. But what about your past? Your family?"

He went cold inside. He'd just wrapped his head around accepting that he was going to be a father. He'd shared more about his past and David's death than he had with any woman he'd ever been with.

Why can't that be enough? he thought irritably.

"Perhaps later."

Her face fell a moment before she drew herself up, her eyes flashing. "I see how this is going to go. You get to hear about all my past, all the darkest parts of my life, but when it comes time for you to share, you're allowed to keep things close to your chest."

"I did share back in Hawaii. And you didn't have to share anything with me just now. That was your choice."

"Doesn't not sharing defeat the purpose?" she challenged him. "I thought this was about getting to know each other because we're going to be raising a child together. You're the one who made the choice to be involved, to push for us to spend time together."

"Yes, but as you pointed out, we aren't in a romantic relationship. Getting to know each other as much as we need to in order to be successful parents is one thing. We both have the right to keep other secrets."

She reared back as if she'd been slapped.

"You're right," she said stiffly. "Thanks for lunch. We'll have to do this again sometime."

A fierce wind whipped through the parking lot as she climbed in her car and drove away, piercing his clothes with icy fingers that left him cold on the outside. He preferred that to the coldness inside his chest.

CHAPTER TEN

A SHARP PAIN radiated up Anika's arm. She swore, dropping the hammer as she brought her hand up and sucked on her thumb. She'd woken that morning to a sky made all the more blue against the backdrop of a ground covered in a pristine layer of white.

The hope that maybe today would go by without anything bad happening had lasted all of seven minutes. She'd walked out onto the front porch and spied one of the thin pillars leaning precariously. The base had rotted through. If it wasn't fixed soon, the roof over the porch was in danger of collapsing. She hadn't budgeted for a repair like this, so she'd pulled out her hammer and tools. Marija had taught her many things, from cooking buckwheat dumplings from scratch to wielding a screwdriver. Skills necessary for running every aspect of a family-owned inn.

She'd waited until the sun had risen a little higher and at least given an illusion of warmth outside before she set to work. She'd managed to get the roof of the porch jacked up and the pillar lowered onto the floor. She'd been working on prying out the rotten base for the past ten minutes. Frustrated with her lack of progress, irritated that her morning was quickly going by, and exhausted from her fight with Nicholas the day before—*not to mention growing a baby*—

she'd made a stupid mistake and brought the hammer down on her finger.

She loved the house itself, loved aspects of her job. But when it came to things like this, balancing all of the to-dos that needed to be completed in order to make the inn successful on top of the administrative duties that awaited her, she didn't care for it. And that made her feel guilty. Guilty because she loved the house, the memories, the one remaining link to her family.

Guilty because the thought of running this place by herself, of putting dreams like traveling on hold while she clawed her way out of this hole, made her feel frustrated and helpless. It was why she had been so testy with Nicholas the day before. She had struggled to answer his questions about her desire to travel because until she'd gone to Hawaii, she hadn't realized how restless she had become. Growing up here as a child after losing her mother, she had craved the stability that living with Marija had brought her. Moving across an ocean to live in a new country had brought its own sense of adventure. She'd been happy here. When she'd first started to help with the administrative duties, she had been so focused on getting the inn back to its original state that she hadn't even been aware of any dissatisfaction.

In the months after Marija's funeral, she had chalked up her increasing negativity to depression, the natural progression of emotions after such a loss. How could the inn be a burden? It had been a connection to her past, to the incredible people wo had come before her, who had survived in this building for over one hundred years. That legacy, that connection to the past, had made her feel a part of something when she had felt so alone. After everything Marija had done for her, she owed it to her to keep the inn going.

So why now did she look at this building and not feel

the excitement, the comfort, the sense of belonging that she used to? Why, when she looked at it as she was growing the next generation inside her, did she feel only defeated and exhausted?

It wasn't just her growing discontent with the inn or Nicholas's questions that had put her in a foul mood. It was his complete lack of sharing anything about himself. The man wanted—no, demanded—that she share herself with him. Yet clearly, he was not going to reciprocate.

As the pain in her hand subsided, she rocked back on her heels and glanced in the direction of the Hotel Lassard. Even with the trees bare of leaves, the woods were thick enough she couldn't see the hotel.

She had been enjoying lunch, even when he'd been questioning her about her feelings on travel. She had enjoyed listening to him when he had shared what little he had. Seeing his eyes focused on her when she spoke, it was yet again easy to see why he was so popular with women when he could look at one and make her feel like she was the focus of his universe.

A dangerous place for her mind to go, given that he had told her multiple times that he had no interest in taking their relationship beyond co-parenting.

Not that she had any interest in anything but co-parenting. She simply had not anticipated that Nicholas would have any interest in parenting on any level. He seemed like the kind of man to offer her a large check, ask for perhaps the occasional photo, and otherwise continue on with his life. That he wanted to be involved had both astonished her and warmed her heart.

However, after yesterday's argument, seeing the extent of how much he wanted to get to know her but how little he was willing to share of himself, she'd wondered if Nicholas might be experiencing a change of heart. If not now, soon, perhaps.

The sound of gravel crunching made her look up. A red sports car pulled up in the circle drive. Her heart leaped into her throat as Nicholas climbed out of the driver's seat and circled around the hood, looking like an ad for men's luxury outerwear in a black peacoat and a scarlet scarf looped around his neck.

"What the hell do you think you're doing?"

Irritation edged out the awareness that had been spreading across her skin.

"Having a tea party."

He stomped up the steps and reached for the hammer. She leaned away.

"If you take this hammer from me, the next thing I use it on will not be a piece of wood."

"It's thirty degrees outside, Anika."

"Thirty-five and sunny with no wind. Makes a difference," she tossed over her shoulder as she turned her back on him and resumed her work.

"It's winter."

"Really? Is that why there's snow on the ground?"

A noise that sounded suspiciously like a growl came from behind her.

"You should be inside resting. Or eating."

"Eating?" She turned and frowned.

"Yes. You need to keep up your strength."

"And I will. But Nicholas, there are some days when I can barely stomach a cup of broth. It's normal." She gentled her voice as she saw the tension in his shoulders, the trace of helpless uncertainty on his handsome face. "I'm not going to do anything to endanger the baby."

He sighed and ran a hand through his hair. "I don't like seeing you work like this."

"Well, tough. This is part of my life."

"Do you want it to be?"

She narrowed her eyes. "I thought you said talking about selling the inn was off the table until further notice."

"It is. I'm not asking about selling. I'm asking if you personally want this inn to be a part of your life. Because the impression I got yesterday was it doesn't make you as happy as it used to."

Stunned, she stared at him. How did this man see so much about her? How did he know her so well, sometimes almost better than she knew herself?

"I'm not comfortable answering right now."

His eyebrows drew together. "Because I wouldn't share yesterday?"

"One, I don't have a good answer. And two..." She swallowed past the hurt. "I'm not comfortable sharing with someone who's only going to take and not give. It doesn't matter if you're the father of my child or my lover or my friend. I'm not confiding in someone who sees our relationship as a one-way street."

He stared at her for so long she wondered if he was going to say something or just turn around and leave.

"I'm going to stay and help you."

She cocked her head. "That's funny. What I heard was 'Anika, may I stay and help you?'"

His lips twitched. "Yes. That."

She let out a breath. "This kind of project isn't my favorite on a good day, let alone in the winter and two months pregnant."

He pulled off his scarf, crouched down next to her and looped it around her neck. That intoxicating mix of cinnamon and wood wrapped around her, warming her in a way the wintry sunshine had failed to do.

"Let me take a turn."

Something in his voice caught her. He held out his hand. Slowly, she handed him the hammer, accepting his offer of help.

"Thank you."

He nodded, something poignant flashing in his eyes before he turned to the pillar. By the time she came back out with mugs of steaming tea, he already had the rotted wood removed and was attaching the new base.

"How did you do that so fast?"

"My first job for the hotel was on the maintenance crew at our flagship hotel in London."

"Maintenance crew?"

He shot her a sexy grin. "Hard to imagine?"

With his coat tossed over a rocking chair and hammer in hand, no, it wasn't hard to imagine at all.

"Did you like it?"

"Loved it." He started to lift the pillar up. "When I was younger I loved tools. Getting the experience, seeing what our employees do, was eye-opening. And I still get to keep a foot in that door. Touring the construction sites, talking to the crew, the engineers, the architects."

She remembered the rough scrape of his palm on hers on the Hanalei Bay pier. "And doing some work yourself?"

He grinned again. "Boys and their toys. Sometimes it pays to be the boss's son and ask to get in on hanging drywall."

The insight into the father of her baby sent a small jolt of happiness through her. Just like their intimate conversation back in Kauai, she was learning more about the man behind the glamour and tabloid stories. A man that she was liking more and more. A man she could easily see teaching their son or daughter how to wield a hammer, how to swim, how to dance.

Her throat tightened. They wouldn't have the kind of family she'd dreamed about. But they could still be a family. Most importantly, her child was going to have a good father.

She held the pillar steady while he reattached the banisters on either side and brought the roof down. She walked down to the yard and looked back at the porch.

"Thank you." She smiled at Nicholas. "What a difference."

He came down the porch stairs and walked to her, stopping in front of her and looking down into her eyes.

"Come on a ride with me."

Emotion fluttered in her chest. "To where?"

"Somewhere special." He held out his hand. "You trusted me once today. Trust me one more time?"

The emotions spread through her, a confusing tangle that tied her up in knots. Hope, want, nervousness. It was a simple ride, not a marriage proposal.

Slowly, she slipped her hand into his, nearly closed her eyes as a sense of rightness filled her when his fingers curled over hers.

"Let's go."

CHAPTER ELEVEN

THE ROAD SLOPED UP, a gray ribbon curving through snow-draped trees. The Audi handled the turns with a smoothness that normally made Nicholas feel confident, in control.

He felt neither of those things today. And it was because of the woman sitting next to him. So close and yet just out of reach.

He'd mucked things up after lunch yesterday. Confiding in her back in Kauai had felt natural. It hadn't hurt that there'd been a solid steel door between them, allowing him to say the words he hadn't confessed to anyone while still keeping some sense of distance between them.

That hadn't been the case yesterday when she'd looked up at him with those big gold eyes, so willing to trust, to support, to offer him everything he'd craved as a grieving child yet had gotten used to doing without.

The possibility of opening himself up once more, of letting the true depths of his pain and fear not only see the light of day but be shared with someone, made him uncomfortable at best, if not downright afraid. What if opening the door to his past sent him spiraling like his mother or running like his father? What if Anika rejected him, agreed with his new and deepest fear—that he wasn't capable of being a good father to their child?

He'd gone over that morning to apologize, to try to put

some of what he was feeling into words, only to find the pregnant mother of his child sitting on the porch in the freezing cold with a hammer. Yes, he'd admired her tenacity. But it had also angered him. Why couldn't the woman just accept help? Why was she so hell-bent on taking care of everything herself? On not letting him lend a hand?

Except she had accepted his help. And not just help on any project, but on her beloved inn. It had floored him to realize how much more impactful it was to help someone like Anika. With Susan and her constant needs, he'd gone from feeling like a champion to a crutch. With Anika, it hadn't just been his own desire to be needed. No, it had been that she trusted him enough to help that had nearly knocked him back on his heels.

He slanted a glance at her out of the corner of his eyes. Sun streamed in through the window, casting golden light on the strands that had escaped the loose bun at the base of her neck. The rich emerald color of the sweater she'd pulled on made her skin glow.

How had he not seen her before? Had he let his pride over her initially indifferent reaction to him blind him to who she was? What she was capable of?

"The castle is coming up," Anika said, her soft voice breaking the silence between them.

Nicholas glanced out the window at the orange-red roofed turret rising above the tree line in the distance.

"I haven't been."

Anika smiled. "It's worth a look. It definitely belongs on your recommendations for your guests."

Surprised, he looked over at her. It was the first time she had brought up the Hotel Lassard of her own volition.

"Why would you recommend it?"

"It's over a thousand years old. Small, but it has a nice

museum, plus a wine cellar where guests can bottle their own wine. The restaurant is amazing. But," she said as her smile widened, "it's the view for me. The view is unlike anything else in Bled."

Nicholas flipped on his blinker.

"What are you doing?"

"What does it look like?" he asked with a grin. "With a recommendation like that from a woman who's basically a local, how can I resist driving by without seeing this incredible view?"

He saw the twitch of her lips even as she looked away. "Don't you have some billionaire stuff to do back at your hotel?"

"Billionaire stuff, no. Reviewing the latest reports on projects in Greece and England, including the status of delayed construction supplies and a summary from one of my engineers, yes."

He didn't miss the line that formed between her brows as he pulled into a parking lot surrounded by trees.

"Surprised I can read?" he teased as he opened her door for her.

"No." She bit down on her lower lip, a simple, unconscious gesture that sent a bolt of heat straight to his groin. "You're very different than what I expected when I first met you."

"I noticed your chilly reception."

She winced. "Sorry. I made some assumptions about you based on the way you dressed, the way you looked, the way women responded to you."

A satisfied smirk stole across his face. "So you were jealous."

"More wary," she said with a small smile of her own. "Bled is my home. I was afraid you were going to change things up too much, not understand the culture here and just blaze in with crystal chandeliers and diamond-encrusted silverware."

"I've never used diamond-encrusted silverware."

She chuckled. "I know. And everyone in town has said nothing but great things about you acclimating to the community. It's just…you're unlike anyone who's ever come here, at least since I've been here. Then when you wanted to buy the inn…" She sighed. "I don't deal with change well."

"I disagree with that." He glanced down, noted the surprise on her face as they crossed a small drawbridge and passed under a stone arch. "Look at what you're doing now, how quickly you adapted to the idea of becoming a mother. Pivoting to be the sole owner of the inn. Moving halfway around the world and adapting to living in a new country. I'd say you deal with change very well."

He glanced down to see her rapidly blinking.

"Anika?"

"Thank you," she finally said. "It feels good to hear that."

He paid for their tickets, silencing Anika's protests by pointing out he had invited her on the ride and counted the visit as research. She grumbled but finally agreed and led the way into the lower courtyard, flanked on either side by the walls of the castle. In front of him, the cobbled gray stones of the courtyard ran up to a short wall with views of Bled, the lake and the mountains beyond. He breathed in, savoring the architecture, the history pouring out from every stone.

"Wait," Anika said, grabbing his arm as he moved toward the wall. "Your first view should be from the upper courtyard. Nothing compares."

He allowed himself to be pulled along, enjoying the excitement building on her face. It reminded him of how she'd been when they'd snorkeled off the coast of Kauai. When he'd gotten his first glimpse of who Anika truly was at heart.

"Why do you think you don't deal with change well?" he asked as she tugged him past a well with a shingled roof toward another stone staircase that curved back into the depths of the castle.

"Maybe a more accurate description is I don't like change," she said. "I used to. I used to feel adventurous. I wanted to travel the world like my mother, but I also wanted that home to come back to in between. But being away from the inn and Marija…" Her voice trailed off as she frowned. "Sometimes I felt scared, like if I was gone too long something would happen. Other times I felt guilty, that wanting to travel and not be as invested in the inn as Babica was made me a bad granddaughter. So, I'd come back and work twice as hard to make up for my absences."

"Based on everything I've seen, you're more than invested."

"I like parts of it. But other parts… I feel like I have to," she said as they started up. "Like if I don't keep the inn alive, I'll have let down the woman who was my family for over half my life and everything she worked for. Like I'm letting the last bit of my family die."

Before he could stop himself, Nicholas wrapped an arm around her shoulders and drew her close. She didn't even hesitate as she leaned into him. Their steps harmonized as they neared the top. Even as he kept her tight against his side and indulged in the sudden, fierce sense of possession, dread pooled in the pit of his stomach. He'd thought Anika's obsession with the inn had been a matter of pride, of not liking him and not wanting him to have it.

Learning the full extent of her reasons for not wanting to sell took his carefully laid plan that she'd already disrupted and tore it into tiny pieces. It didn't negate the fact that without a major intervention, the inn wouldn't survive.

Anika's shoulders relaxed beneath his arm as they neared the top. Feeling her against him, sensing the trust she was placing in him, was enough for now. The hotel would open in just a couple weeks, with or without the inn. He needed to focus on that, and the baby, for now.

"Are you ready?"

He glanced down at Anika, who smiled up at him with the same unabashed joy he'd first glimpsed back in Hawaii. His chest tightened as he entertained the idea of leaning down and brushing a soft kiss across her lips. The need to taste her, to mark her as his for everyone around them to see, shocked him to his core.

"I am. Although if the view doesn't live up to the hype, you owe me a drink."

She arched a brow. "And if it does, what do I get?"

"A full-body prenatal massage at the Hotel Lassard spa."

A sigh escaped her lips. "That sounds heavenly."

So did the idea of being the one to offer to massage her from head to toe. He bit back the invitation. Moments later they emerged onto the stone floor of the upper courtyard of Bled Castle. To the right and left were stone walls covered in barren vines, topped off by reddish orange roofs.

And in front of him…in front of him was heaven.

They moved to the stone wall at the edge of the courtyard. He released her and placed his hands on the cold rock, leaning forward to inhale a deep, cleansing breath of winter air. Beyond the wall there was nothing but a plunge straight down to a tree-covered slope several hundred feet below. The lake glimmered beneath the early afternoon sun. The church stood proudly on the island, and beyond that he glimpsed both the inn on the southern shore and the roof of the Hotel Lassard next door. Mountains rose beyond, smaller than the steep peaks to the north, but no less beautiful in the gentle rise and fall of their majestic summits.

"The first time I saw this lake, I felt like I was at home."

He felt Anika tense beside him. He didn't look at her, couldn't. Not if he was going to get through this. He kept his gaze focused on the snow-draped hills, the wispy clouds clinging to the tops of the taller peaks.

"David died when he was seven. We were riding bikes and a driver ran a stop sign." His bare fingers dug into the stone, the roughness grounding him in the moment, keeping him present even as the past tried to pull him under. "The driver was at fault. But to this day I replay that moment over and over in my mind. What I could have done differently. I looked away for a second and David rode his bike out into the road."

When Anika didn't say anything, he plunged forward.

"I know, logically, it wasn't my fault. My parents reassured me of that fact over and over as we sat in the hospital, waiting for David to come out of surgery, then waiting for him to wake up."

The memories washed over him. The incessant beeping of machines, the sharp scent of antiseptic, the tightness of his mother's grasp on his shoulder.

"That first year, we beat the odds. We went to counseling. My dad took us on trips. My parents spent every waking moment they could together. But something changed just before the first anniversary. My mother started sleeping in more. A couple nights I found her in David's old bed. The more she slipped into depression, the more work trips my father took. We existed like that for nearly nine years. The only times we were truly together were on our trips."

He looked down as Anika laid a hand over his. A simple gesture, but one that steadied him enough to continue.

"I haven't shared that part of myself with anyone. I've gotten used to keeping people at a distance because it was how I survived those years. Even after my parents reconciled, I kept them at arm's length." He steeled himself, looked down at Anika. "I don't know how capable I'm going to be as a father."

Slowly, Anika wound her arms around his waist and pulled him against her. He forced himself to relax, resting his chin on top of her head.

"I don't know how capable I'm going to be as a mother," she finally said. "But, from what little I've seen, you've got a lot of potential." She leaned back and looked up at him. She breathed in, then out. "I was scared when you said you wanted to be involved in the baby's life. I'm not as scared now."

It was one of the simplest compliments he'd ever received. Yet it warmed him like nothing else had in his life.

"But still scared?"

"Aren't you?"

"Terrified," he admitted with a small smile.

"Me, too. But you're not as bad as I thought," she replied, her eyes glinting with a teasing light for a moment before her face sobered. "Thank you, Nicholas. For sharing with me."

"You're welcome."

As he gazed down at her, the air shifted, heated between them. His eyes dropped down to her lips. His hands tightened on her hips as he heard the sharp intake of her breath. Slowly, he lowered his head. He didn't just want to kiss her, he needed to feel her mouth beneath his, to possess her once more—

A high-pitched squeal broke through the haze of lust.

His head jerked up. A young man was kneeling on the cold cobblestones, his fingers clutched around a black jewelry box opened up to a glittering ring that a woman with black curls was currently gushing over.

Anika stepped back and looked away, her cheeks flushed. "I should get back to the inn."

Part of him wanted to pull her back into his arms, to finish what they had started. But it was better this way, he decided as they moved away from the wall, to step back from desire. They needed to move slow, not give in to sensual urges that would distract them.

And, he decided as he followed her out of the courtyard, while he had confided in Anika, he needed to ease into whatever this relationship was slowly. Letting down his guard too soon, rushing in, could result all too easily in heartbreak.

CHAPTER TWELVE

ANIKA CLUTCHED HER hands in her lap, her eyes laser-focused on the clock ticking in the doctor's waiting room. Their appointment had been for fifteen minutes ago. She normally handled changes in routine very well. But damn it, she wanted to see her baby.

The door to the lobby opened. Anika glanced up, then did a double take as Nicholas strode in.

"Nicholas?"

The smile he shot her sent her heart catapulting into her throat. He walked over and sat in the chair next to her.

"You haven't gone back yet, have you?"

"No."

"Good." He glanced at his watch. "First time I've been glad a doctor has been late."

"What are you doing here?"

He frowned. "Today's the ultrasound, right?"

"Yes, but…"

"You did invite me," he reminded with a slight smile that didn't quite reach his eyes. "I'm surprised," she finally replied. "Any time we've talked about the baby, you've been… removed." And he had been. Ever since their sojourn to the castle, he'd dropped by twice, once to take her out for tea, the other simply to check on her. He'd even mentioned reading a couple of articles about what to expect in the second trimester. But compared to the relaxed, enjoyable camaraderie they'd enjoyed that day, he'd been distant.

"After what you told me about David, I understand needing some time," she hurried to add. "I just thought this might be too much for you."

He watched her for a long moment before reaching over and settling his hand on top of hers. The slide of his skin on hers made her breath catch.

"I want to be here."

The sincerity in his eyes soothed away her words of protest. She realized that a part of her didn't want him there because she didn't want to get attached. She had started to, that day at the castle. But then he'd disappeared so quickly she'd wondered if she had imagined the deep intimacy she'd felt with him.

She didn't want him to show up, be a part of this journey, only to pull away later when things became real. Things like waking up in the middle of the night to feed a screaming infant or changing what seemed like a never-ending number of diapers. Nicholas might dominate boardrooms and offices around the globe, but somehow, she couldn't picture him balancing a squalling baby in his arms while warming up a bottle at one in the morning.

Still, she wasn't going to make him pay the price for her insecurities. They had months to go before they would face any of those obstacles. At some point in the near future, they would discuss what that first year would look like, the extent of how Nicholas would be involved.

But for today, she was going to focus on finally getting to see the life growing inside her.

The nurse called them back and escorted them into a dim room with a reclined medical chair. An ultrasound technician walked them through the procedure as she laid a towel over Anika's waist and spread a thick jelly over her abdomen.

"So, is this your first?" she asked cheerfully as she picked up a wand with a circular piece on the end.

"Yes," Anika replied, her heart beating fast as she watched the screen.

"Congratulations!"

"Thank you."

"Are you alright?"

Anika turned to see a concerned expression on the technician's face.

"I am." Anika let out a small, self-deprecating laugh. "I've always wanted a family and I just want everything to go well."

"I understand. Your first appointment went well?"

"Very."

"Then I'd say today is going to be great, too," the technician said with a reassuring smile.

Anika heard a rustle, then felt a hand come to rest on her shoulder. She looked up to see Nicholas gazing down at her, his expression serious. He didn't say anything, but he didn't have to. His presence alone settled some of the nervous energy zipping through her.

"Ready?"

At Anika's nod, the technician lowered the wand. She rubbed it over Anika's belly a couple times, her eyes fixed on the screen. Anika watched, waiting, her breathing starting to escalate as her mind whirled—

"There it is!"

Wonder filled her at the sight of the tiny creature on the screen. Pure, breathtaking wonder as she gazed at her baby.

"That's…"

"That's your baby." The technician glanced at something. "Heartbeat at one-sixty, right in the range for healthy."

"So, everything's okay?"

Anika glanced up to see Nicholas staring at the screen, an unreadable expression on his handsome face.

"Everything's great."

His shoulders seemed to relax a fraction. Finally, he tore his eyes away and looked down at her.

"I've never seen an ultrasound before," he said, his voice muted.

She looked back, wanting to soak up every last moment. Her eyes trailed over the rounded head, the swell of the stomach, the teeny arms and legs.

"It's beautiful," she whispered.

"Beautiful and healthy," the technician pronounced. "I'll get you cleaned up and then you'll go back with the doctor to talk through everything. I'll print you off copies of the photos to take home with you."

As the technician shut off the screen, Anika stole another glance at Nicholas. He was watching the printer as it churned out photos from the ultrasound.

"Nicholas?"

He looked back at her, his expression unreadable. Trepidation whispered through her. Had the sight of the baby changed his mind? Seeing it literally in black-and-white?

The rest of the appointment flew by, with the doctor pronouncing both her and the baby healthy, as well as reassuring her that her levels of fatigue and nausea were normal for the stage of pregnancy she was in. Nicholas asked a couple of questions, but mostly kept silent.

At first, his unusual quietness made her nervous. But as the doctor gave her a rundown of the upcoming weeks, her earlier excitement returned and she tuned out Nicholas's presence. If he wanted to share with her later, he could. But she was not going to focus on him. Not right now, when she had so much to be joyful for.

Nicholas walked with her to her car after the appointment. She barely glanced at him, her eyes focused on the pictures in her gloved hands.

"Anika?"

"Hmm?"

"I'm going to follow you home."

She blinked and looked up at him. "You mean 'Anika, may I follow you home?'"

His eyes narrowed even as his lips curved into a reluctant smirk. "Yes. That."

She sighed. "Yes, you may."

Ten minutes later, Anika drove down the lane. She'd barely parked the car when Nicholas appeared at her door and opened it for her.

"Do you have any guests tonight?"

"No. January is our slowest month," she said as he followed her inside. "I need to come up with something for next year's skiing season. Although," she added with a yawn, "I'm not disappointed this year. Half the time I can barely keep my eyes open."

"Why don't you head up to bed? I can lock up on my way out."

"I will in a bit." She hung up her coat and pulled the photos out of her pocket. "I think I'm going to make myself a cup of tea, light a fire in the library and stare at these for a while."

She looked up to find Nicholas watching her intently.

"You're happy, then?"

"Very." She crossed over to him and held up the photos. "How could I not be? I got to see our baby today."

She traced a finger over the tiny head, that sense of wonder returning. It might not be how she'd imagined starting a family. But it was happening. She was going to be a mother.

"I'll make the fire for you."

"You don't have to do that."

"I don't. But I'd like to."

She huffed to cover her spurt of pleasure. "Well, thank you."

By the time she walked into the library, a fire blazed in the hearth. Nicholas had turned on a couple of the banker's lamps, the green glass lampshades glowing in the darkening room. Nicholas himself had stretched out on one of the leather sofas.

Suddenly and inexplicably nervous, Anika walked into the library.

"I'm sorry. I didn't realize you were staying, or I would have brought another cup of tea."

"May I see the pictures?"

"Oh. Of course." She pulled the pictures out of her pocket and handed them over. He took them with a light touch, as if he were afraid he might rip them just by handling them. She focused on her tea as he shuffled through them. He would pause on one, turn it this way and that, then continue on to the next, still wearing that unreadable expression he'd had in the doctor's office.

Finally, he laid them on the coffee table and leaned back into the couch, staring at the fire.

"Is everything okay?" Anika finally asked.

"Yes."

Nicholas turned to her. He reached out, took the teacup from her grasp and set it on the table before turning back and taking her hands in his.

He's going to end it.

Anika sucked in a deep breath, mentally steeling herself. It had been too much, too much seeing the actual evidence that their night in Hawaii had created a child.

"I knew you were pregnant, had accepted it from the moment you told me." He glanced at the photos again, then back at her. "But seeing it…actually seeing the baby…hearing you say 'our child' cemented it." His hands tightened on hers. "I told you before I'm not sure what kind of father I'm going to make. But I know I'm going to try to be the best one I can be. For you and for the baby."

Anika stared at him. She'd been so prepared for him to tell her he couldn't do this, to walk out, that for a moment she couldn't process what he was saying. But as his words sank in, a cautious happiness began to spread.

"You've already been wonderful, Nicholas. The dates, reading articles, all of it—"

"Nice gestures," he agreed. "Ones I will continue to do. But I want to do more. I want to be more."

She gave in to temptation and reached out, cupping his jaw in one hand. "You will be, Nicholas. You are nothing if not stubborn. I know that if this is something you want, you'll make it happen."

His breath shuddered out. "Thank you, Anika. For trusting me. I know that's not the easiest thing."

"Neither is altering the entire course of your life."

"No. But—" a smile spread across his face, stirring heat low in her belly "—after seeing what I saw today, I don't want to be anywhere else but here."

She wasn't sure how long they sat there staring at each other, the only sounds the occasional crackle of a log in the fireplace or a creaking from above as the house settled. Did she move first? Did he lean forward?

Does it matter?

The thought flitted through her mind before their lips joined in a searing kiss.

Nicholas circled his arms around Anika's waist and pulled her closer on the couch. Fire shot through him as she moaned and melted into his embrace, her hands coming up to rest on his shoulders as he kissed her.

It had been two months since they'd last kissed. Two months since he'd held her like this. So much had changed, including the desire he felt for her. Back in Hawaii, he had been consumed by his need to take Anika to his bed. Yet the numerous times they'd made love that night had only made his hunger grow. Never had he let down his guard with a lover before, trusted her enough to take control and surrendered himself to someone's touch like he had with Anika.

The desire he felt now, while still laced with that ravenous edge that threatened to drive him mad, was deeper, even more possessive. Not just a carnal need to have her body joined with his, but a want for the woman who continued to impress him. When he'd seen the joy on her face as she'd seen their baby for the first time, heard the breathless happiness in her voice, something had shifted inside him. Something that now drove him to cradle her in his arms and force down the desire that threatened to overwhelm him.

He gentled his kiss, sliding his fingers into the thick silk of her hair and tilting her head back. When she moaned, he teased her lips with his tongue until she laughed, opening her mouth to him. He teased, coaxed, savored each taste, all the while wondering how he could have lasted so long without kissing her these past weeks.

"Where's your room?" he asked as he moved his lips down to the pulse beating at the base of her throat.

"Third floor."

"Of course." His hands moved to her waist, his fingers slipping under the soft cashmere of her sweater and settling on her bare skin. Just the feel of her sent a hot bolt of need straight to his groin. "Do you trust me to carry you up three flights of stairs?"

"I do, but…" She pulled back, a shy smile curving her full lips up. "Can I tell you one of my fantasies?"

"Considering how hard just hearing the word 'fantasy' from your lips made me, yes."

"I've always wanted to make love in a library."

The woman constantly amazed him. How had he ever thought her stuck-up and cold?

"Then let's make your dream come true."

He gathered her in his arms and laid her down on the plush rug in front of the fire. He pulled her sweater off and unclasped her bra, baring her plump breasts to his hungry gaze. She stared up at him with a mix of shyness and desire that drove him wild. He stripped himself of his own shirt and circled his arms around her waist. She arched up into his touch and pressed her body against his as he bent his head. He captured one nipple in his mouth, sucking and kissing and licking her as she moaned, her fingers digging into his hair.

He continued his sensual onslaught on the other breast before moving lower and unbuttoning her jeans. He slid them off slowly, kissing her from the swells of her thighs down to her slender ankles. But when he moved back up her body, she sat up and put a hand on his chest as he reached for the waistline of her panties.

"I go first this time."

Aroused beyond belief, he stood. She moved to her knees and unbuttoned his pants, sliding them over his hips with torturously slow movements. A groan escaped his lips when she wrapped her hand around the base of his erection. He looked down just as she licked him all the way to the tip.

"That feels so damned good," he growled.

Her smug look of feminine satisfaction made him harden in her grasp.

"Good."

She took him in her mouth, nails scraping lightly along his thigh as she sucked on him. His hands tightened into fists. Part of him wanted to let his body take over, enjoy the incredible sensations to the finish.

Next time, he promised himself as he finally pulled back and sank down in front of her.

"I want to feel you, Anika. All of you."

Her eyes widened as his meaning hit her.

"I guess we don't need birth control anymore," she said with a soft laugh.

"I'm clean." He reached out and grasped her hand, threading his fingers through hers and bringing her up to kiss her knuckles. "I had my annual appointment at the end of the summer. I haven't been with anyone but you."

The slow smile that spread across her face hit him square in the chest.

"I'm clean, too." She sucked in a trembling breath. "I told you I've only been with one other man. I've never made love without a…" A becoming blush stole over her cheeks. "Without protection."

That sense of possession returned, burned bright in him as his hand tightened on hers. "Neither have I, Anika." He turned Anika's hand over and kissed the sensitive skin of her wrist, savoring the shudder that ran over her body. "I want to make love to you without anything between us."

Slowly, she nodded. "I want that, too."

He lowered her back onto the carpet. Firelight bathed her body in a golden glow. She gazed up at him with faith in her eyes. His heart shuddered. Never had a woman looked at him with such trust.

It unnerved him as his gaze drifted down to her belly. He could take care of her, and the baby. Financially, he could ensure they wanted for nothing. But was he capable of being the man they needed, the father they deserved?

Anika raised her arms up, reached for him. The simple action banished his unvoiced apprehensions. He couldn't have resisted her for anything in the world.

Their lips met, melded together in a kiss blazing with heat and some unnamed emotion that added a sweetness he had never known he craved until now. He pressed his body against hers, groaned when her naked curves molded to him. He reached down, placed his erection against her wet core and slowly slid in.

The sensation of sliding into Anika's molten heat nearly undid him. The intimacy of it stole his breath, as did Anika's sharp, beautiful cry in his ear. He dragged out each second, easing himself in inch by inch until he was fully joined with her.

He paused, savored the sensation of being buried inside the woman who had ushered in so much change to his life, who surprised and astounded him on a regular basis with her strength, her confidence, her resilience.

The woman who carried his child within her.

He started to move, long, slow strokes. Anika clenched around him, her hands moving over him restlessly as she rose up to meet his thrusts. When she cried out, he eased back.

"Did I hurt you?"

"Don't stop!" she gasped, her hands coming up to grasp his shoulders in a fierce grip. "Don't you dare stop, Nicholas."

The sound of his name on her lips, along with her urgent plea, sent him higher. Fire built at the base of his spine as he succumbed to the spell woven by the incredible woman in his arms, the intimate setting, the glow of the fire. All of it combined, spiraled upward as Anika arched her hips up and took him deeper. A moment later her body tightened. Her nails dug into his back.

"Nicholas!"

She came apart in his arms, her skin flushed, her cries like music. He followed a moment later, heat spiraling through his body as he spilled himself inside her, groaning her name before he lowered his head and claimed her with a kiss.

He quickly rolled to the side and gathered her sweat-slicked body in his arms. She snuggled into his embrace, her head cradled on his shoulder.

"That was incredible," she murmured.

"It was."

Slowly, his hand drifted down over her breast, her ribs, then rested on the slight swell of her belly. He heard her breath catch, felt her body tense against his.

Then, slowly, she brought a hand up and laid it over his.

Emotion swamped him. The joy he'd seen on Anika's face in the doctor's office had given him a glimpse of a future he hadn't imagined for himself since that day long ago on the streets of Belgravia.

He tightened his arms around her and glanced down. Her eyes were closed, her lashes dark against the paleness of her skin. The steady rise and fall of her breasts told him she'd fallen asleep in his arms.

His gaze drifted down to where their joined hands rested on her belly. Fear drifted up, tried to steal away the moment. Seeing their baby had strengthened his resolve to be a good father. But what if he could never let go enough to experience the same kind of happiness Anika had experienced today? Would he be able to give their child the kind of uninhibited love they deserved?

Heaviness tugged at his eyes. He gently moved away, pulled a blanket from one of the nearby couches and lay back down, draping it over them as he tugged her back into his arms. He pushed his fears away and allowed himself to relax, drifting off to sleep in front of a roaring fire with Anika safe in his arms.

CHAPTER THIRTEEN

ANIKA CURLED HER legs underneath her and sank into the plush embrace of the window seat in her room. She'd indulged in new pillows, a knitted throw from one of the shops in town and a small shelf she'd hung to hold her favorite books. Between the coziness of her nook and the deep blue waters of the lake stretching out before her, she was in heaven.

Her hand drifted down to her belly, her fingers spreading out. She didn't want to wish away her whole pregnancy. But she also could barely wait to feel the first flutters, the little movements as her baby grew. It had been two weeks since the ultrasound, and she wouldn't get another until she was twenty weeks along. She huffed, then let out a soft, exasperated laugh.

"I can't wait to meet you," she whispered down to the hint of roundness just below her navel.

Her gaze strayed toward the trees that separated the inn from the Hotel Lassard. Tomorrow night the hotel would have its grand opening. People from all over Lake Bled were invited, not to mention the entire world. Getting to know Nicholas, to see how much he invested in his work, had made it easier to talk about, and eventually become interested, in the Hotel Lassard at Lake Bled.

Unfortunately, it had also raised uncomfortable questions

for her. Part of the reason why she had resisted Nicholas's offers before was because she had thought he simply wanted something because he wanted it. But seeing the passion that he had for his company, the passion that he brought to his guests and the time and attention he put in, altered everything. What if selling the inn to him was actually the best solution? Given what she knew about him now, perhaps he would do the right thing and maintain the integrity of the inn while doing all the things that she alone was not capable of. Her grandmother had wanted nothing more than for the inn to succeed. Was selling and letting someone else take over the reins to see it reach its full potential the right thing to do? Especially if it meant giving her more time to pursue not only motherhood, but her own hopes and dreams?

She shook her head. That line of thinking still felt foolish to her, still felt too much like severing the last remaining connection that she had to her family. The further along her pregnancy progressed, the more she desperately wanted to preserve at least something for her child. Something of her history and her roots, where she came from.

Now was not the time to think of it anyway. She should be focusing on more immediate things like her growing relationship with Nicholas. Ever since the ultrasound and that night they first made love, they'd spent time together almost every day. From her cooking him meals to taking walks around the town and surrounding area, they had started to develop what felt like a real relationship. That she had spent several nights in his bed, and he in hers certainly, hadn't hurt.

A smile crossed her face. She'd woken up that morning to his arms wrapped around her, their bodies pressed together in her bed. Never would she have imagined Nicholas Lassard of all people falling asleep in a cramped queen bed inside a centuries-old inn. But when she had rolled over and found him looking deeply into her eyes, felt his hand caress first her face then drift slowly down over her bare breast, arousing her to heights of passion she never could have fathomed, it felt right.

Except, despite the growing intimacy between them, he still held back. Anytime she brought the baby up in conversation, whether by asking if he'd thought of a name or sounding him out on any ideas he might have about what he'd want to do the baby's first year, he would give a quick answer and then quickly turn the subject to something else.

She sighed. She needed to give him time. After all, he'd only been back in her life for about a month. Yes, she wanted more resolution, a clear idea of where they were going and just how involved he saw himself being. But they still had nearly six months to figure that out. Given all the progress they had made in such a short time, she needed to be patient and trust in the man that she was starting to learn more about.

Dimly, she heard a doorbell ring. Sighing, she tossed aside her blanket, thrust her feet into a pair of slippers and padded downstairs. She opened the door to a delivery worker, a silver box topped off with a red bow in her arms.

"Are you Anika Pierce?"

"Yes."

"Rush delivery. I need your signature that you received it."

"I'm not expecting anything," Anika said with a frown.

"It's from a salon in Paris," the delivery worker said with a wide smile. "Maybe you have a sweetheart."

Heat suffused Anika's cheeks. She signed for the box and took it back upstairs, setting it carefully on her bed.

She stared at it for a full minute, working up the courage to open it.

Finally, she huffed.

It's just a box. Open it.

The box was packed with red tissue paper, the same vivid hue as the bow. Sitting on top was a white envelope addressed to her in a strong masculine handwriting. What did it say about her, she mused as she picked the envelope up, that just the sight of his handwriting was enough to make her belly quiver?

She opened the envelope. A simple, plain card greeted her with the words "Thank you" emblazoned on the front. She opened it, her hands trembling.

The grand opening is tomorrow night at seven. It would honor me if you would join me as my guest.

She pulled back the tissue paper and gasped at the dress beneath. Slowly, she reached in and gently slid her fingers into the pile of frothy teal fabric. She moved to the mirror and held it up. With an off-the-shoulder neckline, diaphanous sleeves and a bodice that flowed out into a sweeping skirt, it was the kind of dress that would make a woman feel like a princess.

Not going and not supporting the man who had become so important to her in such a short amount of time was not an option. That he had taken the time and effort to do something like this, something he probably thought of as simple with the kind of money he had at his fingertips but that felt so generous with everything else he had going on, spoke volumes to her.

Yes, she told herself as she laid the dress out on the bed and stared at it with adoring eyes, there were still lots of questions to be answered. But for right now, the father of her child was thinking about her. He was including her in his life. And that was enough.

* * *

The hotel ballroom was packed. Guests in evening wear by Versace and Gucci milled about. Waiters slipped in and out of the crowds with silver trays loaded down with some of the finest delicacies European and Slovenian cuisine had to offer. Music from a string quartet drifted over the room, weaving a winter fantasy of airy music that enticed guests to linger and enjoy. It was exactly the kind of opening night Nicholas had envisioned.

Yet as he glanced around, he was disappointed. With how close he and Anika had grown over the past couple of weeks, he'd been confident she would have accepted both the invitation and the dress. They had still avoided the elephant in the room, the future of the inn. But he'd thought the relationship had progressed enough that she would at least attend.

"You look far too morose for someone who just launched one of the most successful hotels in Central Europe."

Nicholas turned and greeted his father with a smile and a hearty handshake. Henry Lassard surprised him by pulling him forward and wrapping him in a hug.

"I was just looking for someone," Nicholas said with a smile. "I can't be too upset when our reservations from April through the end of the summer are booked solid."

"I expected nothing less."

Nicholas returned his father's smile even as a thread of discomfort wound through him. He and his father had reconciled when Nicholas had approached him about pursuing a career in the family business. But there was always a faint distance anytime they spoke. It wasn't something he had paid much attention to, not until he had met Anika. Not until he had opened the door to his past. It was sobering to realize that he had never fully forgiven his parents for

emotionally abandoning him in those years after David's
death. It unsettled him, too, to realize that he had kept himself emotionally distant from his parents as well as from
other people around him. A defense mechanism to not only
protect himself from the pain of losing someone as he had
lost David, but also as a safeguard against ever suffering
the emotional tragedies he had when his parents had chosen their grief over him.

He grabbed a flute of champagne off a passing tray. If
he was still holding on to this pain and resentment after
twenty-plus years, was he capable of letting go and being
the kind of man that he wanted to be for his child? It was a
question he had been able to ignore as he had savored his
time with Anika, everything from the intimacy of waking
up next to her to simple things that he had never expected
to get joy from, like looking across the table at breakfast
and seeing her face smiling back at him.

But every relationship had its honeymoon period. And
to date, every relationship that he'd been in had eventually
lost that bloom of infatuation, of excitement and anticipation as it gave way to the cold realities of life.

"I hope Mother's fundraiser is going well," he said, trying to change the subject and focus on something other than
his own morbid musings.

"The library had raised at least ten thousand pounds when
we last spoke." Henry glanced down at his watch. "That was
over an hour ago. Knowing your mother, that amount has
doubled, if not tripled by now."

The pride in his father's voice, the slight smile about his
lips, stood out to Nicholas.

"Are you happy?"

His father blinked. "Happy?" he echoed. "But of course.
Why wouldn't I be?"

"There was a time in all our lives when we were extremely unhappy," Nicholas pointed out. "I was just wondering if you and Mother are still in a good place."

Henry tilted his head to the side. "What's brought all
this on?"

Nicholas shrugged. "Just curious."

His father looked down at the floor. "I would say, overall, yes, we're happy."

Coldness slipped over Nicholas's skin as he watched a
small frown mar his father's brow. What was his father holding back? Had the past years been a lie, a front to hide that
his parents had never truly moved on?

Before his father could answer, a glimpse of teal at the
corner of his eye made Nicholas turn his head. His heart
thudded hard against his ribs as Anika walked into the room.

The dress clung to the curves of her breasts, the sleeves
whispering over her arms. The skirt fell in a fairy-tale froth
of fabric to pool at her feet. She had kept her hair simple,
lightly curled and pulled back from her face with silver pins
to reveal her beauty. She glanced around, the nervousness
clearing from her face when she saw him. The smile she
gifted him brightened the room in a way no amount of crystal chandeliers or candles could do.

"Who is she?"

Nicholas turned to see his father's head swinging back
and forth between him and Anika.

"Anika Pierce. She lives next door and runs the inn."

His father's eyebrows climbed up. "The owner of the inn
you've been trying to buy?"

"Yes."

His father glanced at Anika once more. "Just don't lose
sight of what's important."

Nicholas's chest tightened. Was he losing focus? He never

would have thought that anything could derail him from his career goals, or his plans to propel the family brand higher then higher still. Yet someone had. Or rather, two someones.

The more involved he became, the more he would need to give of himself. He had committed to that, had thought that if his parents could achieve at least some healing, he could, too.

But now, as he watched his father be pulled away by a guest to discuss business, he couldn't help but wonder if he was reaching for something he was truly incapable of attaining. Every time the subject of the baby came up, he tried to summon enthusiasm, anticipation, something. Yet it was as if there was a wall built around his heart, an obstacle that no matter how hard he rammed himself against, he couldn't break through.

Would he ever be able to?

Anika approached him.

"You look beautiful."

"Thank you." She looked down, her fingers drifting over the skirt. "I've never owned something so beautiful. I can't thank you enough."

"You being here tonight and supporting the opening is thanks enough." He reached out, took her hand and pressed a kiss to her knuckles. "I know we haven't been talking business lately, but I appreciate you coming. I imagine it's not easy."

She cocked her head to the side. "A few weeks ago you would have been right. But the more I've gotten to know you and understand the reason behind why you do what you do, the more I've come to respect what you've accomplished here."

Never had someone's words meant so much to him.

"Thank you, Anika. Would you care to dance?" He

smiled wolfishly. "Because I recall we never got to finish our last dance."

Anika rolled her eyes. "After everything we've been through, you still bring that up."

"I do have a reputation to live up to."

He led her to the dance floor. Two-story windows lined the wall and gave incredible views of the lake. With the faintest bit of color still splashing the night sky beyond the ridges of the Alps and the church on Bled Island standing proudly against the growing darkness, it truly was an enchanted setting. One brought to life by the woman in his arms.

This time as they danced, their bodies close together, the music winding around them, there was the sensual awareness of her body, of her breasts pressed against his chest, of her waist and how fragile it felt beneath his hands. But there was also knowledge there, knowledge of the woman and not just her body but her mind and her heart, resulting in the most intimate dance that he had ever shared with a woman.

Satisfaction spread through him. His latest hotel had opened to rave reviews. The event itself was a massive success. And he was dancing with a woman that he truly cared about. The woman who was carrying his child.

As they passed by a pillar, he saw his father speaking with an older couple. His pleasure dimmed. What had his father been about to say before they were interrupted by Anika's arrival? Were his parents still truly happy? Or was there something else going on beneath the surface, something that he had missed? The last two weeks, even as he had struggled to open himself up, he had reminded himself that his parents had walked through hell and come out on the other side. Scarred, yes, but alive and moving forward.

But what if they hadn't? What if they were simply putting on a show? If they couldn't overcome the grief of losing David, would he ever be capable of overcoming it himself? Capable of finally letting down his own barriers and allowing himself to be the kind of father their baby deserved? Of being the kind of man Anika deserved?

Anika's hand tightened on his arm. He looked down at her and returned her smile with one of his own. There were plenty of questions to be answered, yes. But not tonight. Tonight was about celebration, about joy, about looking to the future.

A future that, if he could just let himself feel, might include the woman in his arms.

CHAPTER FOURTEEN

EXHAUSTED, ANIKA LAID her head back against the chair in her office. Reservations had continued to climb, enough that she had been able to hire a handyman part-time. He was making improvements on the interior and had replaced some of the rotting boards on the front porch. If the weather forecast held and next week got as warm as they were expecting, the porch railing and trim might be restored to its ivory glory by the weekend.

Slowly but surely, she was reclaiming the inn bit by bit. Larger projects like replacing all the beds were still a ways away. But if she continued to make enough changes to bring customers back and kept up with marketing, the inn would survive.

It was an accomplishment, yes. But as her relationship with Nicholas grew, deepened, she was beginning to contemplate more and more the possibility of selling. Of starting a new chapter in her life.

Or, as she'd started to think of it recently, their life.

Don't jump in too fast.

Yes, the last few weeks had been wonderful. But it was just a beginning. There was still so much that had to be discussed and decided upon.

She'd stayed with Nicholas the night of the grand opening and woken up to an empty bed. Not surprising given all there was to do with the opening. She'd experienced a momentary flick of fear, along with a heavy dose of guilt. Had it been like this for him when he'd come back into his room in Kauai and found her gone?

But Nicholas had banished her fears by returning with a breakfast tray and sharing pancakes with her in bed before he'd planted a searing kiss on her lips as he'd headed out to a meeting.

The rest of the day had rushed by, ending on a somber note when Nicholas had received an urgent phone call about an emergency with his new property in Greece. He'd left quickly and she'd returned to the inn, not quite comfortable with staying in his suite without him there.

She walked out into the lobby. The thick burgundy-and-cream rug she'd found online stood out against the dark wood floors. Replacing some of the older lamps and having the handyman bring down some chairs she'd found in the attic had already altered the atmosphere from worn to cozy. Blankets made by a local artisan were stacked on one of the built-in shelves by the fireplace, inviting guests to relax by the hearth.

Regardless of whether she decided to sell or not, she was very proud of the work she'd managed to do in a short amount of time. If she sold to the Hotel Lassard, an idea she was entertaining more and more, she could bring the baby back for visits. She imagined picnics on the dock, walking through the fields of snowdrops in the spring and watching her son or daughter run chubby little fingers over the white petals, and was filled with a joy she had never experienced.

She glanced out the windows behind the desk that overlooked the lake. The island stood proudly in the middle, the church spire white against a pale gray sky. Snow clung to tree branches. The lake was still, smooth as mirror glass.

A peaceful tableau. One that reflected the growing peace

she felt about the future. Things were certainly going in a different direction than she'd ever thought possible. But she was finding happiness in these unexpected turns, joy in moments she'd never envisioned. The more Nicholas did for her and the baby, the more she relaxed. When he did things like send her a basket with teas from a local shop she'd told him about in passing, it made her want a future with him in it. Not just a sideline participant who occasionally popped into her child's life to bestow the occasional gift before departing again for his bachelor life, but a man involved in the raising of his child.

A man who might want a life with her, too.

She moved to the fireplace, tossed in another log and sank down into a chair. Was she being foolish, picturing a future with Nicholas and their baby? They hadn't talked at all about the changes happening between them. But surely he wouldn't have said what he did at the opening if he didn't feel at least something for her.

I just need to talk to him.

As nervous as she was, a frank conversation would be in both their best interests.

A sudden rolling sensation in her belly had her on her feet and rushing for the bathroom. Dimly, she heard the bell ring over the front door, but she couldn't stop. She barely made it into the little room off the entryway before she was sick.

As she knelt on the floor, fire burning in her throat, she felt warm hands on her back.

"I'm here, Anika."

She closed her eyes against the hot sting of tears of relief that she wasn't alone.

"You're back early," she croaked as her stomach spasmed.

"Shush," he ordered. "Just focus on you and the baby right now."

For once she had no rebuttal, just listened as she heaved up the contents of her breakfast. Nicholas stayed with her through it all. When it was finally over, he escorted her back to the chair by the fire. She watched as he disappeared down the hallway toward the kitchen. When he emerged several minutes later, he had a glass of water in one hand and a cup of steaming tea in the other.

An odd sight, she thought fondly, to see the wealthy Nicholas Lassard dressed in a dove gray Tom Ford suit with a royal blue tie, serving her tea. He set the drinks on the end table next to her.

"One moment," he said with a smile.

Bemused, she watched him walk away again, only to come back with a small plate laden with crackers and slices of cheese.

"In case you need to replenish."

Touched, she swallowed hard. Then felt her world shift as he leaned down and pressed a soft kiss to her forehead. When she looked up to see him smiling down at her, the truth hit her.

She was in love with Nicholas. From his trusting her with his darkest memories to how tenderly he'd cradled her belly after they'd made love, she'd been falling for him bit by bit for some time.

Shaken, she picked up the teacup and nearly spilled the hot liquid on her hand.

"Careful." Nicholas stepped forward and took the cup from her. "Are you still feeling sick?"

"Just a little unbalanced." She took a deep breath. "I think I'm okay now."

He handed her back the tea and sank down into the chair opposite her, glancing around as she sipped the lemony brew.

"The changes are nice."

Pleased he had noticed, and needing something else to think about other than her personal revelation, she smiled.

"Thank you. I got the new bedding in while you were gone. Took me a little longer to get the beds made, but they look wonderful."

He frowned. "You made the beds?"

"Yes."

"I thought you hired a new housekeeper."

"Part-time. I can manage until we get a little more money. Which should be soon," she said with a smile. "The spring reservations are up. Those nonrefundable fees have been a lifesaver."

Nicholas nodded, his own smile slight. One hand came up, fingers curling into a fist that partially covered his mouth. As if he were physically holding himself back from saying something.

Surprised, she tilted her head. "What?"

"I'm glad you're happy, Anika."

"But?"

"I am concerned that continuing to manage the majority of the operations is taking its toll on you and the baby."

She suppressed the irritation that bubbled up inside her. She'd agreed to Nicholas being involved. She had ultimate say over her body, but she wanted to be able to have these conversations, especially when it involved their child, and consider Nicholas's thoughts and feelings.

"I appreciate the concern. I have cut back a lot. I've hired a handyman from Bled to take care of things like painting that aren't safe for me right now. I also have a front desk clerk and several more maids starting at the beginning of March, when business picks back up again." She took another sip of tea. "But right now, when it's just the occasional guest here and there, I see no reason to spend money on ad-

ditional employees when I'm perfectly capable of launder-
ing bedsheets and laying out a breakfast spread."

Nicholas's jaw hardened. "Noted. But how long are you
going to go on like this?"

"Like what?"

He sat up and leaned forward, his body hard, his face intense. "How much longer are you going to play at innkeeper?"

Cold settled inside her chest.

"Play at?" she repeated, her tone frigid.

"We still need to discuss what happens after the baby
is born."

"Yes, we do," she replied through tight lips. "And I have
some ideas about that, some changes I've recently considered. For now, though, I have plenty of room here to raise
the baby. And with the additional staff—"

"No."

Her spine snapped into a rigid line. "No?"

He gestured to the empty lobby. "You're by yourself a significant amount of time. How are you going to raise a child
while caring for an inn that's on the verge of collapsing?"

Hurt spurted through her. "You just said the changes
were good."

"Cosmetically, yes. But you can't keep going on like this,
Anika. I think it's time you moved in with me."

Her jaw dropped. "Excuse me?"

"I have several more business trips in the coming months.
I don't want to leave you alone here." He looked around
again, his lips curled into a faint sneer as if he could barely
stand to be in the room. Her heart twisted in her chest. "I'll
book the penthouse at the Hotel Lassard for the foreseeable
future. It's at your disposal."

"But I want to be here. In my home."

He pinched the bridge of his nose. "Your home is over

a hundred years old and falling apart. Let me take care of this for you."

His words catapulted her back to autumn, when he'd stridden into her office like he already owned the place and pushed her to sell him the one piece of her family she had left.

"This isn't one of your business deals, Nick." She took some satisfaction in the flicker of displeasure that crossed his face at her use of his nickname. "After all we've been through the past few weeks, how could you think I would just accept you making a decision like this without talking to me first?"

He frowned. "This isn't about pride or holding out against the big bad wolf trying to buy your inn. I want you closer, where I know you're safe."

For a moment she faltered. He had gone about it in the most horrible manner possible. But was something else driving his actions? Was this all because he wanted to keep her and the baby safe? Protect them the way he felt like he hadn't protected his brother?

"And no matter how many pieces of furniture you replace, you can't run this place by yourself, especially once the child is born."

Her heart cracked. Had she thought that he had changed? Because he hadn't. He was still the same arrogant, conceited playboy used to getting his way.

"What do you propose I do then? Sell to you?"

"That's one option, yes."

"The preferable option," she shot back, anger filling her until she could barely speak without wanting to shout at him. She wouldn't tell him now that she had been considering doing just that. "Is that what all of this has been about? Your initial goal of buying my inn and fulfilling your whim of having property on Lake Bled for your precious hotel?"

"Don't," he warned as he leaned down and placed his

hands on the arms of her chair, caging her in. "I didn't sleep with you so you'd sign away your property."

"No, you just slept with me because I was the next available woman." Furious, hurt that he could know so little about her, she pushed him away as she stood.

"You and I know there was much more to that night than just sex."

She crossed her arms, refused to look at him. "I don't know what I think anymore. I thought you knew me. I thought something more was developing between us."

Silence stretched between them, the awkwardness shifting into a painful, gut-wrenching stillness punctuated only by the occasional hiss of the logs in the fireplace. Had it been just a few weeks ago that they'd lain in front of another fire, his hand on her stomach, all of the beautiful possibilities of the future stretched out before them?

He ran his hand through his hair. "I told you before, Anika, there's only so much I can give you. I'm giving you everything I'm capable of."

"No, you're giving me everything you're willing to let yourself be capable of."

His eyes flashed. "I find it interesting that you judge me so harshly when you're not being honest with yourself."

"Excuse me?"

"You're working yourself into the ground. You're putting your health at risk, and our baby's, and for what? What do you want out of this place, Anika? Do you want to restore it to its former glory? How are you going to do that?"

His question hit her hard.

"Step by step," she finally replied.

"And why? So you can honor a family legacy? A legacy you told me you don't even really want to preserve?"

"If that's what you think, what you took away from what

I shared with you," she said coldly, "then you don't know me at all."

"Oh, but I do." His tone was low, dangerous, as he advanced on her, his usual carefree expression dark, brows drawn together and eyes narrowed. "Pride. Not wanting to surrender control, to accept help."

"That's part of it," she admitted, taking a step closer to him. "But do you know why that pride matters so much? Because this is all I have left of my family. My mother grew up here. My *babica* was born here, married on the shores of the lake. If I give this up, I have nothing left."

As soon as the words left her lips, she wanted to snatch them back. Judging by the darkening expression on Nicholas's face, she'd gone too far.

"Nothing?" he repeated. "Not me, not our child?"

"The baby is my future. This place is my past, my present."

How could she make him understand how important this was? How much it meant to her to have this last connection to her family?

"You're holding on too tightly to the past, Anika."

"And what about you?" she countered.

"Me?"

"You act as if you've moved on. I appreciate everything you've done for the baby and me, Nicholas. But don't stand there and pretend like I'm the only one struggling with her past."

He glowered. "What am I not doing? I went to the ultrasound appointment with you, I've bought gifts for you and the baby, I showed up today when you needed me."

"All wonderful things, Nicholas. But when I ask you what we should name the baby, you pull away. When I ask if you think it's a boy or a girl, you change the subject. You do amazingly well at concrete things like buying things and reading articles. But you're keeping our child at arm's length."

"You know my history," he ground out. "I told you, I'm giving as much of myself as I can."

"But are you working on giving your all?" When he just stared at her, she plowed on. "I can be patient with you, Nicholas, just as you've been patient with me. But," she continued when he opened his lips to speak, "I can't move forward with my own personal development when you're essentially telling me that you'll never be able to fully commit to our child or me."

He stared at her for so long she wondered if he'd even heard what she'd said.

Then, finally: "And what if I can't? What if I can only offer you and the baby pieces of who I am?"

How was it possible for her to realize she was in love with the father of her child and have her heart smashed into a thousand pieces within the span of a few minutes?

She stared at Nicholas, her pulse beating so fast she could barely catch her breath. Her eyes caressed his handsome face, the hollows below his cheekbones, the straight slant of his nose, the faint stubble that had so entranced her the morning after they'd made love in Kauai.

She loved him so much. But loving someone didn't mean accepting less than what she deserved.

A cramping in her lower stomach interrupted her spiraling thoughts. Her breath caught as her fingers tightened on her belly.

Something's wrong.

Panic clawed up her throat.

"Nicholas…" She bit back a sob and reached out to him. He was by her side in an instant.

"What's wrong?" he demanded.

"The baby. Something's wrong with the baby."

CHAPTER FIFTEEN

NICHOLAS SAT BY the hospital bed, Anika's hand clasped in his. She'd fallen asleep sometime just before dawn.

The doctors had run a series of tests but found nothing wrong. The doctor had diagnosed the most likely scenario: normal muscle cramps exacerbated by stress.

Every moment in the hospital had made Nick remember the dark days when his brother had passed. The beeping of the machines, the distant sobs, the cold feeling deep in his belly. Every time a doctor came in, he'd tensed, fearing the worst news possible. He tried to maintain a brave face for Anika's sake. But as he sat there watching blood being drawn from her arm, watching her fingers fist the sheets at her sides as she waited for the next doctor to come in, all he could think was that once again he had caused someone pain.

And not just anyone. The mother of his child.

Tonight, when he had walked into the inn and seen her so pale, he'd been angry. Angry that while he had been off managing a ridiculous disagreement with one of the construction firms hired to work on the hotel in Greece, she had been working too hard, putting not only herself but the baby at risk. He'd been anxious to get back, to see her, to spend time with her.

Only to walk in and see her looking like death. He'd been

scared, yes. Scared that she would work too hard, that something would go wrong. But he'd also felt guilty. He'd been sleeping on a brand-new bed on Egyptian cotton sheets while she'd been tucked away in that ramshackle building. One of the few things he could offer without reservations, or ties tethering him to the past, was his wealth. And he'd done nothing with it aside from a few token gifts.

When he said that she should move into the hotel with him, he had truly only been thinking of her. But her reaction to his proposal, her immediate jump to her initial accusations of the past, had brought out the worst in him.

Or had he merely lived up to her expectations, or lack thereof? He scrubbed his hand over his face. She had spoken the truth when she had accused him of not being able to fully commit. He had tried. He had tried to open up the lock he kept on his heart, to let go of the fear.

He had failed.

As much as he had come to care for Anika, as many times as he had thought about what it would be like to hold the baby in his arms, he still could not allow himself to feel about her the way he was beginning to suspect she felt about him.

How cruel, he thought as he turned to look at her once more: the dark brush of her eyelashes against her pale skin, the slight curve to her mouth, the protective hand lying over her stomach. The sight of it sent a jolt of longing through him, but he quickly squashed it. Of course he would be feeling something in the moments after he had the terrifying scare of hearing her calling his name, asking for his help. Of seeing her eyes wild with panic, her teeth gritted in pain.

He hadn't known fear like that since the ambulance had sped away with David in the back. The day that his entire life had changed.

He had learned the hard way that people could act one way in the midst of a crisis and then, once it had passed, go back to being themselves or even become better versions of who they used to be. Sometimes, though, they became worse. Like his parents. After David's death, they had pulled together. Those first few months they'd been there for him, for each other.

But as the first anniversary of David's death had rolled around, something had changed. His mother had withdrawn from both of them, her depression taking her farther and farther away from her husband and only living son. His father had responded not by fighting for her, but by taking more and more trips to get away from the dark melancholy cloud hanging over their home. Leaving Nicholas to wallow in his own guilt.

When he talked with Anika at the castle, when he'd unburdened himself and she had done nothing but listen and accept him as he was, he'd felt cautious hope and a desire that went far deeper than just the physical for the incredible woman who just months ago had despised him. The way she had looked at him when he helped her with her porch repairs had made him feel more accomplished, more appreciated and more valued as a man than anything else he'd done to date.

And when they had made love that first night after the ultrasound, when he drifted his hand down to rest on her belly, he'd experienced the same sense of wonder he'd glimpsed on Anika's face when she'd seen the baby on the ultrasound screen. The time they'd spent together had drawn him further into the fantasy. Meals shared, walks taken, business ideas discussed, all with a woman he genuinely liked and was coming to care for. How much he'd missed her while in

Greece had made him wonder if he could possibly change. If they could be more.

And then he'd walked into the inn and destroyed it all. Proven to himself and to her that he was not cut out for this. If he let things continue, allowed the relationship to go any further, he would just be hurting both of them. Marriage and family were never a part of his future. That he had felt anything beyond a simple liking and desire for Anika was an achievement in itself. But she wanted more.

No. She deserved more. So did their baby.

His chest clenched. The right thing for all of them was for him to let them go, even if the thought of someone else being with Anika, of being around his child made him want to throw something at the wall.

Wasn't the proof that he was emotionally incapable of being a father or a husband right in front of him? Once again, he had been so caught up in himself, in his own hurt, his own pride and confusion over Anika's obsession with the inn that he'd added to her stress. Even though the doctors had assured them that it was normal for women to experience dizziness and cramping in the first trimester, he still had not been able to shake loose the insidious guilt that he had caused her episode.

Anika started. Her eyes fluttered open and latched on to his face.

"Hey," she whispered softly.

"Hi," he replied, giving her hand a gentle squeeze.

"Have the doctors been back in yet?"

"No. But a nurse came by. The tests have continued to show everything as normal." He gave her hand another squeeze. "The baby's okay."

Tears pooled in her eyes and ripped open his chest.

"Thank you for coming. For bringing me here and staying."

"You don't need to thank me," he responded curtly.

She blinked and he inwardly cursed his sharp tone.

"I'm leaving." He sucked in a deep breath. "Once you're settled back at the inn, I have to take a trip to London."

A look of sadness passed across her face, one that gutted him. He wanted nothing more than to stay with her, to take her back to his hotel and tuck her into his bed, lie beside her all night.

"I won't be back for some time."

She frowned. "For how long?"

"At least a few months."

Her mouth dropped open. "Months?"

"I've been thinking about what you said." Slowly, he released her fingers and pulled back his hand. "You and the baby do deserve more. You deserve someone who can care about you more than I can, who can experience their emotions and not hold back. I'm not the kind of man who can commit to you that way."

He watched what little color was in her cheeks drain away.

"What are you saying?" she whispered.

"I still want to be involved in the child's life. But the majority of that involvement should be from a distance. I'm not good at getting emotionally involved. You told me your biggest dream was to have a family. The kind of family that you'd have with me wouldn't be the kind that made you happy. It would be one where you're constantly wondering if you're at fault, if there's somewhere else I'd rather be, if I'm actually going to stick around."

Her face twisted into something that looked far too much like pity.

"Is this about you," she asked gently, "or is this about your parents and what happened after your brother died?"

His body tensed. "A lot of it, yes. But it made me who I am today. I remember what it was like for those years after David died. How stilted everything was in the house. How I wondered if I was ever going to be enough, if we would ever be happy again." He ran a frustrated hand through his hair. "I'm not going to put you through that. I certainly will not put an innocent child through it just because I can't heal from my past."

Her lips parted. He stood before she could say anything else, before she could tempt him to stay, to put everything at risk once more and possibly fail.

"I've made my decision, Anika. I'll be in touch about financial arrangements and visitation."

She absently plucked at the hospital blanket draped over her legs. Slowly, she raised her gaze to his. Pain radiated from her eyes and stabbed straight into his heart.

"I understand."

It would be so much easier if she didn't understand. If she were like the other women in his life who would have been angry or frustrated or given him a big show of tears. But that wasn't Anika. It was one of the many things that he liked and appreciated about her—how much she cared for others, including him.

"In light of that, I agree this is for the best. And you're right." Her hand settled on her stomach. Regret washed through him that he hadn't touched her more, hadn't whispered to the tiny swell of her belly, hadn't had the guts to indulge her just once and talk about details like names and nursery colors. "The baby and I do both deserve someone who will be fully present, not just physically but emotionally." Her voice grew heavy. "I never thought I'd say this. But I wish it could have been you."

He hadn't thought he could hurt anymore. He'd been wrong. Grief dug its talons into his skin, clasped his heart and twisted. It was like David in some way, seeing her lie right in front of him yet just out of reach in this damned hospital bed. Yet it was different, worse, because this time he knew exactly who was to blame.

"I have really enjoyed getting to know you these past couple of months." Her small smile nearly killed him. "You're far much more than I gave you credit for."

"As are you, Anika. Our...the baby is lucky to have you as its mother." He swallowed past the tightness in his throat. "If you're comfortable, I would still appreciate seeing ultrasound photos. And a text every now and then. Knowing how you're doing."

She nodded once, the movement stilted.

He wasn't sure how long he stayed there, hands clenched at his sides, his gaze trained on her as if he was trying to memorize every detail of her face.

Finally, he turned and walked away.

CHAPTER SIXTEEN

NICHOLAS STARED DOWN at the paper in front of him. The contract he had been coveting for over a year finally signed on the dotted line.

There was no satisfaction; there was no excitement. There was only the hollow feeling that he had lost something far more precious than seeing his dream for the Hotel Lassard come to life.

His extended trip to London had lasted all of two weeks. He had arrived to evaluate one of the new properties going up on the north end of the city, only to find that a shortage of supplies had postponed the project indefinitely. He visited several other properties, staying for a day or two at a time. But all along he'd felt restless, a yearning to go back to the place that had started to feel like home.

He finally convinced himself that he was missing the shores of the lake: the distant Alps and the sight of the mystical castle standing guard over the town. Except when he had arrived and driven up the road leading to the hotel, he'd experienced nothing but a cold, bitter disappointment.

Home was no longer a place. Home had become a person, a woman he missed with every fiber of his being.

It would change, he kept telling himself. This was exactly what had happened to his parents, and to him, after David's death. Something in him would change. This sense of loss would lessen, leaving him a shell of what he needed to be to be the best person for Anika. The best father for their child.

For the most part he kept to the hotel, using the office to oversee the other properties. He booked a few visits to their resort in Dubai, the hotel in the Caribbean, the new resort going up on the peak of the Rocky Mountains in the middle of the United States. Everything he had been working for the past few years was coming to fruition.

Eventually it would satisfy him again. He just needed to get over this bump.

"Sir?"

Nicholas looked up to see his secretary standing in the doorway.

"Yes?"

"There's a woman here to see you."

Nicholas's heart hammered against his ribs. Slowly, he stood and walked to the door, keeping his pace as casual as possible.

"Darling!"

Nicholas's mother, Helen Lassard, walked to him, a wide smile on her face that dimmed when she took in his expression.

"I'm sorry, have I come at a bad time?"

He forced a smile onto his own face. "Not at all. I'm sorry, I've just had a lot on my mind. It's great to see you, Mother."

They hugged. She looked good, probably the best in nearly twenty years. The gauntness that had chiseled out her cheeks and made her look frail had disappeared. Her auburn hair was cut and colored to perfection, a classic bob around her heart-shaped face. A few more wrinkles here and there. But he was grateful to note the more noticeable ones were at the corners of her eyes and on the sides of her lips.

"Smile lines," she had told him in the fall. There had been a time once when he had thought she might never smile again.

"Your father's been bragging about the Hotel Lassard at Lake Bled. I had to come and see your success for myself."

He took her on a tour of the hotel, showing her everything from the glamorous spa with its Roman bath–inspired grotto to the restaurant with its floor-to-ceiling windows that overlooked the lake. He took pride in her compliments, acknowledged the accomplishments that he had made with his latest hotel.

"And how goes your quest to secure the property next to the hotel?" she asked as they walked out the front door and into the coldness of a February morning. "The last time we spoke you wanted to add it as an expansion for the hotel. You were quite enthusiastic about it."

"I received the signed contract this morning."

He felt his mother's gaze on him.

"You don't sound too happy about that."

He shot her another forced smile.

"It's nothing. Just tired. The traveling I've been doing, the grand opening and now the addition of this contract, while very welcome, will mean longer hours trying to get everything prepared for next summer."

Whether she bought his excuse or not didn't really matter. He just wanted to get in the car and drive as far away as possible. On cold mornings like this, if he looked out the balcony doors of the penthouse to the west, he could see the weather vane on top of the inn's tallest turret poking above the branches.

He took his mother into Bled. They walked along Cesta Svobode, peeking into the various shops, pausing to grab lunch at a café alongside the lake.

"Oh, that castle," Helen said as the waiter brought him

the check. "It looks so beautiful. Have you had a chance to tour it yet?"

"Once. The view is incredible."

"Do you have time to take your mother up there?"

He'd rather do anything but revisit the place where he'd first made himself vulnerable to Anika. Where their almost kiss had rekindled the passion that had been smoldering since Kauai and reawakened the desire she had stirred in him.

But he would have to get used to being in Bled, seeing the sites that he had experienced with Anika and not letting it ruin his day. He would also have to get used to the possibility of seeing Anika herself with their son or daughter, especially if she stayed here after the sale.

They drove up the winding road. Helen chatted on about the various things going on in London, his father's latest developments with the hotels that he managed, some of her old friends and everything that their children had accomplished.

"Linda's son recently got married," she said as they pulled up to the castle.

"Armand?" he said with some surprise. "I never would have figured him for the type to get married."

"Neither would I," Helen said with a laugh. "But he's very happy. It's amazing what finding the right person can do to change how you might think about your future."

He slanted a glance at her. Had his father told her about Anika? Had they somehow found out about the baby? With the way that she was looking around at the scenery, her face serene, he doubted it. He'd always known that his mother had wanted grandchildren, had hoped that he might find a woman he could settle down with. If she had any inkling of what had been going on, she would have said something by now.

They toured the castle, coming out to stand on the same parapet where he had poured out his heart to Anika. He moved to the wall, his hand settling on the cold stone, his fingers scraping against the roughness. From this vantage point, he could see the inn perched on the edge of the lake.

"Is that it?" Helen asked as she came up to his side. "The property you just bought?"

He nodded once. Hard to believe that at one time buying the inn had been so important. Now the victory felt hollow.

"All right. Enough with the playacting."

He turned, surprised by the firmness in her voice.

"What?"

"I don't know. You tell me. Something's been bothering you since I arrived. You've never been one to mope, but it seems like you've just lost your best friend."

Nearly, he thought to himself. Anika had been everything he had ever wanted in a woman: kind, supportive, feisty, strong.

"I have lost someone," he finally said. "Someone that I care very deeply about."

His mother's eyes turned sad. She laid a gentle hand on his arm.

"Would you like to tell me what happened?"

He looked down at where her hand rested on his arm.

"It's not a happy story. I made a lot of mistakes. Too many," he murmured as he turned his gaze back to the inn.

"Not all stories are happy," Helen finally replied. "I've come to realize that over the years. That doesn't mean that they can't lead to joy later on."

He took a deep breath.

And then he told her everything. He told her about Anika, his quest to buy the inn. About his numerous run-ins with the spunky owner in the past year, culminating in their encounter in Hawaii, although he left out the more intimate parts. He started to tell her about Anika surprising him at the hotel and that his mother would have a grandchild before the first leaves of autumn fell. But something held him back. He didn't want that kind of news to be shared during such a dark confession.

Instead, he told her about how he and Anika had argued. How he'd hurt her.

"Did she want you to leave?"

Nicholas paused.

"I'm not sure what she wants," he said. "I don't know if she even knows herself. When we were in Hawaii, I saw another side of her. It was like the Anika that I saw here in Bled was muted, weighed down by all of her problems. But in Hawaii she…it was like watching her come alive."

A slow smile spread across Helen's face.

"You love her."

He stared at her. "What?"

"You love her."

Her words went round and round in his head, then settled in his heart with a brightness that he had never experienced.

"I do," he finally said. "I love her. But how can I possibly stay with her knowing I'll never be able to love her without restraint?"

Helen cocked her head. "What are you talking about?"

"I can't be the man that she needs me to be. After David…" His voice trailed off as pain spasmed across his mother's face. "Forget it. I shouldn't have brought this up."

"Don't." Helen held up a hand, took in a shuddering breath. "How many years did I not allow you to experience your own pain? How many years was I so focused on my own feelings that I failed you as a mother?"

Nicholas stared at her.

"That's what it is, isn't it?" she said softly. "You're worried that when something happens, she'll change or you'll change and things won't be the same. That there's the risk of going through what your father and I did. All those years apart, all those years of us being miserable."

Her words gave power to his deepest fears.

"Yes," he said. "We were happy before David died, and then for so many years…we weren't. Even now…"

"Your father and I are happy," Helen replied softly.

"Are you? Or is that just a line you trot out for your and others' benefit?"

He regretted the harsh words as soon as they left his mouth. But Helen didn't back down.

"We are. There are difficult times, yes. There always will be. You can't survive something like that without the grief popping up at random times and trying to pull you back under." She looked out over the idyllic tableau spread beneath them and sighed. "Those years after David's death weren't your fault, Nicholas. It was your father's and my fault. We should have gotten help far sooner than we did. That was our responsibility as your parents, as adults. It was something that we failed at. But it doesn't mean that if you and Anika were ever to experience a loss that's how you would handle it. Don't deny yourself a life with the woman you love because of my mistakes."

When she put it like that, it was hard to argue with her.

"What about your father and me?" Helen continued. "I know you love us, but what if something happens to us sooner than you expected? What about when something does happen? Are you going to keep us at a distance simply because of the possibility of what might happen?" Unshed tears glimmered in her eyes. "Please don't follow your father's and my mistakes. Learn from them and be better than we were. Be happy."

"When you phrase it like that," he admitted with a slight smile, "it does sound foolish. But I'm not sure if I know how to open myself up to someone."

"I know." Helen sighed. "I suspected you kept your father and I at a distance, too. Not," she added as he started to speak, "that I blame you. I should have said something long ago. But I told myself I was analyzing too deeply, that you wouldn't call or visit as much as you did if there was a problem." Tears glinted in her eyes as she raised her chin up and looked at him. "I'm sorry, Nicholas. For all of it." Her hand came up and rested on his cheek. "But please don't let my mistakes take away the possibility of what you might have with this woman. It's foolish not to allow yourself to love her as much as I think you do."

"It is," he agreed. "But it's not just that." His gaze slid back to the inn. "I've already made so many mistakes. I don't know if she could trust me. It's always been about me telling her what I think is best, always me coming at it from the angle of either wanting to buy it or wanting to take it off her hands. Wanting to help make things better."

"I think you get that from what you experienced with your father and me. Even as a young boy, you always wanted to fix things. Admirable, if you go about it the right way. For me, I withdrew. For your father, it was easier to give you things, to take you on trips, than it was to deal with his depression."

His stomach rolled as he thought of what he had offered Anika: the money, the gifts…and the one thing that he hadn't. The one thing that Anika had asked for above all else, for him to open himself up to the possibility of truly loving their child.

"I'm not just saying this because I want to someday see you married and to give me grandchildren," Helen said with another smile.

Nicholas suppressed the quick surge of guilt at his mother's words. He would tell her eventually, but he wanted it to be a happy announcement, one that he could share with Anika by his side.

"From what little you've told me, son, she sounds like an amazing woman. One that you should be fighting for. I've never seen you this interested in anyone. For someone to do what she's done, to run an inn single-handedly by herself after so much loss, speaks volumes to her strength and character."

And it did, Nicholas realized with a surge of pride. He hadn't even taken the opportunity to fully admire what Anika had accomplished.

"I need to go to her. I need to fix this." Panic spurted inside him. "What if she doesn't accept my apology?"

"One step at a time. Yes, it might be hard for her. Whether she forgives or not is up to her. But," Helen added softly, "she sounds like a woman capable of such forgiveness. Give her the chance to choose."

Nicholas squared his shoulders. The inn gleamed like a jewel on the southern shores of the lake.

"I told her once that I don't lose." Determination hardened in his veins. "I certainly don't intend to start now."

CHAPTER SEVENTEEN

ANIKA WALKED THROUGH the lobby of the inn, smiling at a couple of the guests clustered by the roaring fireplace. Lori, one of her new hires, walked by with a tray of tea and biscuits.

Everything was running smoothly. Anika hadn't yet told the staff about the pending sale to the Hotel Lassard. She would eventually, and hoped that her requirement that the hotel retain all of her staff while providing them with a generous pay raise would soothe any concern they might have.

It was funny, she thought as she walked to the tiny little nook at the back of the kitchen that overlooked the lake, she had expected to feel sadder about finally signing her name on the contract. Instead, all she had felt was relief. There would be some sadness. She would miss things like arranging excursions for the guests, growing the inn the way Marija and she had dreamt about. But she wouldn't miss the day-to-day operations, like having to get up in the middle of the night if a guest needed her or reviewing the books and making sure all of the accounts balanced.

A yawn escaped. She was exhausted, but every time she closed her eyes at night and tried to fall back asleep, her mind raced. She had hurt Nicholas. All because she didn't want him to hurt her first. Because she was scared of falling deeper in love with him when he continued to hold back.

Because she hadn't been patient enough to give him time. Perhaps they would have realized that they weren't meant to be together. But perhaps, with more time and patience on her part, it could have been something beautiful.

Her eyes drifted back toward the trees that separated the Hotel Lassard from the Zvonček Inn. Should she reach out to him? Give him space? Or accept that, whether or not she was open to trying a little longer, he was done?

The thought tightened her throat and she turned away. If that were the case, she would do what she always did— adapt and move forward. Perhaps she and the baby could go somewhere else where she could take on a role that combined the things she loved. Maybe a job in marketing or excursions, with fewer demands on her schedule allowing her to be fully present as a mother. That and, as the baby grew, time to travel, to share adventures with her little one.

All thoughts for another time, she decided. For now, she would focus on waiting to hear back from the Hotel Lassard's lawyers. She had sent the contract through the business channels, even though part of her had wanted to reach out to Nicholas to explain why she had finally decided to sign.

As painful as it had been, her conversation with Nicholas had opened her eyes to how she was hanging on to something that needed to be let go. The inn was not her family. Yes, it represented a rich history, and yes, it had been Marija's dream. But it wasn't hers, and Marija had always been nothing if not supportive of Anika going after her own dreams. Keeping herself tethered to the inn out of a sense of loyalty was not what her *babica* would have wanted, and certainly not the right fit for Anika or her child.

Letting go of her pride and placing the inn in the hands

of someone she trusted to do it justice was the hardest thing she had done to date. But it was the right thing.

Suddenly restless, she slipped on her red boots and gray coat and slipped out the back door. Snow crunched underfoot as she drew closer to the dock. Steam drifted up from the water, creating a hazy, magical mist. Brilliant sunshine, so bright it almost hurt, made the world glow white. In the distance, the church spire stood proudly against the sky.

Her pulse beat in her throat, each hard thump making it harder to hold back her tears. A week before the grand opening, Nicholas had suggested going out to the island. But she'd already scheduled the handyman for more work on the inn, including some projects she'd needed to walk him through.

Next time, she had promised.

She tilted her head back and looked up at the brilliant blue sky. What could they have been if she had asked him to stay in the hospital room? What could they have been, not just as parents, but as a couple, as partners, if he could let go of his past and she could have not been so damned stubborn?

A crunch sounded behind her. Irritated that a guest was intruding on her grieving, she swiped a hand at her cheek in case any wayward tears had escaped and turned around.

Her heart stopped. Nicholas stood in front of her, mere steps away, dressed in black pants and a black winter coat, the red scarf he'd worn the day he'd helped her with the porch wrapped around his neck. The black reminded her of what he'd worn that fateful night in Kauai when they'd danced on the patio with the wild ocean roaring just beyond the cliffs. She'd thought him a demon then, or perhaps even the devil.

But now, as she looked at the handsome face that had

become so familiar to her, and felt the pain in his eyes as if it were her own, he reminded her more of a fallen angel.

"Sorcha."

She blinked. Of all the things she had expected him to say, that was not it.

"Sorcha?" she repeated.

He took a step closer, his movements slow, as if he were afraid she'd run away at the slightest provocation.

"It means 'bright' or 'radiant.' Scottish, although it's used in Ireland, too."

The tiniest flame of hope flickered to life in her chest.

"I'd have to think about it. But I like it."

"And Geoffrey if it's a boy," he said as he moved closer still. "Geoffrey David Lassard."

She swallowed hard. "Now, that one I don't have to think about. It's perfect."

Slowly, he reached up, cupping her face the way he had in the hotel hallway, with such tenderness it made her want to weep.

"I've barely been able to sleep," he whispered. "All I can think about is you. You and…" His other hand came up, paused, then rested on her belly. "Our child." He leaned down, rested his forehead against hers. "Anika, I've been such a fool."

She rose up on her toes and flung her arms around his neck. His arms came around her, crushing her to his body before he loosened her.

"The baby—"

"Is just fine. Don't let go, Nicholas. Please don't let go."

He threaded his gloved fingers through her hair, pulled her head back and crushed his lips to hers. She returned his kiss with every ounce of passion and love she had.

"I missed you," she whispered between kisses.

"And I you." He lifted his head but kept her enclosed in his embrace. "I'm terrified, Anika. I told myself in the beginning that I needed to go all in if I was going to be involved in raising our child. But every time I tried to let myself experience the joy I saw on your face that day you had the ultrasound, it was like there was a wall I couldn't get past. I told myself it was because I wasn't capable. But it wasn't." He let out a harsh breath. "It was fear. Fear and years of unresolved resentment and anger toward my parents."

Her heart broke for him. She had suffered loss, too, but she had never doubted that her parents or her *babica* had loved her.

"That's on them, Nicholas. Not you."

He smiled slightly. "My mother told me the same thing."

"Your mother?"

"She came to visit. We had the first truly honest conversation about David's death and what happened in the years after that." His fingers traced a pattern on her cheek, his eyes never leaving hers. "She told me that fear of what might happen in the future was a poor reason to hold oneself back. That whenever she thought of that time after David's passing, she would always mourn, but she would never regret the work she put into getting better, nor the life she's found after loss."

Anika reached up and brushed his hair back from his forehead. "How do you feel about that?"

"Good. Sad, but good. It'll take a while for my parents and me to fully repair that relationship. I had always thought I had been the most successful one to move on from David's death. But I did the same thing they did, losing myself in school and sports, then university and work."

"You were a child yourself," she reminded him with a

little heat in her voice. "You shouldn't have been left to deal with that on your own."

"No. My parents made mistakes. But as an adult, I have the choice to do things differently now. Starting with an apology. I'm sorry I walked away from you, Anika, and our child. I'm sorry I pushed to get what I wanted, to not truly listen to your reasons for wanting to hold on to the inn."

She smiled through her tears. "But you were right, you know. I was holding on to it for the wrong reasons. We were both holding on to the past. It was safer to focus on the inn and the connection I already had than risk forging a new one. I was so focused on what I might lose by selling the inn that I couldn't see all the wonderful possibilities in front of me. Although," she added, "it was very satisfying in the beginning telling you no."

He smiled. "I hope you'll have a different answer for my next question."

Her breath caught as he dropped to one knee in the snow. He reached into his coat pocket and brought out a small black box, opening it to reveal a beautiful ring with delicate strands of silver winding over the most incredible sapphire she'd ever seen.

"I love you, Anika. I never thought I'd be capable of loving someone the way I love you. And I can't promise there won't be days I still question whether I'm capable or not, whether or not I'm doing things right. But I can promise that I won't give up and I won't stop trying to be the kind of man you and our child deserve."

Tears streamed down her cheeks as she looked down into the face of the man she loved.

"Yes." She barely choked the word out as he slid her glove off and put the ring on her finger.

"I picked the sapphire because it reminded me of the way

the ocean looked in Hawaii." He stood, looking down at the ring as his hand curled around hers. "How blue it was when you jumped off the pier looking like a mermaid. How it felt when you reached out and grabbed my hand while we were snorkeling. How untamed it looked when we watched the storm from the balcony." His eyes came up to capture hers, the heat and passion stealing her breath. "I knew I wanted you before we went to Hawaii. I wanted you like I'd wanted nothing else before. But it was the moment you held my hand under the waves, and then when you smiled like you had just seen the most spectacular thing in the world, that I started to fall in love with you."

"Funny," she said as she reached up and laid her bare hand on his cheek, the ring glinting in the sunlight, "it wasn't too long after that I started to fall in love with you. The night of the gala, when we danced, when you called to check on me, when we sat and talked in the dark…" She leaned up on her toes and brushed her lips against his. "I realized how much more there was to you than fancy suits and smug smiles. And you saw me," she murmured against his mouth. "You saw me and told me how special I was, and I felt myself fall right then and there."

He kissed her again before he leaned back and pulled an envelope out of his pocket. She took it, frowning at the unexpected weight.

"I was hoping I could offer this to you as a wedding present." She opened it, pulling out little square cards with different paint colors on them. "Instead of the Hotel Lassard purchasing the inn, I'd like to help you renovate it. Bring it back to its former glory."

Tears fell again, making the envelope crinkle as they hit the paper.

"Nicholas…"

"I should have offered this to you a long time ago." He brushed a hand over her hair. "I was so focused on my dream that I disregarded yours."

"And I appreciate that. More than I can express." She ran her fingers over the paint colors, indulged in a brief fantasy of what it would be like to see the inn with a fresh coat of paint, a new roof, a renovated front porch. Savored the image.

Then let it go.

"But I'm no longer the right person to run it. My heart isn't in it. I want to travel and, most importantly, I want to be there for you and our baby." She glanced over his shoulder at the inn. There was grief in letting go, but also a hint of excitement. It would be a fresh start for all of them, a chance to truly move on. "After seeing how you run your hotels, knowing the reason behind why you do what you do, I knew signing the contract was the right thing to do."

He turned and together they studied the inn.

"I had planned on making Bled my home base, at least for a few years," Nicholas finally said. "Would you be comfortable living here in Bled and traveling with me for work?"

Anika smiled. "Yes. That was always one of the things I struggled with. I had my mother's wanderlust, but Babica's love of having a home to come back to. And," she added as she looked back over her shoulder at the town perched on the north shore, "Bled has been my home for so long. Knowing we'll always be able to come home will make the adventures that much more enjoyable."

"Then I would appreciate having you play a part in the renovation of the inn, ensuring that the vision of the Hotel Lassard brand blends with the legacy of your family."

Her heart swelled. "Thank you."

He turned her in the circle of his arms. "And at least a couple of stays every year, for quality control."

"Of course."

His smile faded as he looked down at her with a serious expression. "I love you, Anika. I'm not sure what the next few months are going to be like. But I do know I don't want to be anywhere but with you."

She cupped his face in her hands and rose up on her toes.

"I love you, Nicholas. And I know it's not going to be perfect. But," she said just before she kissed him, "I have a feeling it's going to be our best adventure."

EPILOGUE

THE ORANGE AND red leaves glowed beneath the rays of the autumn sun as the gondola pulled up to the dock. Nicholas stepped out onto the wooden boards and turned, his breath catching at the sight of the woman still seated in the boat.

"Are you ready, Mrs. Lassard?"

Anika smiled up at him. Her dark hair fell in loose curls past her shoulders. The ivory gown she'd selected for their intimate wedding at the castle bared her shoulders, adding a hint of sexiness to an otherwise elegant dress that clung to her body all the way down to her knees before flaring out into a cascade of silken folds.

He held out a hand, hot possessive need flowing through him at the sight of the silver band on her finger. An hour ago, they'd exchanged vows in the upper courtyard of Bled Castle with his parents and a couple of close friends in attendance.

And their daughter. *His* daughter, who had watched over the ceremony in a little white dress that brought out the golden brown of her eyes and a gummy smile.

When he looked back over the transition he'd undergone in the past year, it amazed even him how starkly things had changed. He'd offered to purchase the inn and have it made into a home. But Anika had stayed firm: she wanted the inn renovated to be enjoyed by guests. Zvonček House, a Hotel

Lassard property, would open in the spring and was already booked a year out.

As they'd balanced traveling in her second trimester for his work and overseeing the renovations, they'd stumbled across a home tucked away in the mountains with a two-story living room, massive windows that provided a jaw-dropping view of the lake and acres for their little one to run around on. The words "I love it" had barely escaped Anika's mouth before he'd told his realtor to make the deal.

The painters had just finished painting the nursery adjoining their bedroom a pale lavender when Anika had gone into labor four weeks early. When he'd first held Sorcha Lassard in his arms, his wonder had been offset by a resurgence of his old fear. She'd been so tiny, so dependent on him and Anika for everything, that it had been a struggle to stay present and not give in. It hadn't been easy, but he'd kept his vow to Anika and their child. From rocking a wailing Sorcha at midnight to learning how to change diapers and bathe a tiny infant, he'd tackled every task he could to be there for his daughter and help Anika.

It had been after one of those baths just a couple weeks ago that he'd lifted Sorcha out of the little baby tub, wrapped her in a tiny towel and watched a smile bloom across her face as she looked up at him.

And just like that, he'd experienced the same wonder he'd seen on Anika's face at the ultrasound appointment. He'd hollered for his wife, begged Sorcha to do it again and laughed when she'd proven to have both her parents' stubborn streak and refused to smile for another three days.

And his wife—*his wife*, he thought with masculine pride—had given him the time to get there, supporting and loving him through the highs and lows of those first tumultuous weeks of parenthood.

"Are you sure you can do this?" Anika asked as she joined him on the dock, casting a skeptical glance at the stone steps that climbed up the hillside of the island.

"I'll try not to take that as an insult."

She laughed. "But it's ninety-nine steps! I don't think I could even walk that without needing to rest."

He pulled her against him, savored her sharp intake of breath as their bodies collided. He would never tire of this rush, this desire mixed with the intimacy of loving someone as he loved Anika.

"Trust me?"

"Always."

"Well, then, Mrs. Lassard..." He leaned down and scooped her up. A laugh followed her initial squeal of surprise as her arms flew around his neck. "Onward and upward."

He carried her up the entire flight, kissing her soundly at the top before setting her on her feet. They walked into the church hand in hand. The chapel, complete with wooden pews and gold-framed paintings on the white walls, was small but beautiful. While Nicholas had included it in his recommendations for guests at Anika's suggestion, waiting until now to actually experience it himself had been worth it.

Anika approached the rope hanging from the ceiling. It connected to the wishing bell she had spoken about the first time they'd had lunch after she'd told him about the baby. She smiled at him.

"Ready?"

"I am."

They grasped the rope and pulled once, twice, three times. The bell tolled, a rich sound that echoed off the arching ceiling. Anika looked up, her eyes crinkling as she laughed.

"This is incredible." She looked at him then with such love shining from her eyes it nearly knocked him off his feet. "Thank you."

He moved to her side and swept her up into his arms.

"You don't have to carry me back down the stairs," she said with another laugh as he carried her out of the chapel. "The legend says you just had to make it to the top."

"I know." He grinned at her. "But I don't want to let you go."

She shook her head even as a blush stole over her cheeks. "I can see why all the women fell for your charm, Mr. Lassard."

"You're the only one who matters, Mrs. Lassard."

He carried her out into the sunshine and back down the steps. By the time they reached the bottom, the gondola carrying his parents and Sorcha had arrived. His father cradled Sorcha in his arms, pointing out various sights around the lake, while his mother looked on with happiness radiating from her eyes.

"Did you make it up?" Helen asked.

"He did," Anika said as she kissed his cheek.

"Impressive, son." Henry grinned at him with a teasing glint in his eyes. "Didn't know you had it in you."

It was amazing, Nicholas thought as he took his daughter in his arms and kissed her forehead, how quickly he and his parents had healed. After learning they were gaining not only a daughter-in-law but a grandchild, they had made frequent trips to Bled over the last few months. Trips that had included long talks, tears and apologies.

There was still work to be done. But Nicholas could honestly say it was the first time in over two decades that all three of them were truly happy.

Sorcha curled into the protective curve of his arm, her

eyes fixated on his face. Her tiny lips tilted up and his chest grew warm.

"We have the *pletna* for another hour," Henry said. "Then it will take us back to the castle."

"With plenty of time to rest and refresh before the reception," Helen added.

"Then go and enjoy the island," Anika urged. "I've never been to a two-hundred-guest wedding reception before, but I imagine we're all going to be very busy tonight."

Henry and Helen walked up the stairs hand in hand, and Nicholas cradled Sorcha on his shoulder as he tugged Anika closer.

"Do we have to go to the reception?" he whispered, savoring the way she shivered as he gently kissed her on the neck.

"It is *our* reception."

His hand drifted up and down her back, the heat of her skin seeping through the thin material.

"But if we left early we could—"

"Little ears!" Anika said as she cut him off with a laugh.

"All right. But you owe me at least one dance."

"You know what, I like you so much I'll give you two." She kissed one of Sorcha's chubby cheeks before she looped her arms around Nicholas's waist. "So, what did you wish for?"

"If I tell you, doesn't that mean it won't come true?"

She wrinkled her nose. "I suppose that's true."

"I can make an exception, then, because I didn't make a wish."

A frown crossed her face. "You didn't?"

"No. Because," he said, just before he kissed his wife, "you already made my wish come true."

* * * * *

COMING SOON!

We really hope you enjoyed reading this book.
If you're looking for more romance
be sure to head to the shops when
new books are available on

Thursday 4th January

To see which titles are coming soon, please visit

millsandboon.co.uk/nextmonth

MILLS & BOON

Introducing our newest series, Afterglow.

From showing up to glowing up, Afterglow characters are on the path to leading their best lives and finding romance along the way – with a dash of sizzling spice!

Follow characters from all walks of life as they chase their dreams and find that true love is only the beginning...

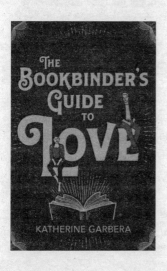

MILLS & BOON®

Coming next month

THE BUMP IN THEIR FORBIDDEN REUNION
Amanda Cinelli

'Sir, you can't just–' The nurse visibly fawned as she tried to remain stern, her voice high with excitement and nerves as she continued.

'She knows me.' The man stepped into the room, his dark gaze instantly landing on her. 'Don't you, Isabel?'

Izzy froze at the sound of her name on Elite One racing legend Grayson Koh's perfectly chiselled lips. For the briefest moment she felt the ridiculous urge to run to him, but then she remembered that while they may technically know one another, they had never been friends.

It had been two years since Grayson had told her she should never have married his best friend, right before he'd offered her money to stay away from the Liang family entirely.

She instantly felt her blood pressure rise.

True to form, Grayson ignored everyone and remained singularly focused upon where she sat frozen on the edge of the exam table.

When he spoke, his voice was a dry rasp. 'Am I too late…have you already done it?'

Continue reading
THE BUMP IN THEIR FORBIDDEN REUNION
Amanda Cinelli

Available next month
millsandboon.co.uk

OUT NOW!

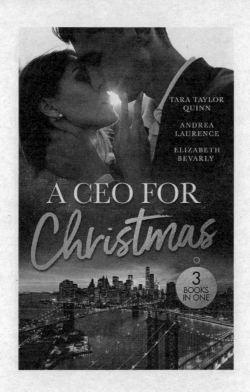

TARA TAYLOR
QUINN

ANDREA
LAURENCE

ELIZABETH
BEVARLY

A CEO FOR

Christmas

3
BOOKS
IN ONE

Available at
millsandboon.co.uk

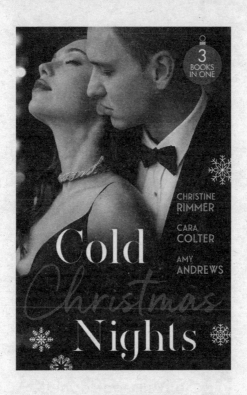

LET'S TALK
Romance

For exclusive extracts, competitions and special offers, find us online:

f MillsandBoon

X @MillsandBoon

◉ @MillsandBoonUK

♪ @MillsandBoonUK

Get in touch on 01413 063 232

MILLS & BOON

THE HEART OF ROMANCE

A ROMANCE FOR EVERY READER

MODERN
Prepare to be swept off your feet by sophisticated, sexy and seductive heroes, in some of the world's most glamourous and romantic locations, where power and passion collide.

HISTORICAL
Escape with historical heroes from time gone by. Whether your passion is for wicked Regency Rakes, muscled Vikings or rugged Highlanders, awaken the romance of the past.

MEDICAL
Set your pulse racing with dedicated, delectable doctors in the high-pressure world of medicine, where emotions run high and passion, comfort and love are the best medicine.

True Love
Celebrate true love with tender stories of heartfelt romance, from the rush of falling in love to the joy a new baby can bring, and a focus on the emotional heart of a relationship.

Desire
Indulge in secrets and scandal, intense drama and sizzling hot action with heroes who have it all: wealth, status, good looks... everything but the right woman.

HEROES
The excitement of a gripping thriller, with intense romance at its heart. Resourceful, true-to-life women and strong, fearless men face danger and desire - a killer combination!

To see which titles are coming soon, please visit

millsandboon.co.uk/nextmonth